DREAM BABY DREAM
SUICIDE
A NEW YORK STORY

DREAM BABY DREAM
SUICIDE
A NEW YORK STORY
KRIS NEEDS

OVERLOOK OMNIBUS

This edition published by Omnibus Press and distributed in the United States and Canada by The Overlook Press, Peter Mayer Publishers Inc, 141 Wooster Street, New York, NY 10012. For bulk and special sales requests, please contact sales@overlookny.com or write to us at the above address.

Copyright © 2017 Omnibus Press
(A Division of Music Sales Limited)
14/15 Berners Street,
London, W1T 3LJ, UK.

Cover designed by Fresh Lemon

ISBN: 978-1-4683-1444-1

Every effort has been made to trace the copyright holders of the photographs in this book but one or two were unreachable. We would be grateful if the photographers concerned would contact us.

Printed in Malta.

A catalogue record for this book is available from the British Library.

Cataloguing-in-Publication data is available from the Library of Congress.

Visit Omnibus Press on the web at www.omnibuspress.com

For Helen and Mari

CONTENTS

FOREWORD

By Lydia Lunch

To come full circle, like the noose we attempted to cut free of by severing the connective tissue from a life we were forced into living, and a life that felt like it was living us, we turned the beating around and struck back and attacked; not only the enemy within, but the ever present enemy surround... with sound.

We used music as an assaultive weapon that furthered the divide between those who were built for abuse because, not only could we take it, and not only could we fucking dish it out but, like a hysterical manifestation of preverted/perverted archetypes, we were created to fully inhabit it. We bore the burden in our bloodline of all of history's misguided lovers, hate fuckers, witches, wretches and wastrel minstrels who troubadoured through the trenches in search of other extreme outsiders that even a coven was too restrictive to contain.

There are certain tribes that stand completely outside of everything and everyone else. In that isolation there is a sense of freedom, desolation and longing.

This was not a caterwaul for the collective, but a personal exorcism of the most gloriously murderous romantics, whose blood longed for blood as our bones were broken and shattered once more, as if fated upon the breaking wheel.

Where what has been done shall be done and done again until you sever the chains and decode the secret language which reverses the repetition of the endless cycle from which only an agonized scream of merciless negation into the darkest and most lonely of all those dark and lonely nights might actually rip a new black hole into your personal cosmos. And when upon hitting that most excruciating and soul shattering, god-forsaking pitiless howl, can the soul truly be set free to reclaim and reconfigure the damage already done to our battered psyches which bear the pain of all man's inhumanity done in the name of a terribly addictive love, an unquenchable greed or an obsessive and forever unsatisfied lust.

Suicide... all this... and the inverse too. How fucking beautiful.

True contrarians. For as terrifying as they could be on 'Frankie Teardrop', 'Harlem', etc, they also composed outlandishly tender psycho-saccharine love songs like 'Sweetheart', 'Dream Baby Dream' and 'Cheree'; psychobilly grindcore – 'Jukebox Baby', 'Johnny', 'Ghost Rider'; driving, post-trance ranters – 'I Don't Know' and half a dozen other genre-defying reconfigurations which would help me to define my own coming musical schizophrenia.

I met Suicide in 1976 at Max's Kansas City. I crawled out of my bedroom window in Rochester, New York, jumped on a Greyhound bus and ended up staying in a loft that Lenny Bruce's daughter Kitty had just evacuated in Chelsea. I went to New York searching for like-minded miscreants whose sense of true romance meant blood-soaked sheets and long slow screams that would shatter what remained of the night I never wanted to end. Suicide was the first show I saw, Alan and Marty were the first people I met (other than the flock of hippies I connived into taking me in) and to a violent 17-year-old hate-fuelled art terrorist in training, their performance was one of the most inspiring events of my life. Suicide. I thank you.

INTRODUCTION

The idea for this book was planted around five years ago when I was trying to get a CD-book series called *Watch The Closing Doors: A History Of New York's Musical Melting Pot* off the ground. My humble plan was to tell, decade by decade, the history of New York through its music, giving the vanishing city an eternal monument before it totally became a corporate rich kids' playground. It was also something of a love letter to the city which had so grabbed me at an early age that I ended up moving there in the eighties, and it still refused to let go after I'd left. Now that I'd stopped traversing New York's streets amid pivotal times from the inside, I could look retrospectively at its broader history from the outside, fired by a more scholarly self-education which could only reach fulfilment through doing such a project.

I'd also been doing another CD-book series called *Dirty Water: The Birth Of Punk Attitude*, which sought to uncover the earliest manifestations of the punk spirit which, I always maintain, didn't just happen one day in a bums' bar on the Bowery, but went back to blues and bebop. Suicide had pride of place on the punk sets and would have had on the New York series if it had got as far as the seventies. (Although reactions to *Watch The Closing Doors* were unusually positive, the plug got pulled on the project for the simple reason the music cost too much for the independent Year Zero label to license.)

I first met and became friends with Marty Rev and Alan Vega amid the violent chaos of the 1978 Clash tour, which was followed by various encounters over the years, including a marathon interview for a film about them that never happened in 2007. When I was doing the New

York compilation, Rev came on board as a kind of technical adviser and the coolest embodiment of New York's multi-hued musical heritage you could wish to meet. He had grown up with doo-wop and rhythm and blues, before elevating his teenage soul with jazz, and cutting his musical teeth with the movement's fearless trailblazers. He still lives on the same East Village street he moved to in the early seventies, and from where he continues to forge his electronic masterpieces. Crucially, the first volume of *Watch The Closing Doors*, which covered the years 1945 to 1959, got Marty's seal of approval. He called it "a major work of total uniqueness and scholarship. I'm sure it's the first and definitely the only one of such depth and breadth of knowledge". The clincher came when he called its accompanying hard-back book "an important historical volume" and suggested the notes from this and the future releases be printed together in major book form.

Although the series stalled, the book idea remained a personal obsession, which grew when I noticed just how often Suicide are marginalised in so many accounts purporting to document the city's punk history or the broader movements they pioneered. When the original New York project started looking too colossal to even comprehend pursuing, I told Marty I must be mad to even be considering it. "No, the best things come from madness like that," he said. "That's actually sanity."

Those words were still ringing in my head after I asked Marty and Alan if I could try and tell Suicide's story, set in its proper New York context, and both gave their enthusiastic blessings. Marty, in particular, became closely involved as the book grew into the story of two quite different individuals, who together strove to combine and transcend the outer limits of art and music, despite finding themselves cursed by dull dictates such as the one which declared a band calling itself Suicide should not be allowed in. By the time that world caught up with them, they had already spawned several musical movements they weren't credited for, yet were now being recognised as one of the most influential bands of all time.

There's a scene near the end of *Downtown 81*, the era-capturing movie starring Jean-Michel Basquiat, where a yellow cab is cruising the ruins of Alphabet City as the sun starts to come up. Suicide's 'Cheree' swells up, with Vega's yearning vocal and Rev's twinkling synth firmament weaving their supernatural rhapsody over the dawn skyline in a time-stopping New York moment. It seems to define so much about them. Suicide embody everything that was unique, dangerous and epoch-making about that city during the last century. Together they ignited New York's most defiant cultural strands, as they caught the blackened mood of a country shattered by the war in Vietnam. Forty-five years since they came together, this confrontational, idiosyncratic performance entity are finally being recognised and given their rightful place in musical history.

ONE

"Where are all the other so-called successful bands now? They have their run of a few years and then they're gone forever. We've gone for the long haul. We're still here." – **Alan Vega**

For over one hundred years, authors and artists have been fixated with projecting their visions of a future New York City. In 1906, a writer called Van Tassel Sutphen, usually known for golf-related musings, published a true romance sci-fi tale called *The Doomsman*, which was the year's strangest but most provocative novel and destined for cult status. The story was set in twentieth century New York City, in the year 2015 to be precise, but oddly couched in clunky Olde English dialect. It portrays the now ruined city as "a wilderness of brick and mortar", huge holes pockmark the avenues, the financial district ruled by owls and the Flatiron Building used as a sighting edifice by archers.

Since the mysterious Terror of 1925, the world has been split into three tribes: the Painted People, House People and marauding Doomsmen, who sport medieval armour, ride horses and practise archery on anything that moves. At its centre, Manhattan is now the "gigantic, threatening, omnipotent" city of Doom, one of the few places not torched in the Terror, ruled by post-apocalyptic godfather Dom Gillian.

Doom uncannily presages urban life later that century (and movies such as *Escape From New York*), overrun by "human rats" pouring in from abandoned jails now sounding closer to the almost unbelievable fate that befell Detroit but, for several decades, could have been New York's Alphabet City or South Bronx. Broadway is now the royal avenue to

4

Citadel Square (the former Madison Square), and its foreboding temple, where an old subway power station dynamo has been converted into an idol called the Shining One. Every day at noon, the generator starts giving off a menacing, subsonic hum, its alien drone attracting fearful worship as the "sinister quality" of its monotone invokes gusts of "superstitious terror" in the House-dwellers, who believe their city is not only inhabited by inevitable outlaws but "by demons of many a grewsome sort and kind... of invisible hands that plucked at the rash intruder's skirts; of monstrous shapes that leered and gabbled behind the traveller's back and were only blocks of stone when he turned to face them; of bloodless creatures that one might meet in the full flood of day... of vampires and ghouls and fair women with enchanting voices, who enticed their victims into blind passageways and then changed suddenly to foul, harpy-like monsters."

If those words could easily fit into one of the more florid accounts of our own two heroes assaulting the Mercer Arts Center or Max's Kansas City in the early seventies, one thing Sutphen couldn't have predicted was that, by his year of 2015, two outlaws calling themselves Suicide would be standing, still proud and defiant, among the few remaining survivors of the seismic social, political and cultural revolutions which really did rock New York City later in the last century. And, far from being a ruin, Manhattan would be in the corporate grip of an ongoing gentrification juggernaut turning it into an opulent island affordable to only the very rich.

Starting Suicide in order to make a confrontational art statement while America was killing its youth in Vietnam, Alan Vega and Martin Rev then spent the next 45 years producing rapturously extreme inner city blues, braving unimaginable abuse, and surfing short-lived fads diluted from their innovations. While internal conflicts, self-serving greed, fatal self-abuse, or just the inexorable ravages of time have relentlessly claimed former allies, friends and contemporaries, Vega and Rev have rarely let up in the creative missions they have been unflinchingly pursuing, both together and solo, for around half a century. Suicide is literally the last band standing from the incendiary seventies they came up in. Slowing down is inevitable, but voluntary retirement or selling out to the nostalgia market would be off the agenda even if the pair were ever likely to have a band meeting.

Vega and Rev are underground music's timeless paragons, restlessly disparate but innately telepathic; two highly idiosyncratic personalities still kicking against the pricks. The year 2015 saw them revive the 'Punk Mass' tag of their earliest shows, at London's Barbican.

The first gig I ever saw was Tyrannosaurus Rex at the Royal Albert Hall in 1968; another classic duo made up of two contrasting figures who complemented each other visually and musically, until they fell out the following year. Marc Bolan was the bopping elf engaging the crowd, while bongo patterer Steve Took perched next to him, stoned impregnable in shades, but stripping off and shouting at audiences on the disastrous US tour. "I loved them, man, but they bombed when they played New York," remembers Alan.

Ten years later, I saw Suicide for the first time, and witnessed the fearless livewire Vega cajoling and ultimately conquering ugly crowds of catalogue punk grunts bellowing for the Clash, while Rev stood immobile behind a Perspex screen, sporting much bigger shades than Took, unleashing ferocious, futuristic rock'n'roll and juddering electronic pulses from his self-invented Instrument. Nightly, these two alchemical brothers faced down potentially life-threatening globs of pig-ignorant humanity and came out on top, laughing to disguise their disdain.

While Simon & Garfunkel, Sam & Dave or the Everly Brothers famously couldn't stand each other but synced on stage, the fierily intense Vega and eternally cool Rev could seem like polar opposites, doomed to clash and splinter. But the pair share a deep bond and understanding, which has always proved indestructible at the most crucial times. Born out of solid, working class families, they are essentially cut from the same cloth, and could trust each other immediately. Neither reports childhood abuse, life-threatening bouts with hard drugs or booze, or major delinquency beyond that of any self-respecting teenager. Both enjoyed early awakenings to art, music and literature, discovering its essential history and roots, to be used as launch-pads in their respective journeys. Suicide have never split up and, even if they haven't seen each other between the last gig and the moment they walk back on stage for the next, whether it's been months or even years, they will instantly plug into the same infernal magic which crackled between them at those first rehearsals 45 years earlier.

Vega and Rev were both irresistibly lured at early ages to Manhattan, which glimmered enticingly across the East River. Although the city claimed both their souls as teenagers, the ever-questing lives and obsessive artistic paths each pursued were vastly different before they collided in a SoHo loft in 1970 – the point at which their creative big bang occurred.

Lazily describing Suicide as "electro-punk" or "industrial" pioneers has no place here as, like they've repeatedly proved, Vega and Rev have always been a law unto themselves, going further out than anyone while remaining beatifically unique and defiantly unclassifiable.

Alan was already in his early thirties when he met Marty and Suicide cranked into life. Despite starting adult life as a regular sports-loving Brooklyn guy on the way to a normal blue-collar life, his hardwired artistic DNA and seething social conscience were compounded by seeing Iggy Pop perform in 1969. When he was born Alan Bermowitz on June 23, 1938, at the Bronx Hospital, his parents were still living in the thriving Jewish community of New York's Lower East Side.

On March 13, 1881, Czar Alexander II was assassinated in St Petersburg, setting back political reform in Russia by decades and having a calamitous effect on the Empire's Jewish population as they were blanket-blamed for the killing. The incoming Czar Alexander III was an anti-Semite, who persecuted Jewish enclaves all over Russia, the Ukraine and Poland, resulting in enormous numbers of Eastern European, Yiddish-speaking Jews fleeing to New York in the mid-1880s. By the end of the century, the Lower East Side had become the largest Jewish settlement in the world.

Alan's family were both of East European Orthodox Jewish origin, his father a first generation immigrant who settled in the teeming slums of the Lower East Side after entering the US through the imposing Great Hall on Ellis Island (then processing 200,000 immigrants a year). The Lower East Side now boasts some of the most expensive real estate in Manhattan but, by the late nineteenth century, was infamous as one of the most overcrowded slums in the world. Families crammed, sometimes several to one room, into the dark tenement blocks which had proliferated after the first high-rise was constructed at 65 Mott Street in 1824.

That particular seven-storey building (now a Chinese pharmacy) laid out the first tenement blueprint of two apartments on each floor, although developers soon found more effective ways of squeezing more people into the same amount of space, stretching to the common four apartments per floor format which rapidly infested the Lower East Side and beyond.

When Alan was three, the Bermowitz family, which included his younger brother Robbie, joined the exodus from the sardine-like LES and moved to Brooklyn in search of a better life with more space. For most of the last century, Brooklyn was portrayed as the preferably ignored, sometimes maligned, outer borough whose teenagers longed to make it over the bridge to Manhattan. Nobody came to New York with the intention of settling in Brooklyn. It seemed stuck in a time warp, until the gentrification which got under way in the nineties started driving hopeful settlers and cash-strapped long-time occupants away from the Lower East Side and East Village to Williamsburg, an area which itself now sports real estate prices comparable to Manhattan. Around 70 square miles, Brooklyn only became a New York borough in 1878.

Brooklyn was New York's most populous borough by the early forties, when the Bermowitz family relocated to Bensonhurst, in its southwest. Named after the former president of Brooklyn Gas, who previously owned the land, Bensonhurst is surrounded by Dyker Heights, Borough Park, Bath Beach, Midwood and Gravesend. While it became known to many as home to the Cramden family on untouchable TV comedy show *The Honeymooners* in the mid-fifties, Bensonhurst was later the backdrop for TV sitcom *Welcome Back Kotter*, which starred the young John Travolta, his cinematic disco smash *Saturday Night Fever* and Spike Lee's inter-racial love story *Jungle Fever*. The famous car chase in *The French Connection* took place along 86th Street.

When the Bermowitz family first moved to Bensonhurst, the area was equally divided between Italian and Jewish families, until the former increased in number, resulting in the neighbourhood becoming known as the Little Italy of Brooklyn.

Talking to Alan now at the age of 76, specific details have faded, but he has come to cherish certain memories of his Brooklyn childhood, talking about it with great affection. "I've loved boxing since I was five years old," recalls the voice still steeped in rapid-fire Brooklyn twang. "Smoke-filled boxing rings, men smoking cigars, the whole family there in Brooklyn. Then my father in front of his TV screen. We'd watch the boxing every Friday."

When Alan starts reflecting on his family, he regrets not expressing his feelings more when they were around. "My father was a nice man. My mother was really beautiful, too. They were good, tough, working class people. I'm really sorry I never had a chance to say 'I love you,' and to tell them how much I loved them and appreciated what they gave to me, because they really did give me a lot. But by the time I got to think about it, they had died, and I never said the things I should have said. My brother Robbie's dead too. He died in 1999. My brother and I used to share a room together."

Alan's father worked as a diamond setter. Not just any diamond setter either. "He was an artist," recalls his son, who cites his father's skill at setting diamonds in a ring, using only three prongs instead of the normal four to make the stone appear larger than it was. His clients included the rich and renowned, names such as the Rockefellers.

Alan goes on to stress, "I really loved the neighbourhood in Brooklyn. I was hanging out on the streets with my friends, and doing a lot of sports. I loved the parks and playgrounds. I loved sports; basketball, football, baseball. Typical New Yorker, typical schmuck. But I think about how the old neighbourhood is now and it's like a joke." He went back to see the old family home on 84th Street ten years ago. Unsurprisingly, "Everything seemed smaller. It had changed dramatically."

Alan attended the "half-Jewish-half-Italian" Lafayette High School at Bath Beach, in the town once known as Gravesend. The school opened in 1939, and famous alumni include Italian-American actor Paul Sorvino, of *Goodfellas* and *Law And Order* fame, suspenders-sporting TV broadcaster Larry King, and baseball legend Sandy Kouvacs, who was two years older than Alan, before he went on to his glittering career pitching for the Brooklyn Dodgers in the mid-fifties. Throwing himself into sports, Alan got to know Kouvacs and the baseball scouts. "They looked out for me. I knew 'em all. Sandy Kouvacs was Italian and I was half Jewish. I played ball, a lot of sports. I wasn't really that tall, so I was too short for basketball. Baseball really suited me well. I was a good baseball player, I could pitch really well. In fact, for a while I thought I was going to be a ball player."

With art and music not yet an issue, Alan's parents expected their son to achieve maximum marks so he could become, "a professional that didn't have to work with his hands. I got pretty good grades, so at least I could stick at school." At the same time, Alan had to deal with the "ghetto mentality" which divided the Italians and Jews and led to skirmishes and rumbles. "At first it was strange. I made new friends but I had to watch out all the time. I had to have eyes in the back of my head because of the way it was with the Italians and the Jews, and the *this* and the *that*. You were supposed to stay with your own, but I liked the Italian kids because they were tougher. I hung out with them a lot, although I wasn't supposed to."

Alan doesn't have any clear memory of deciding to write, or even a particularly burning desire to read books. "I didn't think much of the intellectual things, like reading. I didn't really give a shit. I liked comic books, and the comic book culture. I enjoyed the teachers. In the last year in high school, my English teacher told the class, 'I really wanna to tell you, this guy really looks like a writer.' That was me! I said 'What, I don't know how to write!' I don't know why she chose me. Of course, *now* I became a writer. She said some really great shit, so I really had to start writing then. Who knows what I was writing? A writer? I had really hated literature, but I must admit I started to really read a lot in high school, then college. I didn't think anything of it, although I absorbed it somehow. I *must* have absorbed it."

Alan's real cultural awakening happened when he started attending nearby Brooklyn College at Midwood in the mid-fifties, studying physics. Established in the thirties as the Brooklyn branch of the City College of New York, Brooklyn College was the first public co-educational liberal arts college in New York, and was called "the poor man's Harvard" because of its low tuition fees and reputation for academic excellence.

At home, Alan remembers the mantra "science, science, science", but art "slowly but surely" entered the picture. "That first year at college, I excelled in math and science. My lowest grade ever was art. So who knows why something changes, why something happens? At 16 or 17, I started getting into other things. I started reading the Beat writers; Jack Kerouac, all those writers. But it was weird, I didn't really think about it. I didn't think, 'That's my reading, that's my writing,' but I really enjoyed it. I read all the Beats, got into abstract expressionism, that whole thing. It was like a whole different world. Camus is my favourite writer of all time."

After World War Two, under the Presidencies of Harry S. Truman, then Dwight D. Eisenhower, the US was at its most affluent. Inspired by notions of the 'American Dream', increased consumerism led to an industrial boom, automobile mania and the radio giving way to TV as the prime source of home entertainment. This apparently prospering nation was also in the grip of Cold War paranoia, which resulted in the nuclear arms race and McCarthyism: an almost Stalinist form of artistic censorship which crippled many artists across the board by blacklisting them. Many social and cultural shifts had started by the late forties and early fifties, including the civil rights movement, the birth of rock'n'roll, abstract expressionism, method acting, bebop jazz, contemporary folk and the Beats – who raised a middle finger at conservative America through their radical lyrical expression. Allen Ginsberg smashed taboos inspired by his life as a homosexual while redefining poetry with *Howl,* although Alan's favourite, Kerouac, became a drunken parody of the degenerate image foisted on the Beats after scoring a best-seller with his epic *On The Road* in 1957. Kerouac had come to New York in 1939, discovered sax titan Lester Young, and passionately identified with his musical values. Even Ginsberg's *Howl* was inspired by Young's 'Lester Leaps In'.

Alan describes reading *On The Road* as a "life changing event", along with his devouring of Henry Miller's literary game-changer *Tropic Of Capricorn,* and his discovery of the crazed splatterings of action painter Jackson Pollock.

Although he didn't realise it at the time, the Beat writers were Alan's port of entry into New York's subterranean underground. He remembers being friendly with Gregory Corso, who appeared in the late fifties, although he repeatedly emphasizes that no specific life path had yet opened up for him, even though he was inspired by all this. Alan's journey into a life of art, rather than the science route mapped out by his parents, accelerated when he started hopping on the D or N train to Manhattan at the age of 17.

Then along came Elvis, Alan's earliest musical hero. It was his "voice from the heavens" which first did it for him. So far, Alan had grown up to a musical soundtrack of his mother's beloved Frank Sinatra records, opera, classical and Liberace, plus his dad's country & western. Although Elvis had cut his history-changing version of blues man Arthur 'Big Boy' Crudup's 'That's All Right' during his first session at Sam Phillips' Sun Studio in Memphis on July 5, 1954, Presley's full devastating impact didn't hit nationally until January 1956's 'Heartbreak Hotel', which crucially brought his unique, other-worldly charisma to TV screens for the first time. Today, Elvis' music, and those images, have been heard and seen countless millions of times; one can only imagine what it must have been like experiencing Elvis and rock'n'roll for the first time *as it was happening.* Unprecedented, undiluted and unlike anything the world had ever seen. As Pete Frame puts it so beautifully in his definitive tome about the era, *The Restless Generation,* "everything about him was unique and mysterious, more thrilling than anything teenagers had ever heard or seen or read about before... we only saw pictures but we soon knew he was wilder, younger, more graceful, more sexual, more lithe, more grease, more beautiful, more tender, more respectful, more vulnerable, more sensitive, more soulful, more exquisite, more animal, more naturally elegant, more sussed and more us than anything else that was ever likely to visit our planet. The God of rock'n'roll, Elvis Presley, was going to change the world."

The 17-year-old Alan Bermowitz joined the smitten masses, recalling, "For me it was first seeing Elvis. He has one of the greatest voices of all time. I couldn't go to school unless I put on an Elvis record like 'Blue Suede Shoes' to give me the will to get there. I also loved Little Richard, Roy Orbison and Fats Domino. I'd listen to all that under my covers at night. There was a station coming out of New Jersey which used to play all this stuff. I didn't want my parents to hear me listening to this, so I'd be under there with a flashlight listening to all this great shit." The idea of the teenage Alan Vega hunkered beneath a blanket trying to stifle his adolescent euphoria under threat of parental wrath, as unholy rollers like Elvis, Fats and Richard howled their forbidden southern hoodoo, is priceless.

Pat Boone had already released his milk-doused rendition of Little Richard's 'Tutti Frutti' (which was about gay sex) as part of the ongoing white pop goon's heisting of black rock'n'roll, making it easier for mass consumption and a way for the mainstream to break into this lucrative new market. What started happening in the mid-fifties was actually the loudest explosion in a trail which began in the late forties, when there was a rocking new phenomenon going on in black music ignited by New Orleans piano pounder Roy Brown, who harnessed his chanting lyrics and rhythmic hand-clapping to the blues-derived prototypes being conjured by Big Joe Turner and Louis Jordan. Roy sang about black street life, the pleasures of drink, blow-jobs, rocking the joint, and tearing its roof off. His 'Good Rockin' Tonight' was the first song to use the term "rockin'" as universal good time declaration, rather than a clean way of saying "fuckin'". The thriving chitlin' circuit gleefully celebrated wild new names, such as flamboyant Macon teenager Richard Penniman, who would sashay between the Tip In Inn, where his dad sold bootleg whiskey, and the Church of God, where his family sang in the choir, hatching that taboo-groping meeting of the sacred and the profane called Little Richard. Black music enjoyed its own street-level watering holes which would change music, decades before CBGB and Max's Kansas City did the same for another generation.

When Wynonie Harris' cover of 'Good Rockin' Tonight' became a national 'race' hit in 1948, a new genre lit up black theatres all over the

US (and the song would be a hit again when Elvis covered it five years later). Roy's revival meeting-like crusade around the country helped prod *Billboard* into renaming its African-American music chart from 'Race' to 'Rhythm & Blues' in summer 1949, which saw the blues-derived revolution inaugurated by Louis Jordan earlier in the decade taking over the black pop charts. After Elvis came out of Memphis, rock'n'roll became defined as what had happened that time in Sun Studio when black rhythm and blues mated with white country & western music, but when Roy Brown was rocking back in 1949, white consumers were still bathing in aural saccharine, and country & western fans were yodelling along to waltzes and steel guitars. The twain couldn't hear each other, let alone meet, until 1954 when that bunch of Memphis white kids started playing like musicians they'd seen or heard on the radio, forging a new style through absorbing blues, country, pop and gospel, churning them around with teenage energy, then disgorging them as simple, blistering rock'n'roll, in its most basic rockabilly incarnation.

These were the original musical ructions which first grabbed Alan around 1955 (and would palpably reappear in his early eighties solo albums), and Marty a few years later, when he also plunged hook, line and sinker into the doo-wop form. Alan immediately identified with rock'n'roll's rebellion. He names James Dean as an early hero, although the young star was killed in a car crash before his ground-breaking teen trauma vehicle *Rebel Without A Cause* hit the screens in 1955, establishing him as the first teenage rebel anti-hero and posthumous cult icon.

Directed by Nicholas Ray, the film presents a harsh picture of the restless urban teenager, and shows just how wide the generation gap had become. Dean's Jim Stark starts the movie lying drunk on the sidewalk before being dragged into the juvenile division of the local police station, where he meets Sal Mineo's Plato and Natalie Wood's Judy, who's been mistaken for a hooker in her red dress and hauled in. School goes badly for Jim, who clashes with meathead jocks, climaxing in the fatal chickie run on the cliffs, shootouts and tragic curtains for Plato. While Alan recalls being told he looked like Mineo, he cites the film as a crucial early sighting of the new breed of young urban rebel, along with *Blackboard Jungle*, which also appeared that year with theatre-wrecking consequences.

Blackboard Jungle debuted rock'n'roll on the big screen, often the only part of the cinema left unscathed in the seat-destroying rampages and jiving in the aisles which broke out at many screenings, including in the UK. Based on Evan Hunter's novel about teenage delinquency in a tough, inner city school, the opening and closing credits over Bill Haley & the Comets' 'Rock Around The Clock' almost certainly sparked these early teenage riots because rock'n'roll was being experienced on big speakers for the first time. Alan describes the film as "mindboggling". *Blackboard Jungle*, no matter how dated it may seem now, kickstarted the rock'n'roll revolution. The producers craftily presented it as a public information document, giving the storyline sociological weight in the film's opening reel, assuring viewers that this was not an exploitation film but a serious look at the growing epidemic of "juvenile delinquency" infecting America's schools. After war veteran teacher Richard Dadier (Glenn Ford) turns up on his first day to find his multi-ethnic class of kids from the wrong side of the tracks jiving to Bill Haley, they subject him to a savage campaign of abuse, although he bonds with a black kid called Miller, played by Sidney Poitier, who shows him the often grimmer problems he has to face outside of the classroom. Of course, there's gonna be a showdown, but 'Daddy-O' (the first use of the term on celluloid) wins on the strength of his teaching and communication skills.

The film introduced the masses to a new hip vernacular, teenage rebellion and rock'n' roll; stereotyping it as the domain of leather-jacketed, knife-wielding street punks with outrageous hair, anti-social attitude and bleak futures. Lives were changed and battle lines drawn for the next few decades. At least subliminally, Alan now had seminal influences to draw on when he took to Manhattan's downtown stages with Suicide in the early seventies. What was the original Alan Suicide but the most hellishly extreme manifestation of this alarming vision of American degeneracy and 'moral decline'?

Although Elvis never appeared on *American Bandstand*, Alan's daily shot of Dick Clark's TV show, which saw teenagers frugging to top 40 music of the day, with at least one act coming on to lip-sync their latest hit, helped fuel the fire started by the King and *Blackboard Jungle*. Rock'n'roll was now firmly embedded in Alan's soul while he experienced downtown Manhattan's late fifties beat-scape and avant garde artistic community. But Brooklyn wasn't going to let him go that easily.

TWO

While Alan Vega loomed up front as the crowd-baiting agitator and crooner-from-hell delivering Suicide's nightmare urban missives and damaged love calls, Martin Rev was the mysterious, insect-shaded figure to his side, extracting anything from heaving cacophony to twinkling doo-wop eloquence from his self-customised heap of electronic keyboard circuitry, taking what he called the Instrument into areas rarely ventured into by the avant garde, let alone the synth-pop he's known to have blueprinted.

As this book neared completion, Marty started contemplating how he was going to approach the upcoming Barbican event billed as a 'Punk Mass', after Suicide's earliest gigs. It was almost possible to hear his unquenchable questing spirit and inherent sense of mischief battling against the fact that some punters might just be coming to take selfies against 'Ghost Rider'. But Marty's life philosophy is born from his jazz upbringing as a refusal to stand still and emulate anyone, least of all himself. It's the oil that has kept Suicide's machine turning while Alan expresses the mood and the message. From his earliest experiences singing falsetto to doo-wop records and improvising piano from jazz sheet music of the fifties, Marty's life has been a fearless musical odyssey and one long lesson, whether knocking on drumming legend Tony Williams' door, sitting next to greats such as Lennie Tristano, or facing the crowd at New York's legendary Five Spot as a wide-eyed teenager in a band of seasoned black jazz men. With Alan Vega, Marty found an opposite but perfect partner to venture into terrain no normal rock band dreamed existed, even in their worst nightmares.

Quietly aware of the importance of image, Marty started sporting his trademark huge shades in the seventies, during which time he was perceived as a laconic genius, who preferred to retreat to the company of lifelong partner Mari when things got too intense. When writers have dealt with Suicide in the past, they usually focus on the 'shocking' first album or the axe-throwing abuse crowds subjected them to, which were ultimately just two vital but routine parts of a far more layered picture. I first became aware of Marty's knack for expounding with humble, soft-spoken eloquence on the music that inspired him when I was putting together the New York music history compilation. It then became clear to me that his extensive knowledge and quietly assured outlook provide a necessary foil to Alan's outgoing intensity. Talking to Marty is an endlessly fascinating roller coaster once he opens up, as he is capable of riffing through stories of doo-wop, modern jazz, electric keyboards and the inner machinations of Suicide in the time it takes to play a game of pinball.

In many ways, Marty adheres to his declaration that the basis of a person's direction, no matter what transpires later, "is still imprinted from what you had between one and six, or one and ten, at the most". His earliest memories of his father start with the musical jam sessions which took place at the family home every Sunday afternoon, with dad leading on the mandolin, and also pay tribute to his old man's days as a promising young actor and "working class guy" who became a union leader and made sure his family never went short.

When his father, Milton, whose own parents were first generation immigrants from Eastern Europe, was born, the Reverby family were living four miles from downtown Boston in Revere Beach, which was established as America's first public beach in 1896. The oldest of three brothers, Milton came to New York City when his parents moved to Brooklyn. He initially held ambitions to become an actor, enrolling in classes at the same Brooklyn College later attended by Alan Vega.

By the thirties, Milton had become semi-professional, studying with the influential Group Theatre, which was formed in 1931 by directors Harold Clurman and Cheryl Crawford, along with method acting pioneer Lee Strasberg. Gathering at various New York venues, the Group Theatre attracted actors, directors, writers and producers who learned the artistic acting techniques inspired by Russian actor-director Konstantin Stanislavski, staging works by important American playwrights for ten years before mutating into the seminal Actors Studio.

"Stage acting was what he was gonna do," says Marty. "He was with his peers, like John Garfield and Lee J. Cobb. All those guys were at the same stage. They were young and planning, doing classes, trying to get roles." But Milton's thespian career was cut short when the Depression kicked in and, being the oldest son, he had to get what was called a proper job. "He had to leave everything. It was impressed upon him as what he had to do as his responsibility to his family as the oldest brother, and he felt responsible enough to do it."

Milton started working as an organiser in the unions, "from the time before they were legal and were still building the labour movement in America from the ground up. You would go on strike and could go to jail. He was involved in the department store union, very prestigious in terms of their values, outlook and vision. They started out working in the Lower East Side in little places where you'd get a job packing up what they called dry goods. It used to be down around Orchard Street, where there were little shops selling linens and clothing and this and that. You can still see some of it now. They were run by poor local working class kids basically, many who ended up becoming very big, like the people who created Bloomingdale's and Macy's. The big chains started out with these bosses in these little stores."

Milton relocated to the Bronx after he met and married Marty's mother, Louise, "a Bronx girl, and also a musician. As a girl she studied piano for several years, which was unusual in her circumstances because they were all poor kids." Joining older brother Laurence, Martin Reverby was born on December 18, 1947, at Lutheran Hospital on 144th Street and Convent Avenue, Morningside Heights. He will allow that he is a Sagittarius.

Marty spent his first four years in the family home on Anderson Avenue, a few blocks up from Yankee Stadium. August Darnell, the future Kid Creole, whose path would cross with Suicide's in the late seventies, was growing up in this part of the Bronx around the same time, giving it credit for his attitude to life, people and genre-demolishing music. "I couldn't imagine being what I am today," says Darnell, "without having been brought up in the Bronx. It was a true melting pot, Irish, Jewish, blacks, Puerto Ricans and Italians, all cramped into this small area. As a child I never saw any conflict between races or religions. For me the Bronx was a fantastic place to grow up, realising that the world comprised different colours, shapes and ideologies without leaving your borough. That's the greatest lesson life can give."

The Reverbys then moved to a house on 225th Street, in Bayside, Queens, near Little Neck Bay and a few blocks from Union Turnpike. "Luckily for me, I was born into a bit more comfort because by that time my father had achieved lower middle class status so they were able to move a little out of the city," he recalls. "Not anything tremendously fancy or big, but I never knew any economic duress. Sometimes my father took me when he went to the strikes at department stores, to give my mother a break. It was probably before I started at school; 'Take Marty out'. I would find myself on those lines, holding the signs."

If political awareness was instilled at an early age, the Reverbys also encouraged a musical household. "My family all played music unprofessionally. It still amazes me how incredible a musician my dad was. He was one of the most innately talented musicians I've ever known in my life. Every Sunday, he would pick up a mandolin and just play song after song, all from out of his head. The songs were well-known folk songs from his childhood. He always amazed me. I saw him once years later, when we were up in a loft where I was living with Mari. One of the jazz musicians was keeping his vibes there. My father casually walked over and started playing around with the sticks. Within three minutes he was picking out songs. Although he could not play a note, he had that kind of ear where he could play an instrument like that, without any knowledge. He never studied. He told me later he wanted to study violin when he was a kid, but his parents wouldn't let him because they were poor and needed money. He had a mandolin in a case and would just pick it up and play one song after another, with my brother Larry on accordion. I was still quite a baby but I heard that."

Marty remembers getting into the band by shaking some marbles in a plastic container, "like a rattle or a shaker. I joined in when they were playing, like the drummer. Once in a while, they'd have conventions where my father worked, up in the mountains in upstate New York. People would take their kids. You could go into these late shows with comics and singers, where the adults used to go and drink. Dad would go to a bar in the afternoons, in the grounds of these resorts, where they'd all be drinking. If one of the kids walked in, nobody's gonna say anything. There was a jukebox, which again was so relevant because the music was more real. It wasn't formatted or anything like that. It was very exciting."

Marty's mother sorted him out with piano lessons at a young age, her natural love of music also rubbing off on him. "My mother was the kind of person who, if she was driving in the car in the afternoon, the radio was always on and she was always singing; not loudly, but always completely into every song that would come on; the songs of the day, the pop songs, doo-wop, whatever. She'd be humming and singing along, just naturally. I started playing piano that way. I was given lessons that I wanted to quit immediately, or at least for the next year or two. They just got in my way when I felt like going and playing ball on a Friday afternoon, and I didn't wanna do it."

Although he stuck with the lessons, like Alan Bermowitz over in Brooklyn, and millions of other American kids, the young Rev was glued to the radio and excitedly watched *American Bandstand* every day. It was the age of rock'n'roll, doo-wop and unfettered rhythm and blues, if you knew where to look. "Elvis, rock'n'roll, *a capella* and doo wop was basically what I was brought up on," says Marty. "My pre-teenage years were rock'n'roll. That was my environment. I had a little transistor radio in the fifties. We went to the prom and did dances. I would watch *American Bandstand* every afternoon when I got back from school."

Even before Elvis' arrival, white American teenagers had twigged that the sanitised pop they were being force fed paled against the records being made for the 'race' market. By the end of 1954, such major tunes as 'Earth Angel' by the Penguins and 'Sh-Boom' by the Chords were riding high in the charts, having swaggered in from the black rhythm and blues substrata. The main purpose of the US charts at that time was to keep stores in the loop on what records were flying out. The demand for black music snowballed, exacerbated in New York City when high profile radio station WINS hired DJ Alan Freed to host its rock'n'roll programmes, which bolstered the bridge between R&B and rock. Freed was responsible for exposing countless white teenagers to R&B, putting on vast extravaganzas featuring artists of the day, which removed racial barriers in music for the first time. Rev's newfound love of doo-wop would lodge much deeper in his soul than any passing childhood fad.

Unlike today's sensorily deprived internet bombardment, every music fan of a certain age remembers their first time going into a record shop and handing over real money for the hot fave they'd heard on the radio. It was like entering a magical new world, every hard-earned purchase an event. Marty vividly remembers acquiring his first two 45s when he was around ten years old. First came 'At The Hop' by Philadelphia vocal group Danny & the Juniors, which topped the US charts in January 1958. The song, about the scene at a record hop, was notable for combining the two most popular hit formulas in fifties rock'n'roll: 12-bar blues and the 'doo-wop' progression. It was originally called 'Do The Bop' until Dick Clark suggested the name change, which secured the appearance on *American Bandstand*, guaranteeing overnight success. His second single was 'Get A Job' by the Silhouettes, a towering example of animated doo-wop magic, which topped the charts in February 1958. This was punk-presaging social commentary, written by the group's tenor, Richard Lewis, after he returned from the services and his mother nagged him to find employment. The group, also from Philly, came up with the "Sha na na" and "Dip dip dip" exclamations which would grace hundreds of doo-wop tunes.

"Doo-wop was the music of my time," enthused Marty when he stepped up as my adviser on the subject for the New York music series in 2011. "It was coming right out of the neighbourhoods, off the streets and from the corners. You heard it when you went to school, when you went to dances, when you turned on the radio. Doo-wop was our music. The thing about doo-wop was that it was such an idealised thing. It was *religiously* romantic. All this stuff comes out of the church anyway with gospel, just in different interpretations. The love songs border on pure prayer, aspiring to something celestial. It was an incredibly romantic time to be brought up hearing that stuff. It was the music you fell in love to, the soundtrack to incredibly in-depth emotions of love. You combine that with being a teenager."

Doo-wop's heartbreaking confessionals, courting struts and yearning skyline serenades were the sound of young black New York in the late fifties. Running parallel with jazz, it was a proper product of the streets, the poetry of inner city life evolving on rooftops and in empty subway stations, as disaffected teenagers escaped their overcrowded homes and demoralising poverty by singing in harmony about subjects close to their hearts, usually girls.

Having gripped Alan too, doo-wop is the not-so-secret ingredient in Suicide's incandescent future-blues, providing the vulnerable human element and underlying romantic swoon that lifts them somewhere special. Rev's later solo works would strive to capture doo-wop's angelic beauty and sound like a transmission from a distant, purer time.

"It was the kids on the streets who were making the music," states Marty. "The music business was just starting to build too, so it was all fresh and open. The record companies were just starting to cut 45s, then going to the DJs and pressing to get them on the radio. It existed before, certainly, but not in terms of this generation and this music. Before it was all 78s and now there were 45s. There was always race radio up until the early fifties. Here in New York, it was really starting to become more of a mix though. It was right off the corners. It wasn't yet corporately controlled or formatted, although they tried to dismember and dislodge it for many reasons, just like punk."

Predictably, record labels tried to brush doo-wop off as a fad, before its implications in post-war integration between black and white audiences, and also street gangs, emerged as it started gripping the charts and sparked huge events. Marty named the heavenly serenade of Cole Porter's 'In The Still Of The Night' by the Five Satins as a crucial late fifties New York anthem. The masterstroke is the languid saxophone solo which slides in midway, there to be air saxed, eyes closed, head tilted, imagining the lights of Manhattan twinkling above like the stars of love. Asked to name the song that sums up the whole era, Marty immediately cites 'Why Do Fools Fall In Love' by Frankie Lymon & the Teenagers. "That song was very big. He was the quintessence of New York at that time. He was a New Yorker, from Spanish Harlem; just a kid, 14 years old." If only the group's own story could have been as innocent as the song sounds. Lymon was born in a Washington Heights tenement in September, 1942, when the neighbourhood, which Marty would later count as home, was a hotbed of prostitutes, junkies and dealers, so he grew up getting into trouble, hustling prostitutes by the age of 13 and OD'ing by 1968. He also rated the Charts ("they had great songs, like one called 'Desirie'"), the Channels ("a truly great group"), Dion & the Belmonts and, particularly, the Paragons and the Jesters, whose *The Paragons Meet The Jesters* could be the genre's definitive album.

The Paragons were far removed from the smoother doo-wop that could slide easily into the mainstream. The style, sometimes called 'greasy', was big on the East Coast, primitively recorded with simple, pumping piano, while vocals soared and swooped like exotic birds weaving through dark tenements. It was an unusually untamed sound with rough edges, which, according to the group, arose because they didn't really know how to sing and taught each other. Forming in 1955, tenor Ricky Jackson, bass Al Brown and baritone Donald Travis hailed from Bed-Stuy, while second tenor Gable 'Ben' Frazier hailed from nearby Brownsville. The four Brooklyn kids lived for practising harmonies at the Ralph Avenue subway station, on the intersection with Fulton Avenue in Bedford-Stuyvesant, or at their school, Thomas Jefferson High. Donald's sister recommended the melismatic falsetto of Julius McMichael. Taking their name from the Paragon Oil Company, the group were inspired by the Drifters, Flamingos, Moonglows and Continentals. An unproductive stint with Harlem-based manager Hiram Johnson led the Paragons to legendary 125th Street entrepreneur Paul Winley, who many first encountered in the late seventies through his *Super Disco Breaks* bootleg albums and labels such as Enjoy, which gave artists such as Afrika Bambaataa and Grandmaster Flash their first platform.

The Paragons Meet the Jesters was released in August, 1959, and has since been hailed as the ultimate late fifties New York doo-wop soundtrack, with Winley using the two groups to evoke street corner singing battles and show competitions. The sleeve might be the first gang-related album cover, although Mort Goode's cover notes point out "There'll be no gang war here. …This is a rumble on the beat." The Jesters were students at Harlem's Cooper Junior High, and had honed their harmonies under an elevated station near 120th Street, before being discovered by Winley when they won Amateur Night at the Apollo. Their hits included 'So Strange' and 'Please Let Me Love You', sitting on the album with the Paragons singles.

Rev remembers the album's impact. "*The Paragons Meet The Jesters* is one of the classics, but it was lesser known at that time because they didn't enjoy the radio success that others did. The tracks on there are just celestial, like 'Twilight', which is just extreme."

So great was its impact on him, the album became a real fork in the road for Marty's future musical direction. "I was now thinking that I'd like to be a falsetto," he confesses. "I was getting to identify with the vocal groups so much; my heart was more into that. I used to listen to that record all the time." At this point, Marty spontaneously bursts into his own rendition of 'Twilight', before continuing "To me, that was the direction I wanted to go in, but I also had this heavy instrumental background I wanted to keep going with too. In the end I didn't attach to becoming a vocalist, I attached to jazz."

Things might have turned out very differently if Marty had followed his teenage heart along the upper registers of the doo-wop route, but jazz was already waiting for him on the next big corner, snapping its fingers, puffing on a cigarette and in no hurry, safe in the knowledge it would dominate his entire musical adolescence and oncoming decade. It came with a grounding and education in socio-political awareness, which started at home.

"I think I was there anyway," Marty now reflects. "It was the times, and coming from a family like I did. My parents were not unconscious people. They were very clear what they felt about what was going on. They understood economics, the systems of class and racism, all those things. If I had questions, they would answer in a broad context. They weren't complacent, like those people who didn't really know or care. They knew, at least from their vantage point, exactly what was happening. Naturally, I got some of that from them, because I never felt they were hypocritical. Like when you see your father say something to his friends, and you feel it's really genuine. When you feel your parents are being phony, it's another generation, but when you feel the sincerity, it goes right into you. Then you can identify with them in any generation. Their choice of books definitely helped, along with the music."

When Marty was ten, the Reverby family moved to a house on Goethals Avenue and 167th Street, the other side of Union Turnpike, in Jamaica, Queens. Marty attended Jamaica High School on Gothic Avenue. At that time it was the largest high school in Queens, with over 4,600 pupils. Alumni include the Cleftones singing group, composer Gunther Schuller, cartoonist Art Buchwald and film director Francis Ford Coppola.

The books which Marty devoured around the age of 12 had a strong impact on his adolescent outlook. Some dated from during the Depression, sitting in the bookcase waiting to be opened by the next generation. These included controversial African-American author Richard Wright, who'd left years of racism growing up in Memphis and Mississippi to come to New York in 1937, where he joined the Communist *Daily Worker* before being exiled to Europe. Howard Fast, whose most popular works included *Citizen Tom Paine*, a fictional account of the life of the 18th century activist, *The Last Frontier*, about an attempt by the Cheyennes to return to their native land, and *Freedom Road*, which concerned the lives of former slaves during reconstruction (made into a film starring Muhammad Ali in 1979).

"They had a lot of stuff that was very important to them during the Depression, a lot of meaningful social fiction," recalls Marty. "I remember I read *Scottsboro Boy* by Haywood Patterson, which moved me incredibly. I could not put that down. The times were still that way; the civil rights struggle and situation in America was still there even if people didn't want to think about it, and had no sensitivity to it. *Scottsboro Boy* is like the thirties, a true story, but so relevant and so incredible. I also started getting into non-fiction legal stuff for a while, like Clarence Darrow's play *Inherit The Wind*, and Sacco and Vanzetti's trial."

This particular input extended to a natural love of black music, or as Marty puts it, "I was already listening to pretty much everybody I listen to, whether it was rock, doo-wop, and then jazz, which was then people of non-majority. They were called people of colour, to put it in the nicest way. Racism had been going on constantly in the country, with lynching and segregation, and the struggle in the fifties before I knew what was happening, like Eisenhower trying to protect a little girl going into school and the vehemence of the reaction down there. It was in the newspapers, it was all around you. Then you realised that in your environment, your world, in New York, everything was so separated. So-called black people living in apartheid in a totally separated situation. You felt it on the street if you passed a kid of colour. You felt the tension, you saw him and he saw you, and you knew you were in two different places, even if you weren't rich or anything. Because the society was so divided. That was the environment."

Marty's young mind was particularly caught by *Cell 2455, Death Row: A Condemned Man's Own Story*, the first memoir written on Death Row by convicted robber, rapist and kidnapper Caryl Chessman in 1954, who had been sentenced to the gas chamber in 1948 but maintained his innocence. Becoming the poster boy for the movement to ban capital punishment through his writing, he won several stays of execution, and world fame. "That was an incredible story," remembers Marty. "The guy spent much of his entire life on Death Row, and became an incredible scholar and writer. He claimed his innocence. He told everything that happened between his accusation, and the horror of his life going into that accusation. You're talking about someone who'd been on Death Row for years, then the fact that he had shown such an incredible evolution. The whole book was a testament to the fact that you can't execute this guy. Eventually they executed him, the motherfuckers. They just wanted to. Those were very impressive books to me."

After choosing piano over doo-wop singing, Marty returned to furthering his technique, which he soon had down to playing songs he heard on the radio. "When I started doing that, then I could take my own direction, and start to improvise, like boogie woogie stuff. None of that was far from the times. It was out of Big Joe Turner, although the forties was like the Middle Ages. Music that came beforehand was now all fed into Bill Haley & the Comets and Little Richard. It got on the radio for that whole teenage phenomenon. Teenagers had existed before, but after the war the whole technology came in with cars and the emergence of the middle class."

Marty gained a futuristic aspect to his outlook from the rapid evolution of technology, "The product explosion; washing machines, electric vacuum cleaners. The cars were incredible. As a kid, you couldn't wait until the new Cadillacs and Chevys came out. Every year they were so innovative and sci-fi, all trying out new things, bigger, crazier. This was before there was any worry about size and energy conservation. I never had any urgency to get a car, but I loved the designs as they were so exciting. Nothing was done for practicality, it was all done for style, and the look of the future. I guess it was sci-fi when it became the vision of what may happen, what was in the air. That was what we would fantasise about. High sci-fi stuff in the twilight zone."

Although "even as a pre-teenager, I'd play some 'Barrel House Boogie Woogie' when called upon to concertise", by 1962 Marty had become good enough on piano to play local gigs, "like rhythm and blues things. That was fine, but I didn't feel there was a tremendous challenge. But that was the way I was seeing it, in terms of instrumental rock keyboard at that time. My first ever gig was with a saxophone player I knew in public school. We played for an hour or so in a church. I guess there may have been dancing. After that I did an assortment of R&B and jazz gigs, all with different bands. I would get called by my name being passed around. A year or two later I played with a steady band in venues in St Albans, Queens and uptown Manhattan. These weren't rock bands. Those didn't start until Suicide, although some early teenage summer gigs in the mountains required playing some of everything, and the Beatles were in great demand at that time. But I remember improvising a lot as a kid before I even heard jazz."

So even at an early age, Marty was feeling stifled by the traditional styles of music he was being required to play. He had already started getting into jazz through brother Larry, who was squeezing out radio faves of the day from sheet music, on his accordion. A two-page arrangement of an obscure song called 'Eighth Street Rag' caught Marty's attention when Larry started cranking it through his squeeze-box. He started playing along, and began to improvise.

Previously bound by radio playlists, Marty's musical universe had revolved around hits of the day and whatever he could glean from records, such as "a couple of albums my parents had in the house which maybe came from a club and were just put on the shelf, like a Lester Young." But jazz went out on the radio past his bedtime, like forbidden fruit waiting to be grabbed and gobbled.

Hearing jazz turned Marty's head and provided that magic moment when the future becomes crystal clear. "I wasn't into writing songs at all, but then I heard jazz. You couldn't just sit down and play that. It was beyond boogie woogie and everything. It was incredibly sophisticated by the time you got to the late fifties and early sixties. That's when I said to myself, 'How do I do that?'"

His new obsession skyrocketed when Larry acquired a reel-to-reel tape recorder. In the early sixties, this was regarded as an exclusive pathway to the future through state-of-the-art technology. For the just-turned-teenage Rev, it was "like the greatest invention", especially when Larry started "taping these jazz programmes, which were on the radio too late for me to be up, and started compiling these reels, which I heard him play. I already felt that improvising was what I was gonna do for a couple of years. I was going through the jazz fake books after my brother got one. I asked him to show me how to make chords and then started figuring out, in a very basic way, the chords to all those songs. The modern jazz fake book had all these very hip songs from Miles and Gerry Mulligan. So I was doing that, and playing all the time."

While Larry favoured saxophonist Mulligan, three pioneering giants struck Marty enough to become his inspirational cornerstones through the upcoming decade: Thelonious Monk, John Coltrane and Miles Davis. He had some catching up to do, which is part of the fun, but steamed in with the kind of possessed enthusiasm that would fire any musical path he now followed. "I'm like that when I embrace something. When I get into something that excites me, that I feel I wanna learn and be able to do, I tend to jump into the deep water and try and embrace it all as a true believer. Eventually, you come to shore the other side and have taken everything you've been through with you."

Even by the end of the sixties, Marty would still be swimming a furious crawl to land he wasn't even looking for yet, such were the intoxicating diversions and inspirational figures he would encounter on the way to hitting a monolithic island named Suicide.

THREE

Suicide was a product of the revolutionary sixties. While Marty followed the jazz trail, Alan spent much of the decade zigzagging between his working life in Brooklyn and the clubs and art galleries of Manhattan, which only served to stoke the budding creative dynamo he was fast becoming.

After graduating from Brooklyn College as an art and science major, Alan initially followed the same path as most local men of his age, getting married and settling in Brooklyn Heights, working factory jobs to survive. He effectively wrote this period out of his story when Suicide started, along with the ten years he shaved off his birthdate. Ask him now and Alan's allusions to that period revolve around his trips to Manhattan. "Jazz, the Beats... hanging around SoHo, St Mark's Place, that was our home," he says.

"Alan was like a kid who married right out of school," recalls Marty, "He was living in the Brooklyn Heights neighbourhood, making a living like a married guy down there, with that kind of Brooklyn Heights mentality, which was basically middle class."

Alan could have done worse than choose Brooklyn Heights for his first marital home. By the mid-fifties, the classic brownstones of New York's first historically preserved neighbourhood were being renovated by hungry property owners. Today it's one of the most desirable, highest-priced locations in New York state; the landing area for the Brooklyn and Manhattan bridges, flanked by Dumbo, Downtown Brooklyn, Cobble Hill and Boerum Hill. One good thing that came out of ruthless developer Robert Moses' megalomaniac urban restructuring of the forties and fifties

– which included the building of the Brooklyn-Queens Expressway and the flattening of many local brownstones to build huge apartment blocks – was the Brooklyn Heights Esplanade. Few sights on Earth beat the view of the Manhattan skyline from across the East River seen from there at night. Alan spent the next few years working on his sculptures and soaking up the new music coming in, looking at those lights flickering across the water, dreaming of the inevitable.

Martin Reverby had fallen deeply for the jazz lifestyle, from its fearless civil rights stance and struggles against severe odds to its mind-blowing innovations and cool image. By the early sixties, he had transformed from doo-wop hopeful to cool bebop kid.

Brother Larry's tapes opened many early doors. "A lot of the music was from a couple of years before. What Miles was doing in 1954 or '56 still sounded very fresh and important. I got into it and started thinking about this seriously. I'm that way that if I hear something and like it and I can't do it, well let me try and do it! By the age of 15, I was really immersed in the challenge of jazz. As an instrumentalist coming out of doo-wop and R&B, my native music, I didn't find it a difficult thing. I was doing these little gigs with my keyboard already but it was rhythm and blues. Jazz was so relevant then. Socially and politically, it was such a contemporary expression of the times in New York and all over America. It was incredibly deep study to master the forms at that time, because it was in its post-modern period, where you had to be incredibly sophisticated musically. You had to study like crazy to get to that level, but I was really into it."

He started learning about jazz; its history, protagonists, masters and rebels, which led to names like Lester Young and Bud Powell, and to movements such as bebop, the first major post-war musical revolution, whose virtuosos, outsiders, junkies and outlaws changed history after initially being met with abject horror by the jazz establishment. "It was very insular, in many respects, compared to other forms of art; a very small and cool society," says Marty. "The sad thing, but also a factor that made jazz and American black music so great for generations, was that the African-American community was so detached from the mainstream. It wasn't allowed in. In many respects, it was even shut out. They were forced to find their own way of life, but had such a richness of expression through their history, from slavery to the church through to spirituals. They had an incredible vocabulary to draw on, from their own experience."

And a fertile place to express it after World War Two. Shortly before and during the war, New York had seen an influx of European artists and intellectuals fleeing Hitler and the Holocaust, bringing with them new ideas and cultures. Despite it often seeming like they'd been used (in similar fashion to the Vietnam War later), the black presence in the war had still elevated self-esteem and started an unravelling of Jim Crow restrictions, sparking militant reaction when it became obvious these sacrifices hadn't brought any new status. New York had long been a magnet for those looking for a better standard of living, and a unique form of excitement that couldn't be found in rural areas. It became a fertile paradise for aspiring artists and impassioned musicians, as well as entrepreneurs looking to make a fast buck. This sense of mutual invasion, competition and unleashed creativity partly explains the city's highly strung energy, and the deluge of ground-breaking music it produced for the rest of the century.

"New York was like the centre of the arts, just as Paris and Vienna had been earlier," says Marty. "Everybody came to New York; whether opera, classical or dance."

Many who also flocked to New York, uneducated and out of their depth, found it cruel and huge, with cramped, squalid, segregated living conditions and low-level employment prospects. This inevitably inspired underground artistic movements, jazz one of the most unfettered as it started trampling traditions, creating bebop, whose first recordings are generally considered those released in 1945 by Dizzy Gillespie and Charlie Parker. They were experimenting with advanced harmonics, syncopation and chord mutation, shot with solos which might take a swing standard as the basis for a new form. Based on high-speed polyrhythms accented by bass drum 'bombs', bebop brought rhythm to the fore, prodding torrential flights from the soloists as melodic, harmonic and rhythmic innovations went surfing on this fresh new wave. Dizzy met Charlie 'Bird' Parker when the latter arrived in New York in 1942, the pair joining musicians including pianist Thelonious Monk, guitarist Charlie Christian and drummers Kenny Clarke and Max Roach who were hatching the nascent strain at Minton's Playhouse and Clark Monroe's Uptown House, in Harlem. Dizzy brought the new music downtown to 52nd Street, appearing regularly at clubs such as the Onyx, Three Deuces and Famous Door.

Although this first great wave of jazz modernism reinvigorated the flagging New York club scene, bebop (coined from Dizzy's nonsensical scatting) was unpopular with the press, which was then engaged in trying to upgrade jazz's image. The musicians weren't keen on any media tag they hadn't devised (rather like the dismay original punks would express at being lumped into someone else's manufactured craze). But *Downbeat* gamely tried to start a war between bebop and Dixieland jazz and, in 1946, *Time* magazine was describing bebop as "hot jazz overheated with overdone lyrics full of bawdiness, reference to narcotics, and doubletalk", played to crowds "high as barrage balloons". While an LA radio station refused to play bebop because they claimed it aroused degenerative instincts and contributed to juvenile delinquency, Leroy Jones could write in *Blues People*, "If only by implication, bebop led jazz into the arena of *art*, one of the most despised terms in the American language."

Marty was born too late to experience the bebop uprising first hand. He would later find out the jazz he was getting into had experienced its own version of the punk revolution he would be instrumental in pioneering by the mid-seventies. Spawned in smoky clubs, the speedy, aggressive bebop had shaken jazz to its core by stripping away the showbiz and orchestras to attract hip young crowds. It had given musicians a licence to bust out and improvise, paving the way for modern and free jazz forms. It also threw up the enigmatic genius of Thelonious Monk, his biggest early influence and first musical hero.

Marty started going to as many jazz shows and concerts as his age allowed, notably at the Five Spot on St Mark's Place, or the Village Vanguard on Seventh Avenue. Sporting the fearless front of the true believer, he blagged his way in and got known by the staff, as he pursued his snowballing quest to study and master this thrilling new music. Those first gigs, especially in impressionable early teen years, can shape someone for life. "Yeah, when I could get in, I started getting in, although I was under age. I loved it. It was so exciting to be in New York then, in the middle of everything. Everything was alive culturally."

Marty remembers getting into the Five Spot after it had moved from its original location on the Bowery to St Mark's Place in 1963. "That was the one I was familiar with when I was growing up. One time they opened up in the afternoons for Sunday matinees and you could get in under age. That's the first time I heard Monk."

Asked to define jazz for Lewis Lapham of the *Saturday Evening Post* in April 1964, Monk stated, "New York, man. You can feel it. It's around in the air." A sensitive musical visionary, Monk turned any technical limitations from being mainly self-taught into his greatest assets, developing his own time and space approach, splashed with unsettling dissonance, odd intervals, off-centre rhythms, a unique sense of drama and "the child-like approach", which Marty particularly noticed. As a performer and composer, even within bebop, Monk stood alone. He also gave the beboppers and parallel Beat movement a cool archetype and visual pacesetter with his hat, glasses and goatee.

Monk's six-month residency at the original Five Spot, running from July 4, 1957, helped establish him as a true innovator, bolstered by his sax player, John Coltrane. The Five Spot at 5 Cooper Square had officially opened for jazz the previous November, giving Cecil Taylor a place to play. Salvatore Termini had sold the bar, originally called the Bowery Café, to his sons Joe and Iggy in 1951, who renamed it and started putting on live music after the city tore down the Third Avenue El in 1955. Piano-playing neighbour Don Shoemaker told the Terminis he'd provide the music if they stuck in a piano, resulting in the venue acquiring its knackered old upright. By this time, artists were taking advantage of the cheap rents in the area and the Five Spot, with its pock-marked bar along one side of the dimly lit room, rickety tables, watery beer and jug wine, started attracting a noisily conspiring crowd which included Herman Cherry, Franz Kline, Willem de Kooning, Larry Rivers and Joan Mitchell, along with Ginsberg, Kerouac, Corso, Leroy Jones, Frank O'Hara, and musicians such as Dizzy, Mingus and Roach, plus many more jazz fans and scenesters. Anything went at the Five Star. Billie Holiday is said to have sung there one night; Norman Mailer sat, enraptured and high, five feet from Monk as he played; Leonard Bernstein got up to play; David Amram backed Kerouac's readings, and so on. After Ginsberg presented Monk with a copy of *Howl*, the pianist commented "It makes sense". By the end of the decade, the Five Spot was the hub of downtown bohemia.

Monk's Five Spot stint established the club as the most significant niterie in jazz history, while the pianist had become an internationally feted name by the following year. After signing to Columbia in 1962, he released *Monk's Dream,* his biggest selling album. Sadly, although he became an enigmatic sixties icon, Monk's bi-polar mental state led to a breakdown, the loss of his recording contract and, eventually, his death in February 1982.

"Monk was my biggest influence," reveals Marty. "As a kid hearing Monk, he was such an incredible individual, the way he looked, his personality, and his brilliant music. I guess Monk was like an older father figure to the other guys; very New York, very mature. He was our accepted leader. Everybody went to Monk for things. It wouldn't go the other way round. He was the essence of hip, of cool. They used to call him the high priest of bebop. Monk was the quintessential innovator, and the ultimate hipster, in the best sense of the word. Cool jazz to the rest of the world in that period was really Monk and Miles. But Miles was quoted as saying his teachers were Monk and Dizzy. Monk was the really great composer of that period. He had such a personal style of expression. In a way, he was more contemporary avant garde, more Bartok. He approached the piano as pure colour and sound. On his best playing, like 'Monk's Dream' and recordings like that, he's just playing pure splashes of sound."

In the early sixties, the new jazz was next to get histrionically pilloried. Even figures like Coltrane and Eric Dolphy, who *Downbeat*'s John Tymon attacked in November 1961, huffing, "Coltrane and Dolphy seem intent on deliberately destroying (swing)… bent on pursuing an anarchistic course in their music that can but be termed 'anti-jazz'." Far from being anti-jazz, Coltrane redefined the genre. His supernatural outpourings reach for ecstatic catharsis as he uncurls his ascending essence like a snake charmer for the soul. As Marty puts it, "Coltrane became, without saying a word, literally the spokesman of everything that was happening at that time, just by way of what was coming out of his horn. He actually embodied the whole civil rights movement. He was so vibrant and of the time, it was part of the fabric of what was happening in society. That's why you can't just manufacture these things all over again when you want to." (A point he likes to raise whenever Suicide are called to revisit their own era-defining works.)

Coltrane's musical journey came into its own after he signed to Bob Thiele's happening new Impulse! label in 1961, releasing *Africa/Brass*, then *John Coltrane: Live At The Village Vanguard*, complete with 'Chasin' The Trane', which saw Coltrane influenced by Sun Ra's squalling sax lieutenant John Gilmore. The track is widely considered to be the major milestone of sixties avant garde jazz. When future tenor titan Archie Shepp heard the track, he instantly joined the numbers rallying around the new

32

sound, and played on the recording sessions for 1964's transcendental landmark *A Love Supreme* (although his sessions didn't make the final cut).

Coltrane's former boss, the untouchable Miles Davis, shows up in Marty's story in various ways, whether as inspiration, real life figure or simply the most charismatic jazz icon of the last century. "I was fortunate to see Miles play a few times," he says. "He was a creator and everything he touched had to be thought out with an incredible amount of intelligence."

After growing beyond bebop, leaving Charlie Parker's band, hooking up with kindred spirit arranger Gil Evans (precipitating one of the last century's most influential musical partnerships) and igniting another movement in 1957 with *Birth Of The Cool*, Miles kickstarted another jazz genre called hard bop with 1954's 'Walkin'', which was more bluesy and less frenetic than bebop. Miles had come out of the heroin addiction he had just beaten sharper but shorter-fused, as his music became brooding, reflective and even more ground-breaking. Using the Harmon mute, his trumpet floated the haunted, disembodied tone that would dominate his playing for the next few years, starting with the great quintet which included new sax sensation Coltrane and pianist Red Garland (another Rev favourite).

Marty remains in awe of Miles' style, crediting the influence of pianist Ahmad Jamal on how his playing developed. "It was mostly the notes Miles left out. In terms of finding himself, his style started appearing very early on, just as soon as he got his feet on the ground after playing with Charlie Parker. Apparently, Ahmad Jamal was a great influence on Miles. He used to go to the clubs and just sit and listen to him. Jamal's approach was so incredibly cool and no one had played like that at that time; so infectious, so understated."

Rejuvenated, Miles signed to Columbia and replaced Garland with classically influenced young pianist Bill Evans, sculpting jazz milestones such as his heart-demolishing reading of George Gershwin's ghetto opera *Porgy And Bess*, whose time-stopping 'Summertime' shone on the first volume of my New York series, prompting Marty to comment "It's a perfect example of one of Miles' great attributes which, although it isn't talked about much, is the way he personalises the melody. He did that with 'Round Midnight' and 'Straight No Chaser'. He had this talent for playing something exactly the way he wanted to and making it sound great." It didn't stop there as Miles rounded off the fifties with *Sketches Of Spain* and *Kind Of Blue*, the best-selling jazz album of all time.

This was just some of the music Marty was catching up with as he felt his way through a new world in a new decade. Though he regrets being born too late for 'Bird'. "Unfortunately, he was a little bit before my time. I'd love to have seen him but I was a baby really, six in his last year. He spent most of his last years right around here where I live on the Lower East Side, on Tompkins Square." But the late Eric Dolphy was one trailblazing giant Marty was lucky enough to catch at the Five Spot. Although not one of jazz's more mainstream names, he's up there with Coltrane, Mingus, Ayler and Miles as one of its most revered, yet another genuinely innovative talent who died too young.

Dolphy was a dream sideman, respectful and sympathetic. He took part in Ornette Coleman's landmark *Free Jazz: A Collective Improvisation*. In 1963, Dolphy and a producer called Alan Douglas conducted sessions for his *Iron Man* and *Conversations* albums. Douglas later became a controversial figure after his involvement with Hendrix, but his eye for talent was keenly revolutionary, as he released these two albums on his own label which, in 1970, would unleash the seminal first Last Poets album, the birthplace of rap. In 1964, Dolphy signed with Blue Note and recorded the stellar *Out To Lunch!*, with trumpeter Freddie Hubbard, vibraphonist Bobby Hutcherson, bassist Richard Davis and drummer Tony Williams, who'd been shaking the foundations of Miles' band for a year and would become another major figure in Marty's musical coming-of-age.

Rev still remembers the life-changing impact of this miraculous band in action at the Five Spot. "I remember going there and hearing Eric Dolphy and Bobby Hutcherson. A group like that was incredible! That was just before Eric went to Europe." Tragically, Eric never came back. After touring Europe with Charles Mingus' sextet in early 1964, he intended to settle in Paris with his ballet dancer fiancee, but died mysteriously in Berlin on June 28, at the age of 36. The usual explanation is diabetic coma, although it's been said he was administered a shot of insulin which would have been stronger than the US dose, causing shock and death.

Marty's expanding circle of jazz friends got him into several major shows at this time. "I was about 15 or 16, and fortunate to know people who were exposed to the underground. You could call them 'heads', with a heavy bohemian influence. Everybody used to get high." After just turning 16, Rev witnessed Albert Ayler infamously clear the Lincoln Center with Cecil Taylor's Unit on New Year's Eve 1963, sandwiched on a bill opened by Coltrane and Dolphy and closed by Art Blakey's

Jazz Messengers. At that time, the Philharmonic Hall of the new Lincoln Center For The Performing Arts had been open for a year, built on the site of an over-crowded section of the west 60s known as San Juan Hill, whose empty tenements were last seen as the backdrop for Leonard Bernstein's New York gang Romeo and Juliet musical adaptation *West Side Story*. Another Robert Moses sweep, clearing out black and Latino residents, the massive complex also included opulent homes for the Metropolitan Opera House, New York Philharmonic, New York City Ballet and Juilliard School.

"They talk about it now as a classic gig, but we didn't know who was going to be on," recalls Marty. "I was really into that stuff and I'd already seen some people, but seeing Coltrane and Eric Dolphy and Taylor and Ayler live on the same bill? Sure! That's the kind of stuff you used to see in New York a lot then."

While he wasn't anywhere near as big an influence as Monk, Marty still considered Taylor's attack improvisations to be "an important book in my mental library". Taylor had studied at Boston New England Conservatory in the early fifties, where he discovered the likes of Schoenberg, Webern, Berg, Bartok and Stravinsky, consequently appreciating the way piano innovators Lennie Tristano and Dave Brubeck brought in European avant garde elements. While not averse to opening a concert playing the strings inside the piano, as he did at New York's Judson Hall in December 1963, Cecil was disdainful of European avant garde composers such as Stockhausen, whom he recalled using "Storm Troopers" at a New York concert, "shuttling everybody around and trying to look like they were going to punch somebody in the mouth if they didn't love the music". As he told A.B. Spellman for his 1966 book *Four Lives In The Bebop Business*, he tried not to snigger, but couldn't help himself, and got such a "salty" reaction from the zealous audience he did it again. Cecil maintained that "jazz improvisation comes out of a human approach", while Stockhausen was like "a meticulous, slow worker who knows each instrument, but he doesn't create any music."

This human element is a vital key to the sound of Marty Rev, and also Alan Vega and Suicide, no matter how machine-dominated their music is portrayed as. Suicide might have started as a performance protest art happening, but the heaving emotions being expressed, by any means necessary, were all theirs. "I remember people turning me on to Stockhausen in the sixties," recalls Marty, "and from there I discovered

Varese's electronic stuff, but in New York at that point I was between rhythm and blues and jazz." By now, Marty's days were increasingly spent traversing the thoroughfares of Manhattan, looking for music to electrify the mind and the body.

Taylor encountered practically the same problems that would befall Suicide the following decade. His uncompromising attitude could see him go months without a show, working as a dishwasher to support himself. Club owners hated that some of his pieces lasted 90 minutes, leaving no breaks for patrons to even acknowledge the existence of the bar, and feared for the safety of their pianos. He found a willing venue at the original Five Spot in November 1956, when he opened it up for jazz, but practically reduced the battered old piano to matchwood. Many sat in befuddled awe as Cecil pummelled the broken keys, stoking the reputation which would dog him from now on, but stood him in better stead when raw expression became more accepted the next decade. Even then, when he played his first ghetto show at the Coronet in Bedford-Stuyvesant in 1962, the crowd got aggressive and he was fired after one set. When Cecil protested, the manager drew a knife.

Cecil gave Albert Ayler his first break, Marty catching the last time the uproarious tenor sax colossus played with him at that Lincoln Center show. Ayler's ceiling-cracking skronk now stands as the most extreme example of cathartic self-expression in jazz, his apoplectic torrents navigating spirituals, standards, Salvation Army bands and even the French national anthem. Originally hailing from Cleveland, Ohio, Ayler used the hardest reed available, a plastic Fibrecane number four, to produce the loudest, fullest, most bull-throated sound ever to roar from a sax. Because he was shifting such a wodge of air through his tenor, he could work up a sonic boom like feedback from a guitar, bolstered by the R&B horn hooligan technique of growling from the back of the throat.

When Cecil hit Stockholm, Ayler asked to sit in. Taylor declined him but he got up anyway, stunning the pianist to the extent he sat back and let him blast. After releasing his first album on a Danish label in early 1963, Ayler settled in New York, playing with Cecil at the Take 3 club and getting befriended by Coltrane and Dolphy, who were appearing at the nearby Village Gate. By mid-1963 Ayler had been forced by Cecil's paucity of jobs to go back to Cleveland, returning to New York when the opportunity arose to live in a house his aunt owned in Harlem.

The Lincoln Center show was his last with Cecil, in a band also including drummer Sunny Murray, bassist Henry Grimes and alto player Jimmy Lyons, who tore through Taylor's 'In Fields', 'Octagonal Skirt' and 'Fancy Pants'. This time the bar did great business.

"I wasn't aware of Albert before that," says Marty. "I'd heard his name as the new agent provocateur on tenor, but I wasn't listening to him. There was a lot of excitement around him. All the musicians were whispering, 'Ayler, he's the one. He's the new evolution of the revolution.' I went to this show and it started with the John Coltrane Quartet with Eric Dolphy, then the Cecil Taylor Unit with, lo and behold, Albert Ayler. They played for about an hour non-stop. Nine tenths of the audience just walked out and went into the other rooms. That was the first time I heard Ayler. He was incredible. I was very moved, he was so striking. One honk, one big blast of that tenor and you knew why he was causing so much controversy. He *was* the next word. After that Art Blakey came on and the crowd returned. I respected Ayler, but he wasn't one that I took so internally. I was very aware of him, of course, absorbing so much of the so-called avant garde in jazz."

Although the most searing manifestation of the pain and protest coursing through the sixties, Ayler was also greeted with indifference or savage hostility during his short career. Reviews lamented his "violent provocation and senseless aggression", while catcalls emanated from the same foetid well which splattered the electric Dylan and was filling up for Suicide the following decade. But Albert still managed to make his defining statement the following year when he signed to nascent independent label ESP-Disk and released *Spiritual Unity*, now one of the cornerstones of the free jazz movement. It featured his renowned trio with Murray and Californian bassist Gary Peacock. *Spiritual Unity* would be Ayler's breakthrough album, unleashing a honking behemoth speaking in tongues through his instrument, accompanied by Peacock's swallow-diving bass flurries and Murray's ever-restless drum tapestries replacing steady beats with wildly embellished pulses, the trio seemingly suspended in their own space-time continuum.

When the late activist wordsmith and rap pioneer Gil Scott Heron first arrived in New York City as a teenager in 1962, he hit the street and asked a brother on the avenue, "Where can I find the blues?" "Well hey, you don't have to do anything," came the reply. "Just stand there." Although the 12-bar form had long ago been dismembered, all black music and, in

Suicide's world their own music too, was still just a form of blues. As Ayler told an interviewer, "The music we're playing is just the blues...a different kind of blues. This is the blues. The real blues. The new blues. The people must listen to this music because they'll be hearing it all the time, because if it's not me it'll be someone else who's playing it. It's the only thing that's left for musicians to play. All other ways have been explored."

This new blues, the new thing, free jazz, energy jazz, whatever it was called, continued to thrive in New York through the early sixties, brandished by names such as Ornette Coleman, Pharoah Sanders, Frank Wright and many who appeared on ESP-Disk. Jazz purists were faced with a concept which appeared to dismantle their entire platform of virtuoso chops, replacing cool expertise and chord sequences as the basis for improvisation with anarchic chaos and force 10 cacophony. Club owners were reluctant to jeopardise the jazz dollar, while critics felt undermined as their reference points for scholarly expounding were demolished with their chastity belts. Confronted with free jazz, they were lost for words, apart from insulting ones, thus invalidating their status unless they started blaming it on disintegrating social conditions. To civil rights activists, this sonic distillation of rage and turmoil was sweet music, echoing rising ghetto protest, channelled directly from gut emotions churning with militant fire. "It is the jazz issuing from the friction and harmony of the American Negro with his environment that captured the beat and tempo of our times," wrote Eldridge Cleaver in *Soul On Ice*.

By soaking up the new thing as a 15-year-old kid from Queens, Marty had already set out on the path he had decided for himself, even resisting, for now anyway, using free jazz as an excuse to dive into Cecil Taylor-style annihilation of his keyboard. First he wanted to learn the rudiments, theories and foundations of jazz and his chosen instrument. "What I was really trying to do was master what was happening before that, trying to be able to play on the level of Herbie Hancock, Bill Evans and Red Garland, while studying musicians like Bud Powell. That took such an incredible sophistication. That's what was challenging me. I eventually evolved into the avant garde and playing totally free, then, of course, to electronic free playing, then back to my roots, which is rock. But I didn't wanna jump right into it."

In 1963 Marty discovered that another seminal, but often overlooked, jazz piano great was living in his neighbourhood. Not only that, he gave lessons.

FOUR

One weekend afternoon in early 1963 Rev found himself traversing the leafy avenues of Queens' Jamaica Estates not too far from his home. Finally, he found the address on Palo Alto Street and knocked on the door of a big old house. He was here to play for Lennie Tristano, the blind piano iconoclast who had been bebop's most controversial innovator. By many accounts, a notoriously selective teacher.

Marty was let in and ushered into a closet-sized downstairs room, containing an upright piano. "That's where he would listen to you and decide if he wanted to teach you. I went right in and played for him." It must have gone well as, for the next two years, Marty visited Lennie's house every weekend for his lesson, establishing a rare bond with his softly spoken but firm new mentor as he learned exercises and techniques he would use for life, and in Suicide's engine room.

As Marty started learning who his new teacher was, he discovered he was in the presence of greatness. "I hadn't even heard of Lennie, and wasn't necessarily looking to find a teacher. When I started to look into and discover Lennie, I saw that he had incredible significance in the past. He had a unique approach that was very influential. He played with Charlie Parker, and just about everybody in that period. They had a tremendous respect for him, as he did for them."

Tristano is usually glossed over in Suicide-related writings; few have heard of him and he's never been a hip name to drop. He's generally ignored or sidelined in many jazz history books (like Suicide in accounts of seventies New York). When Lennie died of a heart attack in 1978, jazz had long been celebrating innovations he had made but not bothered

39

claiming, from free improvisation to studio overdubbing. As Ted Gioia writes in *The History Of Jazz*, Lennie was "something of a Nostradamus of the bop era: when the future of jazz finally arrived, it bore a striking resemblance to how he thought it *should* be."

Born in Chicago in March 1919 (his dad was Italian and moved to the US as a child), Lennie lost his sight through childhood flu and glaucoma, attending the Illinois School for the Blind between 1928 and 1938. Something of a prodigy, he studied at the American Conservatory of Music in Chicago, and was teaching by the early forties. In 1946, after teaching and playing in clubs with Chicago alto player Lee Konitz, Lennie moved to New York, where he played in bands with Dizzy, Max Roach and 'Bird', who loved his rhythmic complexity and the ground-breaking techniques he derived from classical music. "He kind of combined Bach with Bud Powell," says Marty.

When tenor saxophonist Wayne Marsh started studying with him in 1948, Lennie called Konitz and formed the sextet that recorded *Crosscurrents*, spontaneously presaging free jazz, and even Sun Ra's space music, on track such as 'Intuition' and 'Digression'. Lennie's music was even more complex than bebop's intricately racing free-for-alls, clustering beats in odd combinations and casting harmonies at strange angles. The rhythm section anchored the music, leading to accusations of being cold and alien, but Lennie was simply linking bebop to modern jazz, then that to free jazz that didn't exist yet. (Konitz also played on the two sessions that formed Miles' *Birth Of The Cool* album.) In 1951, Lennie recorded the first overdubbed, improvised jazz recordings, 'Ju-ju' and 'Pastime', released as a single on his short-lived Jazz label. 'Descent Into The Maelstrom' from 1953 was another innovatory venture, translating Edgar Allan Poe's story using multi-tracked solo piano.

Lennie founded his New York jazz school in 1951, the first of its kind. He recorded his self-titled first album for Atlantic Records in 1955, conducting further experiments in multi-tracking on 'Turkish Mambo', and tape-speed manipulation on 'East 32nd'. Teaching then took over as Lennie moved his home and studio to Queens, although 1961 saw his second Atlantic album, *The New Tristano*, complete with sleeve announcing no overdubs or tape fiddling. This is where his innovations in left-handed bass patterns, block chords and counter-rhythms came to the fore as the idiosyncracies that most influenced Marty.

Something of an outsider in the jazz world, Lennie was probably his own worst enemy, refusing to milk commercial trends, self-promote or play mundane gigs to earn a living. He preferred to celebrate jazz as a special, uncompromising vehicle, stuck with those convictions and never sold out.

Ultimately, his influence was felt through his former pupils, including Konitz, Marsh, Charles Mingus, future David Bowie pianist Mike Garson, Dave Liebman and Martin Rev. Gioia says Lennie's standards became so high in later life that "few could live up to the demands Tristano placed on his devotees", so his "inner circle found fewer and fewer new acolytes". Now Marty had played his way into Lennie's confidence, he got his first close-up look at what it was like to be ahead of your time but rarely recognised, and even lambasted for it when you were. Jazz composer-historian Gunther Schuller deemed Lennie *too* far ahead of his time in 1946. It was a statement Marty got used to when Suicide needed to be described in a few words.

The introduction came when Marty's father had organised a "a little get together" at home, and one of the guests – who happened to be president of the Musicians Union – could hear his son play. "That's how you got to Lennie," recalls Marty. "My father asked me to play so this guy could hear me. He saw my interest was very concentrated. The guy said, 'Take him to Lennie Tristano!' My father followed up on that and it turned out Lennie lived only a few miles from where I did. My father wasn't familiar with him either but the working musicians and the guy from the union certainly were. That's a good enough reason."

Lennie's three-storey house was full of pianos, upstairs and downstairs. There was the big room with the grand piano, another with a baby grand, and the little audition room. On arriving, pupils sat on a couch in the hall and waited to be called up to Lennie's teaching room on the second floor.

"Lennie was a very nice guy, but he was very clear about what he felt," recalls Marty. "He had a very individual way of teaching. You were in and out in ten minutes. He'd dictate the things he'd want you to work on, and you'd keep doing them every week. Like he'd give you certain harmonic and finger things, scale things, to do in all the different inversions. He would say, 'Okay, play me where you're up to now on those', then 'Go further', or 'Do those again, do it more' and advance you from that. You had about three or four things you were working on at the same time. Once he gave you the essential of what he wanted you to practise, he'd call out one of each category, and review it with you. He had certain people that he felt were the great artists of the music, so you studied them."

Marty's first lessons revolved around Lester Young, the tenor icon who'd sprung to prominence with Count Basie and blown the smooth blueprints for cool jazz. "Lennie started with Lester Young, who he felt was one of the most important improvisers, which he was. I hear Lester as the major influence on cool and on Miles Davis. He was already doing cool music at a time of such hot swing music. Lennie felt it was essential to learn from Lester. If you stayed with Lennie long enough, you went up to Charlie Parker's solos as Lennie felt the same way about him. I didn't stay that long! Bud Powell was a very significant keyboard player in Lennie's book. I would hear Bud Powell as a kid but I wasn't so familiar. He was definitely a chapter in that history that you didn't want to avoid. Once you tried to master bebop piano as closely as you could to Bud Powell's technique, you could see that every great pianist after was influenced by him: Sonny Clarke, Red Garland, Wynton Kelly, Herbie Hancock, Bill Evans. He had a whole school of players, who all ended up at Lennie's place."

Marty remembers meeting Mike Garson coming down the stairs one day with Brooklyn-born saxophonist Dave Liebman, who went on to play with Miles and Elvin Jones in the seventies. "Mike stopped and started talking to me. I guess he was just curious about other students." Mike still remembers Marty from the three years when, every Sunday, he would spend four hours travelling for his lesson from Lennie. "Martin is very talented and creative," he says, adding, "Lennie was quite the taskmaster. I had to memorise three thousand left-hand chord voicings in the first year, then play all kinds of scales with bizarre fingering, like using only the fourth and fifth fingers to strengthen those weaker digits. The lesson was 10 minutes and I travelled four hours every Sunday for this discipline." He adds, rather ruefully, "Lennie never played for me once."

Lennie's rigorous regime paid off as Garson, who also had the front to ask Bill Evans for lessons, went on to graduate from Brooklyn College with a music major in 1970, then played on Annette Peacock's seminal *I'm The One*. The album's startling synth-voice explorations propelled David Bowie to sign Peacock to his Mainman organisation. Annette had come up through the avant garde, marrying Ayler bassist Gary Peacock, collaborating with Paul Bley, hanging with LSD guru Timothy Leary and being turned into a hologram by Salvador Dali. Enjoying the Bowie circle's lavish lifestyle for a year before bailing out, she coerced Garson, who'd never heard of Ziggy Stardust, into the *Aladdin Sane* line-up for a then-astronomical $800 a week. "I procured Garson for Bowie, but Bowie ultimately plagiarised my music as I had been warned he would," Annette told me. "Still, it was quite an affirmation from an icon whose judgement had been proven, that when I'd made *I'm The One* I had, in fact, gotten it right." Garson's lustrous avant-cascades would enliven more Bowie albums than any other musician. He memorably elevated *Diamond Dogs*, *Aladdin Sane* and *Young Americans*, but he never forgot his original teacher, recalling, "I saw Lennie live many times at the Half Note with Lee Konitz and Wayne Marsh. He was phenomenal; fresh, creative, different, and with a whole other approach to jazz and improvisation. He was an unsung hero, who still hasn't received his proper recognition, like Monk, Ellington or Bill Evans have when he might have been the most creative of all of them, in some ways. To top it off, he was blind!"

Marty was also impressed at how Tristano dealt with his disability. "Lennie was like this romantic loner figure, an outsider artist for most of his life. The fact that he couldn't see. There was a movie about a blind jazz musician when I was a kid. It was incredibly moving, realistic stuff. Lennie definitely had his own school, very strong views on the value of music in society, and what the roles were for certain musicians, like the rhythm section. As a keyboard player he was incredibly developed. Of course, I didn't agree with everything he felt, but I understood it. I think about him often, and the things that he said. He had a great influence. He was a brilliant, innovative musical mind, no doubt about it."

Lennie also instructed Marty on old school jazz etiquette, scolding him after he displayed his rebellious streak in an audition. "I wasn't going to play schlocky," insisted Marty. "To me, that was the way of doing that stuff." He thought Lennie would be proud but was shocked when he protested, "No man, you shouldn't have done it that way, you should have done it their way! If you went to that kind of gig, you should have played it that way, not your stuff." But Lennie did admire how Marty handled money, once declaring, "Man, you're very good at that shit," when he was only paying for his lesson.

One afternoon, Lennie sat down with Marty and said "Okay, here we are six months down the road, play something for me, I just want to hear where I've gotten to with your playing." Marty played one he'd written himself, around jazz standard 'Don't Blame Me', which brought a smile of satisfaction to Lennie, who exclaimed "You're blossoming like a flower." Marty still sounds chuffed. "He was real complimentary. I think he was very pleasantly surprised." Marty now felt he was getting there and, "for the first year, I started to develop a lot," particularly "that left-hand bass-line thing", which was going to come in handy when he took to the electronic keyboard and recalled his left-handed bass-line training for early Suicide compositions such as 'Rocket USA' and 'Ghost Rider'. "Lennie was one of the only ones who made playing a solo piano with bass prominent," says Marty, explaining how the low end had become the role of string bass players, "which moved everything up higher. There wasn't anything in the bass area. The rhythm had that smooth propulsion because the bass player was enough to keep that going on that level. The way pianists could voice everything using their left hand was very fresh and new, and I wanted to do that. With Lennie I got into doing bass lines, which I loved to do and did for a long time, although it's more of a solo piano thing."

Future Suicide blueprints aside, by 1965 Marty was becoming naggingly aware of the changes sweeping jazz. Despite the priceless value of Lennie's lessons, he "wanted to learn a lot of other stuff that was happening that I'd heard on records. The developments were coming like crazy. *Everything* was so crazy. I wanted to get it all. So one day I said to Lennie, 'I'm gonna split'. When I went to him in 1963 I was 15. Two years with Lennie and I was really developing. He had said to me I was blossoming, which was a really beautiful thing to hear but, even though he was teaching a method which was totally right and innovative, it was *his* method. There were other things I wanted to learn that maybe I could pick off records, but I wanted to study them more specifically. I wanted to have all that newer stuff too. I told Lennie I was leaving. He wasn't crazy about the reason, but didn't discourage me. I think he had a certain respect for me that way."

Marty's parents had split up when he was 16. "It was traumatic at first, but I got adjusted to it in a short time; at least on the surface." Focusing even more intently on his jazz studies, Marty had answered an ad in the paper placed by veteran jazz arranger Hall Overton, who he recognised from orchestrating Thelonious Monk's historic February 1959 concert at New York's Town Hall. He knew little else of Overton when he turned up at the dilapidated but, as he soon found out, fabled Jazz Loft on Sixth

Avenue, just past 28th Street in the Flower District, where you might have to step over a sozzled bum to get to the door. Born in Michigan in 1920, Overton had studied theory and composition at Chicago Music College, then Juilliard Music School. He moved into the loft in 1954, counting renowned photojournalist W. Eugene Smith as his neighbour.

Overton continued to write classical compositions, but became deeply involved in jazz, recording with names including Stan Getz and vibraphonist Teddy Charles. In 1957, he drew shapes to start the young Steve Reich composing. In 1959, Monk picked him to orchestrate his works, as heard on *The Thelonious Monk Orchestra At Town Hall*, a highly successful career peak for the pianist. Going on to teach classical music at Yale and Juilliard, Overton carried on giving jazz theory lessons in what turned out to be his final year at the Jazz Loft (a heavy drinker, he died in 1972 from cirrhosis of the liver). By now, it was considered a pilgrimage to study with the chain-smoking college professor who taught jazz piano at night. Marty was thrilled to sit down at the same upright Monk had worked on before the Town Hall show. Overton told Marty that he and Marty rarely spoke a word as they worked, communicating instead through glances, finger signals and the music.

"When I went to Hall Overton, I didn't know that was where they rehearsed the whole Town Hall thing," says Marty. "In (Eugene Smith's) book of photos you can see Monk playing that same piano Overton taught me on. In a sense, he was a total opposite to Lennie, which was why I went to him. He had a filing cabinet full of transcribed solos, chords and harmonic rudiment stuff taken off Monk and Bud Powell. When he gave you the standard lesson of an hour, he said he wanted you to work on something, then he'd go over to the filing cabinet, pull out a transcription, which he did by hand then Xeroxed. That is exactly what I was going for and I got it from him for about a year. In that time, I set myself up to play in a setting of what was being done then, what Miles was doing then, which is really what the standard was for my generation of pianists."

During this time, Marty made frequent club sorties into Manhattan, including Sunday afternoon matinees at Birdland. Situated on Broadway and 53rd Street, this was the "Jazz Corner of the World" (named in tribute to Charlie Parker), which had opened to much fanfare in December 1949 with a bill including Bird himself, Lester Young and Lennie Tristano. Attracting a star-studded clientele, the club became a microcosm of New

York's fifties jazz scene, but blighted by drugs, mob tactics, prostitution, police hassles and violent incidents, it was forced to close in 1965. When Marty saw the club was holding Sunday afternoon matinees, he said, "Wow, let me go down there."

He remembers the afternoon when five groups played, including one featuring Paul Bley and Gary Peacock. Another included Archie Shepp drummer Joe Chambers, and was fronted by an 'older singer' – "because he's already in his thirties!" – who sang Monk songs with his own lyrics.

After leaving Jamaica High, Marty spent two years at Queens College Music School "before I felt I had to drop out". Here he met budding jazz musicians including trumpeter Art Williams and drummer Charles Brackeen, who would both go on to play with Cecil Taylor, along with playing with precocious double-bassist Steve Tintweiss, who would soon play a significant part in this formative period.

During the summer of 1966, Marty journeyed daily to a union building on Astor Place, which had an old piano on the tenth floor. "I just knew the place and almost everyone there knew me, from when I used to run around, barely out of diapers! I just went there and started practising. I knew exactly where the piano was, and the floor was usually empty. The piano was all out of tune, all the way at the top, but I said, 'Hey, I just wanna get in the city every day and start playing.'"

When Marty took a break in the afternoon, he was confronted with the Five Spot on St Mark's Place and, over on Third Avenue, a big old neighbourhood bar, whose sign just said 'Bar' but "was known by the hip as the Four Spot". (It later became local rock venue the Continental.)

"That was the hippest bar," he remembers. "I looked in and saw a dark, smoky, almost empty room with a bar going down it, tables in the back, and a jukebox playing the hippest shit; Miles Davis singles, all jazz stuff coming out, and this is like three in the afternoon! There's maybe 10 people in there, the real neighbourhood gentry. The ambience was incredible, so I walked in." Sat at the bar was the Monk singer from Birdland, who turned out to be Bazzi Bartholomew Gray, the future narrator on Archie Shepp's *Attica Blues* a few years later. Striking up conversation, the pair got along famously. "He said he was looking for a piano player, maybe I wanted to come by, and told me where he lived on the Lower East Side."

Next day, Marty returned to the city, locating the two-room railroad flat where Bazzi lived with his young Swedish wife, "but there was a back yard in that building, which was nice. He was on the first floor so you could go out there." More excitingly, Bazzi had an upright piano. "The first day, he gave me the keys to his place, and said, 'Come down and practise any time, and if I'm not here, just come in'. I would come in and just play for a couple of hours. I was doing that every day, literally."

Bazzi wanted Marty to play keyboards for a band he was putting together to play at the Five Spot at the end of August. "He started preparing for it, we started going over tunes. While that was going on, people were coming in and out of his place, because he knew everybody on the scene, all the musicians. I met Kenny Dorham and Leon Thomas, who was a wonderful cat. They all treated me so incredibly well. It was such a great environment for me." Marty also met former Miles saxophonist Rocky Boyd, striking up another friendship. "He was just sitting on the couch."

With Cecil Taylor sitting in the audience, Marty's first high profile jazz show went well, the band around him including Sun Ra bassist Ronnie Boykins and in demand tenor man Roland Alexander. Marty visibly glows thinking about it. "Bazzi was a great guy, I used to love that guy. I knew him for years after, I used to see him in the neighbourhood." Now, he's reminded of that magical time every day when he looks out the window of his apartment. "I can see the back of his building when I look out of my window."

Ten years before Suicide strafed the clubs of Greenwich Village, before Marty tramped its streets through the sixties looking for jazz, or even before that when it was another vibrant pit-stop on Alan's Beats-seeking visits to Manhattan, the area between Broadway to the Hudson River and Houston to Fourteenth Street became the music business launch-pad for one of the key figures in this story. Peter Crowley was Suicide's first major champion, booked them into their first regular club venues, provided the duo's first opportunity to get on record and be heard outside of New York's downtown underground, and gave them the break which led to recording the first album. His early life is a lovely New York story, contemporaneous with Alan and Marty, and has never been told, but led to him becoming a pivotal figure in the city's underground cultural history, after he "came to rock'n'roll in a weird kind of a way".

Speaking from his home in Florida, where he was forced to move in 2002 by New York's escalating rent situation, Peter recalls his Norwegian immigrant grandfather was an artist who "zipped around on a motorcycle drawing pictures of fires and newsworthy events" for the *Daily News* before it started printing photographs, then his father born in Greenwich, Connecticut, and his mother from Hackensack, New Jersey. Both were artists, living in Greenwich Village when they were first married, but forced to take what work was available during the Depression. Despite her degree in library science, his mother became the over-qualified manager of the book department at Macy's, before his father took a management job at a cotton mill in Providence, Rhode Island, where Peter was born in June 1942. The family moved to Vermont when his father got promoted to superintendent of a cotton mill, his mum getting a job teaching at the Austine School for the Deaf in Brattleboro.

Peter remembers growing up "isolated from everybody" near the 500-acre apple orchard, living for his visits to the city. When he was 17, the family went to see the Clyde Beatty-Cole Brothers Circus when it came to town ("the biggest show in the world at that time"). Peter was smitten, running away from home with the circus for the summer as an electrician's assistant. After dropping out of school the following year, he hit the road and landed in New York, just as the fifties were coming to a close. For the first weeks, he stayed with his uncle, who gave him $10 every day to look for a job, but Peter spent his days at Coney Island, hanging out under the boardwalk ("You've heard the song, it's pretty accurate"), and nights in Greenwich Village and Times Square, "learning all the street stuff." After his uncle twigged, Peter lived in various furnished rooms, clerking for the likes of American Express, the National Biscuit Company, chemical firms and warehouses. "You could get a job at the drop of a hat, which would pay $55 take home, and rent an apartment on the Lower East Side for $17 a month. You could buy a restaurant meal for a dollar. Unlike today, the poor weren't poor in the fifties." But he always got fired for coming in late or too tired to work, having been out the night before.

Peter had discovered the action going on in Greenwich Village which, in the early sixties, was dominated by the coffeehouses and bars of MacDougal, Bleecker, Third and Fourth Streets, including the Gaslight, Kettle Of Fish, Gerdes Folk City, Café Wha?, Café Figaro, Caffè Reggio, Café Bizarre, and many more forgotten hole-in-the-wall joints. Of course, the turning point for the downtown folk scene came on January 24, 1961, when Robert Zimmerman blew in from Minnesota, in search of Woody Guthrie but determined to make a splash in his own right. One day in the early sixties, Peter was ambling through MacDougal's vibrant hubbub and spotted a sign saying "Drag Wanted" in the window of a coffee house, a few doors along from the Gaslight, called the Why Not. This meant they needed someone to stand outside and drag tourists inside. Hired on the spot, he found entertainment being provided by the young Stephen Stills, David Crosby and Richie Havens. Within weeks, Peter had risen to manager, finding himself at the heart of the Village coffee house community, befriending legends such as Fred Neil and members of Andy Warhol's crowd. By 1965, he was making ice cream sodas at the Night Owl, where bands such as the Lovin' Spoonful and Blues Magoos held court. After spending 1966 travelling, he tried opening his own coffee house called the Café Tangier on Bedford Street. Despite regular custom from the Warhol crew, the venture failed, sending him to the West Coast. "You have to understand it was like San Francisco's North Beach and Greenwich Village were next door to each other, even though there was 3,000 miles between them. Everybody was going back and forth." After some months in Tijuana, Peter built electronic golf carts in Anaheim, California, before moving to West Hollywood, where he helped design and construct a club, whose owners were marketing the new Coloursound machine, which professed to translate music through lights. The venture didn't last long after neighbours complained, but Peter was compensated with a dozen of the machines. He had spied on the guys operating the psychedelic light shows at the Fillmore West, so returned to New York with a car load of Coloursound boxes, a new innovation to light up the city.

A lot had happened while he'd been away, especially with his friend Warhol, who was becoming the sixties most celebrated and infamous artist since his New York Pop Art show at the Stable Gallery on East 74th Street in November, 1962, which included the green Coca Cola Bottles and Campbell's soup cans. Alan Vega remembers seeing the soup cans as "one of the breakthrough times in my life", and was watching the emergence of this new art culture with great interest.

In January 1964, Warhol took over the fourth floor of the former Peoples Cold Storage and Warehouse building on 47th Street, calling it the Silver Factory after his ex-lover and right-hand man Billy Linich, aka Billy Name, covered it in aluminium foil. Warhol's new HQ hosted an ever-growing enclave of artists, writers, musicians and 'superstars' who, in the next few years, would include Gerard Malanga, Mary Woronov, Ondine, Edie Sedgwick, Joe Dallesandro, Jackie Curtis, Ultra Violet,

Candy Darling, Holly Woodlawn and Viva. Warhol started staging shows at Leo Castelli's East 77th Street gallery, joining contemporary artists such as Roy Lichtenstein, Jasper Johns and Robert Rauschenberg in establishing the Pop Art movement. (One of Castelli's main associates was Ivan Karp, who would soon play a major part in Alan's own artistic emergence.) Warhol was about to bridge the gap between art and underground music by swivelling his artistic vision from objects, canvasses and films to staging events around a band he had taken over as manager and sucked into the Factory's amphetamine-fuelled whirl.

The bad seeds of the Velvet Underground were sewn in 1964 when in-house Pickwick Records songwriter Lou Reed from Freeport, Long Island, and Syracuse University, who loved doo-wop and liked to catch Ornette Coleman at the Blue Note, was put together with an angry young avant garde musician called John Cale, by the former's boss, in the hope of cashing in on the huge pop group market opened up by that year's arrival of the Beatles.

Hailing from the Welsh valleys, Cale had been immersed in the polar opposite to hit-factory conveyor belts, arriving in the US in 1963 with a Leonard Bernstein scholarship, sponsored by Aaron Copland, after studying classical music at London's Goldsmith College. Hitting New York, he was immediately drawn to the avant garde explorations being carried out by John Cage and La Monte Young's Theatre Of Eternal Music, which he ended up joining.

Although a controversial figure, Young is a key figure in New York's experimental legacy, still ensconced in the 'Dream House' on Church Street he moved into in 1962, which Alan Vega remembers influencing his earliest sonic experiments, neatly summed up by his "Holy shit, I loved the drone!" Born in Idaho, Young had discovered and played jazz while at City College then UCLA in the fifties, his bandmates in class and at clubs including Eric Dolphy, Ornette Coleman and Don Cherry. As another example of how the music of this time, and often in this book, links up in various ways, a major early influence on Young's alto sax playing was former Lennie Tristano pupil Lee Konitz, who he witnessed at local clubs, and would bring to study with Indian tambura musician Pandit Pran Nath in the seventies. Young discovered Indian music while at UCLA, injecting raga principles into his undulating soundscapes, along with the serialism coined by Arnold Schoenberg and Anton Webern, which induced him to strip his music down to its core.

By the time he was winding up at UCLA, Young had started on the long sustained harmonies of his 'Trio For Strings', premiered during the first semester of his post-graduate work at Berkeley in September 1958, influencing Warhol's static films, *Kiss*, *Eat* and *Sleep* (enough for him to initially commission Young to compose their scores). Young journeyed to Darmstadt in Germany to study with his hero Stockhausen, but was more impressed by John Cage and struck up a relationship, still looking for something that reduced music to its fundamental sonic essence.

Young's lifelong affair with New York began with the premiere of his 'Poem', being played by Cage and cohort David Tudor at the Living Theatre on April 11, 1960. Young himself debuted his 'Trio For Strings' in New York in October 1962. Young was a big hit in the early sixties artistic community, becoming musical director of the concerts held by Yoko Ono in her SoHo loft between December 1960 and June 1961, hanging out with George Maciunas' Fluxus movement. But Young longed for the long, drawn out sonorities he had explored earlier on the *Compositions 1960* series, and started unleashing drones in mid-1962. He recruited percussionist Angus MacLise, his lifelong partner Marian Zazeela and Billy Name. By 1963, the group included string player Tony Conrad and John Cale. The first Theatre of Eternal Music event, *The Second Dream Of The High-Tension Line Stepdown Transformer*, was an homage to the sound aesthetics of industrial power plants. Ensconced in Young's Church Street loft, the group refined the drone principle on February 1964's 'Pre-Tortoise Dream Music', their hallucinogenic buzzing ethos chiming with the burgeoning psychedelic movement, enhanced by Cale copping mescaline for the performances.

Young's drone ambitions reached a pulsing new plateau with *The Tortoise, His Dreams And Journeys*, inspired by his pet turtle. Its performances were Cale's last before leaving in early 1966 to concentrate on the Velvet Underground. Backed up by the also-departing Conrad, who is still exploring string-drone principles today, Cale felt the scene at Church Street was starting to resemble a cult revolving around Young, who they resented claiming authorship of music they all created.

Anyhow, Cale could cause a lot more damage with what he called his "controlled distortion" where he was headed now, especially with the metal guitar strings and pickups Conrad had fitted to his viola. In late 1964, Cale and Reed had called themselves the Primitives to record dance craze pastiche 'The Ostrich', recruiting Lou's former classmate

Sterling Morrison on rhythm guitar, and Angus MacLise on drums. Cale showed Reed detuning and drones. They first rehearsed in the spring of 1965 at Tony Conrad's loft at 56 Ludlow Street on the Lower East Side. Lou had already written ditties such as 'Heroin' and 'Venus In Furs' but, as demos recorded that July show, they started life sounding like a collision between Dylan and speed-folkies the Holy Modal Rounders. After MacLise left, they recruited metronomic powerhouse Maureen 'Mo' Tucker, who stood striking tom toms and upturned bass drum with mallets, defining the sound of the Velvet Underground. Conrad's copy of Michael Leigh's paperback about the early sixties sexual subculture, *The Velvet Underground*, gave the group its name.

Filmmaker Barbara Rubin and dancer Gerard Malanga brought Warhol along to one of the group's gigs at the Café Bizarre. He immediately saw the Velvets as an aural compliment to what he was doing, and became their manager. He also suggested adding the German actress and model Nico as a cool, Teutonic contrast to their shades and leather moodiness. He then arranged for them to play the annual dinner of the New York Society for Clinical Psychiatry at the midtown Delmonico Hotel on January 10, where illustrious guests envisaged "studying" Warhol's current antics as entertainment, but choked on their roast beef when the Velvets kicked into 'Venus In Furs'. Writing about the event in the *New York Times* of January 14, Grace Glueck reported guests fleeing through the exits and doctors (presaging Suicide's reviews next decade) wailing such comments as "ridiculous, outrageous, painful" and "a short-lived torture of cacophony". In April, the band opened for three weeks at the Polish National Hall, over a bar nicknamed the Dom at 23 St Mark's Place, advertised in the *Village Voice* as, 'The Silver Dream Factory Presents The Exploding Plastic Inevitable with Andy Warhol/ The Velvet Underground and Nico'. "Art has come to the discotheque and it will never be the same again," wrote the *East Village Other*'s John Wilcock about the senses-blasting onslaught of the deafening group, Warhol movies, strobes, mirror-balls, whip dancers, and now lights by Peter Crowley.

Through his Warhol connections, Peter was hired to DJ between sets and bathe the whole ritual with his state-of-the-art lights, "except great sweeps of squishy psychedelic lights wouldn't have fit the Velvet Underground at all," he reflects, "so I did almost like a pinhole effect, where I would set Nico on fire with orange and red pin beams in her blonde hair." If Suicide have been called successors to the Velvet Underground's devastating audio-visual assault, here was their future champion illuminating the originals at birth. He remembers the Velvets seriously trying to drive audiences out of the venue. "They were doing it on purpose. They were doing the S&M whip dance and all that stuff, and set up strobe lights on the stage where the footlights were, which would be aimed at the audience, so they would be blinded by the horrible white lights in their faces. It was designed to piss them off. To me none of that ever seemed off-putting in any way. The strobe lights were irritating because they hurt your eyes, but all the rest of it was really cool, and worked fine by me. They were just about to record their album so were doing 'Heroin' and 'Waiting For The Man'. It was absolutely brilliant. I lucked out. I was in the right place at the right moment. It was absolutely brilliant."

After the first three-week stint, the Velvets launched their offensive on the West Coast, returning to the Dom, now renamed the Balloon Farm, in October. Peter stayed on after the Velvets residency ended, "and they had more hippie bands in there, so I washed the walls with blobs of colour." He quit when the new owner bought the venue. "I was also the DJ in between sets so I was playing weird records. He told me to stop playing weird records and start playing the Supremes. I told him to take his job and shove it and walked out."

In between stints at the Dom, the Velvets had contributed a scathing piece called 'Noise' to an ESP-Disk protest collage album for the *East Village Other Electric Newspaper*, which also featured a recording of President Johnson's daughter's wedding, 'Silence' by Warhol, jazz by Marion Brown, Allen Ginsberg's mantras and poet Tuli Kupferberg, from new ESP signings the Fugs, who were currently causing their own stoned commotion in the East Village, celebrating rampant hedonism and railing against the Vietnam War. Warhol's name as producer had helped the Velvets land a deal with Verve Records, although the actual work was done by Tom Wilson, who had worked with Sun Ra and Dylan. Recording took place that April at New York's decrepit old Scepter Studios. After the album was finished it sat on the shelf while a confused Verve pondered its fate, finally releasing it in March 1967. Something had happened since the original demos, apart from Lou replacing his shrill folk holler with trademark deadpan sneer, now sounding "like a zombie", according to Alan Vega. No other band captured New York

City's glorious isolation from the rest of America at that time. It sold bugger all but, like Suicide would find, its true implications wouldn't be appreciated for decades.

Alan first heard the Velvets' album when a friend brought it round to his Brooklyn home one afternoon. He still remembers the impact of hearing the "incredible" music for the first time, but had little idea the next outfit to sink their plunger into such deep strata would be his own. While declaring, "I always had that rock'n'roll thing, that root", stressing that "I was always a Stones man, I was never a Beatles man", Alan had recently discovered another group whose snarling monochrome simplicity would inspire him in Suicide around a decade hence, remembering, "I used to watch *American Bandstand* all the time in the sixties. They had Question Mark & the Mysterians on there doing '96 Tears'. Holy shit! I couldn't believe these guys. This guy all in black leather became my favourite singer. Those guys are so great. I love them so much, they're really beautiful. They were such a big influence on me in Suicide. A few years ago, they covered 'Cheree'."

Formed in 1962 by Question Mark, drummer Robert Martinez and bassist Frank Lugo, the band took its name from 1957 Japanese sci-fi movie *The Mysterians*, in which aliens from the doomed planet Mysteroid arrive to conquer Earth. They were originally formed as a surf band, adding 14-year-old organ player Frank Rodriguez to create their classic line-up and define their sound with his reedy Vox riffs. Their first single, '96 Tears', started life as a poem called 'Too Many Teardrops', recorded on March 13, 1966 at Art Schiell's home studio in Bay City, and released on the Pa-Go-Go label owned by the band's manager Lillian Gonzalez. After becoming a regional hit in the Detroit area, Cameo-Parkway picked it up and it shot to number one, selling over a million, becoming a classic recorded by countless bands and, at Alan's behest, was destined to stand as the only cover version to remain in Suicide's sets for years, usually introduced as "the national anthem" by "five spics from Detroit".

Alan got seriously into jazz around that time, his epiphany starting with *Meditations*, John Coltrane's 1966 tour de force, which took the revelatory passion of 1964's *A Love Supreme* to the next level.

Or as he puts it so vividly, "I decided to get into jazz. I pretty much had this conversation with myself. I was staying at my friend's house, and he had pretty much every blues record and pretty much every jazz record ever made. He'd sit me down every day to listen to this stuff. It was great. One day he put on *Meditations*. I was sitting on this little rickety wooden chair, and then came the first notes of 'The Father And the Son And The Holy Ghost'. Boom! It was like Beethoven! I jumped back and I actually fell over, man. It's the first time music literally knocked me on my ass. That was amazing. Then I heard some of Albert Ayler's stuff, with his brother Don playing trumpet. Now I was into everything."

When nearby Newark, New Jersey was coming round after four days of riots of the sort sweeping major cities that summer, Coltrane died from liver cancer on July 17, 1967, aged only 40. His funeral was held four days later at St. Peters Lutheran Church in New York City with Albert Ayler opening the service with 'Love Cry', 'Truth Is Marching On' and 'Our Prayer'. Coltrane would now be deified as one of the greatest musicians of all time, and a major influence in rock'n'roll, inspiring the Byrds' 'Eight Miles High', Doors' 'Light My Fire', and the entire ouvre of veteran French experimentalists Magma.

With America plunging further into war and its ghettos on fire, modern music had experienced its first major loss of a bright young life and genius. Compounded by the black-winged arrival of the Velvet Underground, the age of innocence was over.

FIVE

By now the war in Vietnam was casting a malignant shadow over the whole country. At first, the conflict had been a low-level Cold War lunge that took the focus of anti-commie bludgeoning off home-grown artists such as Pete Seeger, as America sharpened its offensive overseas. This south-east Asian conflict saw increasing numbers of America's young men sent to a war about which they understood little.

Protests kicked off when the draft increased from 3,000 to over 200,000 within the space of months in 1965. While those with upper-class pull could swerve the call-up, poor working-class young men were seized on and sent over. When mounting numbers of body bags started coming back, along with tales of atrocities being carried out by US troops on the people they were supposed to be protecting, protests stepped up to the burning of draft cards, and anti-war marches. In March 1966, 50,000 rallied in New York, and in 1967 100,000 marched on Washington.

"We went on the anti-war demos," says Alan. "New York and Washington – that one was really bad, they threw rocks at us, the cops were charging and beating the shit out of us, all kinds of shit." But he managed to beat the draft. "Yeah I did, I didn't wanna die. The war was dumb. I walked into the induction centre and said, 'Okay, give me a gun, I wanna fight, I wanna kill! Give me a gun, I WANNA KILL!' They were like, 'We don't want this cat'. It took me three attempts to get out of it, but they were convinced that I was crazy. I got my 4F and was deemed insane."

Marty was coming to the war from a different perspective as it had started brewing when he was still living at home with his politically aware parents. "I would talk to my father about the war and he would give me a totally clear explanation of everything. Why this is wrong, and what exactly the war was about. I was lucky to have great reference material and alternative information, when I needed it, on what was really happening. I later realised that most kids didn't have that. I had friends who never had that guidance, got confused and made tragic mistakes, like going into the army and getting sent to Vietnam. Most people had parents who weren't that politically sophisticated, so when Vietnam broke out they said, 'I don't know, the country says it's right so I guess it is right. Okay, let 'em go to war.'"

By 1966, Marty had left school and home, first staying at a friend's place on the Lower East Side, then for a year in a studio apartment on 100th Street and West End Avenue, now the Upper West Side, before moving further uptown, above Harlem between the Hudson and Harlem Rivers, to 184th Street and St. Nicholas Avenue in hilly Washington Heights, the highest point in Manhattan, where "I got my own one-room studio apartment, with a keyboard in the middle of the room, which was almost the whole room, and a little kitchen." The birthplace of Marvel Comics founder Stan Lee, and Jerry Wexler, the producer who coined the phrase 'rhythm and blues', Washington Heights had attracted an influx of European Jews escaping the Nazis in the thirties, before becoming known for famous African-American residents, including Paul Robeson, Count Basie and boxer Joe Louis. When Marty moved in, Malcolm X had just been assassinated at the nearby Audubon Ballroom, in February 1965.

During the marathon conversations for this book, Marty was sometimes surprised to discover just who he was hanging out with in his teenage years, including names who went on to stellar careers. Steve Reid is a good example, being born in the South Bronx but moving to Queens as a teenager. He lived in St. Albans, three blocks away from John Coltrane, so stopped off every morning on the way to school to speak to his hero. His first job was in the house band at Harlem's Apollo Theatre, which led to the first record he played on being Martha & the Vandellas' 'Dancing In The Street', after the group heard him playing at the venerable venue. After graduating from Adelphi College he spent three years in Africa, playing with Fela Kuti. On his return, after playing on James Brown's 'The Popcorn', he was clobbered for draft dodging and sentenced to a four-year stretch. On release, he played with Freddie Hubbard, Horace Silver and Sun Ra, by 1974 forming the Legendary Master Brotherhood.

In later life, he relocated to Switzerland, spending his last years playing with Four Tet's Kieran Hebden, until succumbing to throat cancer in 2010. Before all that, "He had a group and asked me to join and we did some shows together," recalls Marty. "We would listen to records together and then I saw him again later in teenage life."

One evening in 1967, Marty and some local musician buddies were strolling down Riverside Drive after enjoying a few beers in a West End Avenue bar. Passing a smart apartment building a few blocks from Marty's, one of the guys piped up, "Hey, Tony Williams lives in that building!" This scored a direct hit. Tony Williams was Miles Davis' drummer, who'd joined his quintet in 1963 as a 17-year-old skins prodigy, after being introduced by saxophonist Jackie McClean. Tony had been like a polyrhythmic rocket going off alongside pianist Herbie Hancock, bassist Ron Carter and saxophonist Wayne Shorter, underpinning one of the richest stretches of Miles' career in one of the finest rhythm sections of all time.

Helped by his bebop musician dad, Tony was known as one of the best drummers in his hometown of Boston by 15, already playing with tenor saxophonist Sam Rivers. Both musicians had been introduced to jazz by local tenor saxophonist Rocky Boyd, who Marty had recently met at Bazzi's and now saw regularly when hanging out at the Village Vanguard. Rocky had moved to New York in 1958, sharing a loft with newly arrived drummer Sunny Murray, who he also encouraged. Boyd was an overlooked but pivotal catalyst who recorded just one album in 1961, with trumpeter Kenny Dorham, although he played with Max Roach's Quintet and Miles that year.

Tony Williams was still only 16 when Jackie McClean noticed him and, with his family's permission, whisked him to New York and trials by fire such as the aforementioned show at Bed-Stuy's Coronet Club. Then Miles saw him, writing in his autobiography that Tony "just blew my mind he was so bad... I could definitely hear right away that this was going to be one of the baddest motherfuckers who had ever played a set of drums." Prompting Miles to bring the rhythm section further forward, Tony played on nine studio and nine live albums, including 1965's *E.S.P.*, 1967's *Sorcerer* and *Nefertiti*, 1968's *Miles In The Sky* and *Filles De Kilimanjaro* and, as his parting shot, the seminal *In A Silent Way*.

Marty's daily routine in the week revolved around practising on the large keyboard set up in his room. One day, when he was "in the middle of the usual daily ecstasy of exalted playing, work studying and playing with records, or whatever I was thinking about at the time, making it even more exalted", a thought kept nagging him; Tony Williams, Miles' great drummer, lived just down the road. The mission became clear. "Tony's like seven blocks away, I gotta talk to him." So Marty duly made his way to the apartment building, scanned the names by the door-bells and, summoning the front which got him into the jazz clubs, rang the one marked 'Williams'. "Hello," said a voice, which had to be Tony. Maybe caught unawares at the simplicity of the operation, Marty quickly thought up an opening gambit. "I'm a keyboard player and I'd like to study with you. Can you teach me?" "Come on up," said the voice.

"It went from there. We were both so young. Tony was only a couple of years older than me. I think he just really liked the idea that I was a keyboard player. I was really serious. I thought it would be a great idea, and I think that's what got Tony's ear too, because I was a piano player wanting to study with a drummer. If anything, it doesn't usually work that way, 'Here's this kid asking if he can study with me'. But he was always growing, and looking to learn too. He was studying keyboard too, so I think he liked the idea of teaching and being close to the piano side. It was novel for him. Sometimes he gave me tunes that he'd written for me to play. Tony was like me, he always had a book in his pocket. He had a harmony book he was always reading, which he'd pull out when he went to gigs like the Vanguard. He befriended me, and literally took me under his wing for a while. Years later, I thought 'How generous he was to do that', because he didn't have to."

The friendship between the driven young keyboard player and ever-questing superstar drummer blossomed over a couple of years, Marty witnessing many Miles shows while continuing mutual discovery sessions with Tony, although any drumming was out of the question because of the neighbours. "I would have loved it, but we couldn't play at his place. He wasn't playing drums in his apartment, but to study that way would probably have been incredible." Marty did get his chance to play with Tony, in front of an audience, and remembers it like it was yesterday, excitement rising in his voice as he recalls the epic jam session they attended at the loft of pianist Art Murphy, who had studied at Juilliard with Steve Reich and Philip Glass, and become a founder member of their respective Ensembles. Jazz was Murphy's true love and, while at Juilliard in 1963, he'd worked with Hall Overton on arrangements for

Monk's big band concert. He was also a close friend of Bill Evans, and had transcribed solos for him.

At weekends, Art liked to kick back with jam sessions, inviting a nucleus of musicians to provide the bedrock for a stream of guests. Marty only knew Art as "a piano player who didn't play out a lot. He was like an insider cat they all knew. Musicians used the occasion just to come in and play with different people. Tony was too young to just fall into one thing, he was always growing. Just playing with Miles might have seemed enough, but he was always looking to do more and experiment, so he'd do that kind of stuff."

Tony invited Marty, suggesting he come by his apartment and they go together the first day. Marty remembers being struck by the woman Tony was living with. "She had such quality, very high class in all the right ways. I was impressed with her right away. She was there, and a couple of friends. We all got along good, kind of kidded around in the street then got in a cab."

There was a lot to take in that first day. Seduced by the heady refreshments and informal atmosphere of masters at play, Marty was content to just watch as Art held down the grand piano, accompanied by a rhythm section of Tony and double-bassist Juni Booth, who had recently blown in from Buffalo, and was currently playing with Art Blakey and Sonny Simmons (and would join Tony Williams in his band Lifetime the following decade). "I didn't play that first day. There weren't many piano players so Art did most of it, but he had a lot of horns. There were so many musicians, a lot of people coming in and out. Sam Rivers came over and stayed for two days."

For the second day, Tony decided to give Marty a piece he had written, to play for his loft debut. Returning to Art's loft, Tony settled behind the drums and, about 90 minutes in, said, "Go ahead Marty, you play this one," and they were off. "That was cool, they'd do that once in a while. I think he wanted to hear something he had written, but it was incredible. By that time, I was so loose and warm, because I was familiar with the guests and the setting. I don't know how it would have sounded the day before, but by now I was very relaxed. When it was time for me to play a solo, it just came out as if from a tube of toothpaste. It just flowed. And Tony's playing behind me. I can still hear it, and feel it. It's a sensation you get when you're playing with certain people. Tony was such a rich accompanist. What he laid down, I had never felt before. One of Tony's innovations was to play the hi-hat cymbal on all four beats, it was usually done in two and four. It was almost like a rhythm guitarist playing on every beat, like a pad, a total mattress under you. He also did this innovation with his ride cymbal. Where most guys went 'dink dink a-dink', Tony was doing about five of those on each beat, so fast and so smooth. With the combination of that, and what he did with a snare, it was like flying in an aeroplane, or being on a cushion of clouds. That one track, and that was it. Art went back to playing, everyone kept playing in different scenarios. Nobody commented on anybody. They just kept playing, trying to do as much as they could in the time that was there. I knew it sounded fine. It was like *there*, you know."

Although Marty took pains not to impose himself on Tony when he was playing gigs, he'd often hang out with the Miles Davis group when they played the Village Vanguard and Village Gate. "I used to go down and hear them at the Vanguard a lot. Herbie Hancock and them would be talking and we were sometimes all in proximity of each other."

One of the few niteries from that time still operating today, the Vanguard is a last vestige of New York's jazz golden age. It was known as the Golden Triangle speakeasy when Polish immigrant Max Gordon took it over in 1935. With the speakeasy concept having demolished gender, race and class barriers in New York's clubland, political posters adorned the walls as Gordon welcomed such dissipated bohemian figureheads as Maxwell Bodenheim and Jack Kerouac, singers including Lead Belly, Woody Guthrie and Josh White, and various stand-up comedians.

Max met his future wife Lorraine in 1948 at a Fire Island club. She was a devoted jazz buff and Monk disciple, who recognised Max as the Vanguard owner and talked him into giving the pianist his first downtown showcase. As Monk was little known in the Village the week-long stretch was poorly attended and it would take Lorraine until 1957 to convince her husband to book jazz again.

The Village Gate on Bleecker Street was already one of Marty's regular haunts. The building it occupied started life in 1896 as a workingmen's residence, then a flophouse called The Greenwich Hotel (where Allen Ginsberg paid two dollars a night to stay in 1951) before it became a Beat-friendly coffeehouse called Jazz on the Wagon. It became one of Manhattan's most legendary niteries in 1958 when it was converted into a club by promoter Art D'Lugoff, who booked in the top jazz names of the day, including Miles Davis.

"I never met Miles but I used to see him," says Marty. "I wouldn't have said anything to him, although we did have an interesting moment at the Village Gate when Dizzy Gillespie was playing." It happened during Miles' August 1967 stretch at the club with his original mentor Dizzy, who was now 50 years old. "This was not too long after Tony and I were in pretty close contact. Tony told me Miles was playing down there. I didn't sit at a table, I sat at the back of the stage, where the dressing room was. There was a long row of chairs for musicians. It was very loose like that, informal. I didn't want to sit at a table, so I sat on a chair. Miles shows up to do the show. You can see he's in very good spirits, looks like he's just come out of the gym with a tight shirt and a smile on his face, ready to play. Everybody's starting to show up, including the musicians."

First Dizzy came on, doing the career-straddling act that was now closer to cabaret, but he was still the daddy of it all. "When Dizzy started playing Miles came out of the dressing room and just watched. By this time, what Dizzy was doing was not modern. I knew Miles knew that for sure, but he stood and watched Dizzy like a kid looking at his trumpet teacher or father with the utmost respect. You could see that he would always look and listen to Dizzy that way, no matter what he did. I noticed that and then, Dizzy went into a carnival burlesque thing where the drummer takes a rubber chicken out of the bass drum and holds it up to a drum roll. It's the comic scene, which was so incongruous to anything in modern jazz. They loved it, the whole place started laughing and roaring, the entire audience is in a carnival. But it didn't make me laugh at all. So I turned my head a little bit to the side, and I catch Miles turning his head to the side and looking me straight in the eye. My eyes caught his looking at me, and I looked at him. I realised that we were the only people in the whole room that weren't laughing. That was Miles and myself totally... crossing paths."

With Alan, events which oddly foreshadowed Suicide itself were taking place elsewhere in downtown Manhattan. He had just discovered the world's first two-man electronic band. They were called Silver Apples, and featured Simeon Coxe III singing over the otherworldly noise he coaxed out of a pulsing heap of arcane electronic junk he called The Thing, all punctuated by highly creative drummer Danny Taylor. Alan recalls discovering the duo in the late sixties, and being first to spread the word in CBGB and Max's about their monumental place in the city's musical history.

"They were so way out, man," he still enthuses. "I loved the minimalism of their stuff. I used to rave about the Silver Apples, but nobody had heard of them. That music was part of me so, from my angle, Suicide stole from the Velvets, Iggy, Question Mark & the Mysterians and the Silver Apples. I remember watching a really early Debbie Harry thing, when she was singing with the Stillettoes, and she came running over to me, and wondered how I was. I didn't even know her then, man. Why are you coming up to me? I didn't know she knew me or anything. Then came her next question, 'Who are the Silver Apples?' I'd been going around telling people about them, and word was getting around that little circle of people."

Although Simeon has today been enjoying the kind of late recognition which tends to hit previously shunned trailblazers, the Silver Apples story contains more than its share of bad luck and tragedy, including Simeon's drastic road accident which halted their short-lived nineties return, and drummer Danny Taylor's death in 2005.

Simeon was born in June 1938 – the same month as Alan Vega – and raised in New Orleans, learning trumpet and marching in Mardi Gras parades. After shining in art as a child prodigy, he decided to try his luck in New York. He hung out at the Cedar Tavern on University Place, the favoured watering hole of the Abstract Expressionists, Beats and musicians, many of whom he engaged in lubricated conversation. Kerouac was barred for pissing in an ashtray, and Pollock was chucked out after ripping the gents' door off its hinges and lobbing it at Franz Kline.

Speaking from his office in Magnolia Springs, Alabama, Simeon remembers, "The Cedar Street bar was the artist hangout in the early sixties. You'd go in there and see people like Bill De Kooning and Jackson Pollock, sitting there drunk and proselytising. One time, Leroy Jones came in with Eddie Fisher and Elizabeth Taylor on either arm, went to a back table and was telling them all about black revolution. New York was an open-ended cauldron of creativity. You were not just encouraged to do something completely different and completely off the wall, it was almost necessary to get anybody's attention. If you wanted to be taken seriously as someone doing something experimental, it had to be pretty blatant. We felt that way so that's the atmosphere we were creating in.

The visual arts scene was exploding in New York. It was like, anything goes."

Simeon befriended composer Harold Clayton, who took him to "absolute junkie trash bar" Slug's Saloon, on Third Street and Avenue B, where Sun Ra and his Arkestra held a residency between 1965-72. Situated deep in the increasingly drug-infested East Village, the long dark room with bare brick walls hosted Sun Ra's crew, who would play non-stop for seven hours until 4 a.m. every Monday, their free-form space anarchy inevitably impacting on Simeon's subconsciousness. Marty recalls frequenting Slug's as a teenager, catching sets by Lee Morgan, Kenny Dorham, Hank Mobley, Marion Brown, Joe Henderson and Bobby Hutcherson.

Simeon was friends with a musician called Hal Rogers, who had attended a Bronx school for exceptional kids, keeping dozens of symphony scores committed to memory, while following the 12 tone and atonal concepts, based on mathematical processes, which inspired riffs and bass lines later used by Silver Apples. Simeon was enthralled by the World War Two oscillator hooked up to Rogers' stereo, "which he played along with Beethoven and drank vodka. I played it with an old rock'n'roll record and was absolutely hooked. That's where my fascination with electronics came in. Without that, I don't know where I would have been. If I hadn't had that exposure to that one electronic instrument, the oscillator, I may have been out in California playing washboard with the Golden Apples or something. I loved the thing, and eventually bought it off him for $10. A few years later, that same oscillator was to become what we called the 'Grandfather Oscillator' in Silver Apples."

In 1967, Simeon joined Village coffee shop outfit the Overland Stage Electric Band, who often appeared at the Café Wha? on MacDougal Street, playing early Doors covers. Already bemused at his reluctance to ape the Lizard King, the band positively balked when he brought along the oscillator. Simeon's noise-generating gadget nonetheless became a draw in itself, leading to the rest of the band departing in disgust, except for laid-back drummer Danny Taylor. Simeon learned basic electronics and commenced a soldering frenzy, wiring in more oscillators he had found on the streets. He fused his tower of electronic debris, suffered regular electric shocks cranking it into life and devising his method of playing its controlling system of 86 telegraph keys, operated with his hands, feet and elbows. The instrument was later dubbed The Simeon by everyone but Simeon, who preferred The Thing, and talked about it like a temperamental diva, prone to grating hums if miffed. Meanwhile, Danny expanded his drums to two kits, tuned so he could complement Simeon's electronic pulses and motifs. "It was basically like a one-man band with a drummer," says Simeon.

The duo started writing songs and called themselves Silver Apples, after an 1897 William Yeats poem '*The Song Of Wandering Aengus* ["And pluck till time and times are gone/The silver apples of the moon"). Simeon explained that Silver represented the moon watching their night-time activities, and the solder which held his setup together, while Apples provided the New York connection. (Coincidentally, Morton Subotnick at NYU's Tisch School of Arts also made an album called *Silver Apples Of The Moon* in 1967. It was the first electronic work to be commissioned by a record company.)

"The amazing thing is they make absolutely mind-shattering music with all this junky equipment," marvelled the *East Village Other* in 1968. But, like Suicide the following decade, Silver Apples provoked hostility from perplexed crowds and players who thought electronic keyboards were robbing "real" musicians of work. Anyway it didn't look normal without a guitar. "Exactly," says Simeon. "People would shout because Suicide had no guitar. We got the same: 'You're not a rock'n'roll band unless you got a guitar'. And Suicide had a drum machine. People thought that was strange and weird too; that there were drums, but no drummer. Danny wasn't playing to normal sounds, so had a clear field to run in and could play what he wanted. I was very fortunate to have a drummer who was so good an audience could identify with what he was doing and latch onto that; feel the rhythm, feel the beat, feel the pulsation of what he was doing. Eventually, they'd get what I was doing but it wasn't as hard for the audience as it might have been for somebody like Suicide, who didn't have that little hook that somebody might get."

Silver Apples' first major gig was in front of 30,000 punters in Central Park, the crowd initially bemused by Simeon's mound of oscillators, effects boxes, guitar pedals and old radios perched on a table, but eventually frugging to the new grooves. They would play more of these free festivals organised by a cultural committee in New York that strove to divert youthful energy from protesting against the Vietnam War.

The duo's favourite home gig was Max's Kansas City on Park Avenue South. "That's where we played a lot," recalls Simeon. "The audience was all artists, poets, actors and other musicians; not just regular types. It was a very art-within-art kind of thing. It was relatively easy to cruise through that environment. You didn't get much off of it, but you could have a gig once a week at different venues to keep yourself going."

Max's was opened at 213 Park Avenue South in December 1965 by Mickey Ruskin to provide a meeting place and watering hole to catalyse the modern art movements gaining steam in New York. The location placed it at the hub of both East and West Villages, and within easy reach of SoHo. A Cornell graduate, Ruskin was already embedded in the city's artistic underground, running poetry-driven establishments for five years from 1960 such as the Tenth Street Coffeehouse, Ninth and Les Deux Megots (sic) on East Seventh Street.

Once described by William S. Burroughs as "the intersection of everything", Max's took over where the Cedar Tavern left off. Patrons were encouraged by a liberal manifesto and intellectually hungry atmosphere which, rarely for that time, welcomed gay customers and turned a blind eye to the pill-popping and shagging going on anywhere from the infamous, red-bathed back room to the phone-booth. Names enjoying its warm alcoves included De Kooning, Castelli, Lichtenstein, Rauschenberg and more as word spread, including as well Burroughs and Ginsberg, and Warhol's menagerie. Andy's freeloading cavorters made Max's their own, and its name known to the rest of the world. "Max's was famous for its freaks," says Jayne County, the regular who ended up becoming the club's DJ and performing there the following decade.

"In the mid-to-late sixties, Max's back room comprised the Factory people, actors, writers and artists," says former Max's face Elda Gentile. "As it gained global recognition, the more famous found it as a refuge for their own personal entertainment. On any night, you could be sitting across from Dali, Fellini, Jane Fonda, Mick Jagger, Jimi Hendrix – who sent a glass of wine over to me one night – and Janis Joplin bumming cigarettes. It was an iconic time and place to be in history for music and all the arts."

Through his Warhol connections, Peter Crowley soon became a Max's regular, loving it so much that, after leaving the Balloon Farm and setting up the first mail order head shop, he rented a loft on 17th and Broadway, just a block from the action. His company, Cosmic Truth, distributed the wares of Head Gear, a firm which manufactured hash pipes and imported incense burners and rolling papers, "the first to nationally distribute that kind of paraphernalia," and "a tremendous success" after advertising in the new *Rolling Stone* magazine. His turnover in the first year was a quarter of a million dollars but, within a year the business had become "cut-throat" whilst, unbeknown to Peter, "the accounts girl was syphoning money into the veins of her junkie boyfriend Joe Dallesandro", the Warhol superstar immortalised in Lou Reed's 'Walk On The Wild Side'. "Buying heroin for him and his girlfriend caused the business to fail, we were bleeding money and I didn't know it," continues Peter. After another staffer got viciously mugged in Washington Square, he decided "New York wasn't working out after all" and moved back to San Francisco; "a really stupid move as the business didn't survive and I had to get a job."

By early 1968, Warhol had moved the Factory to the sixth floor of the Decker building on Union Square West. He was a major Silver Apples fan, suggesting the duo back his 'superstar' Ultra Violet, as the Velvet Underground had with Nico. Simeon and Danny had acquired a manager, business dropout Barry Bryant, who secured them a deal with the independent Kapp Records. To record their first album, the duo squeezed The Thing and Danny's enormous kit into the label's tiny four-track studio. After the horrified designated producer feigned illness, studio virgins Simeon and Danny ended up producing themselves through trial and error. "We just put in some microphones and started playing 'Oscillations'. The result was a total mess. When I think of how good we might have sounded if we could only have had some help from that producer I get angry, because those records are all that survive, not the live performances we did later when we finally got our act together."

'Oscillations', which became their first single, flickers and whooshes over its tribal proto-techno beat, with Simeon singing lyrics by poet Stanley Warren, who had impressed the duo when they met him at New York's Third Annual Avant Garde Arts Festival. While 'Lovefingers' saw the duo use chord changes, most other songs were mono-chord or random. 'Program' predates Holger Czukay's chance-based dial-twiddling with Can, as snippets of Stravinsky and bierkeller broadcasts from two radios filter over the lightly skipping drone-groove.

Once finished, the album was unveiled on the roof of Barry Bryant's apartment, before a week-long stint at Steve Paul's Underground club. The duo could find themselves playing high-school gyms with bubblegum groups such as the 1910 Fruitgum Company, or doing the Fillmore East with the Fugs, nudging the album to 193 on the charts.

Silver Apples really did sound like nobody else in 1968. Even that year's United States Of America album, from LA-based former Fluxus member Joseph Byrd, sounded sophisticated in comparison, betraying formal musical training in complex song structures. Simeon might declare they were "just limping along the best we could", within the technological limitations of the time, but when Silver Apples' self-titled debut album was released in 1968, Kraftwerk were still tootling flutes at arts labs, and even the Velvet Underground were still only amping up conventional instruments. John Lennon was smitten, announcing on British TV in 1968, "Watch out for a band called Silver Apples, they are the next thing."

1969's *Contact* album bristled with extra-terrestrial sound and wigged-out vision, and displayed a new confidence in the studio. "I feel *Contact* is our best work from that period," says Simeon. "By then, we were on the road and most of the stuff that we were doing would be worked up during soundchecks. It's more like what we were doing live. They were really desperate to have something more conventional come out of us, but we never gave it to them. *Contact* was all electronic and drums, and me doing the vocals. By then we were into a rawer, less polished sound. This was because so many of our contemporaries were adding violins and choirs to what used to be rock! We were pissed so we went the other way."

Then there was the cover. Simeon was struck by the yell of "Contact!" when a plane's propeller was cranked into life by hand, applying it to communicating with the people. Kapp's advertising agency had connections with Pan Am, which resulted in the pair being photographed inside a string of cockpits, after all incoming flights to JFK airport were directed to a section of Tarmac to face the sunset on the cover. Simeon and Danny sniggered at the drug paraphernalia they'd snuck in next to the airline's logo. Barry Bryant took the joke further with a shot of a fatal Swedish air crash, the pair superimposed in the wreckage playing banjos. The message seemed to be two freaks piloting a plane with their stash, crashing it, but surviving to strum smiling in the wreckage. Pan Am was apoplectic. Hysteria followed with the album withdrawn and lawsuits, meaning stores never received it.

Barry Bryant cast around for a new deal and secured time at top studio the Record Plant, promising the imagined new label would pick up the tab. Simeon and Danny were booked in between midnight and four every morning, before Jimi Hendrix came in to start his four until eight stint. Obviously there was overlapping between the two, even some swapping of gadgets. When Jimi was whisked to London in 1966, he had wanted to take Danny with him, but the drummer declined. "At that time, Jimi Hendrix and the Blue Flames were just another blues band. He wasn't really a showman, so Danny wasn't all that excited about going to England with him, because he didn't think there was a whole lot to it. Thank goodness, because he ended up with me!"

The friendship continued whenever Hendrix returned to New York. "Jimi would come in and listen to us record and we'd stick around and listen to him. There's several tapes of us just messing around. The only one that I've ever heard is him and me playing the 'Star Spangled Banner', with me on two oscillators. It's definitely a curiosity, but it's not a great piece of music at all."

This is actually the prototype 'Star Spangled Banner' which Hendrix attempted in the studio before unleashing the definitive version at Woodstock the following August. It appeared on 1972's *Rainbow Bridge*, with no Simeon credit. "It was listed as Jimi solo but, if you listen, you can hear me playing six bass oscillators behind three tracks of guitars he'd laid down."

Mayor John Lindsay asked Silver Apples to perform at the Central Park event to watch the US Moon landing on huge TV screens, declaring them "the New York sound" and commissioning a song. They came up with 'Mune Toon', performing it in the rain beating down on the park. "So all during 'Mune Toon' there was this tingling, sexy, frightening, scary thing coursing through my body. I was singing my heart out and Armstrong was stepping onto the Moon, human beings were entering a new era and thousands of people were crying with happiness and soaking wet and singing and hugging each other."

Recording ceased when the studio demanded payment, prospective labels deterred by the Pan Am affair. The lawsuit, record company collapse and third album stalling were enough to squash Silver Apples. In September 1970, while Danny went to work for a telephone company, Simeon sold his amps and shipped The Thing to his parents' home in Mobile, Alabama, where he ended up with wife Eileen after buying a small sailing boat. The following years saw him driving an ice cream truck, working as a news reporter and advertising designer, before returning to painting. If Silver Apples hadn't ceased to exist in 1969, who knows what part they would have played in shaping electronic music as it later evolved. As it happened, all the genres which Simeon might have played a major part in, like electronic disco, hip-hop, house and techno, passed him by as he sailed the Gulf of Mexico.

Simeon also missed out on Suicide materialising the following year and encountering their own, similar obstacles. In retrospect, it almost seems like a metaphysical baton was being passed on as events continued to bring the wayward paths of Alan and Marty ever closer.

SIX

By the age of 20, Martin Reverby's life had been one long quest to take his playing to the next level. He had studied with legends and jammed with downtown's finest, while his social life revolved around witnessing jazz greats ignite various New York niteries. Marty was a regular at the Village Vanguard, and became known by proprietor Max Gordon as quite the obsessed young disciple. "I could just walk in and he'd turn his head, so the guy at the door would be 'Okay'." Marty would slide into a good spot and watch, quietly soaking everything in, usually alone. The last thing he expected was to meet the love of his life.

On a fateful Friday night, Marty took the train downtown to the Seventh Avenue club to see his old hero Thelonious Monk play at the Vanguard. He would always try to check out Monk when he played locally.

"It was a Friday night and a full house, so I didn't want to use up one of Max's tables," recalls Marty. "I was standing at the side from where you could watch everything, on the way to the back where the kitchen and men's room were, basically the dressing room area. There was a wall where you could stand, see the band, and leave enough room for somebody to walk past to the john. The musicians would go by there too when they were done, and just hang out at the back."

When he went to the bar, Marty noticed one of the waitresses collecting drinks on her tray. "Oh wow, who's that?" he sighed to himself, suddenly charged with an internal current he had never experienced before; that once-in-a-lifetime swell which says things may never be the same again. Some call it love at first sight. Right there and then he had to find a way to break the ice and strike up a conversation with her. Marty had thought nothing of ringing a famous musician's doorbell and asking for lessons, but this was an alien feeling he wasn't used to, as he thought to himself, "How can I somehow get to know her? What can I think of to say? I was worse at that time than I would be with musicians."

Marty hatched a plan as he stood by the small bussing station recess where the waitresses dropped off the glasses. He knew she had to return there, and she frequently did. He also knew that all-important opening gambit was going to be vital if this girl, who "was so incredibly striking to me", wasn't going to slip through his hands and out of his life forever. One time when she returned, Marty leaned over, plucking up guts he didn't know he had, smiled and asked, "Didn't we meet in California?"

"It was probably the worst introductory pick-up line anybody could ever think of!" he now laughs. "I don't know how or why I thought of California. I'd never been further west than New Jersey! But I struck a goal. She lit up, and said, 'Yeah, I lived in California'. It rang the perfect bell because it turned out she had lived there as a girl. She had seen Ornette Coleman when he first started out, and knew a lot of musicians on that scene. From there, we just hit it off. I went to the Vanguard again next night, watching Monk again. We went for a coffee, and then it went from there."

Her name was Mari Montgomery. Temporarily staying with a friend in Connecticut, she'd been waitressing at the Vanguard to save money, so she could pick up her young son and daughter, who were living in California with her mother, before moving to New Mexico. Her plan was the only thing that went south. "She decided not to move to New Mexico, and instead, she stayed in New York and we made a life here." Initially, they lived at Marty's place, before Mari got an apartment on the Lower East Side to accommodate her children, Lyn and Greg, who were then three and 10. "Soon we had a family in New York. My place was too small, although we did live there for a while. We then always had two places, because I used to go back to mine every day to play and practise. It was like my studio. We had two children of our own in the first year and eight months, Miro and Elisha. I had a family with four children by the time I was 22."

At this point, this book also becomes a love story, which will be picked up by Alan in the mid-eighties when he meets Elizabeth Lamere, his own lifelong muse and partner but, just as he was hitting his twenties, Marty had met the soulmate who would become the single biggest presence and influence in his life. For some it takes a lifetime to find that magic relationship where sparks fly in every direction on a bright new journey, if it ever happens at all.

Indirectly thanks to Monk, Marty had found the love of his life, and he hadn't even been looking. "After a few years, I was already so far out, but in a way so young, that the chance of even finding a girlfriend my age was slim. All the girls my age were still living at home or at school. After a few years, maybe you can find somebody who's something like you, but it's not always that easy and how far can you go? Most people say 'I can't experience this, he doesn't have any money, so I'll be careful about it', but with Mari there were no limits when it came to learning and creating, as she was already an artist and a musician. I was already living in Manhattan in a flat, very developed in my own direction as an artist, and already far away from the possibility of being in any kind of mainstream! If I took a job it was to get by, so I could keep playing and growing. When I met Mari, she was young and vibrant all the way through, an incredible spirit, mind and intelligence. She was 11 years older than I was, although she always looked incredibly young. She was very pivotal to me, because she created a family around us as two artists who were otherwise so unconnected to mainstream life, and both loners. It was like she gave me my PHD in life at an advanced university. She had read and experienced and listened to so much, which enriched my sensibility incredibly. I wasn't with someone who was saying, 'We got to make a living now'. She wanted me to be as far away from that as possible, so I could keep growing as an artist and a person. She opened the way for me to survive in the fullest way, instead of as a loner which, in many ways, was where I was heading."

Marty never talked publicly about Mari until 2008, when the poignant dedication on his *Stigmata* album, inspired by her recent passing, prompted me to ask about her, and he opened up. But that's 40 years away from that night at the Vanguard. I wanted to know more about this obviously remarkable woman, and this sent Marty off on memories, then some research of his own. Marty discovered that Mari was born at the Harlem Hospital on West 142nd Street – just two blocks from the Lutheran Hospital on 144th Street where he had come into the world.

Not only that, Mari spent her earliest years living only a few blocks away from that hospital. "I never saw that before as I've never researched that region," he marvelled, quietly elated. "We just never connected it, but it was so obvious. I'm really shocked, but positively. I've found the building where she lived after she was born at Harlem Hospital, a few blocks east of Convent Avenue in Sugar Hill. It wasn't a very large avenue, maybe two streets, like a church row or something. I found some old pictures and the buildings are so beautiful and striking. They're just so like her, in a way, like religious universities. It turns out her old building was on 141st Street and Convent Avenue, on the corner on the same side of the street as Lutheran Hospital, which is on the same parallel corner on 144th. That was a revelation! When I was born, Mari was already there."

Mari told Marty about a child piano prodigy she had known in her building called Philippa Schuyler, who was five years her senior. Schuyler's father was prominent black journalist George S. Schuyler, her white Texan mother a Mack Sennett bathing beauty from a former slave-owning family. The couple believed that mixed-race marriage could solve the social problems in America. "She was very similar to Mari, with a white mother and a black father," says Marty. "Mari said she knew Philippa and used to hear her practising. She got as far as someone from that background could go in America at that time."

Philippa was composing by the age of five, soon giving recitals, making radio broadcasts and touring. Although a role model for kids in the thirties and forties, the press liked to suggest she'd been her parents' mixed race experiment. The bigotry that Philippa still encountered in the US caused her to largely continue her career in Europe. By her thirties, she'd abandoned piano to follow her father into journalism, but Philippa died in a helicopter crash in 1967 while covering the war in Vietnam. Her mother committed suicide two years later, still living in the house on Convent Avenue. In recent years, Halle Berry has announced her intention of making a biopic based on Philippa's life, with Alicia Keys in the starring role, although nothing further is confirmed.

Mari started taking piano lessons herself after her family moved to an apartment above her physician uncle's Harlem surgery, where they remained for a couple of years before moving to Michigan. "Mari said that Michigan in the fifties was so incredibly repressed," remembers Marty. "She felt no real connection with anything else that was going on, because apparently suburban Lansing was a very strange place to grow up in. Almost all of the high yellow and Creole community she lived in was materialistic, straight and middle class. Her aunts groomed her to be married, dressed her like a doll, with a flower in the side of her hair, always very prim and proper, never to say too much. She had very little contact or understanding with her immediate family, including her mother. She became a loner very early, and finally split home when they moved to California."

The teenage Mari gravitated to LA's happening jazz scene, where she met and became friends with drummer Max Roach, who was staying in California at the time and had formed his blues and gospel-lashed hard bop quintet with virtuoso trumpeter Clifford Brown. "Mari used to go and check out Max Roach, and they were pretty close," says Marty. "Clifford Brown was 23 and married to a woman named Larue. Mari met them as well."

After Max Roach became one of jazz's most outspoken civil rights voices, he recorded 1960's *We Insist! Max Roach's Freedom Now Suite*, a chillingly provocative concept album tracing the story of slavery and racism, and the most powerfully emotive musical statement from the whole era. The terrifyingly atmospheric 'Triptych: Prayer, Protest, Peace' presages Suicide's 'Frankie Teardrop' with Abbey Lincoln's elemental tour de force of screams, whimpers and agonised banshee wails. It's as if she's wrenching years of cruelty and brutality from her guts and out through her mouth, finishing the song drained, sobbing and almost post-coital. "That's a very strong album," agrees Marty. "That was really a focused record, and probably the best album they did together. I recently heard it on the radio again. 'Triptych' reminded me of 'Frankie Teardrop'. It had never really registered before because I had never focused on it so clearly. But I remember thinking it was from a similar world."

We Insist! was a brave statement at a time when sit-ins were in full swing as a dignified protest, as reflected in the striking cover image of three black men sitting at a lunch counter in front of an apprehensive-looking white waiter. The word 'freedom' got kicked to death in the sixties, but this album was its deepest felt, most extreme statement, and predictably resulted in Roach and Lincoln being blacklisted by much of the US recording industry.

Mari was also a regular at the Hillcrest Club, where pianist Paul Bley was starting his prolific career, and recently deceased sax colossus Ornette Coleman had first hit a major stage. "Apparently Ornette just walked into the club one day," says Marty. "He used to wear a heavy winter coat in the hottest California summer, and looked unusual immediately.

He asked to sit in with Paul Bley, and everyone was astonished at this whole new music coming in. Don Cherry may have been in the audience and would soon do the same thing. That was the beginning of Ornette's professional life."

Although he wouldn't make his epoch-defining *The Shape Of Jazz To Come* until later that decade, the scorching sets Ornette played at the Hillcrest with Bley, trumpeter Don Cherry, bassist Charlie Haden and drummer Billy Higgins got the free jazz ball rolling. Ornette was no stranger to audiences trying to beat him up, or smash his saxophone, and musicians stomping off stage in outrage at the new sounds he was summoning, but there could be no stopping him becoming one of the most revered experimentalists of all time. His high-profile 1959 opening at New York's Five Spot changed the course of jazz.

Mari was friends with Ornette to the point where, for years, as Marty recalls, the pair would stop and talk when they bumped into each other in the East Village. She was also close to Bertha Hope, wife of pianist Elmo Hope, who came of age in the bebop years with close buddies Bud Powell and Monk, toured with Chet Baker and moved to LA in 1958. Marty describes him as "the transition between Bud Powell and the next generation, which could be only three years younger in those days." When Bertha and Elmo moved back to New York in 1961, she worked at the telephone company by day and played clubs at night, while he recorded scintillating albums such as 1963's *Songs From Rikers Island*. After her heroin-addicted husband passed away in 1967, Bertha continued his legacy.

Despite being surrounded by such musical brilliance, Mari was still searching for kindred spirits and her soulmate when she returned to New York in the late fifties. By now, she was pregnant with her son Greg, whose godfather would be Max Roach, after he helped her financially to leave California. "Before she came to New York, she still felt there was no one else out there, until she discovered other artists, and the Beats," says Marty. "The Beat movement was really something then. She knew Kerouac's wife and daughter but not Kerouac as, by that time, he had split up with them and had no contact. It made her feel like there were others like her around. But, although she was of that mentality, she wasn't strictly a Beat generation person. She was beyond that too."

Although Mari had enjoyed working at Judith Malina and Julian Beck's experimental Living Theatre in SoHo, 1967 saw her planning to move out of New York and see what that brought. In the nick of time, she had found her soulmate, and life was about to change again. "Mari knew so much and was like a mentor to me. She had lived and experienced so much, and was so broad in what she knew in terms of music and art. In our whole life together, I always felt she was the most erudite, advanced artist and spirit I'd ever met. I realised later she was actually a child of the Harlem Renaissance, like the next generation from Langston Hughes and an inheritor of that golden period of culture. She had a renaissance outlook to learn everything about arts and science, and combine them in her heart and thinking. She had so much to offer a young, aspiring artist, which is why I always wanted to learn so much about everything in music that I didn't know. I learned it wasn't just about one style so I was lucky, in a way, that I was never successful for a long time in any one niche, until I really found myself."

Marty also recalls Mari as a fantastic writer, always looking for the life beyond racial divides. "I used to try and encourage her to put together her letters to her family in a book, they are so incredible. There's a certain native truth about America and the people of the time which comes through in them. She had been to so many places that she talked about; she had a whole country side and a totally sophisticated urban side to her. She had no brothers or sisters and not everybody was so close, but they all came from very interesting backgrounds. They didn't come through as being black or white, but mixed people who were part American Indian. She loved that she had American Indian and Chinese blood in her, and Welsh blood too. She felt she was part of the future, in that sense, because she saw it as being a mixture of colour and ethnicity. She was brought up in a time of severe institutional segregation and bigotry. She experienced all that growing up, so she knew what that was all about, and experienced it in various ways through her whole life. It wasn't easy. In fact, the whole American experience wasn't that all-embracing for her. That's why she was always looking to leave."

Marty had found his dream girl, his centre and life's inspiration. The next logical step in his personal musical evolution, having cut his teeth with masters, would be to form his own band.

Major eruptions were taking place in Alan Bermowitz's life too, after he left his Brooklyn Heights family home to devote all his time to being an artist. "One day, Alan just jumped up and got going," says Marty. "He still lived in Brooklyn, but with a friend of his, who was an older photographer who had a couple of floors. He was a nice guy, who had a family there and was making a living already. He knew Alan and let him have the basement to live in."

Alan was already aware that SoHo was becoming downtown's arts hotspot, and an alternative to the snootier establishments uptown. The mood of the times needed its own enclave for unshackled expression. The decaying and deserted-after-dark Cast Iron District was so perfect it would become the birthplace of Suicide.

It is often said that Manhattan's real estate boom started in SoHo, but in the sixties it was a 19th century industrial slum. Earlier that century, the area below Houston Street was mainly inhabited by wealthy New Yorkers, who patronised the hotels and theatres on Broadway, along with the brothels on Mercer and Greene. Atypically for New York, its streets had names instead of numbers, titled after generals from the Revolutionary War, including Lafayette, Crosby, Wooster and Greene. Using a technique developed in England in the late 18th century, foundries along the East River were first to manufacture the bespoke cast iron frames which could support tall buildings using pre-determined moulds, rather than the more laborious and expensive method of carving them out of stone and marble. It also meant large panes of glass could be used. The 1857 E.V. Haugwhout store at the corner of Grand and Broadway was the first to incorporate iron into a building's structure, also the first to boast a steam-driven passenger elevator. The modern skyscraper was born, and SoHo soon boasted the world's most impressive array.

Most of SoHo's colossal structures were built before 1890, and used by the textile industry, mainly immigrant workers from the Lower East Side. When the industry shrank after World War Two, the buildings were mainly used for long-term storage, but populated by a few artists attracted by the cheap rents. When New York writer Henry Miller, who'd written the teenage Alan's favourite *Tropic Of Capricorn*, visited painter Beauford Delaney at 181 Greene Street in the forties, his essay in *Remember To Remember* talked about "streets which seem commemorated to the pangs and frustrations of the artist; having nothing to do with art. Shunned by all living as soon as the work of day is done, they are invested with the sinister shadows of crime and with prowling alley cats which thrive on the garbage and ordure that litter the gutters and pavements." There were frequent fires in the dilapidated industrial tundra, which was tagged 'Hell's

Hundred Acres'. More businesses fled the area when the dreaded Robert Moses threatened his proposed 10-lane Lower Manhattan Expressway, which would have run between the Williamsburg and Manhattan bridges on the east and Holland Tunnel on the west, doing a South Bronx-style demolition job through the cast iron cluster, and the neighbourhood's heart. The project was stalled through the sterling efforts of community activist Jane Jacobs, but a damning October 1962 City Club pamphlet deemed the area "The Wastelands of New York City".

New York Commissioner of Planning Chester Rapkin's 1963 Study of 'The South Houston Industrial Area', which is credited with coining the term SoHo, noted the declining businesses, but advised the city not to destroy the buildings, or evict the remaining vestiges of the rag and garment industries, which were a source of tax. By that time, the Artists Tenants Association was petitioning Mayor Robert Wagner for permission to live and work in districts not officially zoned for residential use, or any buildings lacking a residential Certificate of Occupancy. The city agreed that no more than two artists could live in such buildings, providing they stick a sign on the front saying 'A.I.R.' (Artist In Residence), which identified the floors for firemen. Crucially, real estate agent Jack Klein then persuaded neighbourhood landlords to rent their empty buildings to artists. The landlords were only too happy to get income from these "raw space" lofts, with their weathered walls and leaky ceilings, so offered prospective artist owners purchase mortgages, which were repaid directly to the seller as a red-tape short cut. SoHo started filling up with the artists who were undeterred by its scary reputation or lack of grocery stores, schools, pharmacies and churches. Only neighbourhood bars such as Fanelli's on Prince and Mercer nodded at facilities demanded by normal civilisation. Fluxus founder George Maciunas was an early invester, buying buildings and dividing them into artists' co-ops, while Jonas Mekas opened the Filmmakers' Cinemateque on the ground floor of 80 Worcester and the Gay Activist Alliance Firehouse became the first homosexual dancehall.

The cracked, graffiti-splattered streets were littered with discarded wreckage, industrial trash, wood, metal, rubber and construction materials, which came in handy when Alan needed raw materials for the light sculptures he had started making from junk he found in the street, cheap religious bric-a-brac and light bulbs. Soon he found himself part of SoHo's flourishing new arts scene, saying now, "SoHo was the centre of the universe then. Everybody went there, it was the apex, full of artists and also manufacturers, who were hard-working people. I loved it." He joined the volatile Art Workers' Coalition, which brought together artists, writers, filmmakers and critics to pressure New York's art establishments into loosening up their exclusivity, notably the Museum of Modern Art. Formed in January 1969, after Greek kinetic sculptor Vassilakis Takis removed one of his early sculptures from the MoMA in protest at it being shown without his permission or input, the AWC lobbied for women, and a wider ethnic representation. It also pressured museums into standing against the Vietnam War, most famously with the *And Babies* poster, depicting innocent victims of the March 1968 My Lai rape and slaughter by US troops, whose circulation stoked the groundswell opposition to America's war crime cover-ups.

The original consortium which met at the Chelsea Hotel on 23rd Street included Takis, sculptor Wen-Ying Tsai, German conceptual artist Hans Haacke, writer Willoughby Sharp, minimalist artist Carl Andre and *Village Voice* art critic John Perreault. When the MoMA refused to allow the group's proposed public forum about its relationship with artists and society, the AWC held demos in front of the museum and an open hearing on April 10, 1969, at the New York School of Visual Arts on 21st Street, where Alan's friend Howie Wolper was a student. Over 300 members of the city's artistic community, including Howie and Alan, attended the meeting to debate artists' rights, museum policy and political issues, including the Vietnam War. When the AWC organised its 'Moratorium to Art to End The War in Vietnam' that October, the MoMA, Whitney Museum, Jewish Museum and other galleries closed for the day. Although the AWC only lasted until late 1971, its activities brought crucial changes to how museums interacted with artists.

After Paula Cooper established her gallery in a second-floor space on Prince in 1968, the first street-level operation arrived the following year when Ivan Karp opened OK Harris on West Broadway, the neighbourhood's widest thoroughfare (the Sixth Avenue elevated railway had once run over it). Many local artists got their first crack at showing through the cigar-chomping Karp, who saw himself as SoHo's unofficial Mayor. He had grown up in Brooklyn and, after starting as one of the *Village Voice*'s first art critics in the mid-fifties, became Leo Castelli's associate director in 1958, giving early breaks to Warhol, Lichtenstein, Rauschenberg and other Pop artists. He opened OK Harris (which he said was supposed to be a tough American name that sounded like that of a riverboat gambler) in 1969 as the first gallery on West Broadway, showing names including Duane Hanson, Deborah Butterfield, Manny Farber, Richard Pettibone, Nancy Rubins, Malcolm Morley... and Alan Suicide. Karp's main mission was to find and encourage young artists. "Ivan had a way of making you feel good," wrote Warhol in his *Popism* memoir, after Karp had constructively criticised his early work before helping show it to the world in his 10 years with Castelli.

Ivan certainly made Alan feel good the following year when he "came down and saw my sculptures with a Canadian art dealer, who was a big shot at the time, and said, 'I want you to be here at my gallery in two weeks.' It was the start of my career. I still remember signing with him."

Although he had no time for polite gallery etiquette, Alan started getting known for the fizzing, flashing light sculptures he constructed out of abandoned TV sets, fluorescent tube lights he stole from stores by sticking them down his trouser leg, subway lamps, chains, broken glass and electrical detritus he found on the streets which, in a brilliantly Dadaist move, he threw back out on them after the show was over, "ashes to ashes and dust to dust."

Alan remembers a rattled Ivan shouting at him to turn down the four or five radios he had blasting simultaneously, tuned to different stations, and described constructing his tangled monoliths with "a not-give-a-shit attitude about just piling up a load of garbage and proving it could look good too, just throwing a bunch of lights on sculptures." He adds "I was never thinking about having a career in anything. I wasn't really thinking about it. I was just doing it, although I soon started changing..."

Peter Zaremba, future singer with Suicide's later gig and labelmates the Fleshtones, remembers Alan's show as his first encounter with Vega-world. "I first became aware of Alan when I was a student, and stumbled into a show of his sculpture at OK Harris. There were all these big, dangerous-looking piles of dismantled TVs and electronics on the floor, with what looked like live wires sticking out of them. I remember a terrified gallery-going mom racing in to pull out her little boy, who had wandered in while she was admiring some other work in another room."

"Part of Alan's intensity was that he had left a fairly conventional life," says Marty. "He had graduated as an art and science major and was still doing art, including a lot of very unique drawings. When I met him he had left his wife and his job. He had basically left that life. It was the whole Gauguin trip, y'know?"

By 1969, Alan had become a janitor-director at the Project Of Living Artists, situated in a spacious, renovated second-floor loft on the corner of Broadway and Waverly Place. It was funded by the New York State Council for the Arts to provide an open-all-hours space where artists, musicians, poets and radical political groups could express themselves, using words, music, slide shows, or any means they chose. Or, as the council's literature put it, "a centre of cultural activities which sponsors meetings of artist groups, workshops, and exhibitions", with "live sketching, film showings, dance recitals and poetry readings; and free exhibit facilities for artist groups concerned with relating the arts to society."

Alan got $90 a month and a free space to develop his experiments in sound and vision. The Project soon became a safe and welcoming refuge for not just artists and musicians but citizens of the streets with nowhere else to go.

"We had a grant from the New York State government to keep it open 24 hours a day, so that any artist or anyone who called himself an artist who wanted to do something could come into this space and just do it for nothing," recalls Alan. "It was also like a political haven for anti-Vietnam radicals, who had their part-congressional coalition groups. We got a lot of crazy radicals coming there to do their thing, whatever it was, but a lot of great jazz bands came in there too, all kinds of things. The first women's lib meetings were held there. We'd probably been infiltrated by the FBI already, because all these radicals had meetings, but one night, in a joking manner, we decided, 'Let's go kidnap Henry Kissinger', who was Secretary of State at the time, as a joke. Next day they fucking invaded us. The FBI came in on us, man, searching for shit. Unbelievable times. After a while, the crazies tried to take the place over and we had to get 'em out."

Now Alan was in the right place, next came the event that would crystallise his vocation and jerk his destiny into sharp focus. And that's *before* the coming collision with Marty Rev.

SEVEN

The year 1969 was memorable for both Alan and Marty, as it saw events unfold which led to them meeting, and the birth of Suicide the following year. While Alan experienced the life-changing epiphany which propelled him to become a performer, Rev embraced playing electronic keyboards on a big stage for the first time and formed his own jazz arkestra.

Marty had renewed his friendship with his teenage friend Steve Tintweiss, now an in-demand double bassist on the free jazz scene. Since their days at Queens College Music School, Steve had played at Birdland matinees, studied bass with Gary Peacock, learned bowing techniques from Ornette Coleman's bassist David Izenzon, and joined pianist Burton Greene, another of New York's most fearless jazz piano innovators. Steve was in the band when Greene accompanied singer Patty Waters on 1965's avant garde vocal landmark *Patty Waters Sings* and 1968's *Presenting Burton Greene*, the album that marked the first time a Moog synthesizer was used on a jazz record. Greene got the gig after being the only musician to show any interest when Robert Moog tried to promote his new invention at an electronics show in 1963. One thing led to another and, several years later, Greene found himself in a room stacked with Moogs, pampered by five technicians, who carried out his every untutored whim.

Playing in Steve's band and on the downtown loft scene proved an easy way for Marty to ease into new jazz circles, and led to him forming his own band. "Steve had a very avant garde band, which I was in around that time. I used to see him in New York, and sometimes he'd call me up and say 'Do you want to play with my band?' I played about six gigs with Steve. We did some of that outdoor kind of thing."

The biggest was at the Bandshell in Forest Park, the third largest park in Queens (where Steve has now been putting on jazz shows for the last five decades). These earliest shows were Marty's first experience of a big stage, and using an electronic organ. "I remember doing that electronically because there wasn't a piano there. That opened up a lot for me because of the way it sounded going out in a big stadium setting. I don't think I ever rehearsed on that organ but, from the first sound, it was great."

Marty hadn't slept much the night before as he'd been hanging out with Rocky Boyd, the tenor saxophonist who had introduced Tony Williams to jazz in Boston. "I used to see Rocky live and hang out with him at the Vanguard, because he was there all the time," recalls Marty. "We used to meet up and talk and play together at my place, especially when he was staying there. We would go over charts and stuff. He was a beautiful player and a very sweet, mild, spacey guy."

Marty had also taken to hanging out and playing at a smoky jazz loft called Studio We, at 193 Eldridge Street on the Lower East Side. Run by trumpeter James DuBoise and jazz percussionist Juma Sultan, who played the Woodstock festival that year as part of Hendrix's Gypsy Sun and Rainbows band, the old tenement was one of the first significant venues in the loft scene, and nurtured New York's free jazz movement at that time.

As Marty recalls, "Eldridge Street was all neglected, falling down tenements. At that time, the Lower East Side was the slum neighbourhood of Manhattan. It was a very heavy, crime-infested place, but then you had this creatively rich community as artists who didn't have the money to live on the Upper West Side were able to find spaces. New York was able to give seed to new movements because you could get a place for 80 bucks. That's how they were able to get this empty building, and all the avant garde scene at that time used to pass through there. James DuBoise was always there playing with groups, and that was my connection. James played with Steve at some of the gigs I did with him. He was a great dude and a wonderful musician and spirit. The house piano was a concert grand which Burton Greene had put in there, one of those really long ones, and they'd have concerts. I did something at Studio We with Steve's band, where there were five bands going on after one another, a loose loft thing."

The night before the Bandshell gig, Marty was "walking around the Village downtown, which I do very often, and I ran into Rocky, so we stayed up almost the whole night hanging out, then went back to my place. We had to get together fairly early in Studio We, because they were gonna drive us out to the park. I was up for most of the night, feeling really good, which had something to do with where my mind and my head were that day! We drove out to Forest Park that morning and played in the daytime. I felt great, and it was just one of those incredible gigs. Everything about it, the ambience, the electronics, and the organ."

On a roll one evening, Marty ran through some of the other illustrious names he had either met or played with through this vibrant new circle; some known, others lost to loft legend. These include trumpeter Arthur Williams ("a totally avant garde, post-Don Ayler trumpeter"), drummer Laurence Cook (who played with Alan Silva and Paul Bley), reeds man Mark Whitecage, who went on to carve a prolific career after 10 years with Gunter Hampel and Saheb Sarbib, and clarinetist Perry Robinson, "who was also a local, under-the-radar figure but very prominent that time in free music." Forming his own ensemble was a natural move for Marty in this inspiring, balmy time. "I was looking for a name so I took the Reverend from Rev and just added the B. It was funny when I thought about it several years later and realised it was kind of a hip name, in terms of many that came after. It sounded right to me and I just used it."

Fronted by Marty on electric keyboards, Reverend B played at Studio We, as well as in galleries and lofts. The line-up changed with every show, sometimes running to 12 musicians, with up to three drummers. "It was a very avant garde-sounding group, totally free. There was a combination of people that did the shows, different musicians every time we played. It was the kind of band where you'd call up people the week before a show and assemble them. Sometimes eight, nine or 10 musicians, sometimes four or five, depending on who was available."

At various times, Reverend B included future Sun Ra trumpet mainstay Ahmed Abdullah, Mark Whitecage and an oboist called Jimmy Hahn. "Jimmy was there at every show. He was of a very avant garde mentality. One time, he said 'come over and listen to records'. He was living in Queens and I was in Manhattan, so I took the train over and spent about four hours there while he put on avant garde classical records one after another; Stockhausen, Berio, total like Deutsche Grammophon post-modern, post-surreal, and after and before. That was what he was into. It was great for me to hear all that at one time, but I remember when I left, going down the stairs from his apartment building, I was just thinking 'Oh man, I'd really love to hear some rhythm and blues now!'"

Displaying the kind of go-getting approach he would soon employ with Suicide, Marty even arranged an audition at London Records' New York office, getting his first taste of mortifying unsuspecting A&R men.

"It was avant garde, or even post-avant garde. It was more like Cecil at that point. Sometimes, when I was playing the electronic keyboard, I found I would go into a groove kind of thing, something very beat oriented, but with all the horns improvising, and the drummer would follow me. It was closer to fusion then, but with a lot more improvising and intensity because we weren't trying to fuse anything. It just came naturally out of that whole free place. It was all totally fresh and exciting. For the innovators, it was totally open at that time."

Miles had caused another ruckus that year with *Bitches Brew*, which realigned jazz's gravitational focus by using electronic keyboards. Predictably, like its predecessor *In A Silent Way*, the album was attacked by outraged jazz purists, but embraced by a new audience. "At that point in time, Miles came head to head with the electronic explosion," says Marty. "He had, of course, made major, major works before that but, still being a fairly young guy, was still creating. They were finding a big corner to explore which had never been done before."

There were big changes happening in jazz and Marty made sure his band was in the thick of it. "I was always downtown a lot because that's where most of the music was happening," he says. "I'd be with Mari uptown at my place, and I'd get up and do these Reverend B shows wherever I could. *Downbeat* magazine had this listing in the back that had all the events and people who were playing that month. I'd call them up and say 'I'm doing a show here with Reverend B' and they would print it, like a listing. It was my first time of getting anything in print. I'd get the magazine and come back and show Mari; 'Hey look!' I would go back and forth, uptown and downtown."

One day, Marty was jamming at Studio We with Steve Tintweiss and James DuBoise, when he noticed a poster lying on the floor, which advertised an event coming up at the Project of Living Artists, now calling itself Museum. "I remember I was playing there one afternoon, looked down and saw this poster lying on the floor. I thought it sounded like an interesting kind of place and made a note to check it out."

Suicide might never have happened without that two in the morning phone call from Howie Wolper in early September 1969. "You got to turn on the Nightbird now! You gotta hear this!" he barked when Alan, who was luckily still up, answered at home in Brooklyn. Alan punched on the radio, already tuned to WNEW, New York's first FM station, where the pioneering Alison Steele, the Nightbird, played underground psychedelic delights every night. Around then, Hendrix, recording in New York City, immortalised her in 'Night Bird Flying'. Tonight she was playing the just-released debut album by a band called the Stooges.

Alan heard the bludgeoning drums and squalls of overloading guitar, then the voice; snotty, accusatory and nihilistic, ranting about the war and blank social ennui. Next came a song in which the singer slavered about wanting to "be your dog", over more fuzzed-up, dumbed down pounding. Instantly deciding "I love that lyric best in the whole of rock'n'roll!" Alan had an overwhelming feeling that nothing could be the same again, especially his art. Endlessly muttering "What the fuck?" he was elated to discover the Stooges were playing the next night at the New York State Pavilion in Flushing Meadows, Queens. They'd be supporting the MC5, Detroit's high-energy insurrectionists, who Alan had loved since hearing their *Kick Out The Jams* debut album that February, and now describes as "one of my favourite bands of all time". The MC5's album had been a high-energy call to arms, shot with free jazz anarchy, but the Stooges were something else; innocently brutal, gloriously raw but couched in a rare instinctual sensitivity. And they were produced by John Cale, who'd recently knocked Alan's socks off gouging hell out of his electric organ on the Velvet Underground's 'Sister Ray'.

On the evening of Friday, September 6, Alan and Howie travelled to the Pavilion, the last structure in use from the 1964 World's Fair, which was putting on summertime concerts for a couple of 1,000 lucky punters, while many more jostled outside against heavy-handed police. It was the Stooges' first major appearance in New York, although they had been to the city the previous April to record their album at Hit Factory studios.

Opening the night was street singer David Peel, who had released his *Have A Marijuana* album the previous year on Elektra, home to the MC5 and Stooges. After "the marijuana guy", as Alan describes him, had finished his stoner rabble-rousing, beshaded guitarist Ron Asheton, bassist

Dave Alexander and behemoth drummer Scott 'Rock Action' Asheton, took the stage looking like the slovenly gang of Michigan ne'er-do wells they were.

Alan becomes visibly re-electrified as he starts recounting the night which changed his life. "Then, all of a sudden, I saw this figure, standing behind an amp ready to come out. I thought it was a girl, because he had these bangs, like a Brian Jones cut. I didn't know what Iggy was about. I just knew there was a singer, this wah wah guitar that Ron was playing, and this whole crazy beat. Then he was walking out; no shirt, pants like dungarees cut off over the knee, and these stupid looking penny loafers, whatever they were. Of course, he's built magnificently, all wiry; the pre-drug years, man. Then they launch into, 'It's 1969, okay', and he's doing his thing, and they're all doing their thing."

At this point, the band had only been playing live since the late 1967 house party gig where, calling themselves the Psychedelic Stooges, Iggy had wielded a mic'ed-up food mixer and Scott beat Bo Diddley rhythms on oil drums. They mainly played their home gigs at Detroit's Grande Ballroom, usually with "big brother" band the MC5. Like Suicide the following decade, their first songs were sculpted out of free-form noise onslaughts, which Iggy lacerated with a Hawaiian lap steel guitar, its six strings tuned to the same note, a quirk which hadn't been lost on the drone-grounded Cale.

"The next thing I know," recalls Alan. "Iggy's diving onto this concrete floor where people are sitting down, then coming back on stage. The drumsticks are already broken and flying all over the place. Iggy picks up this broken drumstick and starts cutting the shit out of himself, while the bass player starts fucking Ronnie up the ass with his guitar. Twenty minutes goes by and the show ends. That was it. Usually at these shows they would play rock'n'roll songs in between, but not this one. Iggy walks off, there's silence, and you're expecting this shit to come on, but instead the guy puts on Bach's Brandenburg Concertos. That added to it. I was with some friends, and our mouths dropped. What I saw that night was beyond anything I'd seen or heard before. It was like the new art form. It was beyond music, because they involved the audience. The separation between artist and audience was broken down. I was in awe. I couldn't believe what had just happened in 20 minutes. I knew I was in the presence of something great happening. The MC5 came on and they tried hard, but it was just too late."

Alan Bermowitz, aged 21 months, strikes a pose with mom Tillie outside their Lower East Side apartment in March 194

The young Mari Montgomery: future Mari Reverby & Suicide drummer.

PUNK MUSIC by

SUICIDE

and
ZOOT SIMS
15 Pc. Band of the Century 7PM

Sunday, May 9

10PM
PUNK MUSIC
by

Lloyd
at Price's
CRAWDADDY
53rd & B'Way

Flyers for earliest shows, including the night Suicide collided with jazz royalty.

Suicide at the Mercer Arts Center.

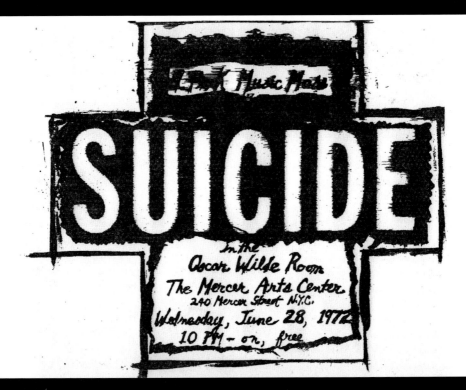

Flyer for Mercer Arts Center, 1972.

NEW YORK FREE MUSIC COMMITTEE

Presents A Concert Event
CHERRY SNATCHERS SUITE

Steven Inkwhite Tintweiss

photo: Victor Pilosof

with

James DuBoise

And N.Y.F.M.C.
MEMBER MUSICIANS

photo: Frank Gimpaya

photo: Susan Robertson

and

Suicide·punk music
Sept. 25   7·9 p.m.

Damrosch Park's
Guggenheim Bandshell   Free
at Lincoln Center · Rain Date·Oct. 3

Produced with the cooperation of the City of New York
Parks, Recreation & Cultural Affairs Adminstration,
with financial assistance to be provided by a grant
from the New York State Council on the Arts

info: 533-2052, Studio We or 472-1003, P.R.C.A.

a free-space music conception

Graphics/Draggan

and Vega in the early 70s.

rty, Debbie Harry, Alan; Times Square, 1975.

The incomparable Lydia Lunch.
JASMINE HIRST

Rather than treat the Stooges as just a great rock show, Alan saw Iggy's kamikaze lightning rod for the audience's confused hostility as performance art destroying the boundaries between artist and crowd. Now all became clear, and he knew what he had to do. "That really got me going. That's when my life changed. Before that I was in visual arts. I was lucky enough to have Ivan Karp as a dealer, I was pretty much up in the world. I was pretty young too. But after that night, I thought, if I was gonna be a real artist and be honest about it, I had to go where Iggy was. I never in my life thought I'd ever get up on a stage. I was totally shy, so it was the scariest place. At the bottom of my list of the 100 things I was gonna be in life was on a stage. But I just knew I had to go that way to be a real and truthful artist, man. I had no idea how I was going to make this happen. I can't perform, much less sing. Be a performer? With musicians? What am I, crazy? I must have been out of my mind."

While Alan tried to deal with his epiphany, the *New York Times*' Mike Jahn attempted to describe the show. After declaring the Stooges belonged more Off-Broadway than in rock'n'roll, Jahn describes Iggy "seeking to represent the malaise of the long-haired, teen-age radical" with nihilistic lyrics, his "simple but tortured gymnastics built around a Midas-like ability to turn everything he touches into a phallic object", and an audience which "reacted predictably. Some seemed fascinated, if only for the same reasons that drive mobs to yell 'jump!' at a potential suicide standing on a ledge. Others reacted with contempt, throwing containers of orange drink at the wriggling performer."

Perhaps the most monumental work ever written about the unique force that was Iggy and the Stooges in their incendiary first flush was Lester Bangs' epic November 1970 *Creem* review of second album *Fun House*, with observations such as, "Iggy is like a matador baiting the vast, dark hydra sitting in front of him. He enters the audience frequently to see what's what and even from the stage his eyes reach out searingly, sweeping the joint and singling out startled strangers who're seldom able to stare him down... In this sense, Iggy is a true star of the most incredible kind – he has won the stage, and nothing but the force of his own presence entitles him to it." Bangs blamed "lazy passive crowds" for rock's current malaise, continuing, "That's why most rock bands are so soporifically lazy these days, and also why the Stooges, and any other band that challenges its audience, is the answer. Power doesn't go to the people, it comes *from* them, and when the people have gotten this passive, nothing short of electro-shock and personal exorcism will jolt them and rock them into some kind of fiercely healthy interaction."

Bangs could have been describing Alan Vega a few years hence (and shows why he would later welcome Suicide with such evangelical enthusiasm).

While still relatively unknown, the Stooges were an unmitigated highlight of a year which saw the demolition of the Californian hippie dream by the nightmares of the Altamont festival and the horrific Manson murders. Released in the same week as the Woodstock festival (which had briefly promised the hippies' utopia), *The Stooges* album stood out like a simple teenage rebel manifesto and, for me personally, nothing sounded so right and spot on at the tender of age of 16. The band boiled rock'n'roll down to its original essence, Iggy's lyrics about basic teenage desires and instincts scribbled as he observed the behaviour of school kids in a local burger bar. Ron built his monolithic riffs on anything from the Yusef Lateef blues which inspired 'I Wanna Be Your Dog' to bass snippets from Pharoah Sanders.

Elektra A&R man Danny Fields had signed both the MC5 and Stooges to the label. His choice of Cale for producer was inspired. Impressed by the Stooges' live chaos, Cale took to the project with diligence, but also relished the avant garde sensibilities which gave the band their edge. Having rehearsed structured songs for the first time, the Stooges hit New York, finding themselves groped in the back room of an adoring Max's and mixing with Cale's hip chums, including Nico, who embarked on a relationship with Iggy that proved artistically inspiring for both of them. Within a week the Stooges had an album which would help shape musical history. Sadly, by the time Suicide released their own seismic debut, the Stooges would be long gone, imploded in a morass of excess.

Alan's own musical experiments at the Project eschewed traditional methods from the start, presaging his solo albums of the next century as he messed around with two-inch tapes, abused circuits from his electronic art and ripped into records as they played on his turntable; anything to scrape out a noise. "I was really crazy. I used to listen to classical music, like Bartok and Stravinsky, and scratch these records to make them even crazier! I used to do all kinds of things. The very first scratch artist that ever lived was Bartok. I'm not kidding! After Iggy, I came around to German electronic music of the late sixties. That's my schtick right there. I came out of visual arts, but I had a great love of this music."

By 1969, Germany was throwing out its own exotic musical sonic concoctions, led by *Monster Movie*, the mysterious first album by Can, who cut another idiosyncratic swathe through the post-psych fallout and had a major effect on Alan. Can was formed in Cologne in 1968 by two former Stockhausen students – classically trained pianist Irmin Schmidt and studio scientist/bassist Holger Czukay. The idea for the group was born when Schmidt visited New York City in 1966 and hung out with La Monte Young, Terry Riley and Fluxus mainstays Nam June Paik and Dick Higgins. On a later trip, he was smitten by the Velvet Underground, and confessed to being impressed by the Stooges, Hendrix and James Brown. It was enough to motivate him into trying to merge the worlds of avant garde minimalism and new American rock and proto-funk, his visions inevitably coloured by his experience in classical music. Schmidt and Czukay were joined by master drummer Jaki Liebezeit, whose uniquely cyclical style was influenced by Art Blakey and North African music, 19-year-old rock guitarist Michael Karoli, and unpredictable New York sculptor Malcolm Mooney, who had fled the Vietnam War to India. On his way back, Mooney met Schmidt's wife, Hildegard, who planned to introduce him to Cologne's art scene until he pitched into one of the new band's rehearsals. Rather than write songs, this disparate quintet spontaneously thrashed out jams for hours, which Czukay captured on his two-track tape recorder then painstakingly edited into tracks drawn from stretches when their supernatural alchemy was at full beam.

After several weeks of sonic exploration and recording, Can finally emerged from Schloss Norvenich, the 14th century castle where they recorded, with *Monster Movie*, another of 1969's great debuts. After hot-wired trance-rock hypno-monsters 'Father Cannot Yell' and 'Outside My Door', side two was devoted to the fearsomely hypnotic pressure cooker vamp of 'You Doo Right', which had been edited down from over 12 solid hours of playing. Can's demanding recording methods demolished Mooney, whose psychiatrist recommended escaping the centrifugal pull of the music. His final gig saw him intoning "upstairs, downstairs" for over an hour, before experiencing a complete breakdown. Mooney was replaced by Japanese traveller Kenji 'Damo' Suzuki, whom the band encountered busking in a Munich street and asked if he would sing at that night's gig. Damo's alien improvisations proved perfect, as Can went on to release more shape-shifting albums, including 1971's *Tago Mago*, 1972's *Ege Bamyasi* and 1973's *Future Days*. I was lucky enough to witness

Can in concert around this time at my local Friars club. For three hours they jammed around album tracks which were only recognisable for a few minutes, before the band's supernatural telepathy took over to steer their creative locomotive to jaw-dropping stratospheric peaks. At the time, I likened it to how it must feel riding in a flying saucer.

Galvanised by Iggy to perform, motivated by Can to reach into the unknown, already inspired by the infinite expressive possibilities of free jazz and electronic detritus of Silver Apples, Alan didn't need any more persuading. It was time to be making his own statements through the mediums of music and performing. Working feverishly in the Project, his startling sculptures crackling into deafening life as he continued torturing circuits, attacked an electric guitar, set off wind-up monkey drummers and manipulated tape. He had been joined by a sculptor called Paul Liebgott who, having picked up a guitar for the first time, piled in with similar untutored abandon. It was a start. Now Alan just needed that vital, like-minded catalyst to join him on the next vital stage and take it all the way.

The turning point of this story started the night Reverend B played its first show at the Project, which came about through a friend of Mari's called Yvonne, whom Marty had bumped into on 8th Street. She told him a friend of hers was holding a political slide-show there and she'd ask the organisers about Rev supplying music. "She called me a couple of days later, and said, 'Now you're with Mari and there are kids you need to do some gigs.' She was really looking out for me, she wanted me to, y'know, start working! It was a beautiful thing. I remember her very fondly for that. She's no longer here but she's from that background similar to Mari's, very progressive. So she spoke to this revolutionary Middle Eastern guy, who turned out to be the son of a Saudi Arabian prince, but no one knew that for a while. He'd show all these revolutionary films, and they'd have discussions. So I went down there and did it, got a couple of bucks, whatever you made in those days. That's when I got accustomed to the place. So it was actually a friend of Mari's who opened up that direction for me. That was great, I'll never forget that night. And through that I would meet Alan."

Reverend B returned to play the Project in early 1970, "at a party for a glamour oriented dude". This time, Alan saw them, although when the group started their set that night, he was uptown doing a light show for an electronic event at Columbia University. Returning to the Project, he found the band in full swing. "What a night! I'll never forget it," he recalls with awe. "I walked in and I saw people entranced, smoking, lying on the floor, sitting up or just dancing. There were two drummers, three saxes, trumpets, clarinetists and Marty was playing this amazing keyboard. I had a tambourine with me, so I said 'Fuck it, he's got people playing in this damn thing so why don't I just stand there banging a tambourine?' They had this incredible sound, man, something like I'd never heard before. They played on and on and on for hours and hours and hours. I got there halfway through and they still played on for another two hours. Everyone was high, crazy, drugged."

After he had finally wound down the monstrous racket, Marty was still bathed in post-gig reverie when he walked up to Alan and told him, "You and I will make music together."

EIGHT

"We had no formula with Suicide. We were kind of starting with a big block of stone, like a sculptor does. We didn't start with a beat or instrumentation, but we were going to find it through chiselling out this total mass of sound. It took a few years. Our sound had its own kind of journey." – **Martin Rev**

"You know like the big bang? There's all this gas which coalesced with the galaxies and the stars. That's kind of what happened with Suicide; this chaos like the universe came out of gas. There was a big bang and Marty and I just merged into this one thing." – **Alan Vega**

Nobody, least of all Alan Vega or Martin Rev, can give the exact day, week or even month that Suicide coalesced into life after its gradual, organic gestation. The first gigs under that name definitely took place in November 1970 at the Project of Living Artists, and were billed as 'PUNK MUSIC BY SUICIDE' on the stark, hand-drawn flyers which littered downtown bars, art galleries and music lofts. In just those four words, Vega and Rev announced themselves to the world, sealed their fates and unwittingly foretold the coming decade, but thought little of it against the much bigger picture that unfolded as their mutual creative electrodes sparked into life, along with the relationship which still endures over 45 years later.

"It didn't happen straight away," remembers Alan, whose janitor's position at the Project gave him the keys to a place to work, hang out and sometimes sleep after the evening's meetings and art sessions had finished. "Marty was very quiet. I only got to know him after a while. He'd walk in while I was playing around with stuff and then he'd walk out. He had a big Afro and wore this blue sweater, all torn and stuff. He looked bohemian, like he might come out writing poetry or something. He wouldn't talk for a while. It was all in body language. He'd disappear, then he'd come back again. This went on... "

Marty recalls revisiting the Project after the Reverend B gig and walking in on Alan, who was crouched on the floor extracting a chafing soundtrack from the mess of speakers and cables spread before him, with Paul Liebgott pitching in on guitar. "One day, I was passing by and I thought 'Let me check out the Museum again', so I took the elevator up and it was open. When I walked in Alan had his amp, trying to hear feedback, and the guitarist was there. Right away I heard what they were doing. I searched for something and found these industrial springs, because it was still like a large industrial kind of a space which had been renovated, and there was stuff lying around. I sat on the floor and started doing a percussive thing. After that we started talking."

Marty knew he had found a kindred spirit in this restless co-conspirator. "Sometimes there'd be 100 people there, sitting around all day getting high, but just having the Project, and the practicality of that space to work in, brought me closer to Alan. That space was essential for me as a place to duck into when I was on the streets, especially during the winter. Now I knew it was there, I would just go up there. We were always the last ones to leave and would walk around downtown Manhattan until four or five in the morning, just talking. We just kind of hit it off. We were as they say, two ships that pass in the night. Perhaps each very close to shipwreck as well. It just made sense to try and do a group. We were both already very developed in our own ways and so intense about what we were doing."

Feeling he had learned all he could from his multi-faceted jazz education, Marty felt ready to take his biggest step yet and wound down Reverend B. His improvisational background synched perfectly with Alan's street art ethos, and they shared a mutual desire to create the loudest, most confrontational statement they could at a time when commercial motives and complacency seemed to be replacing the anger, protest and invention of the sixties. The pair never had any game plan to start the kind of movements Suicide were later credited with inspiring or instigating, and the possibility of mainstream success was a far off, even perverted fantasy in those earliest brainstorming sessions. They were more concerned with the daily realities of survival, along with anger at the atrocities being carried out by the government in America and Vietnam.

"We were just fortunate in the same way that Jagger met Richards," says Alan. "It's basically always a two guy thing that creates a rock band, and Marty just happened to wander into the Museum one day and start banging on the floor."

Mari's son Greg had been lent a set of drums from Yvonne's son of the same name and age, which were in the apartment. Marty threw the snare, ride cymbal, hi-hat and tom tom into a duffel-bag and brought them down to the Project to use in the jams with Alan and Paul. "Before then I was playing sticks on the floor," he recalls. One day Marty dared Alan to try and get a sound out of a trumpet he'd found, with the irresistible words "I bet if you blow through it you aren't going to get a sound at all". Apart from some strained flatulence, that's what happened the first time but, inspired by Miles, Alan eventually took to the instrument with gusto, later enthusing, "Learning how to play that was the best thing. People ask me how I learned to sing... I tell them by blowing a brass instrument. It's the same mechanism." His moment of triumph was hitting "that high note which Miles got and nobody ever achieved... I almost passed out!"

"Alan liked to play the trumpet, and did so with a great energy," confirms Marty. "At that time I think he was listening to Don Ayler, those kind of trumpet players. There were no keyboards at first." Marty found playing drums a liberating experience. "As soon as I sat down and did it I heard so much. Alan used to say 'wow, he's the greatest drummer I ever heard', but I had never played them before."

Alan recalls "At the time he was probably the fastest drummer alive! We'd just play for hours and tape all this shit. After a session of three hours or so we'd listen back to what we'd done and go, 'Are we crazy?' But we were loving it, man. We just jammed, something that nobody does any more. Then it went from there with the singing. We didn't so much write songs, we just kept improvising, let it go where it goes. It all came out like a free jazz thing. I played a little crazy guitar in those days too, some real abstract shit. Marty followed that, then Paul would come in and we would keep going and going."

One night, the noise coming out of the Project's high windows attracted a crowd on the street below. "We played so loud, practically deafening," recalls Alan. "I remember one warm spring night we were just playing away, when all of a sudden we heard people out on the street going, 'More, more!' I look out the window and there's fucking hundreds of kids outside just listening to us blowing this stream of consciousness music. We couldn't believe it. Probably stoned-out people from Washington Square Park."

By November, the trio was ready to play in front of a Museum audience. First they would need a name.

"We went through about 100,000 names and each one was funnier than the next," recalls Marty. "It was like 'Oh man...'." Most writings about Suicide credit Alan's love of *Ghost Rider* comic books (of which 'Satan's Suicide' was one episode), but the first issue didn't appear until 1972. *Ghost Rider* would, nonetheless, provide Alan's most famous lyric. The name Suicide was actually inspired by the artists and jazz musicians sitting around the Project, shooting up smack and nodding out, dead-eyed and pointless. Someone just said 'Suicide' and it seemed perfect for the times and how Alan and Marty felt. They assumed, according to Alan, that "everybody else would be thinking the same thing" and get it immediately, but "I didn't see the name in a bad light. To me, Suicide was a rebirth, a life thing. Very often, you have to commit suicide in your own life to get to a better place than you were originally. I was feeling suicidal a lot because of the Vietnam War and how New York was collapsing. Apart from the Dead Kennedys, it was probably the worst name we could have chosen. It was cursed. In retrospect, we should have called ourselves Life!" When Alan studded the back of his black leather jacket 'SUICIDE' and strutted down the street, he attracted vehement abuse, and knew he had done the right thing.

The night before the first Project gig in November 1970, the trio awarded themselves punk-presaging aliases: Alan was Nasty Cut, Rev was Marty Maniac, while Paul foreshadowed hip-hop with Cool P. The poverty-stricken band wore torn clothes found in the garbage, and thrift stores, which they customised into their own junkie-pimp street fashions, unwittingly inventing the punk look out of necessity, five years before CBGB, let alone the King's Road. Alan recalls cutting the sleeves off a pink jacket and the toes off a pair of socks, which he rolled up past his elbows. Meanwhile, Marty remembered his doo-wop fixation and the New York street gangs which had caught his adolescent imagination, while also favouring a "leather hat with a brim like the rock guys used to wear". There's one grainy black and white photo of that first show, which shows Marty sitting up front behind the drums in his hat, Alan savaging his guitar with the microphone stand, and Paul standing behind the amps with his guitar. Marty remembers Alan speculating that Miles Davis had been in the audience. Despite many reports to the contrary, the crowd was fairly serene. "All that was yet to come," Marty confirms.

Suicide's first gig set a precedent for the next few months by going out under the banner 'Punk Music'. The 'Punk' came from Lester Bangs' *Creem* review of the Stooges' just-released *Fun House* album. Bangs wrenched the word from its long-standing derogatory street putdown status to describe Iggy. Suicide lifted the word from the review and stuck it on flyers for their first gigs, although they had dropped it within a few years – leaving it to be used, abused and irrevocably diluted as the seventies rolled on. But in 1970, 'Punk' meant only one thing: Suicide.

Suicide had bigger things on their mind than trying to upset parents with a new trend. The Vietnam War continued to suck up young American lives and spit back more body bags, as well as horribly disabled returning veterans. The war stoked Suicide's anger into an incandescent energy which Alan was determined to ram into the faces of downtown New York.

"I said, 'Fuck this shit, what about the Vietnam War? Did you forget about it already?' It's true. The Vietnam War was the apex of the whole thing, as far as I was concerned. The Vietnam War was the worst thing that ever happened. We had the worst President in Nixon. Marty was incensed by the whole thing, too."

Marty agrees "Vietnam was a very significant ingredient that gave everything such an extra added intensity. It was driving all those events at the Museum and the artists, especially the ones who were young and just starting out. They were really on the edge, getting more and more intense as Vietnam was eating everything up as the backdrop of it all. We didn't see ourselves as a specifically anti-war band, although we were as individuals. It was very obvious from what we did that we were not happy. As a musician, I'd long been involved in that kind of intensity, all the way back from when I was a kid."

Alan hit on the idea of asking Ivan Karp for a gig at OK Harris. Now that Ivan knew Alan and his work, Suicide could give it a soundtrack. "So we walk in and I've got my drumsticks in my belt and a jacket painted with 'SUICIDE' on the back," recalls Marty. "Alan looked pretty hungry in those days too, and says, 'Ivan, we'd like to play here.' He took one look at us, then turned around to his administrator standing behind him and said, 'Print up cards – Suicide playing on such and such a date, and send them out to everybody.' That was it. They sent out this postcard kind of thing to their mailing list, and the place was almost packed."

The invitation promised "Punk Music by Suicide" at the gallery event on November 20. Marty remembers it as "a very, very intense night, it was total hallucination on everybody's part." Alan recalls it as "a very weird night" in front of an invited crowd who *hated* Suicide. He thinks he might have done acid, while Marty was "cranked on something". After the gig, Alan threw his trumpet into a bin, to his later regret. Although Suicide had not been particularly embraced at their first gig in the outside world, they won a return booking at OK Harris the following April.

Suicide played the Project again five days later on November 25. When Alan and Marty were walking the streets afterwards, cooling off and discussing the show, some friends told them that Albert Ayler's body had been found in the East River. He was only 34. "We were both crushed," remembers Alan. It later emerged that Ayler was depressed following his brother's recent nervous breakdown, being dropped by his record label and stressful financial pressures. Ayler's death wasn't mentioned in the *New York Times* but has been surrounded by inevitable rumours and conspiracy theories over the years: that he'd been shot in the head, some say by the police, or was found with a jukebox chained around his neck, which suggested the Mob had fronted money for his career which he never repaid. What is clear is that Ayler disappeared for several days before his partner, Mary Maria, called the police and the body was found by Congress Pier. Later it emerged he had taken the ferry to Liberty Island and jumped into the river. The death was puzzling after the return to ceiling-cracking form Ayler had displayed at the Maeght Foundation, St Paul de Vence, in July, part of the French tour on which Marty's old friend Steve Tintweiss played bass (captured on an astonishing live album which now sounds like Ayler's soulful eulogy to himself).

When I asked Albert's close friend Annette Peacock about her fallen friend (and her former husband's band leader) she beautifully summed up his magic, and how his fearless music had never been accepted in the times it so graphically mirrored. Some of her response could even apply to Suicide and any artist greeted by ingrained resistance. "Albert was a man of magnificent spirit, vision, determination and few words... But it transpired that he was a warrior engaged in a war he couldn't win.

His adversary was time. During the period when Albert was destined to make his breakthrough, the culture was not prepared to accommodate his overwhelmingly powerful, prescient statement, and therein lies the tragedy. People tend to resist change, industry finds it threatening, but some people can't help being who they are, and that's the gift they give, if we're able to receive it. If met by resistance or rejection, perhaps over the passing of time, history will be kind and offer belated acceptance and a culture may celebrate contributions made. Albert was tormented by disappointment. I suspect he suffered from the betrayal, when he realised that the recognition and success due to him was destined to come posthumously. He looked at me with resignation in his eyes when last we met, as I heard him say these final words: 'I'm not even here.'"

The newly minted Suicide greeted 1971 by looking to play as many shows as they could at any club which would have them, be they rock or jazz venues. Without a manager or agent they represented themselves, as they would for the next few years. "In those days, getting a show was hit or miss," understates Marty, explaining how they would scour the paper for venues putting on bands, then divide the task of trying to interest the booking agents or owners in putting on an act they'd never heard of, which called itself Suicide. Alan took art galleries and lofts, while Marty canvassed clubs wielding the steel pole he liked to carry at the time. "I'd just go down, dressed the way I'd dress in the street for Suicide, with a jacket with the name on the back, hat and shades. Nobody knew you and you didn't know them. I'd say something like 'We're a band called Suicide, can we do a show here?' There were no consistent shows and when there were there was no money involved. Somehow we'd just get in here and there, enough to keep ourselves going." If they got lucky, they made flyers and stuck them around town, running to a $25, one inch ad in the *Village Voice* if they were flush enough.

The first club to bite was the 200-capacity Ungano's on West 70th Street, "one of the major clubs of the sixties" and scene of the previous February's celebrated four-day return to New York of the Stooges. Suicide hit it off with Italian brothers Arnie and Joey Ungano and were given three nights starting on January 7, opening for a long-forgotten outfit called the Sun and the Moon. "Wow, we could get discovered tonight," Marty thought to himself. The first night was empty, apart from a bachelor party, which Alan delighted in taunting. After the first set,

Arnie took Marty aside and said "it was like having 99 Iggys in there". But they returned the following night, this time playing to a full house. Suicide even won a return booking at the end of the month although, by then, the club had closed down.

Thanks to his relationship with Max Gordon at the Vanguard, Marty was able to win Suicide a Sunday afternoon slot. It was packed, and "we blew everybody out," he reports, while Max gave his former teenage regular the thumbs up, although he said, "It was a bit loud."

After two events at the Project billed 'Punk Mass At Midnight', March saw Suicide appearing at the Village Gate, opening for psychedelic folk-rockers Milkwood Tapestry. The billing was somewhat incongruous as the headliners, who had recently released their self-titled debut album, liked to display their love of the Incredible String Band and Jethro Tull on titles such as 'Pink Painted Butterfly', 'Wondrous Fairy Tales' and 'Sunshine Castles'. While Marty relished appearing on the same stage as his jazz heroes at the scene of the telepathic bolt incident with Miles, Suicide's set amped up the violence. "They were aggressive gigs because of Alan's embracing of the total theatre concept of Iggy, which he felt he was getting from the music," says Marty. "We were instinctively very theatre and stage minded. It just came out of us. My image kind of contrasted with Alan's, because I was really being very close to myself and my childhood, but we were finding ourselves."

Around this time, Marty reduced his drumkit to snare and cymbal, having introduced electronic keyboards to the sound in the form of a Wurlitzer electric piano he had bought a while back on the never-never. "I had that with me at my place and eventually brought it down. I set it up with a snare drum in front of me, and the keyboard on the side with a cymbal over it, and played them both together. Then we found a used bass amp, and I plugged into that. I did quite a few gigs that way, with drums and keyboards. I hit the drums so hard that, at the Gate, the large ride cymbal went flying off its stand and went right down into the audience. It was a very high stage too; I'm lucky I didn't kill somebody! Luckily, there weren't that many people, but there was always stuff like that. We were considered aggressive."

Marty hot-wired his keyboard with Electro-Harmonix guitar effects pedals, introduced in 1968 by the New York company started by R&B keyboards player Mike Matthews in the wake of Hendrix. "I was really hot-rodding the keyboard with all kinds of devices, which Alan was aware of too and would tell me about," Marty says. "I was hooking these things up, making this simple electric piano into what it started sounding like, which was more and more close to the sound on the first Suicide album, although there wasn't an organ yet. It was all fuzz and distortion; the way I'm still playing now actually!"

Mari had been joining in at early rehearsals after Marty declared, "I'd like you to come and play drums," although she didn't play at any gigs. "Mari was pivotal to Suicide; she was there when it all started. There was a lot of intensity at that time between my music, Suicide, having very little money and my family, plus the intensity of two artists living together. I was trying to develop every day. I thought it may be good for us when I said come down and play drums, because we had no drummer and thought eventually we should get one. But we already had three people and had to keep the group together. The more successful groups had rehearsal rooms and budgets. We had the place to play, but that was about it. Mari had so much background and knowledge about music that she played great. She was playing the drums and it was fine, but we didn't continue it for long for various reasons. We had a house full of young children too. I knew after she left the band there was no way I was gonna replace the woman in my life with another drummer!"

Suicide's first taste of audience rioting happened when a contingent from a Brazilian revolutionary group turned up. "They were young guys, who really wanted to see us," recalls Marty. "They were all very savvy and excited. During the show, one guy pulled out a trombone and started playing along with us. Then Alan walked over and pulled out the valve in his trombone. They just went crazy. They saw it as such a provocation. They started picking up these folding wooden chairs and throwing them. Everything was flying, it was just chaos. Alan and Paul went down to a bunker in the basement I didn't even know existed. I stayed on the stage, and at some point just stooped under the keyboard for protection, using it like a bomb shelter. It didn't get bloody, thankfully."

After two gigs at a long-forgotten lower Broadway niterie called Supernova in April, Suicide played one of their most infamous early shows at the Gaslight Au Go Go on Bleecker Street. "We started, as usual, with this incredibly intense sound," recalls Marty. "It was so fresh. No one was prepared for that kind of intensity. Thirty seconds in and everything goes off. It turned out the woman who ran the place just threw the power switch, like the sort they have at train stations. The entire place just went black. I was always walking round with my steel pole at that time, that's how far my mind was out then. Between that, and everything that was around and everything you could take, it was a pretty intense time. I was like somebody wandering in the desert with a big stick. I walked back and gave her some kind of prophetic warning announcement about what it meant for her to have done something like that. She just stared at me."

Suicide's name and reputation as a downtown live onslaught like no other started spreading. Alan even found himself invited up to Allen Ginsberg's apartment on East 10th Street for an audience, yet then violently attacked by the venerable Beat. "That was a terrible thing. I got an invitation to meet Allen Ginsberg, and thought I was going up in the world. So I went up to his apartment, and it was all full of books and shit. I'm like 'Wow, I can't believe this, I'm gonna be friends with Allen Ginsberg!' This is the earliest days of Suicide when nobody liked us. So I sat down with him, and he's talking some bullshit, and all of a sudden he goes 'How could you use that word *suicide?*' and starts to attack me!"

Alan makes hysterical wailing sounds and mimes being slapped effetely. "As long as I live, he was crazy, insane. I was like 'Holy shit, I'm being attacked by Mr Beatnik here!' It lasted about 15 minutes, then I just walked out with my tail between my legs. He invited me up there to get the shit kicked out of me! I was like 'Are you crazy?' *Howl* was one of the ones. Maybe it was because Suicide was the real howl. Kerouac was always my man, anyway. *On The Road* changed my life. Suicide then was so literal, and the reality was death. We even managed to piss off Ginsberg."

Alan also remembers fending off overtures from Andy Warhol to join his Factory crew. Alan says: "I never considered myself part of that. People went in there and never came out. It seemed like Warhol gobbled them up." He felt more at home going to the race track with his close friend Howie Wolper, who had accompanied him to his Iggy epiphany and was with Suicide in the earliest days. The pair were frequent visitors to New York's racetracks – Belmont Park, Aqueduct and Saratoga – which Alan says almost became another career option in the cash-strapped early seventies.

New York actually got its 'Big Apple' nickname from the tracks, after the early twenties, when "apple" referred to the big prizes being awarded. After the *New York Morning Telegraph*'s John Fitzgerald started using the term "Around the Big Apple", which he got from jockeys and trainers, the term rubbed off on jive-seeking jazz musicians, who dubbed New York 'The Big Apple' as it was the most lucrative city to play in. The term later got hijacked in a 1971 tourism campaign, which used big red apples as a cheery retort to New York's common image as a dark, dangerous place, and it stuck.

"Me and Howie 'The Horse' used to hang out," recalls Alan. "He went to Brooklyn High School. He and I were a couple of lazy bums. We used to go to the racetrack together all the time. One day I had a triple, and we won thousands of dollars. I don't know how I won so much, I couldn't keep track of it. I was drinking, smoking pot 'cause they had pot coming out of their assholes at the racetrack. I put some of the money in the bank and thought about whether there was a future in it. I could have ended up doing that."

Marty remembers the pair "hanging out together quite a bit when I met Alan. Howie became a friend of both of ours. When we started the group he was like a silent party in a sense; kind of like an adviser, or consultant from the outside. He was very astute regarding scenes, trends, what was happening at the time, and would comment on what we were doing. He was a good friend to all of us. Alan and Howie would go to the track all the time, but it was not something I was into. I went with them once, along with Cool P, but I didn't want to start getting into that because our funds were very short. I had real responsibilities in that regard, so didn't want to start playing around with the little bit of money that I had. Plus, I really just enjoyed watching the horses. Always have dug them the most. I'm a Sagittarius."

When the warmer weather arrived, Suicide played one of Steve Tintweiss' Bandshell shows at Forest Park to their biggest crowd yet. "It was incredible," sighs Marty. "It was like playing Woodstock, with that sound going out again." Thanks to Tintweiss, they also played an afternoon slot in the band-shell in the park outside Lincoln Center. "It was the same band-shell that Sonny Rollins used to play on every year!" recalls Marty. "There were about eight people in the audience just sitting around on these benches but it was cool."

Cool P couldn't hack the escalating carnage at the shows, and retreated to his career as a sculptor. With Mari and now Paul out of the picture, "it begged the question, 'Are we getting a drummer?'" recalls Marty. "But I said to Alan, 'No, let's keep it at two.' Those days were just crazy. My shit was crazy. I was crazier. Now it was just like free electronics. It was such a new, raw sound. Electronics was such a great new world. You could just do a whole free-form thing, try to work in free jazz, rock or anything that happened really. We didn't have songs, just one long, electronic thing. It was all coming out of the amp, which I would stick on top of the keyboard and play the dials, with this gigantic cabinet speaker behind us. In the early days, I was just getting the rhythm from all this feedback. So why get drums when they were coming out of the amp top. That *was* our drums."

During his often thankless travels around New York's clubs trying to secure shows, Marty tried his luck at a place called Crawdaddy's on Broadway and 53rd Street. It turned out to be the former Birdland, which he knew so well from those shows in his teenage years. After closing in 1965, the club had passed through different owners and was currently being run by R&B legend Lloyd Price. Price, who had written Little Richard's hit 'Lawdy Miss Clawdy', was best known for the recording of his song 'Stagger Lee', his biggest hit. "Obviously I liked the idea because it was Birdland, which I'd been to quite a few years before as a kid. I just asked for whoever I could speak to about bookings." Marty was greeted by Lloyd, along with associate Mike Quashie, who was New York's former king of the limbo and once Hendrix's best friend. This "really nice West Indian guy" also became an early friend of Suicide's.

The 500-seater club had tried rock'n'roll in 1969, when future New York Dolls Sylvain Mizrahi and Billy Murcia's first group the Pox had played their mod-inspired sounds to a mixed response. Lloyd hadn't heard of Suicide but agreed to let them play two nights, starting with Tuesday May 4 then the following Sunday when, surreally, the bill was completed by the veteran Zoot Sims and his Big Band. "That was an amazing combination," whistles Marty. "How often did Zoot Sims play with a big band in New York at that time? He'd been living in Europe for several years, but had come over and assembled a large jazz band. I remember we made up the posters and they said 'Zoot Sims Big Band', with Suicide underneath."

Most of the crowd were there for Zoot, but Suicide went down a storm, because "We were from the street and they understood us for what we were," as Alan puts it. Marty remembers the crowd as "mostly the heavy kind of jazz people from uptown, and a bunch of older, harder really in-the-groove New York street guys sitting at a table, and they all loved it. They were laughing and smiling. We didn't scare them at all, and they kind of got a big kick out of it. The room had a big stage and it was just one of those phenomenal gigs. Then Zoot Sims went on with the big band. It was just an amazing combination, but that's how it was in those days. Either nobody would take a chance on you or they would, because *everybody* was winging it."

By now, song titles had started emerging in Suicide's set. Alan got the idea for 'Methedrine Mary' from Mari ("She wasn't using methedrine but she was an inspiration to him. I don't think he had ever met anyone quite like that."). Alan's anguished chant of "I love you" later became 'Cheree', which he says "was the first actual song". 'Speed Queen' and 'Junkie Jesus' were two more embryonic prototypes.

"Alan had lyric ideas that were different," recalls Marty. "He'd go from one to another. We had 'Junkie Jesus'. That could be heard differently because it was a slower kind of Latin thing – in a way. We would do about four or five of those different sections, so to speak, but they all went from one right into the other, so to anyone else I don't know what was discernible, if there even were any differences. It was a wall of noise."

Gigs were still thin on the ground, with the Project their only staple venue. Two shows on the weekend of June 11 were billed as 'Punk Music Mass at Midnight'. Marty now added a battered Japanese organ he had found in the papers for $10 to his arsenal. Now he could place his two keyboards in a V shape in front of him, with snare drum in the middle and cymbal over the keyboard on the right, slamming dense chords with one hand and banging the drum with the other. "I did a lot of gigs like that. I was working quite a bit keeping a really strong beat with the electronics and the keyboards."

Alan remembers Marty's new organ as a crucial element in catalysing Suicide's early sound. He laughs uproariously as he remembers trying to get a squeak out of it before the big moment when Suicide's sound as the world knows it spluttered and roared into its earliest incarnation. "We bought everything for a total of 10 bucks because we couldn't afford any more than that, this cheap Japanese organ that we couldn't get a sound out of. And we had a bass amp, the same basic kind as Bruce Springsteen was using. It was shitty. So we started buying all these treble boosters and bass boosters, these little things for a dollar, which now everybody wants to have. Electro whores! We locked 'em together just to get a sound out. Marty's keyboard would have a whole line of these things, and all these dials and stuff. Shitty is the wrong word. It was beyond shitty. It was magnificent, man! It was a whole sound created out of needing to make a sound because we couldn't get a sound! And out it came. Boom! The big bang, man!"

Marty remembers further developments making their presence felt in Suicide's evolving sonic cauldron during their first year of existence. Maybe the most significant decision was to reach back to the first music which had moved him. He had studied jazz, knew about abstract European forms and appreciated classical symphonic music but, ultimately, "It was out of my time and environment. It didn't move me like a rock'n'roll or rhythm and blues track coming off the radio. That was my time in life. If I hear Little Richard or 'Get A Job' or 'Kansas City', or any of those songs coming off the radio, I'm immediately moved. It's like a soundtrack of my life. I also realised jazz was a step or two removed from my time, even though it struck a very deep part of the very core of me, being so close to the struggle and lifestyle it often represented and the best examples of it being so moving musically. But my innate culture and time was the 45s I bought and *American Bandstand*; a whole different music and sensibility. *That* was the soundtrack of my life when I went to school, or went to dances or fell in love with a girl. I had to come back to something that was closer to me, which was rock'n'roll and rhythm and blues."

This teenage grounding extended to Marty's visual image too. "My own particular theatre was very much me in the image and the way I felt onstage, because it's my background. I grew up at a time where, for people of my generation, it was the idea of gangs and streets. You were dressed differently and there was a different beat. Rhythm and blues and rock were like three chords, which were totally relevant. It shows how any lineage like that is related to the environment and culture it comes out of. Now I really wanted to find a way of playing which would go back to my roots, then all the stuff that I had learned up to that time, and that I was feeling with all the electronics."

Marty was walking around lower Manhattan one afternoon, deep in thought about that evening's practice. He desperately wanted to bowl into the Project basement that night armed with solid musical blueprints for Alan to bite on.

At this time, if Marty needed to write out music or wanted to practise, he snuck into NYU's music practice rooms, west of Broadway. "In those days you could just walk into NYU and go to a certain floor where they had these upright Steinway pianos in all these practice rooms that were really soundproofed," he recalls. "I would just go in nonchalantly, try to be cool and go upstairs. It was so loose, nobody would check anything. Now you can't even get to the front door if you're not a student!"

He felt different that day. "I remember going up there in the afternoon. I was going to hang out a little bit and then go up to the Project. Sometimes I would go through a whole self-assessment, searching, because I was not totally happy with what I was doing. Other times I'd go up there for an hour or two and just play around with ideas, try and find things. This time I wasn't necessarily dissatisfied but I was looking. I was in that frame of mind."

Both Alan and Marty have talked about the dream state Rev can fall into while playing or, conversely, the kind of super-focused creative combustion which gripped him when Suicide were recording *American Supreme* in 2001. Today it was the latter spirit which gripped Marty as he sat down at the NYU piano to dropkick his muse into a vital new phase. "All of a sudden, very quickly, I hit 'Rocket USA'. It was the first one. I hit that approach and, as soon as I did, out it came. I remember it happened right away, in like five minutes. I was just searching to find a way to play everything I was feeling, and how it worked with the two of us. Before it was working in a very free, wall-of-sound way with vocals more like screams. I wanted to find a way of putting Alan into a more singular vocal place where he could perform lyrics that you could hear. It's funny how fast I found it that day. Before then, it was close, but it was not yet totally finding the right riff and approach. I gravitate very much to the bass, not just in keyboard, but in voice, stringed instruments, everything. I love to play in the bass register, it's so rich. I found that 'Rocket USA' was so simple, but so light."

After this instant revelation, it was like he had kickstarted a fire hydrant in a Lower East Side street. While reaching back to Lennie Tristano's left-handed bass technique, Marty also found himself back in his childhood bedroom, looking at the cowboy pictures on the wall. "It's a hearing-seeing kind of thing. I think my orientation always has been, and still is, visual in so many ways. I kind of see music as I hear it. If I listen to a record I see the textures as much as I hear the actual notes or intervals. I immediately started seeing all these images of when I was an infant. I had all these paintings in my room, like these children's western scenes with cowboys; all these kind of American west kind of things in a jigsaw puzzle form, which must have still been very deep inside of me from my infant days. All of a sudden, I could see those things through that riff and that approach; the fact I could do it with one or two notes. It simplified everything that I'd been doing up to that time, and where the next place to go would be in that context."

Interestingly, Rev had worked out Suicide's later electronic milestone on an acoustic piano. "Absolutely, I would go up there and use the piano as my sketch pad," he says, adding "There was something sensual in my eternal fingerprint that day." In terms of personal epiphany and the liberation it brought, Marty cites how Charlie Parker arrived at the trailblazing chromatic blitzkrieg which would crystallise bebop and revolutionise modern jazz while jamming one morning in the late thirties.

Bird always struck a chord with Rev, having worked out his own fantasy of translating the dazzling speed and accuracy of pianist Art Tatum into a surging saxophone torrent, and playing "air saxophone" to his hero Lester Young. Bird heard the near-blind Tatum every night while he washed dishes at Harlem's Chicken Shack, at the same time working on his technique while replicating popular standards at New York taxi dances. The saxophonist also never forgot his basic training in mastering every key of the blues, which he had heard in his early teens on the streets of his native Kansas City, from singers who had worked their way up from the Mississippi plantations.

One morning in Dan Wall's all-night Chili House at Seventh Avenue and 19th Street, Bird was jamming with a rhythm section led by guitarist Biddy Fleet. As they traversed the perennial 'Cherokee', Bird started worrying he sounded stale. Suddenly, he got the idea to play the top notes of the chords instead of the lower or middle ones. Soon he was skimming through chorus after chorus like a pebble bouncing on the waves. It sounded totally strange, and the other musicians looked bewildered as nobody had heard anything like it in jazz before, not even from leaders like Lester Young. But this was all Bird's own invention, and he knew jazz would never be the same again.

The story resonates strongly with Marty, albeit in his own modest fashion. "It's like Charlie Parker talked about that story, where he said he'd been playing here and there but still hadn't found the definitive style he was searching for. Then he said he was playing this jam session and, all of a sudden, because he was so close to it, broke into that chromaticism. Through that he found the whole palette that was so innately him, and could express everything about him at this time. He found it that night just jamming. I found mine because I wanted to focus on certain limitations. If I had been in another context, I never would have found it. I realised that rock'n'roll was the only place that was innately me. It was also the only place that was still an open frontier that hadn't yet finished, and was the youngest form at that time. You could still go on stage and do anything, and it didn't have to be a repeat, especially with electronics. Everything else had a long history and was kind of recycling itself. I just went down to my comfort zone, which was the bass, saw it visually connecting with everything, and found it that way. I came out of that room with 'Rocket USA'."

Marty couldn't wait to hit that evening's rehearsal with his new revelation, which soon impacted on Alan's vocals. "Another thing which changed us happened soon after I started playing more riff-based. One night in rehearsal, when Alan was approaching his vocals the same way as before I suggested that maybe he should try whispering instead of screaming. I could see and hear the more streamlined dynamic of where we were heading. He tried immediately and it was part of the breakthrough on the vocal end.

Armed and now extremely dangerous, Suicide were ready to take on the revolution about to happen, literally, just around the corner.

NINE

For this author in the UK, 1972 was a fabulous year to turn 18. It had started with the first gig by David Bowie in his futuristic new Ziggy Stardust persona, which catalysed the glam movement ignited by T. Rex the previous year. Alice Cooper took American shock rock to number one with 'School's Out', Lou Reed brought Warhol's Factory to the top 10 with 'Walk On The Wild Side' and the whole world suddenly seemed exciting as music was wrenched out of self-indulgent oblivion and repointed at the future. That itself had been given a chilling cinematic portent the previous year by Stanley Kubrick's *A Clockwork Orange*.

The weekly music papers were a lifeline, with any hint of something new and exciting getting the blood pumping. Bowie had reinvented the concept of the old-fashioned idol by absorbing how Warhol's associates smashed sexual and visual taboos, but rock'n'roll still needed a new group to break the monopoly of the old guard led by the still omnipotent but increasingly torn and frayed Rolling Stones. Street level American rock'n'roll had been hit hard by the demise of both the MC5 and Stooges, and New York had been pretty quiet since the glory days of the Velvet Underground.

The *Melody Maker* of July 22 put the city back in the spotlight with a major feature from in situ US correspondent Roy Hollingworth, which introduced a Lower East Side outfit called the New York Dolls by proclaiming: "They might just be the best rock'n'roll band in the world... They can't play very well.... in them, and their kind lies the rebellion needed to crush the languid cloud of nothingness that rolls out from the rock establishment."

The feature's impact was intensified by Leee Childers' startling photo of the band posing at their Lower East Side loft; a defiant mass of hair, lipstick, lurex, big shades and pouting attitude, which even made Ziggy Stardust look clean-cut and studied. Just that piece alone announced that something new and dangerous was happening again on the streets of New York. It came as a blast of optimism for that peculiar breed of early seventies teenage rock fan who prayed for the return of Iggy Pop, or craved a successor to the Velvet Underground.

Unbeknownst to anyone outside of New York, Suicide were the loudest element in that same scene that the Dolls were emerging from, and were now unleashing the most cataclysmic sonic attack the city had ever experienced as reported by a clearly shell-shocked Hollingworth in the *Melody Maker* of October 21 – Suicide's first major press write-up anywhere. I still remember how exciting it felt reading his description of the single, flickering strobe, Alan's face coated in silver glitter, his black leather 'Suicide' jacket, and Marty's keyboard sound, whose "power and effect is startling.... a heady stark trip. The starkest trip I've ever seen."

He goes on to describe Alan stalking the stage, crawling around the sparse audience, whacking himself on the head with the mic, falling into a whimpering heap, shouting about love as "the chords just ooze up, and down... sludgy and dirty... like having a claw rip down your back." Some poor unfortunate makes to leave, but is confronted by Alan. "It was Hell inside there," writes Hollingworth, "... possibly the most frightening blend of music going around today... How two people could create such a thick wall of sound and atmosphere was an unbelievable achievement... Suicide were certainly the most awful sight ever – and yet, in the most bizarre way, it was a therapy for the mind. What has rock created?"

Reading this felt like seeing the future, even if there would be a frustrating four-year wait before the UK could hear what he was talking about as, while the Dolls would soon be on record, it would take much longer for Suicide. But just the idea that something so new, fearless and frightening was going on in the bowels of New York was oddly reassuring, and massively exciting.

By 1972, New York City was caught in a downwards economic spiral, with buildings and services corroding, while crime thrived. There was a dire paucity of happening rock venues in Manhattan, but all that was about to change.

The Mercer Arts Center is as important as any venue in the history of rock'n'roll; a unique one-off which could only have happened at that particular time. It was built as downtown's answer to the Lincoln Center, but went down like the neighbourhood's version of the Titanic; an extravagant monument which (literally) sank after a brief stretch of idealistic glory. While this short-lived product of New York's cultural history launched the New York Dolls, it also gave Suicide their first residency outside of the Project, a stage on which to develop and find their first audiences and brought them into contact with key figures such as Marty Thau.

In the first half of the 19th century, the block up from Third Street, between Broadway and Mercer, had been the site of the Lafarge Hotel, and the attached Tripler Hall, which had presented stars of the day. Restored after a fire in 1854, the venue returned as the New York Theatre and Metropolitan Opera House, before becoming the Winter Gardens in 1859, mainly staging Shakespeare. The building burned down completely in 1867, making way for the vast eight-storey Grand Central Hotel, which had been commissioned by carpet manufacturer Elias S. Higgins.

One of the biggest and most opulent hostelries in New York, the Grand Central's marble fireplaces, crystal chandeliers and catering facilities made it a favourite with the likes of flamboyant tycoon 'Diamond Jim' Brady in the 1890s. After the turn of the century, and by now renamed the Broadway Central, the hotel fell on hard times as high society moved uptown and the neighbourhood declined. By the sixties, it was a dilapidated retreat for hookers and their johns, and had become a welfare hotel run by the owners and city by 1970. Within months, local residents were complaining about the precarious condition of the building, and the rats, junkies, drunks and prostitutes it was attracting. By November 1972, the hotel had been renamed the University and attacked by Attorney General Louie Lefkowitz as a squalid den of vice and iniquity that, in the first six months of 1972, had seen 22 robberies, one homicide, three rapes and untold drug-related crimes and assaults.

The Village Gate's Art D'Lugoff appears again in this story as the Mercer Arts Center was originally his dream. Having already given jazz a local platform, he had unwittingly set the wheels in motion for New York's first musical revolution of the seventies when he started hatching plans to convert the first two floors of the hotel into a performance complex back in 1966, when the lease could be acquired for a pittance. After former racing car driver and now air conditioning tycoon Seymour

Kaback installed the a/c in the Gate, D'Lugoff convinced him to fund renovation of the Mercer Street space, making him a silent partner when it opened for business as the Theater Cabaret.

Art had big ambitions for the new complex and was still talking it up in the press in 1970. However, by early 1971, Kaback had bought him out and was sinking half a million bucks into converting the 35,000 square foot space into, as he told the *New York Times* of November 2, 1971, "a kind of downtown Lincoln Center".

The *Times* piece reported the conversion three quarters done, and theatres "jumbled and stacked together with a kind of jigsaw flair". The Center's brochure announced it catering to "the various performing arts (both live and media), including off-Broadway theatrical productions, film, dance, music, experimental work in video-tape and cable television, multi-media rock festivals, laboratory productions of work in progress, poetry reading, classes in acting, voice and movement, as well as eating and drinking facilities," adding "an evening at the Mercer is impulsive and casual… a natural gathering place for professionals and neophytes to exchange ideas".

The ground floor of 240 Mercer Street boasted the sizeable Hansberry and Brecht theatres. The second floor featured four cabaret theatres – the 300-capacity O'Casey, Oscar Wilde Room, Shaw Arena, and The Kitchen. There was also a bar called Obie Alley, a boutique called Zoo selling glam fashions from London, and the Blue Room cabaret bar-restaurant, which boasted walls, ceilings and floors covered in blue fabric and mirrors. Its futuristic white plastic tables and chairs invited comparisons to the Moloko Bar in *A Clockwork Orange*, as New York Dolls drummer Jerry Nolan told me in 1977: "The Mercer Arts Center was a renovated place. It was a cross between Victorian-looking design and a really spacey modern *Clockwork Orange* type place, yet it still had some of the old things left, like chandeliers."

While construction continued, the grand opening took place on December 21. The theatres hosted successful productions of *One Flew Over The Cuckoo's Nest*, *The Effect Of Gamma Rays On Man-In-The-Moon Marigolds*, *The Proposition* and *Macbeth*, the latter starring actor and Center director Rip Torn.

The previous June, video artist couple Steina and Woody Vasulka had taken over the hotel's former kitchen, called it simply The Kitchen, and started staging events with pianist Michael Tschudin.

The story of New York rock'n'roll is littered with manic exhibitionists, fearless trailblazers and tragic casualties. Eric Emerson managed to be all three in his short life, and the exotic proto-glam rock he performed with the Magic Tramps foreshadowed everyone on both sides of the Atlantic as the very first glitter band. While Eric's anarchic spirit and exhibitionist charisma charmed anyone from cool New York rocker to intimidating Hell's Angel, the Magic Tramps laid foundations for the musical upheavals which shook New York during the seventies. For a variety of reasons, the group never got the breaks which would have taken them outside the few downtown venues they blitzed and seduced.

Born in New Jersey in 1945, Eric was sent to ballet school by his mother. Andy Warhol spotted him dancing to the Velvet Underground in April 1966 at the Dom, which resulted in his being cast in films including *Chelsea Girls*, *Lonesome Cowboys* and *Heat*. That's his ghostly visage hovering over the band on the front cover of the first Velvets album. Short of cash, he tried to claim payment from the record company, but the album was recalled and Eric airbrushed out, like his place in New York rock history seems to have been.

In 1970, he went to LA and joined an experimental rock band called Messiah, whose guitarist Youngblood he had met on the set of *Lonesome Cowboys*. Also featuring drummer Sesu Coleman and violinist Lary Chaplan, Messiah unfurled psychedelic instrumentals as house band at Hollywood's Temple of the Rainbow club. They were offered a record deal, provided they find a singer. Youngblood suggested Emerson, then in LA promoting *Lonesome Cowboys*. "He had long blond hair, wore leather hot pants and tights, carried a whip and had a colourful, song-bird-like personality that demanded one's attention," recalls Sesu Coleman. "He had not been in a band before, but was a perfect fit. We realised we couldn't conform to the label's artistic direction, so Eric suggested we relocate to New York City. He spoke of Warhol, and a club we could play at called Max's Kansas City."

Messiah was renamed the Magic Tramps by the time Eric brought them back to New York in early 1971, all cramming into his partner Elda Gentile's East Village fifth floor walk-up apartment. He didn't waste a moment finding a new venue for the band to call their own, as Sesu recalls, "The very next day Eric and I visited Warhol's Factory. Upon arrival, we met Andy and his film assistant, Paul Morrissey, along with a cast of characters and superstars. Eric told Andy he had brought his band to create a new sound and look in the multi-media arena of New York City. Andy was very happy to see Eric and very receptive towards me."

Morrissey guffawed when the pair explained their multi-media rock ambitions, declaring "Boys, rock'n'roll will never fly in New York City. You need to play cabaret music and theatres. Rock music died with the Velvet Underground. You need songs like 'Swinging On A Star'!" Eric and Sesu took it in their stride, agreeing they could adapt, if necessary, as they crossed Union Square to Max's to meet Mickey Ruskin. Eric knew him well through the Warhol crowd, who kept his club in the news (if not in the black). Ruskin stood up with a big smile when the pair walked into his upstairs office. The grin got bigger as Eric told his story and, by the end of the meeting, they'd convinced him to let them "play a showcase for Andy and the Factory crowd" in the upstairs restaurant, which had lain dormant since the Velvet Underground had played their last shows there between June and August the previous year (albeit their first at Max's, contrary to myth). "So we played, and it really was remarkable," remembers Sesu.

The Magic Tramps commenced their riotous Friday night residency, lapped up by the Warhol inner circle, the famous cocktail of uptown-downtown Max's regulars and the many who were simply bored with dowdy local covers bands. "That was the start of new music in New York," says Elda Gentile. "You never knew what you would see when you went to see the Tramps. It depended on what mood Eric was in. The stage was always draped in black and adorned with candles and spiritual icons; everything from Buddhas to skulls. Sometimes Eric would appear in black tights and a ruffled shirt, and would be draped in a silk cape and top hat. Sometimes he was painted silver, wearing only his signature hot pants. That is when his eight-foot bull whip came out and he would snatch cigarettes from peoples' mouths with it. Eric was the spark that ignited the built-up fuel in New York's need for a new direction when the sixties ended. He was encouraging and supportive of so many artists from the new era, who later became famous."

The residency kickstarted Max's as a live showcase which would go on to host, for example, Bruce Springsteen and Bob Marley on the same bill. Then the Magic Tramps became the first rock band to play the Mercer Arts Center.

"The Mercer was a shambles," recalls Sesu. "Lary Chaplan and I worked cleaning away garbage, broken mirrors and wheelbarrows of trash. We worked out a deal with the manager to let us play in the theatres after the shows if we helped build the stages."

Soon, the Magic Tramps were regularly cooking in The Kitchen. "I sincerely believe we pioneered the early New York City music scene by reopening Max's and finding the Mercer Arts Center, complete with this multi-media room called The Kitchen where you could do video, art, poetry and music," continues Sesu. "Then the Dolls said they were putting a band together and asked if they could open for us. We said 'Sure, we need bands'."

Although they looked and sounded like they hailed from different planets, there were marked similarities between the New York Dolls and Suicide, starting with all the members being born and brought up within New York's five boroughs. They flew that flag loud and proud as their music reflected the streets they struggled to survive on. Both had little regard for artistic convention and would incur untold abuse for the stances they took. The two outfits were also dealing out their own responses to the Vietnam War; the Dolls escaping its shadow with their endless party, while Suicide mirrored the rage and turmoil which gripped many of the country's youth.

The Dolls formed out of a mutual love of rock'n'roll and blues in its purest forms, and sneering disdain for brain-numbing stadium rock. The first line-up solidified in late 1971 after guitarist Johnny Thunders, drummer Billy Murcia, bassist Arthur Kane and guitarist Rick Rivets rehearsed at nights in a bicycle rental shop on 81st Street. They were joined by radical blues and soul bohemian David Johansen, who hailed from Staten Island. David was already a pin-sharp actor, his deep appreciation of roots music instilled by his working class Irish father's regular airings of Harry Smith's *Anthology Of American Folk Music*. They all loved New York's girl groups. David had been in Staten Island bands, but was now working on sound and lighting at Charles Ludlam's Ridiculous Theatre when he tottered into his first Dolls rehearsal. His lung-busting display of Sonny Boy Williamson-style harmonica chops clinched his place as frontman.

The new band played its first gig on Christmas Eve 1971 at a crime-infested welfare hotel called the Endicott, situated over the street from their rehearsal room. Playing Otis Redding and Archie Bell covers to a mainly black and Puerto Rican audience, they went down a storm. When Sylvain returned from Europe, where he had enjoyed a good earner selling his Truth and Soul fashion line, he was incensed to see the band using the name he had coined after spotting a New York Dolls Hospital near the rehearsal studio. He duly steamed in on rhythm guitar after Rivets was canned for being flakey.

After Johnny and girlfriend Janis Cafasso moved into a loft above a Chinese noodle shop on Chrystie Street, in the heart of the Lower East Side, they were soon joined by Billy and Syl. The group survived on thieving missions and holding rent parties to raise the necessary $200 a month. As the Dolls came to life, their parties became notorious. The first proper line-up played through the first half of 1972 at the Palm Room in the basement of the Diplomat Hotel on West 43rd Street, and gay bathhouse the Continental Baths on 74th Street.

David's girlfriend of the time was Diane Pulaski, a former model now ensconced in Warhol's stable, so he knew the inner circle who were hanging out in Max's backroom, which is where he met Eric Emerson. The 'NY Dolls' (as they were listed in the venue's programme as part of an 'Electronic Exorcise') opened for the Magic Tramps at The Kitchen on the night of Friday May 5, alongside fire-eating performance artist Satan, boss of Talent-Recon Inc. – the 38th Street studio where both bands rehearsed. The Dolls ensured the gig was packed with their exotic rent-party regulars, making enough of an impact to convince the Mercer's manager, Al Lewis, to contract them for the 14-night Tuesday residency in the 200-capacity Oscar Wilde Room, which would shape the band and make its name after it kicked off on June 13.

The new scene which sprang up – ruled by drugs, drag and raw rock'n'roll – was hailed as the city's most significant underground happening since the Exploding Plastic Inevitable. "The Dolls were an attitude. If nothing else they were a great attitude," Johnny Thunders once told me. This defiant spunk cast the Dolls at the forefront of a new movement which rejected hoary music industry rules to start a new scene for the modern world. Like the Beatles at the Cavern, the Dolls had their own sweaty gig in which to blossom in front of rabid disciples. As Sylvain told me, "We were totally turned off by the big stadium rock, the Led Zeppelins and all this stuff that was like 30,000 people in the house. There'd be a 25-minute solo on this and a 20-minute gargling solo on that. Who the fuck cares? It was boring as hell. Rock became establishment. It became business. It became no fun. It wasn't sexy. It was all packaged, and repackaged, and shoved down your fucking throat."

Sylvain saw the Dolls as a lightning rod for artists, writers and "all kinds of outcasts put together. We were young and screaming our generation's next move. We never sat down around a big table and worked out a master plan to dress up as girls and shit. We were so far ahead of our time that we didn't even realise it. Everybody else took notes and took it to the bank, but we fell and broke our legs because we were running so damn fast. We were actually inventing it all, not even knowing what the hell we were doing."

The Dolls' impact was indeed seismic for those slothful times, as proved when I was lucky enough to see them play Biba's Rainbow Room in London in November 1973 (although the crowd there was self-consciously cool and inert). Although their repertoire was built on the eternal chords of rock, soul and blues, there was more to the band beyond the image, including the theatrical elements introduced by Johansen who, apart from being a fountain of garrulous, press-friendly sound bites, told writer Lisa Robinson he saw himself as an actor when he was onstage, which wasn't a million miles from Alan Vega's street-war performance art onslaughts.

"I used to see the Dolls around New York in the early seventies," says Marty, remembering "the colour, the glam, unisex, everybody dressed to the hilt in polka dots and high heels. They were literally the dolls of the day in New York. They brought the English look to New York too. Nobody was really doing that Stones and Faces look to that extent. It was such a colourful, party kind of a scene. The girls were dolled up to the skies and so were the guys. It was beautiful."

"I was never crazy about their music though," says Alan. "They had the whole party thing. We had a good time with everybody else but it wasn't like anything new. It was sixties music basically. You didn't go to see the Dolls for the music. You went to see some beautiful women and party."

The Mercer welcomed the downtown dollars pouring into its gasping cash registers, which meant that patrons attending the theatres also had the experience of witnessing the Dolls crowd in the bar. More bands started appearing, including Teenage Lust, Harlots, Luger, Butch, Sniper, Brats, Ruby & the Rednecks, plus a bunch of opportunists who took components they'd lifted from the Dolls and Magic Tramps to the bank under the name of Kiss. The Dolls' first major press came with Ed McCormack's *Rolling Stone* feature in October 1972, which contained Johansen's prescient sound bite, "We like to look 16 and bored shitless." McCormack concluded "Not since the original Velvet Underground has any local band cultivated such a loyal cult following among neo-decadents in New York."

Attempts by the press to pin down the new scene as a glam-rock or glitter craze worked about as well as it did in the equally misguided UK, then enduring a welter of hopefuls adopting the kind of platform boot flash Mott The Hoople had been stomping around in for years. By the time the Dolls' residency wound up in September, Bowie, who had already soaked up the taboo-shattering decadence of Warhol's *Pork* production for his Ziggy Stardust persona, was attempting to take New York at Carnegie Hall, making notes for his next invention, Aladdin Sane, at the Mercer. He also put some of its linchpins on his payroll, including trans-glam diva Wayne County, photographer Leee Black Childers and promoter Cherry Vanilla. Having defined glam once and for all, Bowie was already looking to move swiftly on.

Ultimately, glam was rock'n'roll in louder trousers, played from a greater height. As Sylvain says, "Somebody's always trying to make something out of something. Really it's just bands playing music. When things become movements and whatnot, you're just setting yourself up for a big club to come down on you. Somebody says you're a glam band; who are *they* to? Really, it's just rock'n'roll. We were quite aware of how the business works, but we didn't need it. With us, especially in my case, take away my lipstick or the frilly-loomed nylon tights and it's still just the blues under there. It's three chord progressions. The cool people got it."

The Dolls were getting an exotic new strain of New York club kid on its feet and dancing, even if their blueprint for the future was still hot-wiring the past, under several layers of slap. Party music and genders were being pushed, but sonic boundaries weren't. New York had traditionally been a spawning ground for trailblazers and idiosyncratic innovators, so the ingrained experimental nature of the city's volatile underground *had* to mean the revolution wasn't going to stop with the Dolls' rebooting of rock'n'roll's original manifesto.

Suicide naturally tried to blag a gig at the new hotspot, especially with the Mercer being just a few minutes' walk from the Project. Initially, Mercer manager Al Lewis, who Marty remembers as "a nice guy from the older generation Broadway world, who managed theatres in the fifties and reminded me a little of Phil Silvers," took one look at Suicide in their street gear and gave them a show on Wednesday the 28th. "By accident. Just seeing us, he gave us a date." But he obviously regretted it afterwards, as it was a different story when the pair returned a few weeks later to ask for a return gig.

Al freaked when he opened his office door to find Suicide standing there. Before they could say anything, he yelled "You can't come in here!", slammed the door and ran to Sy Kaback's office in the back. "We could hear him, like in a panic, saying 'Suicide's here again!'" chuckles Marty. Puzzled, they knocked again. Trembling now, Al opened the door a second time, then tried to shut it again. This time, Marty stuck his foot in the way. As their exchanges intensified, Kaback came out to see what was causing the commotion.

"Let 'em in," he ordered Lewis.

Suicide had never met Sy Kaback before. The jovial Mercer mogul looked at the pair of street warriors sat before him in his office; Marty in his leather hat and "long, heavy duty coat, like the kind of thing you'd wear in the middle of winter if you were dressed up", and Alan swinging his chains and sporting his leather jacket studded 'Suicide'. After a few minutes talking about themselves and answering his questions, Kaback came up with the first serious proposition of Suicide's career. "I tell you what, I'll put you in four nights, every Wednesday in the Oscar Wilde Room." He instructed his secretary to draw up a contract. "So it went from Al Lewis trying to slam the door on us, to being offered a contract. It was just mind-blowing how it went from one to the other so quickly. So we said 'okay'. Ten minutes later his secretary came in with two copies of a contract. Alan and me had never seen a contract before in our lives! I was looking at it before I signed, reading it to see what we were signing, but it was a few pages long. Alan was nudging me, going 'Just sign it!' So we signed it, eventually."

A couple of nights later, the pair went to the Mercer "just to hang out, as most musicians would do then." This time, Al Lewis was all smiles when he saw them, exclaiming, "Sy really likes you guys, you remind him of his relatives when they came in off the boat." "His family had been immigrants," says Marty. "They were really hungry too and I guess the way we were dressed, we must have looked the same. Sy got a kick out of that. He liked us, and that's why he put us on. He was a very secure guy, well off from his business, with enough money to build this complex. He was obviously a pretty cool mind in terms of wanting to build this theatrical place, and it was unique. They were very nice theatres, all different sizes, over two floors. The Mercer was incredible."

121

Suicide's residency in the Oscar Wilde Room, where the Dolls had played every Tuesday until switching to the larger O'Casey Theatre, started on October 4, and would extend until mid-November, by which time they were billing themselves as 'Punk Junk Sewer Music'. They sometimes played the Blue Room cabaret bar on the same night as the Dolls, whose audience had to traverse Suicide's electric storm before they reached the exit. "We didn't perform with the Dolls on the same stage. We did the Blue Room a few times, which was like a long, narrow kind of bar, with the stage at the back. It was a beautiful atmosphere, all in blue, including the lights. The thing was, it was central, so it was like the corridor too. To exit any of the theatres, you had to come through the Blue Room."

Alan remembers the unsuspecting Dolls crowds suddenly faced with having to walk through Suicide's inferno with great amusement: "If we were still playing, people were in real fear! The sound alone was so crazy they couldn't get away fast enough. It was like there was some kind of tornado coming after them."

Although Suicide started before the scene got under way around the Dolls, they still found themselves lumped in with the new bands proliferating at the Mercer. While Alan declared "The Dolls' room was like a party, ours was like a death scene," both groups were still essentially propagating their own idiosyncratic takes on inner city blues, lashed with theatrical elements from the street. An affectionate mutual respect and bond grew between Suicide and the Dolls. Sylvain thought Suicide were "fucking weird" but "fantastic", and Arthur took bets on how long it would take them to clear the room. David "was right there with us immediately", according to Marty. He adds, "David became a good friend of mine. The girl who was very instrumental in launching them as far as their fashion went was Barbara Troiani. She had the imagination and was designing their whole look in her little studio on her sewing machine. I was good friends with her too. I met her and her friends, the closest being the Dolls and David, who had his girlfriend Cyrinda Foxe. Barbara used to bring me up to his place. She was a very close friend of his from years before."

The first time David encountered Suicide in action, he joined them onstage and started playing his harmonica. Alan also recalls him sitting down at Marty's keyboard at a break and getting lost in the sound for over an hour. "David came up onstage wearing his hot pants and started playing with us. First I said, 'Why don't I pull this guy's pants down, maybe he's marking us?' Then I said 'No, let him play.' It's pretty cool, actually. He was cool, always has been. He wasn't afraid or anything like that. But everybody else was flying out of the joint, man."

Now Marty says, "We were bringing the war onto the stage. It was an expressionistic thing. It was like two totally different ages. I would describe it as like two world wars; world wars three and four going on at the same time."

But it was the residency in the Oscar Wilde Room which enabled Suicide to stretch out in their own domain, find their feet and really turn it up. Marty had dispensed with the snare and cymbal, further amping up his keyboard setup to conjure feedback so loud some still swear they could hear the drum machine he was three years away from adding to his arsenal. "The rhythm was coming out of the pure feedback from that Fender bass amp," he explains. "I used to take the top off that bass cabinet, which was like a giant speaker cabinet and put all the dials from it on the keyboard as part of the processing. That was my synthesizer. That big cabinet behind me would get all kinds of crazy stuff coming through, like interference and radio and police calls. It was such a big untapped frontier."

Sesu Coleman was a staunch regular in the Suicide trenches, and recalls Al Lewis telling him he wanted to keep the duo in the back room "so the theatre crowd wouldn't get frightened." He says there were four to six diehards in the room when he first saw Suicide at the Mercer. "I sat down and out comes Marty, who walked up to an odd collection of small machines and started a drone sound, which got louder all the time. I soon knew this was different than the other theatres." One couple left after a few seconds. "This was too weird for them. Then out comes Alan, a dark figure with black hair and clothes, looking stern and serious. The machines got louder, pulling you in like a form of hypnosis. You could feel it in your heart. Alan stared out into the dark room and no one moved. He made a few noises, like a haunted soul, then screeched and hit his face with the microphone. The thump echo was so loud you knew he drew blood. Someone else ran for the exit."

Sesu remembers snatches of lyrics, including "America, America's killing its youth", and Alan pulling out a chain and whipping the stage, before ending the set by throwing down the microphone and walking off, followed by Rev, "who leaves his collection of machines squealing."

It was all over in six minutes and, by then only Sesu and Lary Chaplan remained. "I never saw more than 12 people in the room, but I was really digging it as it provoked people," he says. "Lary and I looked at each other not knowing if that was it or to wait for more. I could only say, 'That was great!!' It was punk before punk existed. That was just one night of many. Suicide were always abstract, dark, confrontational and shocking. Alan never jumped offstage or hurt anyone. It was just shocking to watch him hit his face hard, cut himself and draw blood, making animal sounds, while Rev stood stoic, making universal sounds and not talking. It was art, and so different to anything else on the scene."

Sesu returned to experience Suicide's almost ritualistic "room of darkness" bombardments when he wasn't onstage with the Magic Tramps, "sometimes being the only one in there to the end, being taken to an alternate reality. It was so unique and refreshing. Most of the other musicians didn't pay much attention to Suicide as they were too busy with the girls and safer glam in the other theatres. Some shows were six minutes, some 15, some 20, but always different. They were true artists, not rehearsed, as they wanted each show to be fresh and on its own timeline. Alan's stare would scare and Rev was like automaton man. I loved Suicide from the moment I heard them. Little did anyone know back then that they would change music history."

On a more self-conscious note, the *Village Voice* of November 9 ran an account in something called the 'Riffs' column, which kicked off, "What can you say about a duo that calls itself 'Suicide', keeps the audience waiting for an hour, then offers brain-curdling stomps, shrieks and throbbing noises from an electric piano/organ, and highly amplified sobs, moans and 'I-love-youse' from a lead singer who whips himself, is dressed in black leather, hung with chains, sequins, studs and jewellery, with greasy black ringlets framing a face oozing silver pancake, glitter, and fear and which refers to this material as 'punk-sewer-junk' music? What *can* you say?" His answer is to call Suicide "the hippest act around, pure art, worthy of a one-night stand at the MoMA," before lapsing into the old best-in-small-doses punch-line.

Suicide's Mercer stint was gaining them press attention, new friends and rising notoriety as New York's most terrifyingly compulsive live experience. It also led to them meeting another key figure in their lives and careers, who would eventually be responsible for Suicide translating their sound into the studio.

TEN

"When Vega started cutting his forearm with a razor, some brave souls tried to leave the room, but quickly realised they had been purposely locked in the dimly lit Kitchen and were at the mercy of his seemingly crazed hostility. Decked out in black leather, with motorcycle chains draped around his upper body, Vega thrust himself into the appalled faces of the most conventional-looking hapless souls he could find, most of whom were now undergoing a brutal sensory assault unlike any they had ever experienced. Confronting an audience with songs full of lurid, murderous imagery and distressing urban angst, combined with a deafening and immensely physical mixture of droning, rhythmic, electronic grinding repetition, was just part of a show that some bewildered critics didn't understand, and viewed with sneering disbelief and suspicion. But, as masters of their domain, Vega and Rev knew exactly what they were doing." – **Marty Thau**

The world might never have been blessed with the first Suicide album without Marty Thau putting whatever money he had blagged where his razor-sharp New York mouth was. But if Thau's inestimable part in encouraging the downtown scene of the seventies will soon become apparent, his vital role in the Suicide story was still a few years off when he happened on the scene at the Mercer Arts Center.

The year 1972 already seemed like ancient history to me when I first met Marty Thau, along with Suicide, on the Clash's UK tour in 1978. When I got to sit with him in a London record company office in 1980 that tour had already been filed as one of the wildest yarns of the previous decade.

Thickset, with cropped brown hair, mod jacket and shades, large hands clasped in front of him, Marty Thau was every inch the old school record company boss as he emanated brusque New York savvy from behind a big desk at the record company; almost foreshadowing his scene in post-punk movie *Downtown 81*, in which he was to play the role he did best.

Thau started by running through the career he turned his back on to chase dreams he saw more in keeping with the spirit of his beloved rock'n'roll. A native New Yorker born in 1938, he studied business at NYU before starting as a trainee advertising executive at *Billboard* magazine. This led to Cameo-Parkway Records boss Neal Bogart hiring him as his National Promotions Manager. "That year we put 28 records in the charts; not bad for a company that had not had a hit record in four years," crowed Thau. "We had Question Mark & the Mysterians' '96 Tears', Terry Knight & the Pack, the Five Stairsteps, and a whole bunch of bands from Detroit. All through my career I've been persistently involved with young rock'n'roll bands. That year, we were so successful that Bogart, myself and our team set up Buddah Records, where I stayed 1967 to 1971. There we had hits from the 1910 Fruitgum Company, Ohio Express, Curtis Mayfield, Isley Brothers, Edwin Hawkins Singers; 20 gold records or more."

Although Thau swiftly rose to become Buddah's Vice-President and head of promotion, this mainstream business career wasn't what he had originally envisioned for himself. He started to "feel the need to take an evaluation of my career and my life. I felt I knew the answers before I asked the questions; I concluded I had *accidentally* gone into promotion. It wasn't a natural inclination; I needed a job. So I resigned and went towards the area of the industry that had always intrigued me the most, which was the music." He became partners in a production company called Inherit, who released Van Morrison's *Astral Weeks* and *Moondance*, John Cale's *Vintage Violence* and *Church Of Anthrax*.

After two years, Thau spent six months as head of A&R at Paramount, but started feeling too corporate again. "Once again, I'd had a taste of the other side of the desk and couldn't live in the record industry. So I resigned from Paramount and, after a celebration dinner with my wife, walking around downtown New York on a warm spring night, we passed by the Mercer Arts Center. There was this little sign advertising the New York

Dolls, two bucks in the Oscar Wilde Room. I said, 'Sounds interesting, let's go in'. I thought, 'These guys are either the worst group I've ever seen or the greatest.' I concluded they were the greatest, and they were very young, inexperienced and primitive – qualities I liked. They were pretty outrageous. I watched and listened to the Dolls, and I heard their arrangements. I didn't hear wasted lines or excesses. I just thought it was great and to the point. Somewhere in that group one, or all of them, had a very fine understanding of pop-rock music."

Speaking to Thau again over 30 years later, he reflected, "One of the main reasons I signed the Dolls was because of their songs. I had worked at Buddah, and really studied what the ingredients were for a hit." Initially, he wanted to start a label and release killer singles. "I spoke to someone who was going to put up the money. In the course of the weeks that followed, when I made contact with the Dolls and started to get a feeling about them, I was very impressed with their mentality, sophistication, view of people and what it takes. So I shelved the record company idea, and decided to take them on as their manager."

However, after producing demos at a New York studio, Thau's attempts to land the Dolls a record deal failed. The band were simply too outrageous for the times and the conservative US music biz. While bustling and buzzing inside, the Mercer was often picketed outside by anti-gay protesters. Thau concluded this band that was seen as "transvestites, drug addicts and perverts" was too much for the music industry, although Mercury A&R man and noted journalist Paul Nelson got on his side.

Thau figured he might find that elusive record deal in the UK, so their last date was a free farewell show at the Mercer on October 12. Their first trip to the UK would see the Dolls play several dates, including the Empire Pool, Wembley, in front of 8,000 punters waiting to see Rod Stewart and the Faces. Tragedy struck the night Thau was poised to sign a big money deal with Track Records, when the 18-year-old Billy Murcia passed out on downers and champagne at a party, then choked to death on coffee poured down his throat by fellow revellers in a misguided effort to revive him.

The devastated Dolls had returned to New York and were never the same again. Billy was replaced by Brooklyn powerhouse Jerry Nolan and the band greeted like returning heroes when they played the O'Casey again on December 19. "I guess there was a drug-related death and the group were hotter than they ever were," reflected Thau. "Hundreds were turned away and it was like a record industry convention that night, but the presidents still laughed up their sleeves." He blamed the musical climate being geared to singer-songwriters; "very boring and pretentious, that whole LA mentality. The Dolls were just too much against the grain. They were too real. That was coupled with all the misguided confusion about their sexuality."

Thau had first met Suicide the previous autumn, but seemed unaware that they had already appeared at the Mercer when he later devoted a chapter to them in his unpublished memoir, for which I tried to whip up some UK interest before he passed away in February 2014. He recalled "this bedraggled pair of underground boho heroes" approaching him at Bleecker Bob's record store in Greenwich Village in late 1972. "I had no idea who they were, but they recognised me from the many Dolls shows I had promoted at the Mercer Arts Center. We immediately engaged in a conversation about the burgeoning downtown music scene, but when they started describing their personal vision of music and performance art, I was totally intrigued and knew that sooner or later I'd give this intense pair an opportunity to perform in Mercer's Kitchen, the space presenting the most radical artists."

Thau did display a rare ability to describe Suicide as he wrote of Rev's "blend of psychosis and sentimentality encased in a hodgepodge of minimalist electro-rhythm drones… Vega's echo-laden screams, mad shrieking scat lines and incoherent mutterings, all topped with a dash of sugary evil Elvis psychobilly unh-hunhs", declaring, "Suicide was a spiritual ritual and discordant rock'n'roll party rolled into one and possessed a deep awareness of the power of theatricality. Driven by Vega's confrontational neo-Presleyesque, Iggy-like sci-fi vision of gruesome contemporary street life, joined at the hip with Rev's unnerving blend of loud distortion, feedback, recycled jazz, fifties Latin rhythms and electro dance lines, Suicide were an original pastiche of punk's minimalist fervor, disco's hypnotic rhythms, electronica's hi-tech futurism and a harsh barrage of avant-garde ideals designed to capture the hearts and souls of the adventurous."

True to his word, Thau added them (albeit as 'Alan Suicide') to the bill of 'An Endless Valentine's Day All-night Party' which took over the Mercer on February 11, 1973. (By now the duo had binned the punky aliases in favour of calling themselves Alan and Marty Suicide.) This event is now seen as a landmark for New York's underground scene. Although stuck in The Kitchen at this party, it was also the most important show Suicide had done to date. Running from 10 p.m. until dawn, the billing saw the Dolls and Wayne County's Queen Elizabeth appearing in the Eugene O'Neill Room; Ruby & the Rednecks, Teenage Lust and the Magic Tramps in the Oscar Wilde, plus a crowd taking the concept of drag, shock and glam about as far as the city had ever seen it.

Marty Rev recalls, "Thau had known of us since 1972 and seen us before when he was managing the Dolls, but he'd never touch us. We saw him as the establishment. There were bands playing all night, so Marty needed a lot of groups. He booked us that night because he needed us. We went on and played around 2 a.m. He liked us then. He later said he never knew we were so crazily different from what else was going on in the glam rock scene. We could dress that way, but we didn't sound that way. He also said, 'I like them but I don't think they can make records'. That was his orientation. He was a record man."

In 1980, when I asked Thau to describe Suicide's performance that night, he recalled, "There were no rhythm machines then, just an organ. It was totally free-form, wild, whatever the whim of the two lunatics at that moment. Alan had chains on and cut himself up and wore this outrageous outfit of leather and boots. Marty Rev hit one note for 40 minutes."

Alan also recalls this being the infamous set where Rev played one note for the entire performance, along with himself taking the stage carrying a big, cross-shaped hunk of wood he had found. Thau wrote that he was, "pleasantly surprised to see that Suicide had bonded with the Dolls crowd despite the two bands' vastly different musical attitudes." But they also had a terrifying impact on them.

Barry Miles, a key figure of the London underground and co-founder of both the Indica bookshop and *International Times*, reviewed the event for *NME*, confessing he had missed Alan Suicide, "who I'm told has a spectacular act", but commenting that New York was "quite sinister" compared to the "warmth" of London in its velvet and lace. He compared the girls dancing to the Dolls with those moving to 'Fire' singer Arthur Brown at London's UFO club six years earlier, and likened the event to "almost some outrageous parody of the thirties American glamour concept," concluding, "a nation coming out from under 10 years of unpopular war, a history of puritanism and genocide, greets four more years of Nixon with its most potent weapon, Faggot Rock, the music of total drop-out."

By August, Sy Kaback's theatrical supermarket was still doing great business. Although the Dolls had moved on, the ever-growing number of hopeful new bands continued to draw crowds. *One Flew Over The Cuckoo's Nest* clocked up more than 1,000 performances, and other productions were filling its theatres. But Kaback was getting worried about the building. Cracks kept appearing and, despite repeated calls to the hotel's management, had to be plastered over by his own team. On the afternoon of Thursday August 2, fissures started appearing in one of the workshops. Then, around five o'clock the next afternoon, the old University Hotel's walls and ceilings started making groaning sounds before the whole building started to shake and rumble. The Magic Tramps rehearsing in the back were used to earthquakes in LA so didn't take much notice – until plaster started dropping, wooden beams crashed to the floor, and the scene began to resemble one of the disaster movies popular at that time. Panic-stricken hotel residents, from elderly couples to bums clutching bottles, crawled or wheeled themselves out of the front door on to Broadway, while musicians and rehearsing cast members spilled on to Mercer Street. First the top floors came down, then the whole façade collapsed onto the street in a thunderous mass of dust and rubble. The building, said fire chief John T. O'Hagan in the *New York Times*, "fell like a pancake."

"One day it was there, and then the funky old Broadway Central Hotel just came down on the Mercer Arts Center and it was over," says Rev. Alan was actually walking by at that moment and watched the building where history had been made go down. He recalls the Blue Room stage standing bare and forlorn, without any walls surrounding it. Sesu Coleman was next to him, having just fled the collapsing building clutching his drums: "When the Mercer Arts Center collapsed the Magic Tramps were rehearsing inside so we had to scramble out with whatever gear we could grab. As we stood outside in shock, looking up at the remains of the building, Alan Vega walked by, stood next to me and said, 'It's the end of an era'. And it was. It was the end of the beginning."

Tragically, four residents perished. Firemen continued combing the wreckage for bodies the following day, and Mayor John Lindsay ordered his housing and building supervisors to start inspecting the structures of all pre-1901 buildings in the city. Sy Kaback initially hoped his Center could be repaired and re-opened, but it was a lost cause. The buildings at 673 Broadway and 240 Mercer Street were declared unsafe and ordered to be demolished, leaving NYU to buy the block and build the massive dorm which stands there now.

New York City in 1973 was increasingly broke, and was rotting in a sea of vice, crime and uncollected garbage but, after the Mercer's brief supernova, buzzed with a new energy as future artistic offensives brewed in underground pockets. Suicide had welcomed the Mercer residency but had never stopped casting around for other platforms, and were still playing at the Project of Living Artists. By the time of the two 'Punk Mass' shows they played there in May 1973, the Project had moved from Broadway to a smaller 1882 Tuscan building at 133 Greene Street – in the heart of the thriving SoHo art gallery community. This new space also had a leaky basement which afforded Alan a convenient crash pad and Suicide somewhere to rehearse.

On September 29, Suicide played at Talent-Recon on West 38th Street. A Bronx band called Sniper opened. Their singer was one Jeffrey Hyman from Forest Hills. With his gangling height, shyness and yet-to-be-diagnosed Obsessive Compulsive Disorder underlining an other-worldly demeanour, Jeff had spent his first 22 years as a misfit target for bullies and establishment figures. His early life saw him curled up with his rock'n'roll radio, soaking up Herman's Hermits, the Who, bubblegum and girl groups. When he tried becoming a hippie in 1967 he ended up in the mental ward after a bad acid trip. After being thrown out of home by his mother's new boyfriend, he gravitated to downtown's glam scene, renamed himself Jeff Starship, and started writing lyrics about dysfunctional families and mental illness. Alan recalls "this tall, skinny creature with black gloves and glasses who looked like he was on another planet from the rest of the band", and Jeff asking him if he knew a band he could play with. The following year he would hook up with fellow Forest Hills degenerates Doug Colvin and John Cummings and the next time Alan saw Jeff he was calling himself Joey Ramone, sharing the same surname as the rest of his new band.

For decades, the rank old watering hole at 315 Bowery had been the Palace Bar, a last chance saloon under the Palace Hotel flophouse. It catered for bikers and the bums who staggered in at eight in the morning for their daily liveners.

This faded institution was run by a big, bearded jazz and blues buff called Hilly Kristal, who never could have dreamed where his lifelong passions for music and drinking were going to take him when he took it over in 1969. Hillel Kristal's life before the Bowery is another classic New York story, starting when his father and mother's uncle emigrated separately to America from Russia in the early 20th century, looking to farm its land rather than settle in its cities. Hilly's mother was a bohemian jazz fan, who loved to frequent the Greenwich Village clubs, where she met his insurance salesman father. After Hilly was born in 1931, the family moved to the idealistic proto-hippie co-op farm founded in Highstown, New Jersey by his uncle, Benjamin Brown.

Hilly was a talented musician from an early age, learning violin at the Settlement School in Philadelphia between stints working on the farm. Trying to make a living through music, he found a lucrative sideline as a club crooner, but also studied opera and took voice lessons. Moving to Manhattan at 20, he worked various odd jobs, before a stint in the Marine Corps saw him DJing on the army radio station. After returning to New York, he drove cabs and worked in restaurants, before becoming sales representative covering the Lower East Side for a shipping company. His bass baritone voice landed him in the chorus at Radio City Music Hall, singing behind the Rockettes for three fun-packed years.

Hilly then broke into New York's club scene by becoming manager of the Village Vanguard in the late fifties, putting on names such as Miles, Mingus and Monk, before deciding to open his own club. He started with Hilly's on Ninth Street, mixing jazz and crooning with folk nights, then Hilly's In The Village on 13th, concentrating on folk and blues. Then he happened upon the Palace Bar.

The Bowery's booze-sodden reputation goes back centuries, but was particularly exacerbated by the enormous numbers of bars and grog shops which proliferated there in the 19th century, including the huge German-style Atlantic Garden next to the Old Bowery Theatre, and the terrifying McGurk's Suicide Hall, in which six suicides occurred in 1899 alone. By then under the grimy shadow of the Third Avenue elevated railway until the late fifties, the thoroughfare continued to decline throughout the 20th century, although the name was made famous by the Bowery Boys movies of the forties, in which a gang of local kids tangled with mobsters and cops, and Lionel Rogosin's stark 1956 movie *On The Bowery*.

By then the area was the despair-ridden stretch of dive bars, liquor stores and flophouses that the name will always conjure, even after that inevitable day comes when it's been completely consumed by the corporations, trustafarians and self-obsessed yuppie variations who can afford the astronomically priced shiny towers which continue to engorge lower Manhattan. But, back in the early seventies, the number of alcoholics, derelicts, disturbed Vietnam veterans and former mental institution inmates embedded in the area ran into the thousands.

Hilly started presenting live music at his bar around that time. Future Heartbreakers guitarist Walter Lure recalls seeing a friend's country-rock band there around 1971 and former Coltrane drummer Rashied Ali played regular gatherings. Eric Emerson knew about Hilly's through his friendship with the local Hells Angels. Eric had grown up in New Jersey with the future Vice President of the New York chapter, and liked to hang out at their clubhouse on East Third Street. "The Angels loved Eric and he was known as the honorary Golden Angel," says former partner Elda Gentile. "He even had his own pair of feather Angel wings, which he wore when performing, and sometimes just riding a bike through the streets of New York. When Hilly first bought the bar, he welcomed the Angels as a reasonable replacement for the Bowery bums, because they spent plenty of money on booze. So Eric and the Magic Tramps played at Angels' parties there."

"We convinced Hilly to let us play there," recalls Sesu Coleman. "He said, 'This is a biker bar, no one wants to hear rock'n'roll. Besides there's no stage.' The Hells Angels knew and liked Eric and gave their blessings, so we went on the streets to find wood and carpets, and built a makeshift stage. Hilly liked blues and jazz so we opened the club with a jazz band."

Marty Rev knew the bar, recalling, "Hilly lived in his room at the back of the club with his wife and dogs. You could go in there any time of the day and it would still be empty. It was the Hells Angels' place. If they weren't there, there was nobody there except the dogs."

It was a bleak spot to try and launch a club, as Walter Lure remembers, "Pictures of post-war Berlin, or London after the blitz, would pretty much describe the Bowery and most of downtown Manhattan back then, without much of the destruction, but all the bleakness. There were multiple transient hotels for homeless people which were little more than big rooms with 100 bunk beds or mattresses thrown about for people to sleep on for a dollar a night, as well as a few dirty bars for drunks to feed their habits when they begged a few dollars on the streets. The rest of downtown Manhattan wasn't much better with all the slums in the

East Village headed east on Avenues A through D. Danger lurked, with shootings and murders being reported on a daily basis."

While the Mercer was still packing them in, and before closing his other bar on 13th Street due to noise complaints and falling attendances, Hilly was content putting on his low level country, blues, folk and jazz artists. Wayne County and Queen Elizabeth's appearance in December 1973 marked the start of Hilly's stepping up to put on local rock bands (although that month also saw a long-forgotten outfit called the Wretched Refuse String Band).

The mind can only boggle at the regulars' reaction to Wayne's pink afro wig, garish slap, grubby lingerie and high heels; howling about incest while humping a mannequin on 'Dead Hot Mamma', belting out 'It Takes A Man Like Me To Fuck A Woman Like Me', brandishing a double-ended dildo in 'I'm Your Wonder Woman', and other XXX-rated antics which made Wayne one of the most infamous attractions at the time.

Wayne, now Jayne, stands as one of the most fearless, taboo-shattering trailblazers of the last century, and became an early champion of Suicide after sharing the bill with them at the Mercer. When Wayne first appeared with a band in 1971, things taken for granted today, such as men wearing make-up, homosexuality, cross-dressing and swearing in the media, were not only considered dangerous and forbidden, but could be liberty or life-threatening. Wayne took his barbed wit and passion for classic rock'n'roll, then mixed them up with old school glamour and a taste-trouncing apprenticeship in Andy Warhol's inner production circle which spilled into his songs and performances.

Hailing from redneck-ruled Georgia, Wayne Rogers arrived in New York City in 1968, renaming himself after Michigan's tough women's prison and participating in the weekend-long Stonewall riot of June 1969, which launched gay rights in New York. After Jackie Curtis asked Wayne to play a lesbian prison inmate in *Femme Fatale* at La MaMa Experimental Theatre Club (alongside the young Patti Smith as "an Italian Mafia dyke boss with a huge penis"), Wayne went on to write, direct and star in *World: Birth Of A Nation*. "The boys in my play wore women's shoes, make-up, ribbons in their hair... and that's all!" he told me in 1977. "Every second there was something going on...people dying, fucking, killing, police raiding, people cutting each others' cocks off and eating them! Warhol was there and he was jumping up and down in his seat!"

Wayne was in Warhol's 1971 play *Pork*, based on Brigid Polk's telephone conversations which, after opening in New York City, was staged at London's Roundhouse in 1971 to a hail of outrage in the press. "And Bowie just stole everything. His whole look came from us and the cast of *Pork*," protested Jayne later.

While his knowledge of music, especially sixties beat and garage rock, had already secured him the DJ post at Max's, Wayne, as she was still known then, decided to form a "shock rock'n'roll" band, going on to become stars of the Mercer before the landmark Hilly's one-off gig. "I heard about this place called Hilly's from my guitar players at the time, Tommy and Jimmy Marcus. They said it was a hangout for Hells Angels and usually only had folk acts and country banjo players, but Hilly wanted to start opening up the place for other types of music. I was on the cover of *Melody Maker* and known worldwide. I hate blowing my own pussy but I get sick of hearing that same old myth that Television were the first band to play CBGB. Wayne County played four whole months before Television! CBGB was not an empty, barren bar before Television strolled along, then peered through the broken windows and said, 'Oh look, sailors! We have discovered an unknown and unexplored bar, let's jump ship and play there!' That is just not true. I have always had to fight for my rightful place in rock'n'roll history."

Contrary to another myth, Suicide didn't play Hilly's until the following June. By then it had been renamed CBGB, although it would it be another three years before the bar would fully acknowledge Suicide's existence.

Anyway, Hilly was only looking to present the kind of music he liked when he put up a new awning carrying the name CBGB and OMFUG (Country, Bluegrass, Blues and Other Music For Uplifting Gourmandizers). The décor remained as before, and stayed that way, gaining grime and graffiti over the next four decades. But as 1974 started with *The Exorcist*'s vomit-hurling battle between demonic lust and dogged Catholic Bible-waving cleaning up at the box office, downtown was about to be possessed by its *next* major musical revolution; one that should have embraced Suicide as its earliest practitioners but, as is so often the case, would still lionise acts which, although highly individualistic in their presentation and attitudes, were nonetheless still steeped in homage to past forms. Suicide were still just too original.

Television rode into CBGB with their duelling guitars and art-rock aspirations on March 31. "Television got in there before Hilly decided what he was going to do," says Marty. "Richard Lloyd approached him like he was Jesus up the ladder and he was John the Baptist, and convinced him to let them play while he was putting up the letters for CBGB. All these bands were on the periphery looking for places to play. They would find whatever they could because there really was no scene then."

Television's Sunday residency through April provided the breakthrough CBGB experience for many. Patti Smith and Lenny Kaye came the third week and were soon performing there themselves. Elda Gentile and the Stillettoes started playing regularly, laying the foundations for the most commercially successful band to come out of CBGB as co-singer Debbie Harry experimented with her new Blondie persona. "Chris (Stein) calls the Stillettoes the last of the glitter groups," she told me. "It was a sort of campy Shangri-Las/Supremes-type girl trio. We had a lot of fun but we weren't too musical. The record companies at that time were not interested."

Back then, no self-respecting music biz hotshot would have soiled their loafers in such a locale. To the CBs regulars attempting to put their bands together, the decaying isolation and undercurrent of danger added to a tangible buzz that something was happening. "We used to feel we were putting our lives at risk just by hanging out down there," says Walter Lure. "That gave the whole scene the edge that made it feel exciting."

Binky Philips, singer-guitarist with the Planets, who played CBGB over 60 times, recalls, "The Bowery, during at least the first 15 years of CBGB's existence, was the single worst and saddest street in all of Manhattan; the ultimate skid row, complete with the bodies of hopeless, passed out drunks and these pathetic denizens of squalor and misery laying on the sidewalk in front of the club. Perfect!"

"CBs was just like going into somebody's crummy basement," recalls Chris Stein. "There were big, stuffed easy chairs and Hilly had these dogs that would crap all around. It was all very funky." Hilly's dogs were legendary, as Walter confirms, "The best bit was Hilly's dog, which used to wander through the club, leaving droppings for unsuspecting aspiring punk rockers to plough their feet into, bringing them back down to earth a little."

So far, 1974 had only seen Suicide playing what they now called 'Dream Rock' at the Project for two nights that February, as well as performing at a mysterious club called Brandy II. This snake's-arse-level profile might have been demoralising for any other band facing its fifth year of existence, but the ball started rolling again when Alan and Marty developed an unlikely relationship with Brooklyn rock'n'roll band the Fast, which led to them making their CBGB debut.

Formed in 1971 by Zone brothers, Miki, Paul and Mandy, the Fast were Mercer veterans who risked daily mutilation by strutting the macho streets of Italian Brooklyn in their make-up and satin strides, and had been fiercely devoted to the Dolls, Magic Tramps, Wayne County and Suicide. Writing in his excellent photographic memoir *Playground: Growing Up In The New York Underground*, Paul Zone is another brave soul who places himself among the few who enjoyed Suicide's Mercer performances; even after "Alan chased audiences to the exits by terrorising anyone close enough to jump on, kiss, lick or smear his silver face paint on." He recalls how his brothers and their girlfriends would sometimes be the only people to show up at Suicide's Project shows. "We knew they were fantastic, with Alan whispering, crying, screaming, dancing, and sometimes even singing along with Martin's thunderous, crackling and distorted, broken down keyboards… At their best they excited and entertained us with theatricality and genius possessed by no other act in the scene at the time."

In the absence of suitable venues, the Fast booked small theatres and staged extravagant shows. They invited Suicide to share the bill at four shows in March at the intimate 88-seater Townhouse Theater on West 48th Street where Television had recently made their live debut. Suicide were highly appreciative, if fairly stunned, to be given such a rare opportunity without even asking but, as Marty recalls, "The Zone brothers from Brooklyn were into us right away. They used to rent this beautiful little theatre right across from Times Square. They got two weekends and asked us to open for them."

The two bands repeated the exercise at CBGB on the weekend of June 7, which now counted them among the first 15 bands to play the club. Although Alan and Marty got on well with Hilly, as they did with most people, the CBs overseer had a hard time dealing with the noise they made. At least he was pleasant about it, as Marty recalls, "I remember the first time we played CBGB. It was before the scene as we know it had started there. So we did the show, crazy as ever, and went back to the dressing room. Hilly *had* to come back and say something, so he said, 'I don't know what that was, I don't understand it. But I think you may really have something.' Certain bands were something more than he could get with right away. It was a rare show, as CBGB was still three years away from becoming a regular showcase for us, but the gig was great. One of these times, our Fender amp top was lifted overnight from the club before we got a chance to pick it up the next day. Fortunately, word got out that it was ours, and a mysterious phone call was received making arrangements for us to retrieve it."

Two months later, their pal Jeff Starship played CBs for the first time with his new band, the Ramones, having been told about it by Wayne County. When the four misfits in black leather jackets auditioned for Hilly, he described them as the most un-together group he had ever heard, but they soon returned. "At first we played to five people," Johnny Ramone told me in 1976. "Six months later we were playing to 30 people. It was real slow. It didn't seem like the writers were going out to discover new talent. Finally [the writers] came down. Lisa Robinson came to see us, and she went and told other people and everybody came for the second set. In between sets we got more people! After that, everything started building. Mostly we kept playing CBGB, and Max's a couple of times." By the end of the year the Ramones had played CBGB 74 times.

During that time, the scene coalesced and started to mushroom. After the Stillettoes split, Blondie arrived at their first proper line-up in 1975. Talking Heads appeared, drummer Chris Frantz telling me, "CBGB was our musical incubator. The bands were allowed to grow at their own speed until they became good enough to tour the world. If there hadn't been a CBGB, there probably would not have been any Talking Heads." As usual, Wayne County was among its loudest voices, now declaring, "CBGB was a godsend! It wasn't just wanted, it was needed. It helped save rock'n'roll! It gave bands and artists a chance to be heard and seen. It added a magic spark to a city that was crumbling before our very eyes! At that time, New York City was a cesspool of crime, degeneracy, trash-filled streets and raw rock'n'roll, but everyone needed a sort of 'cool rehearsal dump' to play and work out the kinks in their music and image. I was shocked when I first saw it; dog shit on the floor matched with the smell of burnt chilli! I was like, 'What a fucking hellhole!' But playing Hilly's made you want to dress and be trashy, 'cause that was the vibe of the place, not to mention all the future stars getting blasted and passing out in the toilets and on the back stairs. It was really important to have a really trashy downtown bar to play in. A place that would accept new bands, especially ones that were deemed weird or extremely non mainstream, was quite welcome."

Suicide were 'weirder' than any band at that time, and wouldn't play CBGB again until early 1977, but not because Hilly didn't 'get' them. As Marty recalls, "In the daytime, a lot of us had time to kill and would go to CBs and play pool with each other. There were always other musicians there, and I liked to shoot pool, just in the day. I used to go in with Alan. At that time, they had a guy who was managing the place in the daytime, who made a rule that you gotta buy a drink if you're shooting pool. I didn't buy a drink and was obviously not feeling very co-operative, so I just kept on playing. The next day I found out I was banned from the club."

Rather than coming as the kind of major blow which would poleaxe other bands, this petty tantrum from a jobsworth had the opposite effect in the course Suicide sailed through the next few years. A few blocks north lay Max's Kansas City.

ELEVEN

"CBGB was a unique animal unto itself as the place was a right shithole that had this desolation shithole-row type of charm," says Walter Lure. "The place stank and was in a rotten neighbourhood, but that was part of its attraction; the anti-glam factor. Punks always fancied themselves as down and out rebels living drugged-out on the edge. Max's was at the other end of the spectrum. It had been a trendy Warhol gang hangout in the late sixties and early seventies, and really was sort of decadent and glitzy. After the Warhol gang faded away, the punks took over and gave it a bit of street credibility. The place still was a nice-looking club that had a decent restaurant on the ground floor and good music on the second floor."

Max's was much more up Suicide's street with its towering artistic legacy and less self-conscious cliques. Under its next owners and the guidance of Peter Crowley, this would be the club where Suicide's fortunes changed and they first got on record. But in 1974, it was still a struggle for them to get a foot in the door.

While artists still frequented the front bar, the 30 foot deep back room had achieved an elite notoriety after being adopted by the Warhol crowd in the late sixties. Its low-lit ambience still attracted huge stars and artists behaving badly. Meanwhile, the live room had played host to the Stooges (with Iggy famously slashing his chest after returning with *Raw Power*) and Dolls. "Us younger kids, like Patti Smith, Wayne County, David Johansen and the fantastic New York Dolls, who were part of the back room, began to have more relevance," says Elda Gentile. "Max's focus went to music and the days of Warhol's dominance began to wane."

After the Mercer's collapse, Mickey Ruskin started allowing in more local musicians, such as Patti Smith and Lenny Kaye - who supported veteran activist folkie Phil Ochs in December 1973. Max's also broke with its policy of only presenting acts signed to record companies by giving Television and Patti a five day stint in August 1974.

Marty and Alan had asked Mickey Ruskin about playing at Max's a couple of years earlier. Ivan Karp had even sent a letter of recommendation, which prompted a provisional Easter date before Ruskin backed out when Suicide called to confirm. In early 1974, Marty returned and ended up leaving a reel-to-reel demo tape with booking manager Sam Hood, but had still heard nothing after a few weeks. Too impoverished to be flinging reel-to-reels about, Marty decided to go and get the tape back. Sporting his 'Suicide'-studded jacket, hat, shades, and steel pole, he turned up at Max's and found Hood in his office.

Marty soon began to feel like a fly on Hood's coffee cup, recalling how "He only seemed to be hiring guys who'd just made records for Sony, and said, 'I'm sorry, I can't book you'. So I asked him for the tape back. I sat down, thinking 'I'm just gonna sit here until he finds the tape'. He started looking for it, going through boxes, but still couldn't find the tape. I had no other place to go, and I didn't care, now we weren't getting a gig. Then, at some point, I started to nod, like having a siesta. All of a sudden, he decided he would give us a showcase. I guess he had been worried about me nodding out in his office. Maybe he thought I was high or overdosing, or something. I sat there and could see what was happening, so I kept it up. To top it off, he walked me to the elevator. He wanted to make sure I got on the elevator okay and wasn't going to nod out. I don't know why he was so worried. I did not expect that, but it was like getting out of the army. I walked out and said to Alan, 'We got a gig at Max's!'"

The *Village Voice* ad for Suicide's Max's debut on August 6 quoted Roy Hollingworth's *Melody Maker* review, one from *Variety* calling them "the most bizarre act around" and that *Village Voice* review declaring that they were "the hippest act in town."

Suicide had been slotted in over a showcase for a major label glam band. In the audience was Craig Leon, another early fan and vital figure in their story. Born in Miami in 1952 and growing up in Florida, where he opened his first studio, Craig would soon become another seminal presence in the downtown revolution, producing debut albums by the

Ramones, Blondie, Richard Hell and Suicide. He was already working in the studio assisting producer Richard Gottehrer, who had co-written sixties hits such as 'My Boyfriend's Back' and 'I Want Candy'. Gottehrer had also founded Sire Records with Seymour Stein in 1966.

Craig had already done some work at Sire when he found out from his friend Paul Nelson (the man who had signed the Dolls to Mercury) that London Records was planning to launch an American branch of Jonathan King's UK Records in New York, and was looking for an A&R scout. After reasoning "Maybe I'd want that instead of Sire, which was an unknown entity at that time," Craig went for an interview with "this old school, cigar-smoking kind of A&R guy," who assigned him to "go around this weekend, then give me a report, tell me what you've got. If I like your observations, maybe you can work for us instead of Sire."

Craig knew his friend Terry McCarthy, whose apartment he was staying at, was managing a band who were also on the same showcase as Suicide that weekend at Max's. Having long forgotten McCarthy's band, beyond it being "a Roxy Music-Dolls imitation in high heels," Craig was about to leave after their undistinguished set, but impetuously decided, "I'm gonna stay and check out this thing called Suicide that's playing next. There were more people to see the glam band than stayed to see Suicide."

He was glad he did. Speaking now, Craig's most abiding memory is of Alan "swinging these chains and hitting the table in the front row. One of the important things about the gig, that I thought was cool, was that he was going one step beyond Iggy Pop. Suicide were the first people in New York who really coined the punk thing. There were by now only about eight people in the audience, and he was swinging these chains and making a big noise with them. Marty was making like loud Velvet Underground walls of noise, but it had rhythm, although not as rhythmic as it became on the album. Alan had his hair up in a do and was wearing something very sixties R&B, like a leopard skin coat or something like that. He was jamming and doing a kind of James Brown thing over it. I thought they were phenomenal, because it was something totally new. I was very aware of the German bands then, and they reminded me of Can, a lot. Not so much Ash Ra Tempel or Popol Vuh, it was a lot more melodic than them. My favourite Can record was *Monster Movie*. That repetitive thing of 'You Doo Right' and 'Father Cannot Yell' was kind of like what I thought Suicide was doing that night, in a very New

York underground kind of way. Can's singer Malcolm Mooney was kind of like the Teutonic version of Alan, except he was very restrained in comparison. I really thought Suicide were great."

Excited at his discovery, Craig hurtled into London Records on Monday morning, enthusing about this group he had seen called Suicide. He told his prospective boss how they didn't have bass or drums, just a guy playing a keyboard, and another one singing, "except not really singing because it was like hardcore downtown art stuff...I said I thought this band was great, doing something really innovative and new. In my bright-eyed innocence, I thought that something new and different was what the label would be looking for if they wanted a young guy working for them to find new bands. In essence, they did, but they didn't want them quite that different! Obviously the name wasn't right for the label, right off the bat. He said, 'We'll get back to you, kid.' I didn't get the gig, which cemented the fact I was going to stay at Sire, so I ended up not getting a job because of Suicide! I didn't meet Suicide at that time, I just made a mental note and put them on my list."

Although Suicide got to play a return gig, as 1974 progressed, Max's started falling on hard times, exacerbated by three fires and the Warhol crowd drifting on to One University Place and the Ocean Club on Chambers Street. In her book *High On Rebellion*, Yvonne Sewall-Ruskin accuses the glam crowd of taking over the night scene, a move which drove away the more generic arts scenesters who had traditionally patronised the club. "Mickey became bored with his own party. He had filled too many stomachs without filling his own pockets," she writes. "This combination of factors - the fires, thefts, unpaid tabs, and drugs - contributed to Max's demise." The club closed in December, marking the end of an era, and one of the most vital artistic hubs of New York's twentieth century, but it wouldn't be the last the world heard from the venue.

The winter of 1974 saw Marty forced to temporarily move out of his studio flat after Mari had moved in with the whole family, which was then four kids, a cat and a dog. "I had allergies to cats so I split for a while," recalls Marty. "At first, I went to this freezing little room at the Project where Alan had stayed. Now he was living with his girlfriend in Brooklyn, he gave me the keys."

By then the main janitor was artist Joe Catuccio, who "wasn't so happy about seeing one of us sleeping there again. He really liked having that place to himself. Joe used to paint there; these very large, almost modern religious paintings. He was like a Michelangelo of his time. I only stayed there a couple of nights. At night I would go to Max's. Howie Wolper saw me there and said 'You gotta come and stay with me.' He had a loft downtown with his girlfriend, who was Elodie Lauten, the electronic composer. The three of us would sleep on the floor. That kept me going for a while until Mari found another place in Brooklyn." (Catuccio moved out of Greene Street in 1997 and still operates a Project of Living Artists in Brooklyn.)

Still banned from CBGB and with another club gone, Suicide retreated to the Project to give their sound a makeover. One of Marty's most momentous strokes in sculpting his fermenting instrumental panoramas was also his most romantic. After Mari had stopped playing drums at rehearsals, he had stuck to his declaration that she would never be replaced by a human, preferring to explore the rhythmic nuances which congealed in the amped-up feedback roaring out of his overdriven organ, or using his one-man-band snare-cymbal combination. Now it had become time for Suicide to introduce a discernible beat, if only to give Alan a firmer platform to grasp as song ideas continued to form in the lyrical phrases he was playing with.

"One night, it just came to me," recalls Marty. "The perfect idea which was gonna change everything!"

Get a machine to do the drums.

Now that seems such a natural choice but, in 1975, the very concept of replacing a flesh and blood drummer with a box of circuits was alien, audacious and even sacrilegious. Previously, the United States Of America had sprinkled primitive electronic beats on their epoch-making 1968 debut album, but it had hardly been central to the action. The hissing rhythm box underpinning the murky stratas of Sly Stone's *There's A Riot Goin' On* in 1971 fitted perfectly (if often dismissed as a product of his coked-out derangement). That year, I witnessed Kingdom Come, the group formed by madcap singer Arthur Brown after the demise of his Crazy World, play a show bolstered by the mechanised percussion of the Bentley Rhythm Ace, manufactured by Ace Tone, the Japanese predecessor to the Roland Corporation. The band's 1972 album, *Journey*, was the first whole album to feature entirely electronic drums. Kraftwerk's mechanical beats, which were introduced as a robotic component on 1973's *Ralf And Florian*, after 'Kling Klang' on the previous year's *Kraftwerk 2*, came from a preset organ's rhythm box until they started constructing their own.

Marty knew about the rhythm boxes being used by organists at weddings. "I'd always seen these drum machines. Every once in a while you'd get invited to someone's wedding, or confirmation. Those guys would be playing a keyboard piano or accordion, using a rhythm machine, and they'd entertain the whole house. They couldn't afford a band so they got one or two people and used rhythm machines."

These humble, money-saving devices gave Marty a radical new plan to change Suicide's music from the bottom level up. "I could really see it, like it was visual. It was a whole new depth of space, and concept of arranging, where you could just play with the parts. Bands were pretty much in a format at that point, which was starting to dictate the content. If you really wanna change radically, you've got to change the whole thing, the sound of the music itself from its basics, and really get away from it. I didn't really have that all worked out at first in my head but, all at once, I just had this vision of how cool it would be to try."

The first stab at inventing a machine to produce rhythms dates back to Leon Theremin's rhythmicon of 1932 which, after proving too hard to use, lay forgotten until 25 years later when California's Harry Chamberlin created a machine called the Chamberlin Rhythmate, which was stacked with tape-loop snippets of drumkits playing assorted beats. In 1959, Wurlitzer released the mahogany-housed Sideman, the first commercially produced drum machine, intended to provide electro-mechanical rhythmic accompaniment for its organ range by offering 12 different electronically generated rhythm patterns with speed control, which could combine popular grooves of the day such as the waltz and foxtrot. In 1960, New York-based electronic pioneer Raymond Scott unveiled his Rhythm Synthesizer, followed three years later by a drum machine he called Bandito the Bongo Artist, which he used on 1964's ground-breaking *Soothing Sounds For Baby*.

Through the sixties, rhythm machines became more compact than the original floor-standing models, and fully transistorised after home organ manufacturer Gulbransen collaborated with automatic musical equipment company and renowned jukebox makers Seeburg to produce the Rhythm Prince, which was the size of a guitar amp head and used electro-mechanical pattern generators (preceding the Select-A-Rhythm device installed into electronic organs later that decade). The Rhythm

Prince became Marty's first drum machine, after he spotted a second-hand model for sale in the paper, making the journey to Queens to buy it for $30 from a couple whose 19-year-old daughter bought it to accompany her poetry. They told him she had recently committed suicide.

Up until then, Suicide 'songs' had been built on Marty's riffs or chord progressions, which meshed into their own internal pulses, over which Alan sent phrases which coalesced into songs. Now everything changed. "To me, the rhythm was implied in the riff," explains Marty. "At some of those gigs, when we were still doing pure electronics with the amp, the riff and feedback synched up as a rhythm, without steering it in a more recognisably percussive way like it would have with drums. Once I brought the drum machine in, the propulsion was however I interpreted the rhythm, and whatever it meant to me. What made rock'n'roll always work for me, without even realising it, was that rhythmic energy when I heard a great record."

While Kraftwerk despised the preset rhythms found in drum machines, so much so that they ended up building their own, Marty embraced them, working flickering Latin-based grooves into new Suicide songs such as 'Sneakin' Around', which sees him doctoring Cream's 'Sunshine Of Your Love' riff, and 'Space Blue Bamboo'; the first of many quivering garage and R&B riff mutations. In the middle of a scorching hot summer, which was also New York's wettest in recent history, Suicide embarked on a rigorous writing and rehearsal regime in their leaking basement under Greene Street.

"That's where we were spending most of our time," says Marty. "We were always there. Alan was living there at the time. That was like our home away from home. Our hangout off the streets." The new drum machine motivated the pair into recording these first experiments on Alan's two-track recorder, with Marty's Rhythm Prince and organ going through a guitar amp into one input and Alan's vocals into the other. After nearly five years in existence, Suicide finally got down to recording their first proper demos, which Marty likes to describe as "ecstatic adventures, part hallucinogenic; a very powerful new sound suggesting all kinds of visions."

While the yearning 'Space Blue' and eerily weightless 'Speed Queen' appeared on 1981's ROIR cassette release *Half Alive*, along with a spikey missive called 'Long Talk', many more emerged as a great lost record when they accompanied Blast First's 1998 reissue of the second Suicide album. Marinated by time and years in storage embalming this miraculous document like a faded sixteenth century map, the corroded lo-fi ambience actually adds to the haunting intimacy and ghostly atmosphere of songs such as fifties rock-riff-heisting 'Spaceship', techno beat-presaging 'Creature Feature', mysterioso organ-draped 'A-Man' and masturbating stick insect click of 'Do It Nice', where the impact and implications of Marty's new Rhythm Prince becomes most evident. While the malevolent drone-bed and sparking magnesium riffage of 'See You Around' gives an idea how Suicide might have sounded at those early, pre-drum machine shows, 'Into My Eyes' (confusingly mis-titled 'Space Blue' on *Half Alive*) is a shimmering prototype for the first album's 'Che', Alan imploring "sweetheart" over Rev's almost religiously sepulchral organ. 'C'mon Babe' blueprints 'Cheree' and has to be the source of the "I love you" cooings picked up on at the Mercer by both the *Village Voice* and *Melody Maker*.

Throughout these smoky apparitions, Alan's voice billows like stage-whispered black clouds, a hissing demon on Marty's shoulder as the keyboards emit sudden bursts of crackling static and dismembered proto-riffs on truly startling outings such as 'Too Fine For You' and time-suspending 'New City'. One of the most striking factors about tracks such as the luminescent 'Be My Dream' is that, far from being the shattering assault of legend, here was doo-wop soul and cinematic sensibility, awakening in the telepathy between Alan's more considered home recording persona and Marty's melodic tapestries. Although bare wired, shivering and waiting for the train to take it to the next stage, the recordings show that Suicide's sound was now in place, and also suggested that they could make great records.

Suicide also recorded the prototype 'Dream Baby Dream' at New York's Sun Dragon studio around that time. At that point called 'Dreams', it shimmers with a pure glistening soul, sensual rhythm and the kind of innocently simple melody which characterises their best work. Returning to his ongoing sculpture analogy, Marty says "We were really starting now. The carving out process was getting to where there were actual tracks that we could take to record companies as demos to try and get deals. We tried some, but not with any success."

That same year, Lou Reed released *Metal Machine Music*. Its four sides of cacophonous feedback mortified his record company and nonplussed the public, although Alan says it's his favourite Reed album. Whether Lou had meant the album as confrontational artistic statement, or an act of revenge after the disappointingly harsh critical reaction to *Berlin*, it was the most controversial album of his career. Marty isn't sure if Lou had seen Suicide at that point, but *MMM*'s speaker-bleeding barrage was possibly the nearest approximation of what the duo had been invoking at shows for the last five years. *Metal Machine Music* might even have served as a subliminal aperitif for Suicide's eventual appearance in the outside world, just by title alone.

At this point, the cogs in the universe would seem to be shifting at full throttle for Suicide (for the moment anyway). Next, they would find themselves back in a familiar spot, but this time the new weapons at their disposal, along with timing, would start to assure them of their place in the metropolis which had previously snubbed them.

By 1974, the cerebral pull of New York City had proved too much for Peter Crowley to resist. Having been "isolated" in San Francisco since the early seventies, he had missed upstairs at Max's, the Mercer Arts Center, birth of CBGB and gestation of Suicide. After a thankless stint managing the band which turned into Mink DeVille, he returned to find the city facing bankruptcy and imminent collapse (as did Abe Beam, who was forced to make further cutbacks in services when he was sworn in as Mayor that January).

"New York was sleazy and getting worse by the day, which didn't bother me any, but it was," recalls Peter. "When I discovered Times Square in the late fifties, it was sleazy, but the porn was under the counter. You didn't have everything in your face. The police were square then too, and didn't know what we were up to. Then the hippies put everything on the street. We all contributed to putting bohemian culture on the front pages of magazines, which was a major error. It was much more fun when the squares were square, and didn't know anything. I came back around the time of the first CBGB explosion. I had missed the New York Dolls because I was wasting my time in San Francisco, but then I discovered Wayne County at the Club 82."

Situated at 82 East Fourth Street, off Second Avenue, Club 82 briefly filled the void left by the Mercer and now Max's, as one of the only downtown venues willing to embrace glam-leaning local bands. It was first opened in 1958 as a lesbian hangout for Anna Genovese, wife of mob boss Vito, who found it handy for his East Village heroin trade. Now operated by two women going by the names Tommy and Butch, the basement bar was famous for being the one venue where the Dolls actually did drag up for a performance, on their April 1974 tour of New York's clubs. Sylvain recalls "It looked all tropical. The Copacabana goes gay, if you will. The centre of it was the actual stage, like a square. The bar was completely around the stage. We would hang down there."

Marty, who moved into an apartment on Fourth in 1975, recalls Club 82 as "like an after-hours, underground syndicate-type place from the thirties, and a transvestite club for many years. Somebody got in there and convinced them to start doing shows with the neighbourhood bands." Tommy was just about able to stomach the Dolls, but Marty remembers her being so "appalled" by Suicide that she screamed at them to stop ("although she would always be perfectly pleasant when I passed her in the street").

Witnessing Club 82's glammed up decadence and Wayne County in his long blonde wig and gold lamé bathing suit brought Peter Crowley back into the downtown loop. "When I arrived back in New York it was the first place I went to," he recalls. "I didn't know Wayne as a rock'n'roller, only his previous incarnation in the theatre. I ended up becoming his manager. I never expected any commercial success, but somebody just needed to do it. I went to Hilly for a gig and he turned me down. I couldn't understand it. After three attempts, I asked Wayne if there was something I didn't know about. Wayne said Hilly was probably mad at him for not getting back to him about doing another CBGB gig. Anyway, he wouldn't give me a date and I couldn't figure that out because Wayne was one of the biggest draws in New York at that time. So then I went and did Mothers."

Resourceful as ever, Peter visited a "very interesting character" he knew in the Village called Mike Umbers, who "was kind of a gangster without a gang, a freelance guy not connected with the Mob but involved in slightly shady businesses." Peter told him his predicament: "Mike, do you know of a bar where I can put on a show because I have an act that I can't get booked?"

"Not only do I know one, I know one that owes me money!" replied Mike.

The pair hopped in Mike's car and drove up to 23rd Street and Eighth Avenue, locating a little bar called Mothers, over the street from the Chelsea Hotel. The place seemed dead on its feet, as Peter recalls, "Apparently, Mike had fronted money for the guy to open this gay bar and it had failed. Mothers was two small storefronts side by side. The first one had the traditional bar down one wall, a jukebox at the back, then a doorway that went through to the second one, where there was a small stage where they had had drag shows or whatever, silly things. Seated in there were a couple of alcoholic old queens, the owner, who also fit into that category, and a handsome young Thai gentleman who was the bartender. And that was it. There were no customers."

Maybe not too politely, Mike informed the owner that Peter would be promoting shows at Mothers. This was another world from the arty dog-shit ambience of CBGB, being more focused on unfettered fun, and also funkier thanks to its jukebox stacked with juicy disco and flamboyant Warren, "the quintessential gay waiter, who would sashay around to disco songs, with the tray held above his head and wait on all the punk rockers. It was a hysterically funny clash of cultures, and yet it worked because everybody loved Warren, and having disco was better than if you'd tried to have a hip jukebox. It was just a totally funny kind of thing."

Peter made the bold move of putting Wayne on for a week when Mothers opened for business in mid-1975. For a few months, it became a hotspot. "We started off with a bang," remembers Peter. "It was such a small place that, if I had somebody who drew a few hundred people, then I would have to have them for more than one night. I did Wayne for a week and it was packed. Then everybody came saying 'Can we have a gig here?' Blondie, Television, Ramones, the whole CBGB crowd, because they were starved for anywhere else to play. Hilly caused himself all this misery and competition because I never would have even thought to do Mothers if he had booked Wayne. Being forced into finding a venue for Wayne, I made my own. I'm quite willing to admit I blatantly stole all of Hilly's acts, but I wouldn't have done it if he hadn't forced my hand."

Peter couldn't steal Suicide as this was while they were banned from CBGB. When they asked for a gig, as they routinely would of any new venue in town, Peter instantly gave them a weekly Thursday residency, starting in October. Most importantly, they were headlining. Having missed their formative shows, Peter only remembered Suicide from seeing them booed by a conservative CBGB crowd the previous June, supporting the Fast. "I was in California when Suicide started out, so I missed the very beginning. They already had a history of opening for various New York bands, essentially to no avail. People would just boo them or walk out. That happened when I saw them at CBGB. When Suicide asked if I would book them as an opening act, I said, 'No, I won't book you as an opening act because that obviously doesn't work. I will give you your own residency. You're the headliner.' The first time there were a dozen people, the second time there were 25 people, the next time there were 40 people. It worked very well."

"Someone told us Peter was booking Mothers," recalls Marty. "One time I called up and got him on the phone. I didn't know who he was, but he knew who we were. He gave me a date right away, but said 'You guys should headline'. Peter was instrumental in the whole thing. He had the mentality and aesthetic to know exactly what was happening. He had an amazing background and had worked in a lot of interesting domains. He never had any doubts about us and totally seemed to know what we were about right away, in a very positive way."

Suicide enthusiastically took to their residency, commencing the defining stretch of this story, which might have taken a different turn had Peter not spotted something in them which reminded him of his time working the lights for the Velvet Underground nearly 10 years earlier.

"Certainly my having been there at the beginning of the Velvet Underground and similar stuff laid the foundation," says Peter. "For me, these bizarre acts were always going to be marginal. I had no idea they were all going to be so hugely influential. I was probably very pleased to be part of this elite cognoscenti, but I didn't think this stuff was ever going to be *pop*."

Most importantly, Peter Crowley took Suicide seriously, and treated them with respect. It was now five years since that first show at the Project. At last, they had a real champion in their corner.

TWELVE

Nursing a $3 billion deficit, New York City had faced likely ruin as 1975 progressed. If disgraced President Nixon had screwed the country, his hapless successor Ford seemed to be buggering New York, peaking with his refusal of a bail-out. This prompted the infamous *Daily News* headline FORD TO CITY: DROP DEAD, before the G6 summit warned of global economic disaster if New York did fall. Meanwhile, the downtown scene's first golden age finally expired that May when Eric Emerson was found dead next to his motorcycle near the West Side Highway. He was presumed the victim of a hit and run. As one of the key bridges between Warhol, Max's glory days, the Mercer and CBGB, and a pioneering tornado in all of them, it was the symbolic end of an era.

Eric's drug use had been escalating towards the end. He had become more uncontrollable and bitter or, as Elda Gentile puts it, "As Max's had to have its end in '74, Eric began to feel the same about his long-standing spotlight, for the first time."

Thankfully Suicide, although happy to have a smoke or occasional trip, never went the route of their friends in the New York Dolls who were also to implode that year. Marty Thau blamed the split on the record company's failure to grasp the Dolls' essence and potential. By this time, he had stepped back from day-to-day management, leaving the opening for Malcolm McLaren to become their benevolent caretaker and tailor for a few weeks in early 1975.

Malcolm first met the Dolls when they visited his Let It Rock boutique on London's King's Road during their previous UK jaunt. Now he was a fan who wanted to relaunch the floundering band with a new image.

In cahoots with Johansen, he came up with the Red Patent Leather concept, which the Dolls took to an extreme, trumpeting an affiliation to the Communist party which, at that time, was still enough to get you villainised in the US. The demoralised, fucked up band splintered during a thankless stint playing the backwoods of Florida, where the heroin ran dry, which sent Johnny Thunders and Jerry Nolan scuttling back to New York. Here, the pair formed the Heartbreakers with Richard Hell, who had been squeezed out of Television, and sauntered into CBGB as degenerate elder statesmen of streetwise rock'n'roll. By the end of June, they'd gained guitarist, singer and songwriter Walter Lure.

"Malcolm used to love the Dolls," recalled Marty Thau. "I used to see him at their shows and he became a friend. Suddenly he was in New York and trying to resurrect them, but unfortunately it was a little too late. If the Dolls had stayed together and made certain personal concessions I think they could have had all they'd hoped for. They were one of the greatest groups of their time. After Malcolm went back to England, he put all that he had learnt in his exposure to the Dolls to very good use. The Sex Pistols filled the void they had left, although Suicide was really the first new fresh thing to come along."

Blondie would actually become the biggest-selling band to emerge from CBGB. Suicide found themselves quite close to them, initially as fellow rank outsiders of the notoriously back-biting downtown scene. While Alan recalls Debbie Harry as "a total sweetheart", Marty might even have ended up joining Blondie in their doldrums period before Jimmy Destri joined on keyboards, as he recalls, "Debbie and I were sitting among others at the bar at Mothers after one of our shows, just talking. She said, 'Would you like to join the group?' Debbie didn't have a keyboard player yet. We didn't follow it up."

Then Malcom McLaren, who Marty knew through his friendship with Dolls wardrobe overseer Barbara Troianni, came up with a scheme which involved Rev forming an MOR-style duo with Debbie. "Now was the time the Dolls were dressing in red vinyl, so they were all up at Barbara's place getting that whole look created," Marty recalls. "One time, Malcolm said to me, 'I'd like to talk to you'. Mickey Ruskin had another bar after Max's, and we met there. Malcolm sat down and said, 'I've got a great idea! You and Debbie could be like the Captain and Tennille!'" This gleaming Californian couple, who'd met while backing the Beach Boys on tour, had just topped the charts with their first hit – a fluffy version of Neil Sedaka's 'Love Will Keep Us Together'.

The idea of Debbie and Marty embarking on such a wholesomely mainstream project is surreal if delightfully subversive but, according to Marty, Malcolm was serious. "The commercial aspect of it was so clear to him with the way we looked, and he must have liked the way I sounded. I don't think I would've come close to being 'The Captain'. Debbie was maybe a lot more flexible and probably could have gotten over as a new Tennille, if she had wanted to! Malcolm was going by the way we looked and dressed, and I definitely understood. Malcolm always had an eye for what was cool, or what would be successful. I never doubted him, but there was no way I could follow that up, as much as I respected Debbie. I always felt Alan and me were the underground, and were getting no favours. If anything, we were often seen as a sort of conspiracy to the status quo. Therefore, I always felt we were like the Che and Fidel of that scene. Then Malcolm went back to England. I saw him at Hurrah's a few years later when he came to one of our shows. He came over to us outside. We were loading the gear in a rented station wagon with Marty Thau waiting for us at the wheel, when we inadvertently smashed the back window to a thousand pieces."

To the relief of many, Max's Kansas City was reopened in autumn 1975 by Tommy and Laura Dean, who initially sought to re-establish its reputation as one of New York's most vital artists' meeting places. At first, the Deans had little intention of muscling in on the action going on at CBGB, devoting Fridays and Saturdays to a Puerto Rican disco, complete with DJ and flashing lights, which drew a large crowd and seemed to alleviate any need to fork out for live bands. But the rest of the week was barren, the restaurant had failed to find a suitable chef, and Tommy was a rock fan. Wayne County had long been one of the fixtures at Max's, so told Tommy to consult Peter Crowley about booking bands. Peter naturally started by promoting Wayne on a Sunday night. After that was successful, he stretched to Mondays and Thursdays until he was putting on bands every night except Friday and Saturday.

"I was in the right place at the right time again," says Peter. "Tommy Dean's failure as a restaurateur when he reopened Max's saved my life, because I was able to go in and dictate terms to him. I could say, 'Tommy, not that you can't ask me anything you ever wanna ask me, but you can't ever start telling tell me what to do, or I will walk out the door. You have to promise me you're not gonna give me any crap, because a lot of the stuff I'm gonna do, you will never understand, but I'm gonna save your venue.' And I did."

Marty recalls the "Brooklyn, Italian, very New York" crowd which started flocking to Max's, adding, "The new Max's was run by someone much more New York. Mickey Ruskin had been the elite maitre d', all the pop artists had their living room there, and that was the scene which dominated. After Mickey moved on, Max's got much more down to earth. It connected with the Vietnam War winding down and then ending."

The Vietnam War ending had shifted the focus from atrocities going on in the Far East to what was happening at home, in a city rotting with corruption, crime and neglect. "There is some validity to the fact that once Vietnam ended there was no focus," says Marty. "Civil Rights was still very much there. There were really great strides – legally, if not realistically. But the war was over and there was a different sensibility. They weren't the most peaceful of times because of what was going on in the city. It was getting worse and worse and more and more obviously unjust. New York went through a very steep economic decline."

Through running Mothers, Peter now had his finger on the pulse beating under the downtown streets. Now he had a proper platform where it could manifest, inevitably stamped with his passion for the rock'n'roll spirit in all its forms – whether Suicide's extreme noise terror, Wayne County's outrageous trans-punk, the Cramps' unhinged psychobilly, and then the post-punk marauders protesting against new wave blandness. Peter came from the original counterculture, and still adhered to its spirit of smashing societal taboos, plus Max's had been his favourite spot in its sixties heyday. While astute enough to know that glam and punk were short-lived fads, he saw Suicide transcending any movements as they wielded the torch which had been lit by Elvis Presley, then mated all the innovations and insurrection which society and culture had thrown up since to forge a livid new sound for the future.

"Peter never had any doubts about us," says Marty. "He started putting us in slowly to build up audiences. Eventually he got us in at weekends and we started making some money for the first time." Peter confirms this. "By the time I came to Max's, Suicide had enough following to warrant being the headliner. That strategy worked. I don't think a lot of people understood what I was doing, but I continued to do it."

Jayne County now sees the Suicide of that time being too much for most people, regardless of where they appeared on the bill. "Oh yes!" she laughs. "They were known as 'room emptiers!' They would be put on last so people would leave. And it worked – people literally *ran* for the exits. I absolutely *loved* them, but most people usually just didn't get it then."

That started changing after Suicide played their first show at the new Max's on Tuesday, March 9, 1976, followed by the landmark Easter festival, which presented bands of the day such as Wayne County, the Heartbreakers, Ramones, Tuff Darts, Marbles and Blondie between April 11 and 22.

"I stole that idea from Hilly," says Peter. "He had done the underground New York rock festival and I said, 'Why not do it on Spring Break when all the college kids are around?' At that point, Tommy Dean didn't allow me to have Friday or Saturday because he still had a very successful Puerto Rican disco in there. I did the festival for two five-day weeks. I put in our *Village Voice* ad that the party continued at CBGB after the festival. They had Television and Patti Smith, whatever. I didn't ask Hilly, I just put that in there."

Suicide appeared on April 13 alongside Pere Ubu from Cleveland, who were making their much-anticipated New York debut. Talking Heads had been on the bill, but cancelled at the last minute.

In the crowd that night was Miriam Linna, one of the heroines of this story. I first met her in the mid-seventies when she was running the Flamin' Groovies fan club and was already destined to become the Cramps' drummer for their first gigs in New York City. "I had come to visit New York City from Ohio, with my sister Helen, to see our hometown favorites Pere Ubu, who had evolved from the great Rocket From The Tombs," she recalls. "We were so thrilled to see Crocus Behemoth and crew in the 'Big Town'. Suicide was on the bill and they impressed the heck out of us that night. Neither Helen nor myself were fans of electronic weirdness; we were pretty much straight ahead rock'n'rollers, but Suicide was beyond the *beyond*. The pulse and volume and the fact that it was two guys delivering what sounded to us like what we had already determined to be 'the Cleveland sound' was pretty astonishing. We felt like country bumpkins at Max's that night, but that feeling would not last for long."

Suicide's next gig was among a legion of downtown luminaries at Manhattan Center on May 30, all playing a benefit for Wayne County's legal defence fund after he had clonked gay-heckling Dictators singer 'Handsome' Dick Manitoba with a weighty microphone stand and broken his collar bone. On June 5 and 6, Suicide commenced the regular Max's shows which built their legend. Playing two shows a night, between midnight and 1 a.m., then 3 to 4 a.m., the duo hit new heights of claustrophobic onslaught. They were now further bolstered by the metronomic bombs of Marty's drum machine, inspiring Alan to continue honing his demonically confrontational stagecraft. Peter's headlining theory was working, as audiences increased at every appearance.

"The thing with Suicide was to create a situation where the audience came to see *them*," says Peter. "That audience grew fairly slowly, but it doubled every time because people would go and tell their friends, 'You have to come and see this band that's different from everybody else'. Every show had a few more people than the one before, until they were really, really headliners. There would always be the newcomers who would scream and run out of the club, but there was also a contingent of rock'n'roll royalty that loved 'em. Many people still didn't realise they were watching this futuristic thing that has Elvis, the Stooges and doo-wop in it. It was all in there. Willie DeVille and me were probably the biggest rock'n'roll snobs on the planet, totally Muddy Waters and the Moonglows, but both of us were huge Suicide fans."

By now, Suicide had become a firm Max's band, and still found themselves shunned by CBGB. "Hilly wouldn't have got 'em," says Peter. "Hilly was a wonderful guy who allowed a lot of wonderful things but, in my opinion, he didn't have a clue. History just swept him up and took him for that ride, and he went with it, which is very much in his favour but he wasn't part of the weirdo contingent! He was just a little out of touch. He would have watched Suicide being either booed or ignored when they were an opening act, and not realised that they should have been headlining in the first place."

"CBGB wasn't our natural home, but Max's was, in many ways," recalls Marty. "There were carpets on the floors, windows and a dressing room. It was more artificial, in a sense a Vegas kind of décor, but that artificiality was very cool in clubs and much more relaxing. You could go to Max's at any time of night, and sit in a booth with other musicians that you knew. CBs was a rustic, all wooden place that attracted certain people. Hilly was much more of a loner in that he wasn't connected to anybody voluntarily. He was an independent guy, who lived in the back with his dogs; a bright, brilliant guy, very much more of a bohemian. When I went to Hilly's, as much as I respected it, I never felt that it was a place I was going to be lounging in, or maybe looking for a girl you knew, or having a drink with her. It was a harder kind of experience, but some bands gravitated there, like Talking Heads and Television. That was always like their place and they were CBs bands."

Marty stresses that he ended up getting to know Hilly, "as much as we were friends and we respected each other", but points out that CBs "wasn't like Max's with Tommy Dean. He was like a New York street guy, who came out of the Italian working class with a Jewish wife, and they ran the place together. They were from similar backgrounds and neighbourhoods. It was more street. Hilly was more country. Eventually I got back into CBs, but Max's was like our living room, a very Queensy, Brooklynish kind of place, even though it wasn't as 'authentic'. That was our place. We ended up playing there regularly. That's where the audience gravitated to us."

As Alan puts it, "We became much more of a Max's band than a CBs band. That's how we got started. Peter opened up the world." Suicide responded with some of their most hardcore performances to date. Even now, Alan gets quite irate about the young Thurston Moore's Suicide review in Bloomington, Indiana's *Gulcher* fanzine. While he could live with Suicide being described as like "heavy metal Kraftwerk on drugs" and "Two dudes: one with bug-eyed shades who intensified mind-fucking synthesised rhythmic beatings to make your blood clot on a Mooged-out keyboard", he objects to being described as "a lead singer with an old lady's wig who's so sick and gross that he actually burns chicks with his cigarettes and then mashes them to the floor with his sweaty bod. Picks your drinks up and pours them on your head. Pulls chicks across the stage by their hair. I once saw this dude walk on a table at Max's, fall on it breaking all the glasses under him, get lifted back on stage, pull the glass out of his chest and arms, only to slice up his face a bit and heave the sharp pieces at us."

Actually harming the audience, particularly girls, was a line Alan never crossed. "Nobody ever got hurt but me!" he protests. "The guy in Sonic Youth swears I was dragging this girl by the hair. That never happened. The music was psychedelic in a way, man. It was so extreme I think people started seeing things within my performances and Marty's music, and just went into some kind of state. The line between fantasy and reality got blurred. People often used to recall witnessing stuff I know never happened. I never hurt anybody, or dragged a woman across the stage. The only one that would get hurt was me. I did used to stop them trying to leave. I used to jump on tables, upset their drinks, but never hurt them, man. Maybe they got a little wet! I used to have a knife and chain, and used to hurt myself and shit, cut myself. I've still got scars all over the place."

"Alan was going into the audience before we even had those tables," recalls Peter Crowley. "On the live 'Rocket USA' you can hear a glass break at one point. That's Alan taking a sideways swing with the microphone into somebody's beer bottle that was sitting on the table. You can hear the bottle shatter. Once, there was a fellow reading a comic book while they were on, so Alan walked over, took the comic from him, ripped it in half and gave it back, because he wasn't paying attention. Alan was like a cross between Gene Vincent and Iggy Pop."

Queens basement band the Fleshtones were early regulars at Suicide shows. Fronted by singer Peter Zaremba and guitarist Keith Streng, they had sailed through their CBGB audition that May with their rambunctious blend of rock'n'roll and party soul, and became one of the hardest working, but proportionally unrewarded, bands in New York. At this time, Zaremba was living in a loft at 17th and Broadway, just around the corner from Max's.

It was love at first sight, as he recalls, "Suicide was unlike anything I had ever seen or heard before, although I could recognise the pulse of rock'n'roll's heart in what they were doing. They were playing rock'n'roll in its purist form. I also dug the confrontational style, not for its own sake, but because they were forcing the audience to acknowledge they were watching real people; that they were alive too. People had gotten to the point where they acted as if they were watching TV and the 'wall' between performer and audience had become inviolable. Suicide demolished all that. If it meant driving out what little audience that was there, so be it. I didn't leave, and neither did Keith. We had been digging performers like Brother Theodore and Sun Ra, people who reached out to the audience and made them part of the experience."

Max's was the ideal space for Suicide's demolition of this divide between band and audience. Seats were provided at narrow, folding tables, each about six feet long by 18 inches wide, coming out perpendicular to the stage. They were especially tempting to be walked on, and usually collapsed when that happened. According to Peter Crowley, the most glorious table collapse at Max's was by UK rock'n'roll revivalists Crazy Cavan and the Rhythm Rockers, who "went crazy and played at a level they had never played in England. The lead guitarist leapt on one of those tables, doing his solo, and the table's collapsing under him, but he rode it down like a surfboard going into the water. The kids in that audience screamed. It was one of the most brilliant rock'n'roll moments you've ever seen in your life."

Peter kept Max's renowned jukebox stocked with over 100 choice 45s, including imports bought from a guy called Michael Searles at Discophile on 8th Street. "He had the Dr Feelgoods, Roxy Musics and all the interesting stuff which didn't have much of an American footprint. He kept me apprised of what was going on out there. There was also Gene Vincent, Elvis Presley, Chuck Berry, Little Richard and Motörhead. I put the Damned and the Pistols on in the fall of '76, when those records came out."

The first local bands to get their singles on Peter's jukebox were Patti Smith and Television. Currently downtown's hottest property after the previous November's *Horses* debut rode her to stardom, Patti was represented by her Hendrix tribute version of 'Hey Joe' and her own 'Piss Factory', which had been released in 1974 on her and Lenny Kaye's Mer label. The emotionally charged 'Piss Factory' towers as one of the most brutally honest, cathartic broadcasts from that whole scene; a kind of personalised 'Frankie Teardrop' as Patti, accompanied by Richard Sohl's piano, tears through her early poem about the mind-numbing factory job she endured in New Jersey before coming to New York. The song struck a chord with anyone who'd ever endured making such a living, including Primal Scream singer Bobby Gillespie, who once told me, "I totally related to it as a kid and still do. It's working class blues."

With this CBs-centric presence growing on his jukebox, Peter Crowley asked Suicide if they had a 45 to redress the balance. As it happened, they had been asking themselves the same thing.

There is only one known copy of the first record to bear the name Suicide. The seven-inch acetate contains basement prototypes of 'Rocket USA' and 'Keep Your Dreams', the forerunner to 'Dream Baby Dream'.

It's long been worn to a pebble sheen after countless plays, being the very same 45 which Suicide gave Peter Crowley to put on the Max's jukebox in 1976. Safely wrapped and protected, it now sits among the singles on Marty Rev's record shelves.

This is the humble 45 that started it all, after it gave Max's patrons their first taste of Suicide on wax and convinced Marty Thau that Suicide could actually make a record.

It started when Rev heard Television's 'Little Johnny Jewel' scratching out of the jukebox a few weeks earlier. "Wow, that's cool," he thought, and asked Tommy Dean, "Can we put a record on there too?" After Tommy replied, "Sure, just give it to Peter," Marty hotfooted back to Greene Street to tell Alan. This could be a break if they recorded some of the songs which had been rearing up at gigs and rehearsals. Suicide started recording, emerging with 'Rocket USA' and 'Keep Your Dreams'.

The former is a jagged, more relentless prototype of the more ethereal version that would appear on the debut album. Marty mercilessly kicks up the grinding two-note riff, letting it run over the blood-pounding, almost subliminal rhythm box tattoo, which he splatters with radioactive flashes and cathedral organ go-go stabs. Sounding hauntingly disembodied, Alan intones the "It's doomsday" refrain from the same spectral chamber as the demos. Subconsciously grabbed by the relentless pulses which had driven Lennie Tristano's jazz excursions, early rock'n'roll and, most recently, disco, Rev homed in on the bottom end, explaining, "Without doing it consciously, I was making a continuous rhythm totally out of that bass drum in Suicide, like on the first 'Rocket USA'."

Meanwhile, 'Keep Your Dreams' rides a snappier groove than the previous year's more opiated Sun Dragon demo. Marty's billowing organ clouds are now underpinned by those majestic chords which would flower into soul-saving dominance when the track received its definitive makeover as 'Dream Baby Dream' three years hence.

"There were guys on 49th Street in those days that would cut acetates," recalls Rev. "It was a small place that cut wax for people on a walk-in basis. You'd go up there and pay two bucks per copy. It was an incredible place but they don't exist any more. We only had enough money to make two copies of it. One we gave to Max's and the other one went to a radio station, who were doing a half-hour documentary on us and wanted that single."

"They brought back this acetate, and I put it on the jukebox immediately," says Peter. "Both sides were relatively popular, although 'Rocket USA' was played more. We had a very open-minded crowd at that time, and Suicide fit in with all the other odd things I put on that jukebox!"

Suicide's single certainly stood out from the 45s on the jukebox. Marty remembers, "We weren't that close with a lot of the bands, but we were all in the same community. When our record came on in the bar at Max's you'd really hear the difference. 'Rocket USA' stood apart as a whole different concept in rhythm."

Such acetates would soon become essential battle weapons for DJs wanting to try out their latest creation in a club, boasting the exclusivity of the world's only copy. The records were only built to last a few spins before the sound started deteriorating. It would have been unheard of to put one on something in such constant use as a jukebox! "It got so worn out after a while – Scraape! Rurgh!" laughs Alan. "We'd be standing there waiting to soundcheck, someone would put the song on, and the bartender would come over and starting kicking the jukebox, trying to get the Suicide record off. And we were playing there!"

Thankfully for Suicide, not all Max's patrons would feel the same way.

THIRTEEN

After Suicide's jukebox single had placed them in the firmament of downtown's burgeoning scene, their presence was consolidated by a first major press interview, which appeared in the second issue of *New York Rocker*, the monthly broadsheet started that January by former Blondie manager Alan Betrock (Suicide would rarely be acknowledged by the recently launched *Punk* magazine). By that time, I was writing for *Zigzag*, the original UK fanzine started by Pete Frame in 1969, which inspired a legion of titles created by fans who assumed, rather than hoped, that their readership was as crazy about the music as they were, and felt under-served by the traditional rock press. Pete got me to write about the new punk bands, which he felt wielded a similar untamed energy to the unfettered rock'n'roll which electrified his own teenage years in the fifties. Inevitably, he attracted like-minds from around the world, such as the mighty Greg Shaw of *Bomp!*, and Betrock when he started *The Rock Marketplace* in 1973. Soon I would be covering the UK's own punk movement for *New York Rocker* but, in May 1976, was intrigued to encounter the name Suicide again, nearly four years after Roy Hollingworth's *Melody Maker* review.

It appeared that Suicide were still very much alive and kicking. In the *New York Rocker* piece Lisa Jane Persky described the "sexual sado-masochistic rock" which had "a devastating effect on everyone left in its wake". It's good, myth-creating stuff, setting a lifelong precedent as Alan is called on to recount the missiles hurled at him, including punches, cigarettes, bottles and chairs, and he talks about a girl who spent a whole Suicide set smashing her head against the wall before collapsing in a pool

163

of blood. Alan came to check she was okay, then sang to her on the floor, but she got up and ran into the wall again. He compared the days of Suicide clearing rooms to their now growing audiences. This was also the first time Alan revealed his affection for New York City and its inhabitants. From now on, he would regularly expound about his city as it changed around him. These days, as he recently told me, Alan is quite disappointed about the paucity of raw materials for his art to be found on today's clean streets.

Now Suicide needed to get their own art on record. They had recorded demos including 'Rocket USA', 'Keep Your Dreams' and 'Ghost Rider'. The latter was Alan's self-described "apocalyptic vision of the future", inspired by his love of the Marvel Comics phantom motorcyclist. It's probably the song most associated with Suicide. "I was totally into Ghost Rider in those days," he recalls. "Ghost Rider was my man."

The image of the eternally damned ghost rider steering his red-eyed phantom cattle herd through the thunder-stricken clouds was first conjured in the song, '(Ghost) Riders In The Sky: A Cowboy Legend', written by country artist Stan Jones in 1948. The following year saw the tune strafe charts and radio in a stream of cover versions by names such as Vaughn Monroe and Roy Rogers. Frankie Laine's 1960 rendition is often held as the definitive encapsulation of the song's dark, thunder-cracking mystery.

The Ghost Rider character first appeared in cowboy comics in the forties, until Marvel rebranded him in 1972 as the cursed, hog-straddling flaming skull figure encased in a black leather jumpsuit inspired, according to co-creator Roy Thomas, by Elvis in his 1968 TV special. The character first showed up in a 1972 *Daredevil* story before commanding his own strip in the *Marvel Spotlight* series. The following year he got his own comic, which followed the adventures of stunt rider Johnny Blaze, who had made a deal with Mephisto to save his dying father and was now doomed to be possessed by the demon Zarathos. At a time when horror-based characters such as Dracula and Swamp Thing were gripping comics, Ghost Rider was the most truly supernatural hero, born out of an unfathomably arcane evil.

Another promising new song started taking shape around then. Alan described it as his tribute to Jim Morrison, being inspired by the Doors' 'The End' but also the Velvet Underground's 'Sister Ray'. This skeletal first version was called 'Frankie Teardrop, The Detective Meets The Space Alien'.

Suicide's next major opportunity again came through Peter Crowley's ongoing mission to bring Wayne County to a wider audience. In 1976, Hilly Kristal released a double album called *Live At CBGB's: The Home Of Underground Rock*, which gave the world a somewhat flaccid impression of his supposedly happening club. Craig Leon, the guy who'd failed his London Records audition by suggesting Suicide as a worthy addition to the roster, had been called in to helm the project. Hilly had originally hoped the bands he'd allowed to play at his club would return the favour by appearing on his album (not that he asked Suicide). Craig actually did record most of them, envisioning an Alan Lomax-style field document boasting the likes of Patti, Television, Blondie and the Ramones, but they all refused to be corralled into the same compound, and Craig was left with newcomers such as Mink DeVille, the Shirts, Tuff Darts and a few obscure others.

Naturally, Max's wanted its own album. Although Peter Crowley was turned down by the Heartbreakers, Blondie and the Planets, *Max's Kansas City 1976* fared much better than the CBs set. This time acts were represented by studio recordings. And it was the first time the world got to hear Suicide.

For Peter, it would be the only way of getting Wayne on wax with current band the Backstreet Boys. His most recent attempt had taken him to ESP-Disk, former home of the Fugs, Albert Ayler and many of the previous decade's experimental giants, but "We did a whole album at a Brooklyn studio, then brought the cassette tape back to ESP. Bernard Stollman played it and said 'This music is too commercial, we're not putting it out.' By too commercial, he meant everything was in tune and songs had a beginning, a middle and an end. The songs had titles like 'If You're In Luck And If You Wanna Fuck, You Can Stick It In Me', so were hardly commercial! We didn't know what to do. Bernie wouldn't pay the studio, so we couldn't get the tapes. All we had was a cassette. So that was a disaster."

So Peter suggested the idea of the Max's compilation to Tommy Dean, with the argument, "It'll serve to make them more famous, which means more people will come to see them, so it will make the club more famous." Tommy agreed and gave Peter a minuscule budget, of which

Suicide's share was 50 bucks. "We did another version of 'Rocket USA' just for that album," says Marty. "That was our first record."

Other tracks on the album included Cherry Vanilla recording 'Shake Your Ashes', Harry Toledo's 'Knots' and the Fast contributing spirited power-romps, 'Boys Will Be Boys' and 'Wow Pow Bash Crash'. The problem of finding a studio for Wayne was solved by budding disco producer Bobby Orlando. "He was just a kid then, and his daddy bought him a studio," says Peter. "They offered it to us for free, just to get the publicity, I guess. So, basically, I was putting the Max's album together with the primary motivation of getting Wayne County recorded."

There are several incarnations of the album, which all kick off with Wayne's spirited roll-call 'Max's Kansas City', which name-checks artists over a riff blatantly derived from Lou Reed's 'Sweet Jane'. Wayne also supplied feisty rockers 'Flip Your Wig' and 'Cream In My Jeans'. The album also included the first single by Pere Ubu, who had played the Easter Festival with Suicide. "That was when I decided I wanted them on the album," Peter recalls. "I loved that single and asked if I could put it on there. They said 'Sure, why not?' I think that introduced them to England after John Peel played it."

The album was retitled *New York New Wave* and reissued on CBS in 1978, then again in 1981 on the Max's Kansas City label as *Max's Kansas City Presents New Wave Hits For The 80s*. Now in remodelled form, half of side two substituted the original 'Rocket USA' with a stunning ten-minute version captured by Peter at Max's in 1976, "on a tape recorder, which was later stolen when I left it running in the audience. Thankfully the reel with Suicide on it survived. I mixed it years later; only two tracks but I put it through some graphic equalisers so it would have a crisper sound." The track now stands as a priceless earliest document of Suicide live at that formative time, and the most gripping encapsulation of New York's neon-noir streets this side of Martin Scorsese's recently released *Taxi Driver*.

On the same Bicentennial weekend which marked my first action-packed *Zigzag* assignment from Pete Frame – covering the Flamin' Groovies and Ramones on their landmark London double-header at the Roundhouse and Dingwall's – Miriam Linna made the move from Ohio to New York City, taking up the drum stool reserved for her the previous year in the newly formed Cramps.

Miriam recalls the city she arrived in as "hot and smelly as it was bankrupt, a rundown pit with garbage everywhere, rats ruling the overflowing trash cans, bums sleeping in the streets, unwanted punk rockers, gangs and graffiti. It was a perfect world and I was thrilled to find a home." For the next year, she would play around 40 gigs with the Cramps, perched pummelling the skins behind Lux, Ivy and sinister guitarist Bryan Gregory in their living embodiment of an Ed 'Big Daddy' Roth hotrod cartoon. Lux and Ivy, who had the manic devotion of true musicologists, had come to New York City with the ambition of playing CBGB, but their audition gig on November 1 (in fact their first ever gig) did not go well.

Peter Crowley was there, and recalls "I found the Cramps at CBGB. I used to go down to CBs for the auditions, because doing auditions myself scared me. There were the Cramps and they were really terrible. They were so off key they hurt your ears, the songs were falling apart, and I loved 'em! They were *magically* terrible. Hilly walked over and poked me in the arm as they were playing, and went, 'Do you think they're serious?' I looked at him and went, 'I don't know if they're serious, but they're fabulous'. He looked at me like I had lost my mind, then after their show, told them they had failed the audition. I went backstage and they were crying. They thought they were gonna come to New York and be big stars at CBGB, but here they were failing the audition. I said to them, 'Don't cry, you can come and play at Max's.' But I also said, 'You will come to my office with a tuning machine in your hands before I let you do that'. That was no small investment as they were $110 in seventies money, which is over $1,000 today. But they found the money, and duly came to my office with a tuning machine. Then they played at Max's."

The Cramps made their Max's debut less than three weeks after the CBs debacle, on November 21, returning six days later for the first of many nights opening for Suicide. "They were still a bit of a train wreck but at least it didn't hurt your ears," says Peter. "People were going to me, 'What the hell is this?'"

The two bands bonded. "It was similar to Suicide," says Peter, "where you had something that was so wonderful but completely insane. The two bands gravitated to one another, and no doubt I put 'em together just because I figured they were both potentially fabulous, totally crazy and they would like each other. I always mention that among the fans of both of those bands, particularly Suicide, were Willy DeVille, David Johansen and all the people who really understood rhythm and blues, who could watch Suicide and understand that there's a connection to Charlie Parker here and a connection to Gene Vincent there. We had plenty of stupid art-rock bands, but neither Suicide nor the Cramps fit into that category. They were certainly art-rock, in a sense, but they weren't pretentious horse shit."

"It was Peter Crowley who really took the Cramps under his wing," declares Miriam. "Peter was all important. He never judged anyone on anything but who they were as a human being. He would look you right in the eye and treat you as a person, not as a silly girl from the Midwest, or whoever one might be. He was a remarkable person to be in the position of providing a fantastic venue to a whole tribe of kids in bands from so many different places. The bills he put together created friendships between the bands and the fans that would last a lifetime. We were all so lucky that there was a Max's and, more importantly, that there was a Peter Crowley."

By now, Craig Leon had inevitably encountered Marty Thau. In his capacity as Sire's junior A&R man, Craig had first seen the Ramones in the summer of 1975, but had had to work on label honcho Seymour Stein to sign them. While the label dithered, Thau cut a projected one-off single of 'I Wanna Be Your Boyfriend' and 'Judy Is A Punk' with the band, despite turning down managing them in the wake of his Dolls experience. The single, recorded at the same upstate studio used by Bruce Springsteen, was enough to finally convince Stein, and Craig produced the Ramones' epoch-making first album that January.

Thau had been through a tricky year after leaving the New York Dolls, having also gone through a messy divorce. "I was crazed, in need of just silence," he told me. "I decided I'd stay home for about a year, review, rest up and re-evaluate. I moved into the city, struck up a conversation with a guy I'd known in the business for some years, Richard Gottehrer, and formed a production company called Instant Records. He was the producer, I was the talent finder. We brought in Blondie, Richard Hell and Robert Gordon."

Back in 1980, I had asked Thau if he was the man who discovered Blondie, then one of the biggest bands in the world. "Yeah" came his one-syllable reply, although he then elaborated, "I knew about all the groups in their earliest days. I always had this really fine relationship with all the different band members, so whenever they would turn to anybody, they would turn to me. But I couldn't do anything with Blondie or the Ramones because I was so concerned with the Dolls."

Speaking to him again 30 years later, Thau recalled how he became friends with Craig, who had also joined Instant Records. "Craig and I became good friends and discovered we had similar tastes in music, and also people, which was an important part of it as well."

The pair checked out bands at CBs and Max's most nights, deciding Blondie were the most likely to hit mainstream success out of all of them. Craig credits Marty with the foresight, "The band's playing was really slovenly and they were really ramshackle looking. Nobody really took them seriously, but Marty said they were going to be the only band that really makes it out of CBGB. He said they were gonna be the biggest thing ever."

Richard Hell signed with Instant in June. Having now left the Heartbreakers, he was putting together his Voidoids, corralling guitarists Bob Quine and Ivan Julian plus drummer Mark Bell from Wayne County's band. Rev disappointed Hell when he ignored his invitation to rehearse with the new band. That November saw the *Blank Generation* EP, which was produced by Craig with Hell, unveil its nihilist title-anthem on Ork.

By December, Thau and Gottehrer were arguing about money. Craig and Thau had wanted to strike a deal with UK pub-rock imprint Stiff Records, which had released *Blank Generation* in the UK. The pair hoped for an alliance which would see the two companies trading rosters, and might even have Suicide appearing on the UK independent, but Gottehrer stalled and the deal collapsed, along with Instant. "Marty messed up Instant in a big way," says Craig. "There was supposed to be a management company that was he and Ritchie, and a record label that was the two of them and me, but Marty wanted such a big percentage of both things that Ritchie wouldn't give it to him and it never happened."

Thau had his own story, which worked out best for Suicide as events transpired. "About eight months passed in this partnership with Ritchie. I was feeling an economic crunch and Gottehrer was too selfishly motivated. I foresaw that I was gonna end up with the short end of the stick, so I sold out my interest. I thought I'd find another group and go where that takes me. The first group I saw was Suicide again."

On two occasions, with a 30-year gap in between, Thau told me that he believed the Sex Pistols filled the void left by the Dolls, although

"Suicide was really the first new fresh thing to come along". Although he had been impressed enough by Suicide back in 1973 to put them on at the Mercer Arts Center, he hadn't then been convinced they were ready to record. Peter Crowley remembers the night Suicide gained the powerful music business ally they thought would always elude them. "Marty Thau heard the Suicide single when he was sitting down for dinner. Before that he had liked them, but thought they were just a performance-art act you went to see. He didn't think of them as capable of recording, but when he heard the jukebox song he tracked them down and signed them up."

"Marty Thau was at Max's one night and heard the record. After that he used to put it on the jukebox all the time," remembers Rev. "Even though the single was so different, he was really thrown, saying, 'I never thought they could make actual records.' Before that, he had never thought of us as a recording entity."

Thau recalled bumping into Suicide in the East Village one afternoon in late 1976. They invited him to their next Max's show, and to the Project to hear their demo. "A few weeks later, I showed up to hear what I hoped would be something they so convincingly described as a fresh, raw sound...The sound of their demo was primitive and crude, yet offered enough well-conceived lyrical content and innovative musicianship for me to conclude that I should take my growing interest in them to the next level. Short of an apocalypse, nothing was going to stop me from attending their Max's performance."

Thau was also drawn by Rev's jazz background. "That jazz part of Marty is one of the things that interested me about Suicide, and Rev in particular. When I was in my college days, the Village was really hot with Thelonious Monk, Horace Silver, Charlie Mingus and John Coltrane, so I was catching all of those groups when they would appear at the Five Spot or Village Vanguard. We kind of shared an interest, which was surprising because of what Suicide was doing. That was like a separate part of what Marty Rev was about that had really interested me." Thau showed up at Suicide's Max's show and was never the same again. "I thought I had better sign this wonderfully unique duo without delay."

Rev recalls, "There was a weekend in February 1977 when we went to play two nights at the Rat Club in Boston. In those days, we'd get a gig like that and make 25 bucks apiece. One of our Max's regulars drove us that time. We came back from Boston and later I walked into the Project. Alan told me word had got to him that Marty Thau had asked to manage us, and wanted to try and get a record out. He was always looking for something different. That's why he dropped out of the established end of the industry. Hustling had bought him a Rolls and a big house in Westchester. He did the whole thing, then became an independent maverick and lived like that until the end of his life. He found the Ramones and Blondie. Now he was living in a nice apartment, not far from myself. He just started looking for bands, but it had to be what he liked. He wasn't just looking for anybody."

Rev fondly remembers the first time that Mari and Thau met each other. "She and I and two of our children were walking down 8th Street when we bump into Marty, who lived a block away on Mercer Street. We were all going into the food market in the middle of the block west of Broadway. Thau and Mari seemed to get along immediately. I used to carry a score with me most of the time to read when on the metro. While we were in the aisles, Mari pulled out the one I had in my long coat and held it up to Thau, and said, 'Just to let you know what you are dealing with.'"

Thau took Suicide to Mercury, the label which had signed the Dolls. "We did a showcase for them," recalls Rev, "but after five minutes, they covered their faces and walked out with their fingers over their noses. Nothing panned out and nobody was going to sign us because they couldn't see it."

"Marty Thau had so much belief in Suicide," says Craig Leon. "When I was working at Sire he was always on at me about trying to get them a deal – more than the Ramones. He'd just go on and on and on about Suicide, to the point of being quite annoying to hang out with. He literally thought they were going to revolutionise music and, in a way, he was right. My first wife would go bananas and throw him out of the house. She just would not accept it!"

Fleshtones singer Peter Zaremba was surprised to see Thau behind the mixing desk at Max's one night doing Suicide's sound. "I went to heaps of Suicide performances," he recalls. "Alan was quite approachable; he seemed to appreciate someone liking what they were doing. One of the many things we loved about Suicide was they were the only band that was actually louder between songs than when they were playing. It seemed like there was all this primal noise that existed somewhere, maybe in space, or the Earth's core, that they would somehow harness and channel into their songs. Of course, they drove everybody out of the club except a few hardened devotees, so Alan had lots of room to walk out across the tables. There was a rising tide of sound as a song ended, as Alan announced in some bizarre, pseudo-southern accent that they would play the 'national' anthem, written by 'five *Puer-to* Ricans' then shrieking 'But they were spics!' Then they launched into '96 Tears' as Alan shouted at Thau to turn up the echo. 'Turn it up motherfucker, or I'll shove a fucking blowtorch down your throat!' He strode out across the empty tables towards Thau, who was desperately adjusting the settings on the soundboard, as if this could hold off Alan, before abandoning his post. Alan took over the board, sending the volume levels totally out of control, flooding us in a rising tidal wave of feedback, echo and static. At some point, we understood that the set was over, at least in the conventional sense."

Fortunately, Thau was asked by fledgling disco imprint Prelude to start a label which would give them a slice of the new downtown scene. "My own label was always my hope and dream," he told me in 2011, "and now I had someone saying, 'Yeah, we'll finance you.' I sold my interest in Blondie to Richard Gottehrer, and started Red Star Records."

Prelude had been launched in 1976 by Marvin Schlachter, who had worked with Florence Greenberg at Scepter for 10 years, then as label president at Chess. The label was the renamed Pye International, US division of the UK's Pye, which was launching into the discos by signing hot producers such as Patrick Adams, who would score his first hit in 1978 with Musique's 'In The Bush'.

"Marty got signed by these guys who'd been doing business for years and had a lot of great rock'n'roll hits," says Rev. "They saw disco coming so started Prelude Records but, now there was a new scene on the streets, wanted to get with that too, so they hired Marty as president of this new label and said, 'Bring in the people from this scene'. Suddenly, Marty had his own office, and his own label."

By June, Thau had signed Suicide to a one-year contract with options for further albums after the first, giving them a $5,000 advance, which they split. Thau said Alan used his to sign the lease for the Fulton Street loft he shared with artist Anne Deon, his girlfriend at the time.

It was all thanks to Max's. "Yeah," says Rev. "Peter Crowley, Max's and Tommy Dean finally made recording a path for us to go down." Next on that path lay the first Suicide album which, with a touch of delicious irony, was going to be financed by disco!

FOURTEEN

That February, Hilly had finally caved in and let Suicide play CBGB for the first time in nearly three years. Supporting the Ramones, they got their first taste of mass crowd savagery from rock's latest tribe. It happened on the middle of the three dates, when the Ramones had also been booked to open at Nassau Coliseum for Blue Öyster Cult, then breaking big with '(Don't Fear) The Reaper'. Patti Smith was to have appeared as middle act, but was in hospital since falling off stage the previous month in Florida and breaking bones in her neck.

The Ramones planned to blitz through their support set then make it back to CBGB for their headliner, but got lost in the Coliseum car park then jammed up on the Long Island Freeway. Over at CBs, Suicide were incurring the usual abuse they attracted when they supported someone else. The crowd of newcomer punk wannabes, waiting impatiently for the Ramones, couldn't handle Suicide's two-man threat and "booed the shit out of us", according to Alan.

Unbothered, Suicide played their set and returned to the dressing room, only for an uncharacteristically enraged Hilly to appear at the door with steam coming out of his ears. He reckoned Suicide hadn't played long enough and demanded they go back on. When the duo returned to the stage, the booing rose to a herd-like crescendo. This was the kind of situation Alan had for breakfast. "I can't hear you," he taunted, goading the befuddled lynch mob with his knife and chain. After he cut his face, "people thought I was so crazy that they stopped booing." To further make his point, Alan started jumping into the crowd, which fell over itself retreating every time, "like a backward wave."

Eventually, the Ramones arrived and went on. Now back on safe, familiar ground, the crowd probably tried to tell itself traditional rock values had won, but the real victory for punk-style liberation had gone to Suicide. It wouldn't be the last time.

These trials by fire with the Ramones got Suicide back onto the CBs roster, including Friday and Saturday nights, which paid handsomely. Alan still likes to recall going home to his Fulton Street loft with hundreds in single dollar bills stuffed in his pockets.

Brooklyn-born NYU student Jim Sclavunos, now a long-time member of Nick Cave's Bad Seeds, was in the audience at some of these shows, noticing "a conspicuously polar stance from the overtly excitable stage histrionics of the typical punk band". Jim, who remembers his first expedition into the East Village as being in November 1970 to see the Mothers of Invention at the old Fillmore East, was a regular at Club 82 by his late teens; "during that transitional period from late glam to early punk. Shortly after, I enrolled in the NYU School of the Arts, moved to the East Village and started going to gigs at CBGB pretty obsessively. It was right around the corner from where I attended classes, which was rarely. If nothing else, Hilly's dump interested me. Otherwise, I'd make the short trek up Third Avenue and over Union Square to the comparatively elegant Max's Kansas City."

Jim first heard about Suicide through "a review in some local rag of a performance they did in an art gallery. It sounded right up my alley: noisy, bloody, and confoundedly aggressive. I remember the first time I actually saw Suicide play was at CBGB in the mid-seventies. I know it was well before their first album came out because I can remember how much anticipation there was for that release amongst my circle of friends. Alan was beating himself somewhat randomly with the mic, which wasn't unusual behaviour for Iggy-inspired lead singers in those days, but there was an air of bizarre nonchalance to his self-violence that belied the intensity with which he was singing, whooping and glaring at the audience. This Tourette's-like vocal performance contrasted with Rev's cool, immobile detachment. Beyond their unusual stage presence, what also intrigued me was how much Rev's intensely unrelenting repetitive keyboard figures echoed the minimalist music being composed by the likes of Philip Glass and Steve Reich, contemporary composers that were part of a still relatively obscure New York avant-garde music scene then."

Disco was an even bigger movement sweeping New York at this time, and another prime candidate for pointless abuse. I've always loved Bobby Gillespie's declaration that the first two singles he ever bought, on the same day in 1977, were the Sex Pistols' 'God Save The Queen' and Donna Summer's 'I Feel Love'. But this kind of open-minded attitude was rare back then. How that Ramones crowd would have stamped on their toys if they knew Rev had been similarly gripped by Giorgio Moroder's ground-breaking electronic production of 'I Feel Love' when it appeared that May, just as Suicide were preparing to record their first album. Rev was a long-time disco aficionado, and 1977 was a great year for the music.

"I definitely dug disco," he declares. "I would hear it all the time and got heavily into it - Harold Melvin and the Bluenotes, the Moments, the Spinners, the O'Jays with 'Backstabbers' and, especially, 'Disco Inferno' by the Trammps. It was much more word-orientated than what we were doing. It was the urban, inner city expression of the day; a definite sociological expression of American ethnic and economic life. Even though a lot of the songs would be about love affairs, the lyrical content made a very powerful statement that had deep roots in people's struggles and survival. It was the soul music and rhythm and blues of a later generation."

So far, Marty's musical evolution had taken a very pure path, embracing R&B and doo-wop, then jazz and now this latest stage in black music's development. To Marty, disco was part of the same lineage and he had no problem finding divine inspiration in the joyful elegance of New Yorker Tom Moulton's productions for Philly International. "Disco became the music of the day," he says. "In terms of its content, there was nothing really radical about it. That's why a lot of the people who liked rock didn't like disco and just thought it was decadent party music. But I always thought American rhythm and blues was revolutionary because, no matter what the lyrics are about, they're representing the life of the people who are singing them. It's there in their voices. When the Temptations were singing 'My Girl' there was nothing there about their specific social struggle, or how they felt about the system, but coming through the voice you hear such an incredible pathos, which comes out of gospel. The truth of the expression is in the voice, the phrasing and the music, so without having to say 'We're against this and this is what happened to us,' it's innately political music. It was the same thing with disco."

Saturday Night Fever, which was based on Nik Cohn's *New York* magazine article 'Tribal Rites of the New Saturday Night', would seduce the world when it appeared in a mirror-ball swirl in late 1977 but was predictably vilified by stern punks rattled by John Travolta's white-suited target and the Bee Gees' lustrous soundtrack. "*Saturday Night Fever* was actually pretty gritty," says Chris Stein, who himself got untold abuse for homaging disco when Blondie took it to number one with 'Heart Of Glass'. "Travolta and those guys were definitely portrayed as totally outsiders rather than establishment. It was closer to a punk sensibility, even though they were dressing in slick clothes."

The Trammps' 'Disco Inferno', which also appears on the movie's soundtrack, is cited by Marty as a perfect example of disco's vitality and social relevance. "You hear the lyrics, where they're singing about a fire in a disco, but you know there's much more there than just, 'Burn the disco down'. It's pure gospel coming from the people and the streets, in the intensity of the rhythm and expression of the song. Disco was definitely relevant to me. It was the next rhythm and blues."

Then came 'I Feel Love', whose impact on Marty subliminally spiked the first Suicide album and blazed a direct trail to their second one with its electronic drum patterns. "To me, 'I Feel Love' was the first time you had the sense of hearing a rhythm machine playing underneath," says Marty. "There was a connection there for me; not that I wanted to emulate it, but I definitely got ideas from it. That was the beginning of a new sensibility in terms of electronics".

The track came from Summer's *I Remember Yesterday* album, whose evolution concept climaxed with the futuristic sequencer rhapsody of 'I Feel Love'. Obviously influenced by fellow countrymen Kraftwerk, Moroder and right-hand man Pete Bellotte had decided to represent the future with a completely electronic track. While the single climbed to number one in the UK, an excited Eno came charging into the studio where he was working with Bowie on the Berlin Trilogy, stuck on 'I Feel Love' and declared he had heard the future of dance music.

Kraftwerk's use of electronic drums highly influenced the sound that was now sweeping the dance floors of New York, principally through the metronomic electro-cruise of 'Trans-Europe Express'. Although their influence on Suicide was fairly negligible, Kraftwerk helped readjust mass preconceptions about electronic instruments and using machines instead of drummers. Even Silver Apples stopped short of that. If Kraftwerk would later acknowledge New York's influence by trying to engage Francois Kevorkian for a remix project after spotting his name on their beloved Prelude disco imports (and admitting the "ein zwei drei vier" count-in on 'Showroom Dummies' was in tribute to the Ramones), Marty is less forthcoming about them when asked about any influence they might have had on Suicide.

"I actually didn't hear about Kraftwerk until after I'd been doing what I'd been doing for several years. I definitely related to them as significant, but in connection with the German school of electronic groups like Can and NEU! They were just a link in the fact that someone else was doing it that early in the seventies, but I didn't relate to it that much. I understood Kraftwerk, but it was more of a German technological view, which I didn't conceive of having that much to do with what I was doing. I was just playing out of my own roots, which were naturally rhythm and blues and stuff that I grew up with, so it was kind of a different focus, and naturally we had two different environments. They came from a whole different world. All the synthesizers and more sophisticated equipment that they had was something that was really out of my reach. I didn't desire it and I couldn't have afforded it anyway. That helped the way I did what I was gonna do because I *had* to find a way of doing it."

However, Marty could still tell Kraftwerk were "important and even my kids had a copy of *Trans-Europe Express*, which hit over here pretty strong. They were definitely more accessible and got radio play, so there was no way we were gonna scratch the underbelly of that world! People weren't necessarily ready for us at that time, but Kraftwerk could still be a link to the old ways because they were a group, and guys playing drum-pads is closer to a live drummer and stage setup. Kraftwerk wasn't as radical in terms of the format, so there was more understanding and they could bring people in. With us, most people said, 'If this is the future we don't want it'."

Suicide had been walking their own super-voltage high wire for most of the decade now but, as Marty says, "Rhythm machines were still very fresh to me. The first drum machine I bought that we used on our first album was so basic and so right." His rudimentary old Rhythm Prince had been joined by the Farfisa organ he had borrowed then bought from a friend the previous year. In the early months of 1977, "time and disco and all these other influences I was trying" were about to collide as Marty and Alan prepared to record Suicide's first album.

While the discotheque provided an open-minded experimental social environment in which these electronic masterpieces could cause ecstatic havoc, Suicide had meanwhile been courting danger; operating in the face of the rock world, they shamelessly deconstructed the norm with their idiosyncratic approach to instrumentation and performance ethics. As a result, many of their contemporaries looked on Suicide as pariahs. The duo had waited six years to make their first album. Marty recalls, "When we were going into Ungano's in 1971, I was saying to myself, 'Wow, we could get discovered tonight.' Six years later we're finally making the first record. During all that time, we'd been playing that whole album's worth of tracks whenever we could."

Thau had booked time at Ultima Studios, upstate in the small town of Blauvelt; "in the middle of nowheresville", as Alan describes it. Thau had discovered the studio when he lived in nearby Nyack and produced the first Ramones tracks there. It had been opened as 914 Sound Studios earlier in the decade by engineer Brooks Arthur, a music biz veteran from Thau's past. Arthur saw it as an affordable alternative to increasingly prohibitive New York studios, and had entertained names such as Janis Ian, Dusty Springfield and Blood Sweat & Tears. Bruce Springsteen had started using 914 in 1972, after his manager Mike Appel took him there to record *The Wild, The Innocent And The E Street Shuffle*, and some of *Greetings From Asbury Park, New Jersey*. Bruce laboured for months at 914 on his epic new song 'Born To Run', before his producer Jon Landau decided he didn't like the sound in this "beat up old funky studio" and shifted the sessions to the upmarket Record Plant in New York.

At that point, Suicide could only dream of making an album in such a techno-palace as the Record Plant. Nevertheless, when they walked into Ultima on that first day, they were thrilled. They would have been happy to cram into a dilapidated Lower East Side tenement khazi if it meant getting that first album finally recorded. "It used to be a bowling alley, so it was long, narrow and very wooden," recalls Craig Leon. "It didn't really look like your typical studio, but it was a great place."

As Thau always promised, Craig was hired to produce the album. By this time, Leon was ensconced in an isolated summer home he had rented in Vermont, "'cause I was sick of the New York scene by now. I was going to take a sabbatical and just stay in Vermont for a few months, writing the great American opera. Then I got a call from Marty saying, 'I'm going to come and get you in the car, we're going to go out to this studio and make the Suicide record, and you're gonna meet God!' I said 'I've just left New York'. I liked Suicide, so I was committed to making this record, but I had to go to LA in a few days. He said, 'No, we'll do it and it'll be fine, just stay at my place.'"

Craig gave Marty directions for the four hour trip to his secluded abode. "So he drives up to our house and – you've got to understand that times were freer and less politically correct then – shows up with this girl in the back, who he had picked up hitchhiking in Manhattan. She was obviously on some kind of psychedelic, like mescaline or LSD, and her trip was that she was God. Marty got to the door of my house and said, 'Come out to the car, I want you to meet my friend God here.'" The trio then headed back to New York, making a detour to check out the area in the Bronx where Thau had grown up, "which was now a very rough Puerto Rican/black neighbourhood, still with this girl, who had been rattling on for hours how 'I am God and we are God.'" Thau considered leaving her tied up with paper napkins in a "horrible little Puerto Rican-Chinese restaurant", saying "Look, I'm getting sick of this, if you're God get yourself out of this", but they dropped the girl off, and ended up back at Marty's downtown apartment.

Finally, Suicide, Thau and Leon assembled at Ultima, along with hapless in-house engineer Larry Alexander. They started by setting up Rev's Farfisa, Seeburg Rhythm Prince, distortion boxes and hooked in a transistor radio. Peter Crowley still marvels at Suicide's setup at that time. "They didn't have any money, so Marty had a primitive drum machine and old Farfisa keyboard that had broken keys and a bunch of Electro-Harmonix guitar distortion devices that he plugged in series between the keyboard and amplifier in order to get this really raunchy sound. My belief is that they never sounded better than when they had that broken down stuff."

"Marty Rev had this whole Rube Goldberg (US Heath Robinson) bunch of stuff he'd put together, with the drum machine and all these other things," recalls Craig. "There were no sophisticated synths or anything, it was just whatever he found!"

The unique combination of cheap, patched up components which made up Rev's 'Instrument' (as it's credited on the album cover) played a major part in the album's alien, radioactive sound. Suicide's exploratory survival tactics harked back to the earliest rock'n'roll records, whose raw authenticity was achieved because the musicians couldn't afford shiny new equipment. 'Rocket '88' from 1951 has been called the first rock'n'roll record, but its creators, the Kings of Rhythm, led by the 19-year-old Ike Turner, were used to making do with what they had while coming up in Clarksdale, Mississippi. Ike learned guitar by stringing wires over broom handles, the band tightened their slack piano wire with steel from radial tires, and patched up worn-down horn pads with chamois and soda corks. When the young B.B. King recommended they visit Sam Phillips at his Memphis studio to capture some of the live energy that had been slaughtering local juke-joints, they set off up Highway 61 in their station wagon but hit a bump, sending gear flying off the roof and busting a speaker cone in their amp. Sam told them to stuff wadded newspaper into the damaged cone, which gave Willie Kizart's guitar the distinctive fuzzed-up tone which adds to the grungy roll of this early black crossover hit.

Suicide almost looked like they did onstage when they had set up under the studio's low lights, except Alan was surrounded by baffles. "We just set up and played our set," recalls Rev. "We had been playing everything on the album live for so long, the songs had all developed themselves. After running through the set a few times, we cut the album in the time it took to record, like 30 minutes. We cut everything live."

"We ran through their set several times, because the way that it was recorded was the way they were set up," recalls Craig, who says one of his major feats when producing the first Ramones album was getting the members of the band to start and finish at the same time. "It was all basically coming out of a couple of outputs. There'd be a straight signal, then an amp signal, and it went through like radio electronics and things. Basically, I put out a big mono signal, and you got what Marty was playing and that was it. Then there was Alan. When I told him he was going to get these extreme loopy Elvis things, and these kind of repeat delays from Jamaican records, he was very much into it. He obviously played with that later on, and incorporated it into his sound. By the time you get to the Alan Vega solo albums, that's his style, so he obviously wanted to do it."

Craig had thought carefully about the best way to present Suicide's senses-blasting live act. "I knew what they'd done live, and how unique they were, so this record really had to do them justice. It couldn't just be a blank version of what they did live, so let's go to the other extreme in the effects, and what we do with the sound. I thought the right thing to do would be to use a lot of effects from all the different kinds of music that was influencing them, and things I really liked, and make up the sound with outboard equipment. If you listen to the multi-track, when it was recorded, it would have Marty Rev on a couple of tracks, Alan on another track and everything else as printed effects which were controlled and went down live as they were playing it; all these reverbs and delays, feedback feeding back on itself, all this Lee Perry kind of stuff."

Craig thought back a couple of years to when he was recording blues-rock singer Martha Velez in Jamaica with Bob Marley and crackpot producer Perry. Her *Fiends And Angels* album had been a British blues highlight of 1969 but, in May 1975, Velez went to Jamaica to record for three weeks with Marley; the only American artist the late reggae legend ever produced. This had come about after Craig approached Marley, playing him Martha's 'Living Outside The Law' from her 1972 *Hypnotized* album. Bob was sufficiently impressed to bring in Lee Perry and produce the album which became 1976's *Escape From Babylon*.

While playing on similarities he had noticed between Suicide and Can's *Monster Movie* three years earlier, Craig tried out the dub secrets he had picked up, using the studio's tape-delay slapback and Eventide digital delay unit, adding effects live rather than later at the mixing stage. The studio's "incredible, home-made kind of microphonic desk" helped. "Everything was tuned to the A major chord, frequency-wise, so, if you wanted something that was in A major, you could really EQ it and send it into some kind of feedback or echo, then send that back to itself and get an endless loop, which would just get bigger and bigger until it blew up, unless you stopped it. If Alan went 'huh', it would go 'huh-huh-huh-huh-huh', and get louder and louder and louder. When they were running through stuff, it wasn't so much to get takes for themselves, but of all these different effects. Marty Thau, Larry and me were running around working knobs going to different echoes and delays. Everything you hear on the record was printed live as it was going down. None of those effects are after-effects. It's like a dub mix."

Craig says Rev's original source sound and "everything he was doing" was "what he was putting out through the guitar amp, which was miked as the original source sound. I said, 'Let's take off all your effects, and we'll put 'em on from here. Let's try and record everything straight and clean, without the boxes, right into the board.' If you went back to the very original tape somehow you would get a very dry version of what they did live without all those effects. If you just put up the two tracks of Marty Rev and the one track of Alan, you'd get what they play live with no enhancement. They had their live set pretty much down. I did not, like I did on a lot of other records, say 'How about doing this here?' It was strictly interpretative."

"Craig said take off all my effects and play it straight. I agreed to try it and see how it sounded," recalls Marty. "At the time, I was playing a Farfisa organ and it was a much thicker sound anyway. I was using a little AM-FM radio, which I could turn on and play as an instrument, and used to use live sometimes. Everything else was going directly into the board, which we had never done before. We were always going through an amp."

The radio was a crucial part of the nightmare inferno Marty Rev cooked up for 'Frankie Teardrop', "the album's masterful centre-piece", in the words of Marty Thau. Still the most shattering 10 minutes ever committed to vinyl, Suicide's ultimate tour de force was the only track to go through any kind of time-consuming evolutionary process in the studio, after its inception as a demo the previous year. It was still called 'Frankie Teardrop Detective' that day Suicide blazed through the songs which the album would be drawn from but, later on in the sessions, something would happen which transformed the track into their most notorious statement.

The sessions proved hard-going for engineer Larry Alexander, whose experience of recording electronic music had only run to his own synth-created album of Tchaikovsky's '1812' and 'Nutcracker Suite'. "Larry didn't know what to make of any of it," recalls Craig. "I don't know if he was even in the room most of the time! It was mostly Marty Thau and me. I think he thought I was insane wanting to feed all these things back into each other. He didn't understand what was going on. He was a little too conventional."

Rev recalls, "I did very little overdubbing, maybe just a spot here and there. So the record was like 1-2-3 – done. Then it was all mixing. Craig seemed very happy with it. We all rode back to New York in Marty's car, and he was very positive. We were too where he was concerned, which he countered with 'The producer can only be as good as the band he's producing.'"

Then Craig had to go to LA, "So I made what I thought would be a preliminary two-track mix of what we had, which was basically the sound of everything kind of put up the way that we did it; the music, voice and effects. All you could do with what was recorded was move those effects up or down. You couldn't make new ones or anything. I think the band kind of approved of whatever was recorded by the time that I left. I don't know what happened during that time when Marty Thau decided he was going to become Lee Perry!"

There are several accounts of what happened next and what mixes ended up on the album. What is known is that, while Leon was away, Thau came out to play. Although he had never produced an album before, he decided to do a mix at Ultima with Larry Alexander, with Suicide on hand for approval and a large bag of weed for inspiration. In his memoir, Thau wrote: "Taking into account all the obstacles Craig had to contend with, like the technical limitations of the recording studio, a very small budget and Suicide's recording inexperience, he did an unbelievably great job. However, after carefully scrutinising his discerning and highly substantive interpretation of Suicide's music, I felt his mixes were too subtle for a group calling itself Suicide. I wanted to be touched, thrilled and intimidated in equal measure by Suicide's over-the-top psychodrama, and needed to experience their poetic sophistication, as confrontational I suspected it might sound to establishment cynics."

Thau added that, when he played the original mixes to his partner, Marv Schlachter, he asked, "'Where's the beat?' The groove was the sensibility of the day. All one had to do to appreciate that observation was to spend a night dancing at Studio 54. So I did. As much a punk activist and music fan I was, I was truly impressed with the passion that disco fans exhibited. Marv's informed disco observations prompted me to return to the recording studio in Craig's absence to remix 'Ghost Rider', 'Rocket USA', 'Cheree' and 'Girl'."

"So Marty said, 'Hey, why don't I produce it?'," recalls Rev. "Marty had never produced before. We had a great time because we would drive up to the studio every day. It was about 45 minutes out of Manhattan. For us, it was like going to the country because we hadn't been out of the city for so long! Craig was an experienced, polished producer at that time, but Marty gave some of the things a heavier, rougher, maybe more street angle; not that there was that much difference to the two. There couldn't be, because it was all exactly the way we played. Marty was more of a punk, so we could be more involved. He would sit at the board, and Alan and I would relax on the floor of the control room.

Marty would just sit and go through every track, one at a time, EQ-ing. Then he'd add the next track to that, then the next track to that. By that time, we were so incredibly stoned. Then after he got through all of them, he'd put 'em all together. When you do that it's such a beautiful sound, like a big orchestra. Every time he'd finish a track, he'd turn to us and say, 'What do you think?' We'd say, 'Okay, it sounds good,' because we were all very high on the whole experience, and whatever else was going through our bloodstreams. We were all in a kind of positive state of ecstasy."

"My approach was to strip the tracks down to their basics and then rebuild each one while adding unheard of combinations of exaggerated effects, in some cases using ones that were already installed by Craig, that were then coupled with other eccentric electronic sounds that I created to suggest a dramatic futurism," explained Thau. "I broke all the rules but somehow my tinkering succeeded."

As the trio further explored these novel mixing techniques, the atmosphere in the studio became extremely hands-on, enhanced by Thau's freely circulating marijuana stash. As Rev recalls, "Marty was trying to explore all the equipment in the studio, like the big phaser that we used after the album was cut, on the remix of 'Cheree'. It was the state of the art one, at the time. He only had two hands to do all this stuff so we'd be dividing it up. I would be doing the phasing, while Marty was mixing it down. Alan might be doing something too, or just listening to see how it sounded on the outside. Not being a producer, Marty would push things, not knowing how far he could go. We were getting more and more stoned. He didn't know any of the methods. None of us did. The only one who knew anything was Larry Alexander, who was very experienced, but was resisting and getting his nerves frizzled."

"It was driving us crazy," recalls Alan. "One day it was so hard in the studio, man, I was seeing treble. I went to open the door to go outside to the car and saw three door knobs! It was so intense. The shit that was going on between the two of them and then asking us what we thought. But Larry Alexander is the guy who went insane. He said, 'I gotta get out of here!' He went crazy with this record."

The sessions got crazier still when Alan decided to redo his vocals on 'Frankie Teardrop' with new lyrics after reading a newspaper story about a factory worker who lost his job and, in desperation, killed his wife, kids, then himself. "I changed the lyrics," he recalls. "Before, it was about a

nday morning on the Bowery.

Marty Thau: The Chairman.

ART—RITE

SPECIAL # 13 BY ALAN SUICIDE $1.00

an edited the January 1977 issue of Edit deAk and Mike Robinson's *Art-Rite* periodical, presenting images of Iggy, Ghos
der and sports figures to focus on "the romance of the under-culture: horse racing, white trash, greasy rock 'n' roll,
uscles, motorcycles, and the end of civilisation".

Suicide live '78.

the FACTORY

for directions see over

FRIDAYS
at THE RUSSELL CLUB
Royce Rd, Hulme, Manchester

Friday 21st July
CULTURE
PLUS
TRADITION

Admission 2·50
Advance tickets from
Virgin·061 236 4801,
Paul Marsh, Moss Side
Shopping Centre·
061 226 1000.

Friday 28th July
SUICIDE
+Joy Division
AND THE ACTORS
admission·
a quid at
the door

doors
open 8pm

TELEPHONE   01·387·0428

MUSIC MACHINE
Playing times 10.30 pm and midnight
CAMDEN HIGH St. OPP. MORNINGTON CRESCENT TUBE·N.W.

Wednesday July 12th   £1
BRAM TCHAIKOVSKY'S
BATTLE AXE
+ Warm Jets
Free admission for one with this
advert before 10.30pm

Monday July 17th
JAPAN
+ Support
Free admission for one with
advert before 10.30pm

Thursday July 13th   £1.50
ROKOTTO
+ Heart Stealer

Tuesday July 18th
C.G.A.S.5
+ Berlin
Free admission for one with
advert before 10.30pm

Friday July 14th   £2
THE TOURISTS
+ The Invaders

Saturday July 15th   £2
RACING CARS
+ Rumblestrips

Wednesday July 19th
SORE THROAT
+ Blazer Blazer

Monday July 24th Tuesday July 25th
Wednesday July 26th Thursday July 27th

THE CLASH
+ From New York SUICIDE + The Specials
Advance tickets £2.50 from box office

LICENSED BARS · LIVE MUSIC · DANCING
8PM - 2 AM   MONDAY TO SATURDAY

Suicide at their first solo London show, The Marquee, July 18 1978.
EV ARCHIVES

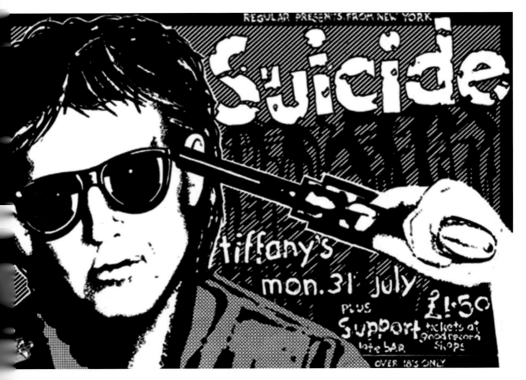

er for pivotal 1978 Edinburgh show.
DSAY HUTTON ARCHIVES

Alan Vega, dressing room, Irving Plaza, NYC, July 28 1984.

Alan and Marty backstage at Irving Plaza, NYC, July 28 1984.

an and Suicide's greatest living champion Howard Thompson, sometime in 1980s New York City.

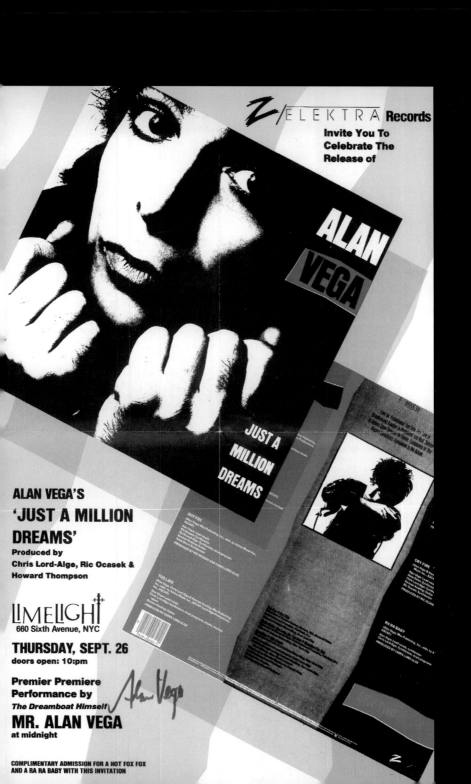

detective at the racetrack, because I went to the racetrack a lot in those days, but then I saw this story in the paper about this factory worker who died, so it became a whole new thing, and a lot more relevant." In two improvised takes, Alan placed himself in the heads of both killer and victims, ending up tormented in hell, while Rev whipped up a disembodied electrical storm, which was given another sinister dimension through his radio. The track now almost become like Alan's psychopathic answer to Patti Smith's 'Piss Factory' as his new lyrics were also inspired by his years working shit factory jobs in Brooklyn. "Lots of 'em, just trying to survive. That's what 'Frankie' is about. It's a self-portrait, of everybody. 'We're all Frankies, all lying in hell'."

Screams had never sounded so nerve-janglingly terrifying, having only previously been pushed to the forefront on Brit-experimentalists White Noise's 'Black Mass: An Electric Storm In Hell' in 1969, to ultimately comical effect and, much more seriously, with Abbey Lincoln's devastating performance on Max Roach's 'Triptych'. "I really got into it, because the music had so much of an effect," Alan recalls. "I almost blacked out with those screams I did. Marty put on some static from the radio, which really made it. That bloodcurdling scream still gets me when I listen to it, especially if you're sitting there all quiet and it comes on. I hadn't listened to it for a long time and when I did it really scared the crap out of me. The music leading up to it is kind of subdued in a weird way. All of a sudden the scream comes out of nowhere, it's like 'Holy shit!' All that reverb or echo, it goes on and on. That's one of my longest screams there. Putting myself in the guy's mind was genuinely disturbing. I always think it's the song Lou Reed wishes he would have done."

Rev recalls that, when it came time to mix the new version of 'Frankie', it took Marty, Alan, Larry and himself to harness the monster they had created as it appeared on the album.

When Craig returned, he was shocked to find a rather different album to the one he had recorded, recalling, "Marty had really overdone it, smoking a couple of joints and really gone nuts on the effects. That's all that you *could* do – either raise Suicide or raise the effects. If you went through every effect individually you'd have to have been on some other planet. He had destroyed the sound by fooling around with it. You didn't hear the original source. I was thinking, 'God, my name's gonna be on this!' What is this that he's done here?' But there was a conscious effort to do that and the guys had to agree with it. It wasn't like 'I wanna do all of this stuff'. It was 'What do you think? They kind of wanted to do it, they just didn't know how to do it."

According to Craig, there were no ambitious edits on the album. "I think some of them were doubled up in sections where there was a four-bar instrumental and they were made into like eight or 16 bars between vocals. It wasn't like Little Richard, where we'd take one song and make it double. There'd be a section with no vocals which was originally only two to four bars and then, because we had all the different effects, we could do four bars with one effect, four bars with another, but I don't think there was any radical editing. Whatever take felt good was it, as far as I can remember."

When it was time to master the album, Thau and Leon met at the venerable Frankford/Wayne studio, where Prelude cut its disco classics. "Marty still wasn't sure which mixes should be used," recalls Craig. "He brought both sets to the mastering, which I was in New York to do with him. We went through the stuff that he had done, because there was a dispute. I don't think any of his stuff actually ended up on the album. I couldn't put my hand on a stack of bibles but, if anything made it, it was 'Cheree'. The mastering engineer was going, 'You can't put this out, quality control wouldn't press it!' I persuaded him that we should go pretty much with what the band said. There's pretty much of a consistency on the album in terms of levels and where the effects are on each track and all of that."

"Actually, I remember it a bit differently," says Rev. "I know that we used ours and Marty's mix of 'Frankie Teardrop', 'Ghost Rider' and 'Girl' and probably, as Craig said, 'Cheree'. They were very close. With due deference to Craig, I don't remember us not liking *any* of his stuff. And those Thau/Suicide mixes couldn't have been too bad, 'cause around the same time we also cut the remix of 'Cheree', 'I Remember', 'Radiation', 'Ice Drummer', which Alan ended up covering on his first solo album, and a new take of 'Keep Your Dreams', all of which came out on record and quite extensively."

Suicide's first album was finally ready; created for a minuscule $4,000 in an atmosphere of cathartic intensity, stoned experimentation and often under the kind of DIY circumstances which might have floored other bands. The final track listing went 'Ghost Rider', 'Rocket USA', 'Cheree', 'Johnny', 'Girl', 'Frankie Teardrop' and 'Che'.

Over 38 years since they were recorded, these seven songs feel branded into my soul like eternal footprints, waiting to combust into glorious life when summoned. They now sound as alien and weirdly arcane as a Robert Johnson blues recording. The journey will always start with those two supernatural cruise missiles which set the scene with Alan's speedway anger juddering through Marty's spectral R&B motifs. 'Cheree' still swells like the purest declaration of lovestruck awe as New York's heart pounds below and its lights twinkle above. Then it's Rev playing with an Elvis riff he heard as a child on 'Johnny', and 'Girl''s finger-clicking bedroom sashay and nonchalant passion. Side two and 'Frankie Teardrop' will always invoke that unbearable tension and swelling terror leading to opening the gate into its teeming Bosch-like maelstrom, before the album closes with the desolate descent of 'Che', which sees Alan mourning like an ectoplasmic spirit in a place no one had ever seen, over Marty's colossal tomb slabs and Bach-like organ flourishes.

Suicide was a once-in-a-lifetime alchemical combustion of disparate personalities on a mutual mission. It was Alan and Marty's story so far, but cursed to be a monolith for the future to appreciate when the present could not. Even in 2015 – *particularly* in 2015 – no other album comes close.

Now came the hard part.

FIFTEEN

"The first album was and is a very moving, haunting, and genuinely ground-breaking masterpiece. Even at the time, it instantly came across as an enduring classic. I love all the Suicide albums without exception, but their first is still my favourite and never fails to transport me back to the visceral thrill of when I first saw them perform." – **Jim Sclavunos**

With their album glowering in Red Star's firing pods, Suicide spent the rest of 1977 ping-ponging between headline slots at Max's and CBGB. The CBs set of September 29 is just one of the priceless field recordings to be found in Blast First's *Suicide Live 1977-78* box set, where it nestles with several other complete performances captured on cassette in New York and Europe by Howard Thompson and Eric Mache.

Maybe it was because it was Suicide's first headline set at CBGB that Alan and Marty sound on fire in the unusually full-blooded sound. It's like they're responding to every indignity and catcall they have ever suffered. Marty Thau continues to relish his new world of knob-twiddling via the Roland Space Echo, dousing Alan in shuddering reverb and fuelling Rev's flight path. The latter's organ has gained a serrated buzz-saw edge and bottomless resonance, while his rampant drum machine seems hot-wired by a road-drill, although it puts out a startling Latin-voodoo groove on 'Cheree'. Having such a flaming hog to ride brings out the beast in Alan, who treats every song like 'Frankie Teardrop' (itself introduced as "a song about every one of us"). The set continues to scorch through 'Ghost Rider', 'Rocket USA' and a techno-stomping 'Johnny', which finishes a 25-minute set charged with enough snarling defiance and pure electricity to light up New York City in the recent blackout.

That night at CBs, Suicide had the novelty of a band supporting *them*. Suitably, it was Lydia Lunch's Teenage Jesus & the Jerks, who had debuted at CBs that June and played Max's the previous month. Lydia Koch had first hit downtown New York in 1973 as a precociously volatile 14-year-old from upstate Rochester who, as she says in the *Blank City* movie, wanted to see the New York Dolls. She finally ran away to the city at 16; hustling, go-go dancing, sandblasting polite gatherings with spoken-word tirades, and finding her first friends in Alan and Marty, who she remembers giving her vitamins and encouragement. Marty remembers Lydia showing him her words: "The poetry was so sharp and so strong I knew she had to do something." After being instantly smitten by Suicide, Lydia started carving out her own uncompromising niche, which owed nothing to the retro-rock now being punted in the name of punk. She preferred to rip the music's stomach open and rearrange its entrails in her own likeness, starting with Teenage Jesus & the Jerks. At first she was joined by Japanese bassist Reck and single-snared drummer Bradley Field, who had followed his friend Miriam Linna to New York from Ohio and met Lydia when he found both girls sharing an Alphabet City apartment.

That December, I had the pleasure of witnessing Teenage Jesus after they had used Freddie Laker's new Skytrain to invade the UK. At the behest of a visiting Peter Crowley, the trio supported Wayne County at London's Vortex club, which had replaced the Roxy as the capital's punk crucible. Teenage Jesus were spiky, enraged and stank of New York's bad side, as the scarily charismatic Lydia caterwauled in black rubber. In their 10-minute set, she venomously cut to size the disgruntled macho elements whose comfort pogo-zones were under threat.

Suicide would soon be hailed as godfathers of the malicious after-punk movement that Lydia was inadvertently kick-starting with performances such as these. The previous year, she had met former conservatory student James Siegfried from Milwaukee at a Suicide gig. Alan recalls the future James Chance approaching him at CBs, having just arrived in New York, with the words "I'm from Milwaukee, I know who you are, can you tell me anything?" James became a Max's regular and was entranced by Alan and Marty's rise to power during the duo's seminal 1976 performances. "Suicide were one of my ultimate favourite bands," says James. "I used to talk to Marty about jazz sometimes. He was one of the few people in the rock scene who was into that. Alan wore these smoking jackets, and had this combination of elegance and violence that I really liked." Alan recalls Chance reminding him of an early Frank Sinatra and Marty remembers "I used to have a lot of conversations about jazz with him."

Chance could barely contain the energy he absorbed from the anarchic New York of this time. He soon became a quiff-topped distillation of Ayler, Vega and James Brown, telling me, "New York then was like a sort of perverse playground, where you felt free to do virtually anything you wanted, and there were hardly any consequences for it." He played in the first Teenage Jesus line-up but soon bust out to front his own band with organist Adele Bertei. He named it the Contortions after a *New York Times* review of a jazz-loft gig he had played where writer Robert Palmer cited his "contortionist's acts with minimal musical content" in reference to his penchant for leaping over musicians and sliding along on his knees. By spring 1978, the band boasted its classic line-up of Bertei, guitarists Pat Place and Jody Harris, bassist George Scott (from seminal downtown experimental band Jack Ruby) and drummer Don Christensen. The Contortions' backing singers included Anne Deon, Alan's girlfriend of the time.

Chance embraced jazz, funk and even much-vilified disco in his infernal new brew, and took Vega-style audience provocation to violent extremes. "Alan would antagonise the audience because he didn't think they were reacting enough," James recalls. "I first saw them in 1976 at Max's. Alan was wearing a red smoking jacket, and was flicking cigarettes into the audience. They were absolutely a big influence on me and were my favourite New York band at the time. People in New York then had this kind of studied cool about them and thought they were so above it all. It was so hard to get a physical reaction from them that I felt it was necessary to actually attack them!" To heighten the effect, James made sure he was smartly turned out and the band was drilled with soul-revue precision. "Yeah, sometimes even the jumping in the audience went along with the rhythm! Jump down, hit somebody, jump back up on the stage on the next beat, going back and forth."

Suicide saw in the month their album was finally released with three more CBs headliners in early December. Going on the box-set recording, they were even more wired and unstoppable now, resurrecting early Latin grind 'Junkie Jesus', while Rev seems to have added a malevolent jackhammer to his rhythm arsenal on 'Frankie'. There's even an encore, where Alan dedicates the new (and never recorded) 'Put A Little Love In Your Heart' to the recently deceased Elvis. There was something demonic writhing in Suicide's circuits that night, all climaxing with Marty's home-stretch beat-machine blowout.

This time, Suicide were supported by two bands from Boston; DMZ, who had recently signed to Sire, while the Real Kids were Red Star's other first signing. Naturally, the latter get historically overshadowed by Suicide, especially since they released their self-titled debut album at the same time. Singer, songwriter and guitarist John Felice had lived next door to Jonathan Richman as a fellow teenage Velvet Underground maniac, playing in the first line-up of the Modern Lovers by the age of 15 (although school activities prevented him participating in their 1972 debut album). The opposite of clean-living health nut Richman, John loved booze, drugs and raw rock'n'roll. He celebrated all three when he formed the Real Kids. By the time his band signed to Red Star, John was accompanied by guitarist Billy Borgioli, bassist Allen 'Alpo' Paulino and drummer Howie Ferguson, and had gained a following on Boston's bar scene and at the Rat Club. John had known Marty Thau, who liked their unpretentious trad-rock sparkle, since 1972.

Recording at Ultima, with Thau producing solo, engineer Larry Alexander must have found the Real Kids' energised ditties about girls, first romance and partying easier to deal with than Suicide, particularly when they covered Eddie Cochran and Buddy Holly.

With Red Star up and running, Thau made himself at home in Prelude's offices, which were situated in the 1917 Rodin Studios building at 200 West 57th Street, opposite Carnegie Hall, although he did most of his business in the China Palace restaurant downstairs. He employed writer Roy Trakin as 'Minister of Information' and Miriam Linna as press officer. After bailing out of the Cramps' fiendish laboratory and joining downtown garage-poppers Nervus Rex, Miriam had heard Thau was looking for staff. The Real Kids already counted her as a super fan. When Thau asked them if he should offer her the job, thumbs went up all round.

Although the Cramps shared many Max's bills with Suicide, Miriam hadn't dared talk to Alan and Marty until Thau's introduction, explaining, "I was kind of scared off from actually going up to them and having a conversation. Marty Rev was an anomaly to me. I'd often see him in the street, and he would smile and say 'Hello', but I'd have to look behind

191

me to see if he was acknowledging me or someone else. These guys were stars to me from the git-go. At Red Star, Marty felt they were the most important act ever to come out of New York. Whenever they came by the office, it felt like royalty was coming to call. They were genuine, approachable guys offstage, but a total menace when they took the stage."

Miriam remembers Thau as "one of the kindest people I ever met, and the best boss in the world. He was amazing with his artists, the press, everyone. I was on cloud nine at Red Star. It was destiny to work at a label that built itself on the risk factor. Marty felt that following your heart was more important than following a guaranteed success plan. Suicide was absolutely the farthest-out act in New York at the time, and even now, I consider them the absolute farthest out *ever* because nothing was contrived about them. They were not putting on an act. Those two guys were the real deal, and to us fans, they put out what we all really felt; not so much anger, but fortitude and attitude. They weren't arrogant. They were powerful."

Suicide was released on December 28, 1977, its name daubed in blood on its cover. Few other groups at that time had come along to skewer America's ruined, bewildered post-Vietnam psyche, then held it up to show the squalor, paranoia and quest for oblivion now infesting the country – especially in its ostracised heart of darkness, New York City. The world was only just starting to catch up with the previous decade's first Velvet Underground album as a dispatch from the dark side of the metropolis, the Dolls had suffered dim production then burnt out and the Ramones' dumbed-up speed-pop celebration had already become a much-plagiarised tool to be used for pub-rock conversions. With the decade in its second half, seventies New York had finally got the defining album to be held up in years to come as the shape-shifting masterwork which actually pinpointed the mood of the city at its darkest time.

Alan still remembers getting the phone call from Marty. "They used to have these little record stores in those days. Marty said, 'You're not gonna believe this but the record's in this store!' I went down and, because it's like 12 inches by 12, it looked *big*. The record covers were works of art then. Just seeing it in the store, sitting next to Bob Dylan; I was like 'Holy shit!'"

Inevitably, the album was often viciously attacked when it did manage to seep through any cracks in the wall of ignorance which guarded the blinkered music infrastructure, which was still ruled by stolid tradition and the law of the average. Many didn't even get beyond the name and cover. If they did, they seemed to find it disrupted their cosy dinner party ambience; like a wall-cracking belch of reality from under the table.

Press reaction in the US was largely nasty, as if the record had been given to the writers least capable of accepting any statement which was even remotely radical. "We had every bad word in the thesaurus, every disgusting word they could find," remembers Alan. *Rolling Stone's* Michael Bloom managed to accuse Suicide of being absolutely puerile and idiotic. Yet in 2003, the magazine listed it at 441 among its 500 greatest albums of all time. Bloom wrote, "I've heard stolen riffs before, but this is far worse: raping and pillage of entire concepts…Suicide's songs are absolutely puerile, and Alan Vega's vocal convey nothing but arrogance and wholesale insensibility…persistence doesn't legitimise this kind of idiocy."

The Village Voice, which Suicide had been paying to run their live ads for years, managed a vicious double-header, starting with Tom Carson's 'Suicide is Meaningless', a putdown of their "brutally impersonal electronic music… impassive hostility… abstract-expressionistic pornography." Thau responded by confronting Carson, recalling "another pretentious pundit at *The Village Voice*, whose mean-spirited review prompted me to tell him, in no uncertain terms, that he was the personification of all that was wrong with the *Voice*. Of course, that didn't go over too well with him, but I didn't give a fuck." Alan now says the review was actually helpful because Max's was packed with curious punters the night after it hit the street. He also took on board the comments about his singing being too speedy, and consciously slowed down his delivery.

Robert Christgau, who David Johansen described as "like a fuckin' schoolteacher, who grades your fuckin' records", continued the *Voice's* scholarly derision by giving *Suicide* a C plus. Thau expected it, recalling, "He hated Suicide and referred to them as the Two Stooges. I thought that was actually very funny, but Christgau was damn serious. He thought he was *tres* cool but, in most seventies Bowery circles, he was viewed as a hippie remnant from the days of groups like Moby Grape… The Dean didn't seem to relate to the punk community, but managed to get away with his pronouncements, thanks in part to his power position as the *Voice's* chief music editor."

Although Lydia Lunch flicked her guitar pick in the critic's face when she left the stage of Max's one night, Peter Zaremba credits Christgau with making Suicide sound worth checking out: "He was pretty dismissive of Suicide. He was totally dismissive of the Fleshtones as well, but it was a good enough reason to go and see them!"

Now writing for the *Voice* and *Soho Weekly News* after moving to New York the previous year, Lester Bangs became Suicide's loudest champion. He played the album to a visiting Kraftwerk, who "understood immediately, and practically strong-armed me into giving them both copies of the record to take back to Germany." Rev backs this up. "Lester Bangs told us that, when Kraftwerk were in New York, they were in his apartment and he said, 'This has just come out; now hear this!' Apparently, they were so blown away they took Lester's copy. It hit 'em so potently they just took his record!"

Lester wrote a landmark piece headlined 'The Joy Of Suicide' in the *Soho Weekly News* of May 28, where he proclaimed "Suicide stands at the nexus where bubblegum music, Iggy Pop, Kraftwerk electronics, Eno futurism, New York street jive, and primal scream vocalisations all somehow magically mesh."

But the mass public were polarised. Alan loves to tell the story he heard about the motorist who went apoplectic when 'Frankie Teardrop' came on the radio. "'Frankie' came on and the scream almost made him crash. He hated it, man. He took the radio out of his car and threw it out of his window, then drove his car over it to smash it. But that wasn't enough. He put the car in reverse, and went back over it the other way to make sure it was really fucking killed!" Marty simply reasoned, "We were just singing the new blues, and the blues scares people."

Suicide's only regular Stateside radio exposure was in Philadelphia, where crazies at the University of Pennsylvania would play 'Frankie' on rotation from 3 a.m. until dawn on the student station.

New York writer and former CBs regular Madeline Bocchiaro recalls "being in awe" of Suicide after seeing them play around this time. "It was weird enough seeing only two guys on the stage, with strange-looking machines. We didn't even know what synths looked like at the time. They sounded like Elvis joined Kraftwerk to make soundtracks for horror films. They were so unique, even in a time of incredible diversity. It was like they came out of the fifties with their leather jackets and street attitude. I immediately bought their album, with the disturbing blood splat on the cover. Early electronic music was more progressive and elaborate, with Wendy Carlos and Vangelis; Mick Ronson turned us on to Annette Peacock when he covered her songs; Bowie's synth usage with Eno was atmospheric on *Low* and *Heroes*, so was Iggy's on *The Idiot*, but there was never anything like Suicide, then or now."

Marty Thau remained pragmatic and saw Suicide being embraced in less inhibited climates: "Although I was fairly certain that Suicide's debut record wouldn't sell very well, I did believe that it would favourably impact their career and they'd eventually become an important cult band. Part of me felt their songs were accessible, and that Suicide might even surprise everyone with commercial hits, but very few others heard what I heard and emphatically disagreed with my optimism. As it turned out, the band's great music turned out to be too advanced for America's heartland airheads in early '78 who, for starters, just couldn't cope with the sheer effrontery of a duo who were breaking a lot of the taboos and sacred cows, had no guitars, or bass, and had a drum machine for rock'n'roll, *and* were called Suicide."

It was that name again, as Thau reflected, "One of the popular myths about Suicide is that they were all about nihilism and negativity, but that was not true at all. Some even say that Suicide were the ultimate punks because even the punks hated them, but the truth of the matter is that Suicide redefined punk rock with a sound that was more disturbing and threatening than anything London's radical bands had ever heard, and that just didn't sit well with them."

Thau had also produced the Fleshtones' projected Red Star debut album at Ultima. He brought Alan along to further sessions at Blank Tapes, as Peter Zaremba recalls: "Alan dropped by when we were doing some recording with Bob Blank. We knew a few Suicide songs and tossed them off with him singing. I'm not sure if we recorded more than 'Rocket USA', but that's the one that wound up on *Blast Off*, our would-be Red Star album."

The Fleshtones had been on Red Star since its inception, thanks to Miriam Linna's ravings and Alan bringing them to Chairman Thau's attention (although their album wouldn't see release for years). "Alan brought Marty Thau to see us," recalls Peter Zaremba. "Anyone that Alan recommended was cool. Marty was the only record guy to pay any attention to us. He started recording us right after he had Suicide and the Real Kids in the pipeline."

The year 1978 started with Suicide venturing to the West Coast for the first time, playing San Francisco's Mabuhay Gardens for two nights in early January and earning a page feature in issue five of local fanzine *Search & Destroy*. Maybe bowing to their Californian debut, Alan and Marty are pictured onstage at San Francisco's answer to CBs sporting white jackets. Interviewed by Kamera Zie and Vale, Alan bemoans that Ivan Karp artists such as Carl Andre and Diego Cortez are using the CBs scene for inspiration, and says the black armband he's sporting is in tribute to repressed minorities and the memory of Elvis, who had recently died.

Suicide hurried back to New York to support the Ramones at the Palladium on 14th Street. This pairing never seemed to pass smoothly and Suicide split the crowd the moment they hit the stage. One faction booed and screamed 'You suck!' Suicide fans yelled at them to shut up. Alan hollered, "What're you all fuckin' booin' for? You're all gonna die!" The conflict can be heard on Eric Mache's recording, on which Suicide can be heard ploughing through 'Rocket USA', 'Cheree', a new number called 'Dance' (at that point Alan chanting "All night long" over the 'Don't Be Cruel' riff Marty had kicked about on 'Johnny') and an incendiary 'Frankie Teardrop'. By now, both cheers and boos are deafening.

There were still shows at Max's, including one the following week and a two-nighter in early February. The former is captured in the box set, Rev unleashing the kick facility on his drum machine in a floor-stomping fashion which would make a techno producer look at his dials. The extra pounding adds a mechanised pump to speedy renditions of 'Ghost Rider' and 'Rocket USA', and only takes a breather for 'Cheree' ("a love song for ya"), although eventually the beat becomes heavier than the breathing. 'Dance' has now become like Suicide's thermonuclear answer to 'The Twist', followed by set staple '96 Tears' and a viciously baked 'Frankie' to finish things off.

By now, Thau had secured a UK output for Red Star through Howard Thompson at Bronze Records. When accepting Suicide's *MOJO* Honours award in 2007, Alan made sure he thanked Howard along with his wife and nine-year-old son Dante. Now living in rural Connecticut, Howard has been Suicide's biggest European champion since the first album arrived in his mail in early 1978. After I first met him at Island Records in 1977 his A&R career went on to straddle a golden age in the music industry. The next time I encountered Howard was at the Chalk Farm offices of Bronze Records in early 1978, after he had signed a deal with Red Star; basically so he could get Suicide.

Bronze was started in 1971 by Gerry Bron, elder brother of actress Eleanor. He had dabbled in many aspects of the music business, managing the likes of the Bonzo Dog Doo Dah Band, Gene Pitney, Marianne Faithfull, Manfred Mann and lumpen rockers Uriah Heep, whom he also produced and took to launch his new label. Bronze also released the likes of Juicy Lucy, Coliseum, Osibisa and Sally Oldfield but, by 1978, had become a last-chance saloon of record labels, which would be saved by Howard signing Motörhead. At the time, Motörhead were one of the least fashionable names in rock but went on to record the golden run of albums including *Overkill*, *Bomber* and *Ace Of Spades* and become one of Europe's biggest metal bands.

Howard still remembers the day he first heard Suicide. "I had a friend in Rochester, New York, called Kevin Patrick, who was a DJ on a radio station. We had met when I was at Island Records. I would send him punk singles; the Sex Pistols, Eddie & the Hot Rods, everything that came out that I thought was cool, and he would be the first person in America to play these things. In return, he would send me American punk rock, so I would get Blondie, the Ramones, Talking Heads and Lenny Kaye-type *Nuggets*-era singles. We'd send each other stuff every week or two. One day, I'm sitting in my office at Bronze Records, which was actually the last label anybody would ever go to to get signed. It was the last gasp."

The post that morning changed Howard's life. "A 12-inch envelope opened up. I shared an office with my boss David Betteridge, who was Managing Director at the time. I put the record on the stereo and 'Frankie Teardrop' started. I had put the B-side on by mistake. I thought, 'This sounds interesting, he kills his wife and kids', then there's the scream. My boss, who was on the phone, drops the phone and shouts 'Turn that down!' Whoever was on the other end must have been wondering what the hell was going on at Bronze Records. It carries on and I'm totally locked into this song. I'd never heard anything like it before. David got off the phone, then we listened to the album. Every song blew my mind. It was such a great record; beautifully performed, fantastically well-produced, and said everything I wanted to hear in a rock'n'roll record. So I called up Marty Thau and asked, 'Do you have any kind of outlet for the record in England, and are you interested? And can I come to New York and see the band?'"

197

Howard wasted no time getting the first available flight to New York and making his way to the Red Star offices, where he experienced "the most intimidating meeting of my career up to that point. Marty Rev said 'hello', then not a word during the entire meeting. Alan looked like a terrorist, and was clearly very suspicious of me. He came off like a Brooklyn street tough, all black leather, sunglasses and beret, for fuck's sake! I suppose he was going for the Che Guevara or some Red Brigade terrorist effect. Red Star's Minister Of Information Roy Trakin had already given me a very strong weed joint to smoke, which completely fucked me up. So I'm sitting with these guys, terrified by the silent one and this mean-looking guy over here and Marty Thau, who basically looked like a gangster. I was a little apprehensive and kept thinking I wasn't in the right room! I was high from Trakin's weed and tried to answer the questions Alan sprayed at me. I think, in the end, I probably told them just what they wanted to hear as I half expected Alan to pull a switchblade out of his jacket and stab me if I didn't. But I presumed the meeting went well, as we managed to develop a pretty good relationship."

Seeing Suicide for the first time clinched Howard's devotion. Supported by the Contortions, the duo was playing two nights at CBGB that first weekend in February. Howard's recording appears in the box set, and shows how the set started with five minutes of undulating keyboard drone before debuting the embryonic 'Harlem'. They then career into 'Ghost Rider', 'Keep Your Dreams', 'Dance' and a blood-blenderising 'Frankie'. It comes as something of a shock to hear CBs erupt into enthusiastic applause after the song screeches to a halt, like a derailed subway car.

Howard stood speechless for moments afterwards. "It was just astonishing," he recalls. "That night was my introduction to Suicide and I thought they were the best thing I'd ever seen on a stage, including the Stooges at King's Cross and Burning Spear at the Rainbow; both events that had a profound effect on me and the course of my career. They were as good live, if not better, as on record and I just knew I had to make this deal. I think I was the only person that wanted to release Suicide's record in Europe. I certainly wasn't aware of any competition, so they were stuck with me and over the course of time, we've become good friends. I love them dearly and still think they are extraordinary artists, individually and together. We made the deal very quickly and the record came out."

UK press reaction to Suicide's album showed much greater awareness and receptivity than their home country. The most incisive review had already appeared in the *Melody Maker* of January 21, which had seen Richard Williams, who was the first host of BBC2's *The Old Grey Whistle Test* and whose writing pedigree stretched back to being the first UK journalist to praise the Velvet Underground, give the album a lead review off import. Under the headline, 'Suicide is a solution', he announced: "In what may be the ultimate fusion of seventies influences, Suicide have constructed an album which proposes yet another way out of the much-publicised new wave impasse." While bemoaning Britain still being stuck in its "crash-bash cul-de-sac", he cites America's "weekly solutions", achieved with "brain and spirit" by bands such as Television and Talking Heads, before comparing Suicide to *White Light White Heat*. He cites the sick vocal cut-ups of 'Lady Godiva's Operation', Cale's keyboards and Maureen's drumming, while also mentioning La Monte Young and Kraftwerk's "procedures" as elements. Williams singles 'Frankie' out as "a post-psychedelic classic... the most disturbing creation since 'Heroin'," and points out how the bass line in the "disquieting requiem" of 'Che' is derived from the Modern Jazz Quartet's 'Softly In A Morning Sunrise'. He also manages to liken 'Girl' to Marvin Gaye's 'One More Heartache', Tommy James' vocals and "Miles Davis' recent organ-playing", while homing in on Rev's "fascinating soundscapes".

In 1978, it was refreshing to encounter such a brave, knowledgeable review which totally got Suicide. For its subsequent feature, *MM* sent Colin Irwin, who normally handled folk but also plugged into New York's latest form of people's music. Irwin compared Suicide with the Velvet Underground, Iggy, the Doors and Can although he stressed "basically they're way out on their own".

Suicide was released in the UK in July, along with the remix of 'Cheree' and 'I Remember' as a 12-inch single. Bronze kindly took out a full-page ad for Red Star's first two albums in the July 1978 *Zigzag*. The rather mysterious ad was headlined 'The Sumptuous Chinese hostess brought another round of hors d'oeuvres as the dialogue continued', before launching into a quote from Thau about punk and bringing rock'n'roll back to the radio.

At the bottom, the small print said, 'Suicide in UK with Clash thru July'.

SIXTEEN

"We put them on tour with Elvis Costello in Europe and the Clash in England, then by themselves. For a brief moment, that was the most exciting summer I'd ever witnessed. It was mental. I felt terribly bad for the band that the reaction was so horrifying and violent, but there were some people in the audience that got it and the effect was profound. You couldn't walk out of a Suicide show. You either loved it or hated it. A lot of people hated it to begin with…" – **Howard Thompson**

Never was Peter Crowley's theory that Suicide should not open for another band so brutally proven than on the infamous European visit which Marty Thau dubbed 'Blood '78'. Those gigs supporting Elvis Costello and the Clash around the theatres, universities and clubs of Europe have reached mythical status for seeing the most extreme abuse a band has ever suffered from an audience. Lesser highlighted is the fact that Suicide also kick-started the UK's early eighties electronic revolution at these dates.

By 1978, punk had become a pantomime parody of its original agenda, riddled with the kind of tribal meathead intolerance which condemned it to join comedy stereotypes such as the dopey racist skinhead or ageing Teddy boy. But the reception Suicide received in Europe didn't just come from overnight punks craving toddler din; it simply amped up the witch-burning hostility Suicide had been getting from reactionary rock crowds back home for seven years.

One day Marty Thau got a telegram from the promoters of the Third International Science Fiction Festival, asking if Suicide would be interested in appearing "as the Festival's musical attraction" at the event to be held in Metz, France, on June 9. Expenses would be paid, along with minimal fee, if they co-headlined with keynote speaker Frank Herbert, author of *Dune*, the award winning science fiction novel. Thau saw it as "a timely offer" because of the press Suicide had been getting and John Peel braving death threats to play 'Frankie Teardrop'. "This appearance would get Suicide overseas at minimal expense," Thau reasoned. Maybe Suicide would be welcomed like spiritual descendants of Rev's jazz heroes, who had fled the US to find receptive crowds in Europe.

Gerry Bron had a bronze-coloured private plane, which he piloted himself. At the behest of his label's marketing department, around 10 UK journalists, plus veteran radio DJ Alan 'Fluff' Freeman and *Zigzag*'s John Tobler, who'd been plugging Suicide on his *Rock On* BBC Radio One show, gathered at Luton Airport to make the two-hour flight to Linz, 20 miles east of Paris. According to Howard Thompson, they landed in a surreal scenario. The festival was being held in "this weird little rustic village-hall-type place with wooden chairs that folded up". The power difference between the US and Europe shorted some of Suicide's equipment, meaning a delay which turned the French crowd ugly. The plane party managed to catch 10 minutes of Suicide before having to head back to make the local airport curfew.

"We saw two numbers and then had to leave," recalls Howard, "but apparently this was a particularly nasty French crowd." Alan was surprised to see a Louis XIV-type chair land at his feet, while Marty recalls getting carried away in the sound but feeling a thud in his chest, which turned out to be a boot.

My old (and sadly missed) friend Giovanni Dadomo, one of the earliest punk writers on *Sounds*, was among the journalists. He had already seen Suicide play "a brief but devastating set" at CBGB the previous November. Although Suicide's impact was compromised at Metz, Gio reckoned, "the sound was still a threateningly malicious blend of drone and caterwaul but for most part all the subtleties – and there are plenty of them in this extraordinary team's future-past concoctions – were lost in the overall boom-boom." He still found Alan "one of the most compelling performers I've seen in yonks, a multiple man who's James Brown for a second, then Little Richard and Gene Vincent combined, a Puerto Rican street-slut spitting venomous taunts, and all the time moving beautifully... I think he's right up there with Iggy and Rotten."

Suicide were then booked to open for Elvis Costello on his first tour of Europe, before supporting the Clash around the UK, which Howard had sorted out. "We couldn't have asked for better exposure, because Costello and the Clash were sizzling hot and major Suicide fans," reflects Howard, who drove a Red Star contingent consisting of Miriam Linna, Roy Trakin and tour manager/sound mixer Charles Ball.

Costello was on the speedy rise which followed his second album, *This Year's Model*, presenting a wired new wave bridge between pub-rock and punk on recent hits such as 'Pump It Up'. Mainstream rock fans could plug into his more accessible sound, although he maintained an angry edge. The tour kicked off in Brussels on June 16 at the venerable 2,000-seater Ancienne Belgique Theatre. It degenerated into a full-blown riot. Howard was there with his trusty Sony TC-205 cassette recorder, so it was possible to hear the carnage when the recording first surfaced on a 1,000-pressing bootleg given away in a December *NME*, then as a nine-inch flexidisc with 1980's reissue of *Suicide*.

The crowd sounds quite enthusiastic after Suicide are announced and Rev kicks up the pulsing death-rattle of 'Ghost Rider'. Boos start to rise as Alan sends out his war whoops, and into 'Rocket USA'. While Alan intones "die, die, die" like a mantra of doom, the crowd start chanting "Elvis, Elvis, Elvis". "What you sittin' there for?" shouts Alan as 'Cheree''s snappy woodblock kicks up, quelling the hecklers enough for Alan to ask if anyone's got a cigarette. "Oh, right, you can't smoke," he corrects, before steaming into 'Dance' against the intensifying explosions of discontent. Irate punters were now ripping tiles off the wall and flinging them at the stage. During 'Frankie', someone nicks the microphone, but after the promoter threatens to stop the night, he gets it back with a hearty "Fuck you, man!"

"You could sense the confusion resonating through the audience, who had come to see Elvis Costello but were being asked to endure the full impact of the Suicide culture shock," recounted Marty Thau. "Ignoring the cries of those Euro music fans that had never experienced such a strange guitar-less band, Vega was caught off guard when a belligerent audience member jumped onstage, and stripped the microphone out of his hands to the cheers of the bewildered attendees. Half the audience started to chant what I imagined garbled Belgian farm anthems would sound like, while the other half cheered and applauded... As was the case with the Dolls, it was obvious that you

202

either wholeheartedly embraced Suicide, or vehemently loathed them. There was no in-between."

After Costello's angrily truncated 10-minute set, it all went off. While riot police moved in blasting tear gas, the Red Star seven made their escape through a fire exit into an alley and cars waiting to whisk them to safety. Later, the Red Star crew were greeted enthusiastically by the Costello crew.

"The cops came in with their helmets and tear gas," recalls Alan. "The shit started flying. The cops actually rioted more than the rioters! Eventually, I walk up to the side of the stage and Marty's standing right by me. I'm standing there laughing my ass off watching this, and the shit is flying, and the equipment's getting destroyed. They said, 'We better get the hell out of here'."

Miriam recalls, "I have never been a fan of Elvis Costello, I don't know anything about that kind of music. I knew Suicide was going to blow them offstage. It was exciting to anticipate their X factor in action. They were like a hand grenade at a sweet 16 party – explosive! You could feel the audience get riled up as soon as the lights went up. I was standing beside Marty Thau and he was clearly sweating, his mouth was open and his graduated-tint glasses were steamed up. When the shouting and cushion-throwing began, it felt like World War Three had just been declared on the continent as Marty Rev cranked up his noise box and Alan started taunting. They were like New York City street thugs who had to stand alone against a huge mob. Their music was not far from an air invasion of unwelcome forces. The whole night seemed like a war zone. We had to get whistled out the back entrance into cars that sped away before anyone discovered where those filthy New Yorkers had gone."

Miriam theorised that perhaps Marty's grinding keyboard and Alan as "a forbidding figure, menacing, yet with a voice positively dripping with pathos" was "too stark an image to be fed to a crowd expecting yet another feel-good rock'n'roll band. This was mob mentality, where music actually popped a switch in the collective cranium and made them all crazy! I was so shocked, surprised and stunned that I didn't have a chance to be frightened. I wanted to run, but the combined volume and musical attack of Suicide was in a war-like debate with a ferocious captive audience, hell-bent on destruction... I am a strong believer in the visceral, physical and mental effect of music, but I have never seen it affect people like Suicide did at this venue."

Miriam's words could be applied to most of Suicide's gigs in the following two months. Brussels was followed by Paris, a city long noted as a European bastion of artistic devotion and, from that show at its Olympia, a lifelong Suicide stronghold. Howard's recording shows Suicide going down well which, if anything, slightly confuses Alan, who ups the screams during 'Frankie'. "By '78 we were already mainstream, man!" he laughs now, while Rev reasons, "There was a lot of interaction and a lot of craziness when we played on our first European tour. We had songs and a rhythm machine by then. We were playing places with stages, so Alan's theatre thing was much more direct."

More dates followed in Zurich, Munich, Amsterdam and the Hague, which saw another police riot against a rampaging crowd. Far from being bemused, Elvis Costello loved the way Suicide shook up his crowds. "One night, we did that real nice, big old place with leather seats in the Hague," recalls Alan. "Elvis' band were all going nuts on speed. The day of the show, I bumped into Elvis walking along the street with his bag of laundry. He goes, 'Hey Al, do you think you can give us another riot tonight?' 'Sure, Elvis'. And sure enough I caused the thing. They ripped up and knifed the seats in this beautiful symphony hall. The headlines in the newspapers said, 'Suicide Cause $100,000 Worth of Damage'. Elvis was happy, because it meant his band didn't have to play that night either."

Howard Thompson reasons, "People just didn't know what to make of Suicide, and they weren't prepared to give it a shot because they didn't have guitars and drums." After further Dutch dates in Apeldoorn, Nijmegen and Groningen, the tour reached Hamburg and Berlin's Neue Welt Kane Kino at the end of the month. Going on the recordings, these shows were comparatively well-received, although heckles can be heard rising with impatient hackles, which were further stoked by Alan laying into the Germans about fascism and anti-Semitism. "What outrageous balls, to say something like that in Germany," reflected Marty Thau.

By now 'Harlem' had become a regular fixture in the set, evolving into a psycho-dramatic epic boding well for the second album they were signed to record for Red Star. "It's a black ghetto, they're dying every day on the streets 'cause they got nothing, man!" implores Alan in Hamburg over Rev's monolithic tenement wedges. Like all Suicide songs, 'Harlem' rose out of a vocal phrase, theme and musical idea. The intro then was a riveting piece of street drama, continued by Rev's relentless Latin shuffle. By Hamburg, the track had built into an ominous nightmare, almost replacing 'Frankie' in the set. Suicide seemed to have a blast in Berlin. Alan later reported being told the straight-looking guys watching seriously at the front, who he had been taunting, were Kraftwerk.

The Elvis tour over, the next day saw Suicide back in Britain to join the *Out On Parole* tour (whose name was derived from 'All The Way From Memphis' by Mick Jones' beloved Mott the Hoople). With the Pistols freshly dissolved after most had never seen them, the Clash found themselves the number one punk band. How things had changed since that first gig I'd seen them play in October 1976, where they had supported a long forgotten pub band in front of 60 suburban piss-heads with an energy and passion I had never before encountered in a band. Now the first album had been out for over a year but they still hadn't finished the follow-up, although the new single was the epic '(White Man) In Hammersmith Palais'. Joe's lyrics about the state of punk and new groups not being concerned with what there was to be learned would become bitingly relevant as the UK tour progressed. Most punk bands springing up now in the UK were third-rate bandwagon-hoppers and Clash copyists, which was one reason Mick Jones loved having Suicide open on the tour. He had excitedly played me the debut album when I went round to the mews flat off Portobello Road he shared with Generation X bassist Tony James. Mick and Tony had also read the first Suicide review in *Melody Maker* six years earlier.

"I knew of Suicide from back in the New York Dolls days, but never got to hear them," says Tony. "In a way, that was more powerful, because when I read about them I had to imagine how they would sound. One day, Mick brought the Suicide album back to the flat as the Clash were about to have them on tour with them. At first, I was quite unsettled by their minimalist rock'n'roll drone. Here was Elvis reduced to a howl of anguish over primitive drum machines and tinny synths. It was only after punk that I really obsessed about them."

Support acts were always important to the Clash. When they toured the US the following year, they insisted on giving the country's own pioneers a platform; shoving America's legacy back in its face. Consequently, American punk crowds would be subjected to names such as Bo Diddley and Sam & Dave. The fact that Suicide, New York's most ostracised act, was going to be supporting the UK's hottest new band raised a few eyebrows.

The previous year, Frame had appointed me editor of *Zigzag*, so a typical month could see gigs and close encounters with the Clash, Ramones, Sex Pistols, Slits, Heartbreakers, Blondie, Television, Richard Hell, Wayne County, Siouxsie & the Banshees or Generation X, plus a welter of lesser-known names. It was striking how so many of their audiences looked and behaved like how they'd read they should, including gobbing. Even headliners were spat on in this vilest of youth crazes.

After Suicide regrettably missed the spectacular tour warm-up at my local Friars club, they joined the Clash in Leeds and then Sheffield Top Rank on June 30. In the crowd at the latter was Paul Smith, who would become Suicide's UK record contact and a major champion 20 years later. "I worked at a local record store and can vividly remember punk sweeping in," recalls Paul. "My prog-generation department supervisor quit, so I started getting the promo albums from visiting record company reps. Suicide's first album was a very early item. Then I saw Suicide open for the Clash at a packed Sheffield Top Rank. I wasn't much interested in seeing the Clash and went specifically to see what Suicide was like live. From the front of the balcony to the left of the stage, I had a bird's eye view and have never seen such a feral reaction to a band from an audience. It was far better, or worse, than any of my school years with tribal football hooligans. There was a constant barrage of spit and frugal young Yorkshiremen were rushing to the bar to buy pints just to throw at Vega. I doubt Suicide managed to play 20 minutes. I happily left after watching maybe 30 minutes of the Clash's terrace rock. Punk had already become as codified, nationalistic and intolerant as everything else."

After Suicide received similar treatment at Leicester's Granby Hall the following night, Mick Jones assured Rev, "Tomorrow will be better, right?" Maybe that was the case at Manchester Apollo, but then came July the fourth at Glasgow Apollo, the show which ranks as the most violent the Clash or Suicide ever played, or most of the audience would ever see. This venue was notorious for having the most homicidal bouncers and volatile crowd in the country.

Suicide walked onto the ten foot high stage. Four thousand Scottish punks and skinheads looked aghast at the absence of guitars and drums as Rev kicked up a drone. Then they looked at Alan, sporting his glitter jacket with one sleeve ripped off. He let out a scream and struck a pose.

Someone started a slow handclap and Alan joined in. The crowd thought he was taking the piss. Soon the stage was being pelted with anything in sight although, fortunately, the rows of steel-framed cinema seats being wrenched out of the floor proved too heavy to make their target. While Alan looked down quizzically, a frothing beer can landed nearby. He picked it up and mimed taking a swig. The temperature rose by the second. Whisky-fuelled bouncers started kicking the shit out of punters before throwing them out. At some point, a silver axe whirled through the air and thudded into the stage, a few feet from Alan. After years of taking on New York, it seemed he had to come to Scotland to lose his life, or at least get nastily injured.

While some maintain the axe incident is an urban myth, Alan remembers it as the closest he got to death by audience. "When we played in Glasgow, I saw this fucking axe come flying by my head like one of these old 3D cowboy movies with the arrows coming. An axe! It looked like a tomahawk. No one would believe me for all those years. The Jesus And Mary Chain guys say they were there and saw the axe come flying by me. It was unbelievable, man."

The www.glasgowapollo.com website strives to catalogue everything which happened at the famous venue, which was pulled down in 1985. There's a section on each band which played there, including Suicide. The eyewitness account from one Ian Tyson describes Alan behaving "like Elvis" in the face of torrential abuse, missiles and booing. "I couldn't make out the words... they just echoed round the theatre. He seemed to be taunting the audience, but also speaking with affection and passion. A real emotional explosion. How could it be possible to create such a violent reaction so quickly with just music? And then silence. I thought I saw blood on his face. Whether it was the result of missiles being thrown, or self-mutilation, I don't know. He seemed not to be bothered by it. He still acted like a showman. The music stopped, he said something... but then calmly and coolly he walked off. It seemed like the audience were suspended in silence as they suddenly came to terms with the state of madness they were in. In just 20 minutes they were taken from a state of complacent acceptance of another support act to complete anger, then suddenly nothing. All I knew was I had to buy a record to try and make some sort of sense out of what I had just witnessed. I bought the first Suicide album, and here I am still listening to it, and every other Suicide, Vega and Rev album that followed to this day."

Bobby Gillespie was also there, having turned 16 the previous month. In 2011, he called it "the most violent gig I have ever witnessed", recalling how Suicide "blew my young mind" with "incredible attitude" as "two guys taking on the Glasgow Apollo at its most violent and bloodthirsty. The bouncers were savage that night, the kids and punks just wanted the Clash and no one 'got' Suicide at all. Not saying I did either, but it was like music from another planet and the future to me. But something about it made me watch them. I was fascinated. I loved their attitude, and still carry that memory with me. They looked so freaky, Rev in giant X-Men shades covering his whole face, a sci-fi mutant. Vega smashing himself in the face with the microphone saying 'You and me, man, we're on the same side', to the baying crowd, who were ripping up chairs and throwing them at the stage alongside anything else they had." Scream guitarist Andrew Innes was also there, but confesses, "I would love to say I loved it, but I was a 15-year-old kid who wanted to hear the Clash, not some band that sounded like they came from Mars. Funny, we've been trying to sound like we come from Mars ever since!"

Alan had been dealing with hostile crowds in New York for years, and had dealing with it down to a fine art. He used every strategy he knew on the Clash tour. "Sometimes the audience would be so hostile and we'd get such shit, but I knew how to do this. You'd cut yourself a little bit and because you're sweating it looks like a lot of blood. I'd break a beer bottle, then take a hunk of glass and put it to my face. It would look like I was really doing it. You're sweating profusely, so the fucking blood would start dripping down and the people in the audience would stop their shit attacking us, man, because they thought, 'This guy's insane. There's nothing we can do to him. He wants to die so let's leave him alone.' But you had to know how to do that, man, because it got so bad sometimes."

Joe Strummer was so incensed by the bouncers' attacks that he smashed a lemonade bottle in frustration outside the stage door afterwards and got hauled in by the police. Paul Simonon tried to intervene and got arrested too. Both decided to plead guilty to avoid disrupting the tour. Joe was fined 25 quid for breach of the peace, while Paul was fined 45. "That's what we get for calling it the *Out On Parole* tour," laughed Joe in a dressing room one night.

Suicide had already won the admiration of Strummer, who announced in Don Letts' *Westway To The World* documentary, "Vega is one of the bravest men I've ever seen onstage. No-one in England had ever seen anything like Suicide. The skinheads just weren't gonna stand for it. I seen a man jump up and smash him in the face. While he was singing, I saw a bottle miss his head. He bent down to pick it up and threw it at his own head as if to say, 'You idiots, how about *that?*' He was brilliant. He'd face them off."

Next day was Aberdeen's Music Hall, followed by Dunfermline's Kinema Ballroom. Then came Crawley Leisure Centre, which was hit by Sham 69-loving skinheads. The behaviour of this particular mob recalled footage of howling redneck gaggles in America's south in the sixties. Suicide could have been a-dangling if there'd been a convenient tree. Instead, Alan got his nose broken by a dimwitted study in bulk ugliness.

It should be pointed out that I'd already witnessed several support acts get similar treatment on Clash tours, including French band the Lous (women were an even easier target) and Richard Hell (American, therefore foreign). And it wasn't only those who came to see the Clash. That year, Nico, sitting alone at her harmonium, was treated disgustingly when she opened for Siouxsie & the Banshees; pelted like an alien threat that had to be suppressed.

"Suicide had a tough time," says Mick Jones. "They were a brave group. I greatly admired them because a lot of the time they used to get in real bad trouble with stage invasions and skinheads trying to bash 'em up. In Crawley, one of them managed to get up and hit Alan Vega but they carried on with the show and got the guy off. Afterwards, we went backstage and could see Alan was really annoyed, smashing the dressing room up. We liked them a lot."

The tour went on to Deeside Leisure Centre, Brighton, Bristol, Torquay, Cardiff, Birmingham, Liverpool and Blackburn George's Hall, where Suicide got busted. It was every copper's wet dream to bust the Clash then but their road crew could swerve these efforts with expert cunning. Thau reckoned, "When the police finally realised they weren't going to garner any national headlines arresting the Clash, they shifted their attention to Suicide." The cops found a small amount of what they believed to be hash in Marty's belongings, but it turned out to be Oreganum Wild Marjoram, a mint seasoning, which he'd been sold in Amsterdam. Marty and Alan were hauled up in court.

Howard Thompson testified as a character witness, recalling, "'Mr. Ray' was the name of their arresting officer when they got busted in

Blackburn for a teeny amount of marijuana which, after analysis, turned out to be 80 per cent 'vegetable matter'. I had to accompany them up to the court house there at the end of the tour and be a character witness. Ha! I was very nervous in the witness box, and muttered something about them being good citizens, first offence, pioneering artists, blah blah blah; then the judge fined them £200 each! I was expecting maybe £25 each, which was the usual amount at the time, but the judge didn't like them, and put them in the cells until I could get another £100 wired to me so I could spring 'em. I was over the moon to see the title of the song on the second album include my name [after 'Mr Ray']."

After another Clash gig in Bury St Edmunds, Suicide played their first UK solo shows at Birmingham Barbarella's and Plymouth Metro, plus their first London headliner at the Marquee on July 18. Freed from the shackles of supporting, all the pressures of the last few weeks were dispelled and Suicide turned up the pressure.

Alan recalls another Nazi skinhead incident "one night in a submarine town on the east coast of England. We did the show and the dressing room was behind the stage. In those days, it was the National Front, all the Nazi boys. I'd left Marty to play on for a few minutes and went back to the dressing room. Then about five of these motherfuckers came in, each one of them about 20 feet tall with Nazi swastikas. They hated me. These were the ones that were hating us. I thought I was dead until people started coming backstage and these assholes left."

The Clash tour wound up with four nights at London's Music Machine starting on July 24. The first time I spoke to Alan and Marty on their own was on the opening night while they were waiting at the side of the stage for the signal to go on. The Coventry Automatics, a promising band from the Midlands, had already done their two-toned set, so the crowd was expecting the main attraction. "Clash! Clash! Clash!" chanted the faceless glob of screw-faced skinheads and self-conscious high-street spike-tops; all oddly reminiscent of impatient babies stamping in their high chairs.

Alan was wearing his beleaguered purple sharkskin suit, which had already seen several visits to the cleaners during the tour. Rev sported the largest pair of superhero shades I've ever seen. I was a bit apprehensive about approaching this foreboding pair, but Blondie and the Ramones had told me they were sweethearts and weren't wrong. Alan immediately struck me as streetwise and funny, while Marty was quieter and pleasant.

The bravest, coolest men in this building, they were remarkably down-to-earth and humble.

Then they got the nod. "This is gonna be fun," muttered Alan as he eyed the seething mass before him then made for the solitary centre-stage microphone. Rev positioned himself behind the Perspex riot-style shield protecting his Farfisa-Seeburg Instrument combination from the goonie-phlegm and assorted missiles which start coming as he ignited the floor-shaking generator rumble of 'Ghost Rider'. At that time, there was no other sound like it on the planet and I'll never forget experiencing it for the first time in a large, cavernous venue. It seemed to make the whole building quake, which further alarmed and antagonised the rally-minded mob.

Striking a chin-jutting defiant pose under pencil-beam blue lights, Alan focused his Manson lamps on the crowd while Rev upped the momentum. The merciless rain of spit and beer, joined by coins and plastic glasses, failed to stop the sound from building into a churning, electronic tsunami. Standing firm like a sea captain in a gale, Alan yelped, screamed and crooned, soaking up the aggression, driving his parochial aggressors to fever pitch hostility, while informing them the real target is not the easy one up here but those wreaking misery outside these walls. We should be uniting against the real enemy – the establishment.

Halfway through 'Rocket USA', with Alan Space Echo'd to infinity, Rev upped gear with monstrous avant garde starbursts. After a hip-hugging 'Dance', the set reached its peak with a mesmerising 'Harlem', and Rev kicked up a wired death-rattle tattoo, lashed with jagged splashes, before grooving out with 'Cheree'.

I was still rooted to the same spot when Alan and Marty strode back from the war zone. Rev remained inscrutable, while Alan's purple suit was by now blackened with blood, beer and bodily fluids. He smiled as he went past, another mission accomplished. Just another night to Suicide but, as with every other show on this tour, several lives had been changed. By the end of the week, there would even be an encore.

The gigs earned decent reviews in *NME* and *Melody Maker*, although Alan was more concerned about the state of his purple suit. "Every morning I had to go to a cleaners with my suit on a hanger. They'd look at it and go 'Ergh!' They thought it was pigeon shit, man. Every fucking day. Then that night it would be all clean, then the same way it was before. It was like going in the trenches."

"Seeing Suicide supporting the Clash was a massacre," says Tony James. "People didn't understand them, or how they fitted into punk at all. For me, they were about a coming new generation of music."

After the Clash tour, Suicide headlined four UK dates, starting at Manchester's funky Factory bar the Russell Club, supported by a new band called Joy Division. This was followed by Liverpool's Eric's which, according to Howard Thompson, "seemed like a bit of a breakthrough, as far as UK audience reaction was concerned. I particularly enjoyed that one." His recording shows Suicide getting a heroes' welcome in the old basement club. After the set started with the scathing 'Mr Ray', Alan was moved to say "I love you guys" as the crowd shouted for 'Frankie' and applauded when things got noisy.

Suicide's European visit ended with further triumphs at Edinburgh Tiffany's and Leeds F Club. Packed houses danced and cheered. It felt unreal and even unsettling after the brute hostility of the previous two months. "We had the opportunity to do our own solo thing after the Clash," says Alan. "It was like a change in my life because I'd never wanted to be an entertainer. It wasn't what Suicide were supposed to be about. You come off the streets to be entertained? Forget about it. You come off the streets to see us, you go back on the street again. So we were in this big disco place in Edinburgh. It was very wide and pretty deep and dark out there. We'd done about three songs, and I could see people moving. I was so used to all the aggravation, I said to Marty, 'Watch out, the shit's gonna start flying pretty soon because they're moving now'. Then I go back up to the mike and, all of a sudden, this great big, old style disco ball goes on and I could see everybody was dancing! Fuck, I'm dead. I'm entertaining people! I go back to Marty and say, 'They're dancing to us, man!' I swear to you, I thought my career was over. What am I gonna do now? It did throw me, man. I couldn't believe it. It was pretty much the same everywhere. Wherever we went, after every show, there were all these young kids, who eventually became the Depeche Modes and Soft Cells, packed in the dressing room afterwards. It was scary because it was a sudden thing; all these kids were in love with us after all that shit we took with the Clash."

These gigs laid foundations for the next decade's electronic revolution. Over at *Zigzag*, a single turned up one day from someone calling himself the Normal. 'TVOD'/'Warm Leatherette' was Daniel Miller's first release on his own Mute Records, and had already impressed Alan when he first heard it at a Clash soundcheck. It seemed like a raw British take on Suicide and Krautrock. There weren't many of those about, so I gave Daniel a spread in *Zigzag*. Apart from the fact he'd been inspired by hearing 'Frankie Teardrop' on John Peel, I loved his reasoning that electronic music was the real punk rock, while what was commonly held up as that was pub rock sped up. As Howard Thompson says, "Suicide flew in the face of what was defining punk rock at that time, yet was somehow more disturbing, more threatening and *more* punk than anybody else."

When the Clash tour was over, I set off with Suicide's old comrades Blondie, who were then on their rise to global stardom. The contrast was amazing as they played the same circuit as the Clash to scenes approaching Beatlemania. Just 18 months earlier they'd been treated like shit by Television on their first UK tour. Now Television were already on the way out, and Suicide had gone back to New York to find the most recent movement they'd inspired in full swing.

SEVENTEEN

"Finally, here was a context to play in which didn't necessarily have to fit in with a sixties record industry notion of what the music is supposed to sound like. For example, I first heard Suicide in 1971 when I was walking down Broadway late at night. I thought the sound was fantastic. Pouring out onto the street were thick electronic textures moving violently and continuously, vocals and instruments merging into a raging, composite sound. I stood, mesmerised, outside the window where they were rehearsing for a full half hour. Finally, I worked up the courage to walk in. I told them how much I liked their music and how I wanted to produce them (I worked at the Kitchen at the time). Alan told me how much the Hells Angels liked their stuff and I thought, 'Holy shit! I'll get fired if I produce these guys.' This band has been playing fabulous music for nearly a decade, in every imaginable context. Now, with the new scene, they had a place to fit in."

So wrote experimental legend Rhys Chatham when I let him report for *Zigzag* as a prime mover in what would later become known as New York's 'No Wave' scene. After becoming the first music director at the Kitchen, Rhys had found a scene where his dreams of combining minimalism with Ramones-inspired guitar onslaughts were embraced rather than derided. When Suicide returned – bruised, bloodied but defiantly unbowed – to their safe New York City home, they found themselves hailed as pioneers of the new movement of musical malcontents which had been starting to stir before they left. Finally, Alan and Marty could make as much noise as they wanted, safe in the knowledge that someone on the next block was probably trying to make something even noisier.

214

"The band that had the biggest influence on no wave was undoubtedly Suicide," declares Marc Masters in *No Wave*, his consummate tome on the movement. He's backed up by experimental composer Glenn Branca calling Alan the godfather of the whole movement, and Suicide its biggest influence.

To finally be acclaimed in their home city was just the morale boost Suicide needed after the mixed triumphs and depressing boot-boy conservatism they had experienced in Europe, although they knew they had started *something* in the UK, going on the reactions of the fans who had approached them. This stark new music forged in the broken-tooth landscape of Alphabet City now ignited one of the briefest supernovas New York's musical evolution has ever witnessed, although the post-punk shockwaves it unleashed are still felt today. This was the real Year Zero, bent on obliterating rock structures while embracing extreme DIY strategies, along with broader musical forms often disdained by punk, such as free jazz, funk and even disco. Nothing was sacred, everything was permitted and, of course, it wouldn't last for long. But for now, Roy Trakin was happy to describe Suicide as "the patron saints of no wave" in *New York Rocker*, which had placed itself at the forefront of the new movement after Andy Schwartz replaced Alan Betrock as editor in early 1978. And Suicide's exalted new status would result in them recording a second album.

The no wave movement's name is usually credited to a fanzine called *NO - Instant Artifact Of The New Order*, which was started by Jim Sclavunos and his NYU classmates to promote their punk band Mimi & the Dreamboats, "but that master plan was quickly shelved in favour of writing about the bands that we would catch at CBGB and Max's." Fellow staffers included Chris Nelson and Phil Dray, who later formed a band called the Scene Is Now, and photographer Annene Kaye, who went on to work for *NME*. All had *noms des plumes*, with Jim going out as Joey Brainiac, after Mexican cult horror film *The Brainiac*. "We were blagging our way into shows for free under the pretext of reviewing bands," he recalls, "so we got to see a lot of stuff, not all of it very interesting or inspired. Some of the more oddball bands that didn't fit the punk template, such as Mars, Teenage Jesus & the Jerks and DNA, as well as Suicide and Red Transistor, were vastly more interesting to us than many of the bands that had fostered the scene and that dominated the multi-band bills of that era."

Alan got no wave legends Red Transistor signed to Red Star. Local lore said guitarist Rudolph Grey and bonkers drummer Von LMO's outfit was the noisiest, nastiest and ugliest of all the bands. Seeking to harness the energy of free jazz, Grey might use a power-drill to play his guitar and, at their 1977 CBs audition, a straitjacketed Von LMO chain-sawed equipment. Jim Sclavunos played drums with the band after a brief stint as their roadie, recalling, "I first got introduced to Von LMO back when he was the drummer for Kongress, around 1975. I was very impressed by Von LMO's drumming, not least because I once witnessed him furiously pummelling a double kick drum setup with both his feet in casts, apparently from jumping out a window, before ending their set by demolishing the kit by whipping it with motorbike chains. When Von LMO told my friend Kip and I that he was starting a band called Red Transistor with Rudolph Grey, we eagerly offered our services as roadies. Sometime later, when Von LMO decided he wanted to move up front, he suggested that I play drums, even though I didn't play drums at the time! Nonetheless, I became Red Transistor's drummer for a short while, performing under the name M. They were very exciting gigs: ultra-violent, flamboyant, extremely noisy and unpredictable."

Alan thought they would be perfect for Red Star, even if he was scared of being in the same room as LMO but, unfortunately, the label went broke before Red Transistor could finish the album they'd started.

The scene gained its name after the second issue of *NO Magazine* accompanied its cover photo of a surfer with the motto, 'New Wave, No Wave'. The movement's defining event was held over five days in early May 1978 at the Artists Space alternative gallery on Hudson Street. Bands taking part included Rhys Chatham's Gynecologists (with Jim on drums), Glenn Branca's Theoretical Girls, the Contortions, DNA, Mars and Teenage Jesus & the Jerks.

Mars were no wave's most extreme cold front, formed in 1975 when singer Sumner Crane was joined by guitarist China Burg, bassist Mark Cunningham and sculptor Nancy Arlen on drums; all picking up instruments for the first time. After first gigs supporting Suicide at CBGB in April 1977, and getting chairs thrown at them when they opened for Richard Hell at the Village Gate, Mars released a single, '3-E' and '11,000 Volts', on Michel Esteban's Paris-based (and ZE-predating) Rebel Records. By December 1978, they were playing their final show at Max's.

DNA were formed and named after a Mars song when yowling guitar-scrabbler Arto Lindsay met simmering keyboardist Robin Crutchfield at a Teenage Jesus gig, bringing in unschooled Japanese drummer Ikue Mori. Explaining they were trying to sound like a Burroughs book or possession ceremony, DNA's spluttering, histrionic outbursts sounded like an extreme manifestation of street rage. They were first captured at Ultima Studios for May 1978's Bob Quine-produced single 'You And You', released on Charles Ball's Lust/Unlust imprint Medical Records.

None of these bands sought to group together in anything resembling a movement, but reclaimed the word 'No' from punk and weren't afraid to acknowledge that free jazz could mean ultimate liberation, disco was having the party of its life, and electronics were nothing to be scared of or persecuted for. Unlike the CBs scene, these bands consisted of individuals from different walks of art and culture, including poets, visual artists, experimental filmmakers, sculptors, painters and other avant garde warriors. It was significant that their pivotal event – their Max's Easter festival – was held at an art gallery, and hardly surprising that Suicide, who had played at such establishments nearly eight years earlier, were held as a major inspiration.

Downtown's art scene was split between for-profit galleries, cashing in on the increasingly lucrative stars of painting and photography, and the not-for-profit alternative spaces set up in lofts and storefronts. Founded in 1972 by arts administrator Trudie Grace and critic Irving Sandler with another of those New York State Council grants, the Artists Space provided the no wave incubator, its flag-wavers hopping between there and the scuzzier rock clubs that would have them. But it was also a more extreme reversion back to punk's original DIY spirit of shock imagery and non-schooled musicianship, coming as a gutter reaction against power-pop's squeak, catalogue punk's flailing flatulence and anyone still using verse-chorus structures and carved-in-stone chord changes. Marty Rev saw it as "a valid avant-garde extension of rock… very much the abstraction of guitar-group rock," and now saw electronics as "the next major movement".

By 1978, Lydia Lunch and Mars' Sumner Crane had moved into a whole second floor above an abandoned Chinese movie theatre on Delancey Street. It became a practice space for no wave bands. James Chance remembers the space as an embodiment of old New York. "I remember at one point Lydia and a bunch of people broke into an abandoned synagogue and took all this stuff out of there, all these nice robe type things. You could do all kinds of crazy things, and nothing would happen. Now it's really heavily policed down there, and you have to be really careful not to do anything on the street."

After having to leave Delancey Street, Lydia moved into James' 12th Street walk-up with new acquaintance Jim Sclavunos, who had interviewed her for *NO Magazine* after her set at the Artists Space event. "We had decided we wanted to interview her for our fanzine," he recalls. "The other boys were either intimidated by her, or put off, or just couldn't be bothered, I'm not sure which. Somehow the job fell to me, and we found that we got on quite well." By June, Jim was in Teenage Jesus, playing bass for the first time, starting a relationship with Lydia which would continue through future outfits Beirut Slump and Eight Eyed Spy (by which time he had switched to drums).

Lurking in the crowd at the Artists Space event was Brian Eno who, after cavorting with Bowie in Berlin, had recently released his fifth solo album, *Before And After Science*, then co-produced Talking Heads' sophomore album, *More Songs About Buildings And Food*, which he was in town to master. He was so smitten by the new bands that he ended up staying for months, and produced the anthology which displayed the movement to the world when it was released in November 1978 as *No New York*. The album, which Island Records' Chris Blackwell had originally commissioned from Eno as demos to introduce him to the new scene, eventually paved the way for ZE Records – Suicide's next outlet.

Eno was wide open for something like this. The previous December, I had interviewed him for the release of *Before And After Science*. He described himself as "at a kind of mental and physical low, which I've been in for a few months". He seemed riddled with melancholic self-doubt that day, but almost foretold the revitalisation he was about to receive from New York's anarchic new underground when I asked him about music press attempts to lump him in with *Sounds*' 'New Musik' movement. While Eno understood anyone's desire to break away from "that bluesy feel... that whole tradition of the Stones", he was "a bit fed up" with being lumped in with any new movement where emotions were down on the list. He said he was ready for a change in his "way of working", which had hit home when he was with Bowie, "because he was someone else with a lot of energy and his own movement which I could jump on to and slightly divert or follow". His new plan was "doing some things where I keep further back from being the focal point of what's happening; where I take a much more subsidiary role... I suddenly realised that what I really liked doing most was working with other people."

Taking the Alan Lomax approach, Eno documented the bands in field recording style, live with no frills. He originally had 10 outfits lined up, but went with the Contortions, Teenage Jesus (who released their debut single, 'Orphans', that month on Charles Ball's Migraine operation), Mars and DNA.

But, beyond its cultural significance, the album seemed unexpectedly tame. The bands blamed Eno's timid production, while Jim Sclavunos described the album as "a lost opportunity". This supposedly definitive document fell short enough to help give no wave an early bath. All four bands were gone by the end of the decade, although transience was also a trait of the movement.

The European tour's riots, craziness and life-threatening gigs now seemed like a dream as Suicide returned to playing home venues, starting with Max's on August 25 and 26, slipping in UK drug-bust souvenir song 'Mr Ray', and ever-evolving 'Harlem'. The Fleshtones, whose album still wasn't out, provided support. On the weekend of September 22/23, Suicide headlined two nights at Hurrah at 36 West 62nd Street, in one of the 'Rock & Roll Dance Party' events presented by radio stations WNEW and WPIX (earlier that week the Real Kids had played, while the Cramps and Dead Boys appeared the following month). Suicide's set now included 'Dream Baby Dream' and the new 'Las Vegas Man'.

They were back at CBGB for three nights starting November 2, supported by the Fleshtones, Teenage Jesus and violinist-scenester Walter Steding. More new songs were infiltrating the set, including 'Touch Me' and 'Radiation'. The second night also featured one called 'Four Horsemen'.

They then put in an appearance at the three-day Nova Convention, held over the weekend of November 30 to celebrate the return of William S. Burroughs to the US. The readings, panel discussions, film showings and performances were held at the Enter Media Theatre, on Second Avenue. Performers included Frank Zappa, Patti Smith, Robert Anton Wilson, Brion Gysin, Timothy Leary, Laurie Anderson, John Giorno, Allen Ginsberg, Philip Glass, John Cage, Ed Sanders and Burroughs himself.

Band performances were promoted by Club 57 at the Irving Plaza, where Suicide appeared along with the B-52's and Walter Steding, who was to become Glenn O'Brien's band leader on *TV Party*.

December also saw a show at Max's by a supergroup called the Nothing, which featured Alan singing alongside Heartbreakers bassist Billy Rath, Roy Travolta, Lousy Louie and Trixz Sly. Later that month, Suicide appeared again and debuted a new doo-wop ballad called 'Sweetheart'.

On December 12, Suicide returned to play at Boston's Rat, the club where they had first met Ric Ocasek the previous year. Now having heard Suicide's album, the Cars leader was an even bigger fan.

"The Cars came to see us when we first played Boston," recalls Rev. "They came to our dressing room and told us how much they liked us. It was before their first record came out. Then that came out and it was huge. All of a sudden, Ric was mentioning us in the press. This was a major league band, but he was talking about Suicide all the time."

Ric Ocasek is another major figure in Suicide's story, and maybe the most unlikely, given his band's success with radio-friendly new wave rock. Born in March 1949, he grew up in Baltimore until his dad, a computer analyst for NASA, was transferred to Cleveland. Here he met singer Benjamin Orr, who was in a local band. By the early seventies, the pair had a folk group called Milkwood, who released an album in 1973 called *How's The Weather*. After little success, the band broke up and the pair formed Rick & the Rabbits before the Cars came together after they moved to Boston. Ric sang and played rhythm guitar, Ben played bass and handled lead vocals, and they were joined by lead guitarist Elliot Easton, keyboardist Greg Hawkes and drummer David Robinson. After signing to Elektra in 1977, the Cars released their first album in June 1978, scoring hits with 'Just What I Needed' and 'My Best Friend's Girl'.

"Suddenly the Cars were like mainstream and talking about Suicide," remembers Alan. "We said, 'What the fuck, this commercial new wave band?' So we did the show and it was crazy. Then afterwards, we're in the dressing room and these five guys walk in and it's the Cars. These big pop bands were supposed to be arrogant, all bullshit, but the Cars were very cool guys, especially Ric. I kept thinking, 'Why do they like us? What's going on?' As it turned out, it was great. We're still friends."

Ric said he wanted to produce Suicide, so they agreed to test the water with a single in early 1979, and emerged with one of their greatest songs.

'Keep Your Dreams' had been around for years, having already made one pit-stop on its evolutionary path on the Max's jukebox. Now it would flower into the time-stoppingly beautiful 'Dream Baby Dream'.

Marty Thau had got a deal at Right Track Studios on West 48th Street, founded three years earlier by studio owner Simon Andrews and Power Station veteran Barry Bongiovi. While Ric continued establishing his rapport with Alan and Marty, the man sitting behind the desk translating their sound and ideas onto tape was a young engineer called Jay Burnett. It was his first major session before embarking on the career which would see him making electronic milestones such as Afrika Bambaataa's 'Planet Rock' and early singles on Rick Rubin's Def Jam label, where he forged the drum machine wallop which would define an era with LL Cool J and, notably, the Beastie Boys.

Although born in Philadelphia, Jay grew up in London where he attended the American School in St John's Wood. He moved to New York in the summer of 1976, and studied film-making at NYU. While Jay had found it exciting in London, hanging out at the Marquee, "it wasn't 24 hours. New York was a whole other fucking thing. When I showed up, as far as I was concerned it was like a whole other planet. I left England around the time the Sex Pistols were really kicking off. I knew the whole Malcolm McLaren, Worlds End bunch down Kings Road but New York was just a lot more hardcore! In London you could go out late at night and stuff like that, but you really had to fucking know where you were going, and have a bit of money, whereas in New York, you could just walk down the street."

Leaving the frying pan of a city falling to the Sex Pistols, Jay plunged into the fire starting to rage at CBGB, where he shot the first known footage of Talking Heads. He had gravitated towards recording studios while in London, including Mickie Most's RAK. In New York, he started making an effort to get on the recording circuit and, by 1978, had acquired a $200 a month apartment off Washington Square and a janitor job at Electric Lady on Eighth Street. Jay "never looked back" as he swiftly became an assistant engineer – "winding up the mic cables and stuff like that" – but also got the feel of the desk on anything from "Kiss, and crap like that" to Joni Mitchell's *Mingus* album.

Jay first saw Suicide in early 1977. "I used to hang out at CBs quite a bit and they were one of my favourite bands from that era. I made sure not to stand too near the front! There were a lot of things being chucked off the stage and at the stage at the time, though not as much as you might think." Typically, the first single Suicide recorded in the no wave era was their most accessible work to date, almost an anthemic ballad.

"Marty Thau wanted to cut a single with Ric producing," explains Rev, "and Ric really wanted to produce us. 'Dream Baby Dream' was essentially 'Keep Your Dreams', but I had some other ideas to work in, like this little xylophone. I was pleasantly surprised by how that went down. It's always interesting how people attach so much to that song and read so much into it. I hadn't really thought of it. I just thought it was fine. Something definitely happened with 'Dream Baby Dream'."

Like other struggling engineers looking for a break, Jay knew Marty Thau from the studio circuit. "I knew Thau was basically a bit of a cheat!" he laughs. "If he'd got some free time in Right Track, I'd be the engineer as I'd been hanging around. It was a really weird studio, but at that time it was just starting. They really sorted themselves out and became one of the major studios in New York. Marty was going to give me $500, but I never fuckin' got paid for it!" Although he later became an occasional drinking buddy of Alan's at downtown clubs, this was Jay's first time meeting Suicide. He recalls the brand new Roland CR-78 Rhythm Machine sitting in its box, obviously ordered in by Ocasek, as would become his wont.

"The record was basically all done in one day," recalls Jay, who also did the extended club version. It was something of a contrast to the weed-fuelled Thau marathons of the album sessions. "I think that was the whole point," says Jay. "They liked Marty, but they didn't want him in the studio! Marty was a lovely bloke, but definitely one of these people who developed a sense of un-focus everywhere he went. I was really proud of the track because it was the first full engineering credit I ever got on anything. It was also the first time I ever engineered a whole thing from start to finish. It was basically pretty much done live, with the Roland CR-78 Rhythm Machine plugged into a couple of tracks, and Marty Rev's Farfisa stuff. Alan did vocals separately. I can't remember precisely what the setup was. I just remember trying to separate the drum machine bits out, and not being really able to. There were only a certain number of outputs in those days."

Jay provided the lightning rod which captured the track's heavenly essence as 'Keep Your Dreams' transformed into a shimmering, swirling hymn, charged with optimism, hope and melancholy through Alan's intimately caressing vocal and Marty's heart-melting church-like keyboard tiers, which betray a myriad of subtleties and sublime counter-melodies on close listen. It's all enhanced by the understatedly propulsive beat, over which twinkling textures and the main hook brim with life.

As Alan puts it, "It became our anthem. A band called Suicide is singing dream, baby, dream."

But the single would now have to sit on the shelf for most of the year to await a fate which would eventually see it being adopted by Bruce Springsteen.

Inspired, Suicide made basement demos of more songs they had been performing live, in the hope they would soon get to record another album. 'Love You' was the spectral doo-wop ballad which became 'Sweetheart', 'Cool As Ice' was later honed into 'Touch Me' and 'Chezazze' would eventually be wired up to become 'Shadazz'.

While continuing to appear at Max's (including another Easter festival in April) and CBGB, Suicide started getting shows at Manhattan's newer niteries, starting with the Mudd Club on February 6. The club had been opened at 77 White Street the previous October by Steve Mass, art curator Diego Cortez and no wave dynamo Anya Phillips, who had become closely involved with James Chance and was one of Debbie Harry's closest friends. Named after Samuel Alexander Mudd, the doctor who treated John Wilkes Booth in the aftermath of Abraham Lincoln's assassination, the club ruled downtown as a multi-cultural, counterculture-homaging oasis, complete with Keith Haring's rotating gallery on the fourth floor. Regular bands included DNA, the Contortions, B-52's and Talking Heads, who name-checked it in 'Life During Wartime'. Although there was a door policy, the club became like an underground antidote to Studio 54, attracting names such as Reed, Bowie, Warhol, Blondie, Nico, Lydia Lunch, Jean-Michel Basquiat, Madonna, Amos Poe and Glenn O'Brien.

"The Mudd Club was fuckin' fantastic!" says Jay Burnett. "It was a pretty hardcore club, with people dressed up and weird theme parties and shit. For about a year, it was like a really cool Studio 54. I'd been to Studio 54 a couple of times and couldn't fucking stand it, neither could any of my friends. It was a bit too poncy."

For a while, Jay did the sound at Hurrah, where Suicide played on May 17. Opened by Arthur Weinstein in November 1976 as Manhattan's first large venue to feature punk and new wave bands, it pioneered the use of videos with monitors around the club. Thanks to the astute booking policy of the late Ruth Polsky, one of the most important but overlooked figures in New York clubbing history, Hurrah built a formidable reputation for presenting no wavers, and vital British bands such as the Slits, Bauhaus and New Order, who played their first gig there after the suicide of Ian Curtis in 1980. Bowie filmed his 'Fashion' video at Hurrah.

New York seemed to be entering a more diverse and colourful phase, as August Darnell, one of its brightest central characters, told me, "When it came to the clubs, Manhattan was unbelievable, with every aspect of the musical rainbow that you can imagine. It was extraordinary because you could hear soul music in one club, then two doors down the best salsa in the universe, and two doors down from that you'd have punk. Such an incredibly romantic period where people would go and hang out just for the aspect of going out, all ethnic groups in the clubs having a good time in harmony. If you went to CBGB or the Mudd Club, you'd find a mixture of people that you wouldn't believe. There was something about that brief time that brought people together; hedonism, escapism, let's have a good time and forget the political and racial divides that are destroying other cities and countries."

This trampling of racial and musical boundaries was helped by Suicide's old friends Blondie enjoying a huge last laugh when 'Heart Of Glass', their homage to European electronic disco, became their breakthrough hit during the first months of 1979. Inspired by their love of Kraftwerk and Moroder, Debbie and Chris knew they had been courting the wrath of downtown's snooty elite when they first subtitled a song called 'Once I Had A Love' as 'The Disco Song' on their first demos. Now, through a painstaking process using the same model Roland drum machine which Ocasek had got Rev for 'Dream Baby Dream', Blondie and producer Mike Chapman seemed to be mischievously drawing a line in the sand when they came out with 'Heart Of Glass'. It cemented Blondie's rising stardom and made them the biggest band to come out of the whole CBs enclave.

"We never thought about the word disco when we working on it," says Chris. "We were thinking about Kraftwerk. I guess it represented the establishment to the punk people. We thought it was more electro-European." Blondie knew the song would rile the same narrow minds which threw things at Suicide for using electronic drums, and wore silly anti-disco badges. As with Chris, and indeed Suicide, Debbie had come up in the more open-minded sixties, and laughed at the jibes she got when she went on the town, particularly "death to disco" being hissed at her through clenched teeth. The song was almost like a two-fingered act of mischief against these uptight puritans. "We wanted to be uncool," she shrugged, but declared the song to be "one of the most innovative songs that Blondie ever recorded."

The coming months would see Suicide enjoy the most unexpected upturn of their career, with that long-awaited second album, a maiden Rev solo flight and morale-boosting praise from an unexpected new ally from over the Hudson River.

EIGHTEEN

The stellar new single that Suicide had recorded was forced to bask in limbo when Marty Thau lost his deals with Prelude and Bronze. Red Star started crumbling as 1979 progressed and, after Thau's management contract with the duo also came to an end, Suicide seemed high and dry again.

"I was only at Bronze for a year," says Howard Thompson. "David Betteridge, who took me there with him from Island, was approached by CBS to be its Managing Director and took me there too; into Muff Winwood's A&R department. Suicide and the Real Kids had not exactly set the cash registers ringing and once we had left Bronze that was it."

With Prelude starting to reap success with disco acts such as Musique, Marv Schlachter decided to buy out Thau. He could only shrug, "My partners felt they didn't understand this punk game I was in." Red Star ceased to exist, although Thau hoped it was only temporarily. He signed off by pressing up the Fleshtones' 'American Beat' as a 45. The single was dedicated to Miriam Linna, who reflects, "I was at Red Star for one year. Marty tried to talk me out of leaving, saying I had a career with him, and that things were really going to happen. But I had been in behind-the-scenes meetings, where his funders were blowing their stacks. I felt I couldn't honestly stay there and be friends with the Real Kids and carry on with my job with Marty. I should have stayed but I did not. Things had begun to fall apart and the Real Kids were threatening to leave. If the Real Kids would have stayed, I would have stayed. It's hard being a fan in the biz sometimes, but I got a fantastic training from Marty, and I feel indebted to him. At first, I felt like a rock'n'roll traitor for jumping ship."

By this time, Miriam was playing in her boyfriend Billy Miller's band the Zantees, who became the A-Bones, while her Flamin' Groovies fanzine morphed into *KICKS* magazine, which spawned the mighty Norton Records "to issue music that we believe is the greatest stuff in the world. Decades after I left Red Star, Marty Thau would call regularly to catch up on our personal lives and 'the biz', and always had great advice and encouragement. He was terrific, an outstanding man."

As Norton Records has grown, Miriam and Billy Miller also started its Kicks Books offshoot and, in 2014, she released her sparkling solo album, *Nobody's Baby*.

Things had been moving fast for the Cars, whose second album, *Candy-O*, had driven up to number three in the charts. While Ric Ocasek waited to produce Suicide's next album, he invited them to open for his band at LA's 5,000-seater Universal Amphitheatre on September 4, 5 and 6, and appear in an episode of top weekly music TV show *The Midnight Special* which the Cars were hosting.

Stadium rock was another foreign world to Alan and Marty, and they anticipated having to face their largest crowd of haters yet. Alan recalls Suicide's little car arriving at the cavernous arena, which was littered with the Cars' massive trailers, and getting stick from the venue's crew when they unloaded Marty's humble keyboards and drum machine. The humpers had never encountered an electronic band before. Neither had the beer-guzzling expanse of young Californian jockage, before these "two roaches out of New York City", as Alan describes them, ambled onto the enormous stage. The booing started before Marty had played a note. Soon they were hurling brand new Adidas sneakers, bog rolls and loose change at the two lone figures dwarfed by the enormous stage. The bands had been instructed not to swear, partly because the amphitheatre overlooked Bob Hope's mansion, but Alan's street instincts reacted with a volley of curses.

A news item in the *St Petersburg Times* of September 29 described Suicide's "obscenities and rabble-rousing", songs about "nuclear disaster, fathers killing their families and sexual perversity", Alan's "taunts to the audience" such as "You suck just like your Dodgers", sexual gestures and even a "failed attempt to vomit". The red-faced management had demanded Suicide be removed from the bill but the Cars refused to appear unless they stayed. "They're the band you love to hate," explained Ocasek, who also insisted Suicide support his group in Boston a few weeks later. They were pelted again, prodding Alan to taunt, "What a bunch of pussies, just like your Red Sox!"

With a week to kill before filming the *The Midnight Special*, Marty stayed on to visit his family in San Diego, while Alan returned to New York. "Mari had gone out to California with the children while I was on tour in Europe," explains Marty. "We were kind of going coast to coast and sharing responsibilities. The children were out there one or two at a time, and lived with me too. We were kind of bi-coastal until she came back to New York around '86."

While Alan was in New York, he got a phone call from ZE Records boss Michael Zilkha, who said he loved Suicide's first album and wanted to sign them to his happening post-punk label. Alan "couldn't wait to tell Marty" when he returned to LA for the filming.

Suicide rose to their first major TV appearance, performing 'Ghost Rider' and 'Dream Baby Dream' for *The Midnight Special* episode broadcast on September 28. Flanked by massive-goggled Marty Rev building hymnal crescendos over his pattering rhythm machine, Alan, in black bandana and white jacket, fell to his knees in James Brown reverie and mined 'Dream Baby Dream''s liberated optimism like a soul man. The mind boggles at what conservative-rock America thought when confronted with this apparition. Paul Smith maintains "I swear at the end Vega looks into the camera and 'feels' the nation go 'Err, no thanks lads, we'll stick with what we've got, ta!'" That would probably be a polite way of putting it, but at least Suicide had appeared on national TV.

By October, Suicide had signed to ZE, which bought their unreleased single from Marty Thau to release as a stop-gap. 'Dream Baby Dream' and 'Radiation' appeared the following month, and included Jay Burnett's magnificent extended version on the 12-inch. It turned out Howard Thompson had facilitated the deal when Zilkha came to see him about getting UK distribution for ZE, and dropped off a tape. As one of the few A&R men who got back to Zilkha, Howard had made sure he mentioned Suicide.

By now, ZE had become part of Chris Blackwell's bustling Island Records. Since starting on *Zigzag*, I had enjoyed a particularly close relationship with the label, one of the first independents to focus on eclectic music, since starting in the sixties. Press officer Rob Partridge was one of the best, old school but hip, doing me favours like sorting out the last UK interview with Bob Marley in return for interviewing this new signing called U2. Rob had started raving about this new label which Island was distributing, and whose roster including James Chance, Lydia Lunch, Kid Creole, disco chanteuse Cristina, world music pioneering Lizzy Mercier Descloux, and, most intriguingly, Suicide.

For the next three years, *Zigzag* supported this exotic party label, which drew from an exotic pool of musicians, artists and lunatics to embody New York's panoramic melting pot. ZE fearlessly mated disco's pulsing hedonism, no wave's nihilism, Latin's hothouse power and jazz's ecstatic liberation, often resulting in potent street-pop couched in thunderous dance floor anthems. Rob Partridge called this intoxicating mix of gutter and glamour Mutant Disco – the fresh and funky sound of New York after dark, when the freaks came out to play.

The Z stood for Zilkha and E for his artistic partner Michel Esteban. You couldn't imagine two more unlikely business bedfellows, but both counted their love of Suicide's first album in common. Zilkha had already formed his vision of the duo's sonic destiny, while Esteban was one of their original French fans.

The British-born Zilkha, who had studied at Westminster School, Oxford University and the Lycée in France, was then working as a New York theatre critic. His parents owned the Mothercare baby chain-store empire, which was basically bankrolling the label. "Michael comes from one of the richest lineages in Europe," says Marty Rev. "He was like an heir, incredibly endowed. I believe his family had him on a budget. Once in a while they'd come in from France and go through the books. They probably wondered why he wanted to go into this business."

Michel Esteban's own background was crucial in shaping ZE's artistic ethos, where visual aspects complemented the music, including the yellow-and-black label design based on the old checker cab. "I thought, we were a New York label, so what's the most visual thing in New York? The cab!" After studying at Paris' Arts Graphiques and Milton Glazer's School of Visual Arts, Michel did a Kerouac-style cross-country US road trip, during which New York provided a turning point when he met Patti Smith at the Chelsea Hotel in 1975. "She became a friend and introduced me to everybody on the new downtown scene, including Tom Verlaine and Richard Hell from Television, Talking Heads and the Ramones. I also met Malcolm McLaren, who was managing the New York Dolls. I guess he realised, like many of us at that time, that something new was emerging that would change the face of music in a couple of years."

While he was in San Francisco, Michel had discovered the potential of silk-screening rock T-shirts. Returning to Paris, he started selling T-shirts by mail order through rock magazines, before opening the Harry Cover shop, selling records, merchandising and magazines. The shop's basement became a focal point for the city's punk scene, which Michel heightened by starting *Rock News* magazine to mirror the new music at home and abroad. After being smitten by a band called Marie Et Les Garçons, Michel started the Rebel Records label, releasing their 'Rien à Dire', and also no wavers Mars' '3E' single. Patti Smith had introduced him to John Cale in New York so Michel asked him to produce Marie Et Les Garçons. Cale agreed, resulting in Michel and band landing in New York. Cale ended up releasing the 'Attitudes'/'Rebop' single on his Spy Records (re-recorded for ZE in 1979 as a Suicide tribute called 'Re Bop Electronic').

After Michel and Lizzy relocated to New York, sharing a loft with Patti, Cale asked Esteban to be Spy's art director and also introduced him to Zilkha, a potential investor. The pair hit it off and decided to start a label that brought their disparate worlds together. Needing distribution and promotion, they struck a deal with Island, whose Antilles offshoot had released *No New York*. "By 1978, it was the end of the first new wave, with bands like Patti Smith, Talking Heads, Ramones, Television and Blondie all signed to big labels," recalls Michel. "Lots of new bands were reacting against that wave, and no labels were interested in them. Chris Blackwell had missed the first wave and didn't want to miss the new one. It was the right time, right place. These bands were signed to ZE, then distributed by Island."

Michel was inspired by the city's artistic vibe at that moment in time. "New York was not yet the Disneyland it became in the nineties. It was the background for Scorsese movies like *Taxi Driver* or blaxploitation films such as *Shaft*. Club culture returned in 1977 with *Saturday Night Fever*, Xenon, Studio 54 and Paradise Garage, where it was boosted by gay culture and Warhol-type socialites. For more rock-oriented music you had the Peppermint Lounge, Hurrah or Mudd Club. At one point, punk and dance music all melted into one."

James Chance was ZE's first proper signing. He debuted with the wired-to-the-gills funk and squalling free jazz of the Contortions' *Buy*. "We always left total freedom to the artists because we chose them as *artists*," stresses Michel. "They did what *they* wanted, not what *we* wanted. A good example was the Contortions album. Michael and I were planning to be disco at that time, because disco was fun. We said to James, 'The Contortions will be great but why don't you do something for the discotheque?' He said, 'No, why don't I do another album as James White and the Blacks, which would be that kind of album?'" Zilkha gave him 10 grand to make the album that became *Off White*. As disco was so reviled by punks, the concept sat perfectly with the sax maniac's antagonistic mindset. Donning the kind of white tux and pompadour combination he'd admired on Alan Vega, James was soon polluting glitter-ball beams as the Contortions were joined by Lydia Lunch (as Stella Rico), guitarist Bob Quine and steely muse Anya Phillips.

Shortly after *Off White*, the Contortions split and Chance departed from ZE. "Michael Zilkha was much more creative than the normal record company guys, but at the same time he didn't interfere with the music," recalls James. "He left me totally alone. He didn't have this interfering attitude that a lot of record companies had. Now I kind of wish he had interfered a little more! I was so focused on doing everything myself. Maybe if he had been around more that big break-up wouldn't have happened with the original band. After that, I had a different line-up every few months."

James' job was done in establishing ZE as a magnet for the weird and wonderful in New York City. Ignoring the 'Disco Sucks' movement and 1979's Klan-style burning of black music by yodelling lunkheads in a Chicago football park, Zilkha now envisioned punk's shockwaves colliding with different cultures throwing their music into the same furnace.

He was also fantasising how Suicide might sound if produced by Giorgio Moroder at a glitzy New York studio. Most ZE releases were recorded at maverick producer Bob Blank's Blank Tapes on 20th Street. Bob, who Esteban describes as "ZE's own Phil Spector", is one of the unsung heroes of New York disco, post-punk and house music, having welcomed such names as Chic, Sun Ra, Larry Levan, Arthur Russell, Tito Puente, Walter Gibbons and Lydia Lunch. Marty Thau brought in the Fleshtones and both Vega and Rev would record there.

Bronx-born August Darnell swiftly became ZE's in-house producer after leaving his brother's Dr Buzzard's Original Savannah Band. He describes Zilkha as "a great innovator and discoverer. Through him I discovered a lot of things that I never would have discovered on my own. The marriage between Zilkha and I was magic." Darnell would soon enjoy global success as his self-described "macho, egotistical and well-dressed" Kid Creole creation but, although now often dismissed as an eighties novelty, he could also remix the Contortions, and soon Alan Vega. His mission became to unite his city's disparate cultural enclaves with old-school glamour and a stage show like Busby Berkeley choreographing a gang of Manhattan disco hedonists aboard George Clinton's Mothership en route to the Caribbean, while dispensing his incisive vignettes of street life. When Zilkha signed Darnell, Chris Blackwell granted the full force of Island Records in Europe.

"It was the right mix: no wave and punk meeting pure disco," says Michel. "Then you had something new and interesting. Michael and I were big fans of Suicide from the beginning. 'Dream Baby Dream' is maybe my favourite song on ZE."

But the next record to come from the Suicide camp was not on ZE, nor did it bear their name. During the limbo period between labels, Marty Rev had taken the opportunity to record the solo album he'd been thinking of since Thau suggested the idea in 1977.

"That came about in a funny way because, right after the first Suicide album, Marty approached me and said, 'I want to do an album with you'," recalls Rev. "That was kind of sudden, and surprising for Alan and I. I was up for doing it but Alan, quite rightly in some ways, felt it was too soon. We had just started building the Suicide thing but Marty just wanted to do music; go from idea to idea. We made a note to do it maybe after the third Suicide album, but not then."

When Red Star was going awry, Rev remembered the solo album idea. "It was right after the tour, we were not doing that much, things were kind of slow in the fall, and there was a change of seasons. I was always having ideas and running off tapes of musical sketches. I thought, 'Hey, maybe I could really do it now.'"

Charles Ball, Suicide's sound man on the European tour, managed a web of post-punk imprints under his Lust/Unlust company. "We knew each other and he lived in the neighbourhood," recalls Marty. "Almost like the day when I really thought 'This album is what I'm going to do next', I walked into CBGB, which was pretty much empty, as it often was then, but Charles was there. He walked up to me and said 'How about doing an album for my label?' It was a synchronised moment, which surprised me. We decided to do it as his first album release on Lust/Unlust. I did that in December, right before the second Suicide album. It got released right before too."

Rev's self-titled album actually appeared on Infidelity, which had already seen 45s and EPs by Peter Gordon's Love Of Life Orchestra, Mars and Don Christensen's impLOG, whose 'Holland Tunnel Dive' is one of downtown's weirdest electronic milestones, with its fizzing pulse, Glenn Miller brass and warped narrative.

Marty recorded at Al Fierstein's Sorcerer Sound at 19 Mercer Street. "It was an eight track studio, so I used what they had and just made the tracks in the studio. It reflects a kind of New York sound, and the instrumental possibilities of pure sound I had uncovered through Suicide."

Basically, the album is the sound of Rev stretching out in his cerebral playground and seeing where he ends up. Touchingly, the first track on Marty's first solo album was a sparkling electronic tribute to his wife and muse, titled 'Mari', which is dominated by a playfully wistful melody and traverses similarly uplifting ground as 'Dream Baby Dream'. The track's lush, synthesized undergrowth is underpinned by a metronomic rhythm box (at a time when using them in this way was still a pretty alien concept). The guttural bubblegum vamp of 'Baby O Baby' is the only track to sport vocals, and sees Marty intoning with lascivious monochrome intent in a dark contrast to the opener's bolt of light. The sound disassembles into unchartered realms on 'Nineteen 86', where a latent Suicide riff snakes under woozy church bells chiming a hymn-like melody, while beset by electronic creepers. That was side one.

'Temptation' bears the nearest resemblance to a Suicide backing track, with its disarming main melody tapped out on Marty's beloved xylophone while the undertow snarls, whooshes and disgorges a deep counter-melody. 'Jomo' is a melange of splashing, diving pulses over Nico-like harmonium drone; as if *The Marble Index* had been dropped into Fritz Lang's *Metropolis*. 'Asia' closed the original album with piano-lathered layers rising like lurid gas from an East Village ruin.

Even if it was released now this album would sound fearlessly new. In early 1980, there had been nothing like it and it more than held its own against any releases which tried to proclaim themselves as being ground-breaking or experimental. Writing in the May 1980 *New York Rocker*, Roy Trakin described the album as "particularly revelatory in capturing the man's left-field genius".

"The first and second Suicide albums are at two extremes to each other," understates Marty Rev. After the live DIY innovations of the debut album, everything about the album which became *Suicide: Alan Vega And Martin Rev* was different and new; including its record label, producer, the state-of-the-art equipment it was realised on and the studio it was recorded in, which was one of the most expensive in New York City. Suicide knew they had been given a once-in-a-lifetime opportunity, so grabbed it and made the album which many consider to be the real peak of their career.

Michael Zilkha loved Suicide and desperately fantasised about hearing them produced by Giorgio Moroder, with Rev steering the cut-glass sequencer glides of 'I Feel Love' under Vega's quivering Elvis croon and volcanic yelps. Zilkha saw this as an audacious future sound which could legitimise disco and captivate the crossover crowds he was targeting with ZE. But Ric Ocasek had already taken Alan and Marty under his wing and into the studio to produce the masterful 'Dream Baby Dream'. Their staunch sense of loyalty plus the potential of this new relationship meant it could only be Ric's arse sitting in the producer's chair when the time came to record the next album. Instead, Zilkha contented himself by presenting Ric with a copy of 'I Feel Love' as a template.

"That was Michael's life," says Marty. "He led that life. He wanted us to be successful and cross over into that. He was bright enough to know there was something there in Suicide, even though it wasn't his personalised sound."

Since first embracing disco as the latest manifestation of the spirit and struggles which had drawn him to R&B, jazz and conscious soul, Marty had been keeping up with the electronic innovations running riot in the music during the late seventies. "I couldn't help absorbing it," he says. "By the end of 1979, a lot of things had happened. Punk had established itself internationally, and we had had the first record out and toured Europe. Then you had the intonations of new things being used in electronics, which had started with Donna Summer and Giorgio Moroder producing disco in Europe. Disco had a big effect and even more technology was now being used. You could now feel disco coming out of the neighbourhoods very strongly. With me, it went in, so a lot of it was subconscious, and a lot of it was conscious. 'Oh man, I can drop that in without doing it in an obvious way.' Anybody in the seventies was attaching on to this thread. It was the fashion. I wasn't interested in doing it that way, but if I heard a riff that I liked, or a rhythmic feeling, I could bring it into what I was doing."

Suicide and disco were both targets in the late seventies. Of course disco, like punk, soon got seized on and watered down by the business and bandwagon jumpers but, by this time, was producing some of the era's most innovative sonic soul. Robert Fripp, the King Crimson guitarist who had recently been lending his searing tones to Blondie, Bowie and Eno, presented an eloquent case for much-maligned disco when we sat in a London record company office in April, 1979. "First, I enjoy disco," he declared. "Secondly, I believe it's now a common currency... It is a valid musical form. The disadvantage in disco at the moment is it's being seized by record companies as successful and therefore being restricted as a form of musical expression." Fripp saw the rise of disco as a result of the sixties counterculture and civil rights movements' failure to change the system by working within its framework and the ineffectuality of "the so-called punk explosion, which basically says 'Fuck the system, it doesn't work.' Very negative, very antagonistic... Now what we have in disco, instead of saying 'Screw the system, it doesn't work', it says 'The system doesn't work, we will ignore it', and the political platform is the dance floor. Summed up, disco to me is a political movement which votes with its feet."

Apart from disco's social resonance, Marty was drawn to its technological innovations, which could super-enhance the beat to outer space or the bedroom while taking its sonic textures to the heavens. "Technology had somewhat flipped out since two years before," says Rev. "All of a sudden there was the Prophet-5 synth and these drum machines. Disco came out with this kind of high-tech, lo-tech rhythm section, which kind of paralleled and had some sympathy to what I was doing. I felt aligned to it, to a certain extent. I got ideas from it. A lot of good, catchy stuff came out of the disco world and I was listening to it all. There were a lot of 45s I picked up on. I know that had an effect on what I was doing, for sure."

At that time, Grace Jones, New York disco's provocative reigning queen, had become an Island Records labelmate of Suicide, and recently covered the Normal's 'Warm Leatherette'. Like the ignorant aggression thrown at Suicide for using electronic drums, Grace was getting flak for using tapes at her shows which, she told me "missed the whole philosophy. Disco's *all about* technology and stuff! It was those outside disco who'd walk out in disgust. Nobody else minded." She also reminded me of Alan when she declared, "With the audience I just come right out and say 'Fuck you guys! Sit down!' I knock 'em on the head while I sing, grab them, rip their buttons off and shake them up! I totally involve them with direct contact."

Ocasek was something of a tech-boffin himself, as shown at the 'Dream Baby Dream' session when he ordered in the brand new Roland C-78 drum machine for the session. To provide further state-of-the-art kit to record his dream disco album, Zilkha gave Suicide a $10,000 equipment budget, which was more money than they had seen in their lives.

"We got all this money," says Alan. "It wasn't a ton of money, but it was a lot of money for us. For us it was like Rockefeller! It was fucking amazing. Ten grand to spend at Sam Ash, accompanied by the Cars' roadie, buying keyboards and guitars."

"We could get anything we want," adds Marty. "I was like a kid in a candy shop. Ric said to me, 'There are a lot of great instruments around, what do you want to use?' He told me what was around and showed me pictures, so I could pretty much order anything I wanted to use in the studio and then I could start using it live."

Zilkha booked Suicide into the Power Station, one of the top studios in New York. In effect, the Mothercare baby empire was financing the most dangerous group in history. "Basically!" cackles Michel Esteban. "Everybody was broke and Michael was the only one who was rich. Nobody got in the Power Station, because it was so expensive, but it was easy for him to sort out. When Alan Vega came up with that proposition it was completely ridiculous, but the album was absolutely brilliant so…"

At that time, the converted Con Ed power plant on West 53rd Street was New York's most revered high-tech studio, renowned for its wooden-domed ceiling, 42-track desk and acoustics which seduced names like Bowie, Lennon, the Clash and Aerosmith. The then-unstoppable Chic were in residence. One of my most treasured memories is the evening in 1983 when, at Nile Rodgers' invitation, I visited the Power Station and witnessed Chic at work. The studio was plush, low-lit and funky, and I couldn't help trying to imagine how Suicide must have felt the first day they walked through those hallowed portals.

At first, they must have been surprised because, sitting at the control desk on their first day was the same Larry Alexander who had fled in terror from the first album sessions. He was now in-house engineer at the Power Station. "Who's sitting at the board but Larry Alexander!" laughs Alan. "He sees us walking in and goes, 'I quit, I gotta get out of here!' He just went crazy. But we were with Ric now, so he cooled out. But

I'll never forget his expression when he saw us walk in. He freaked. He could not deal with the thought of us again."

For the album, Marty's principal analog battle weapon became the Prophet-5 synthesizer, introduced by the San Jose-based Sequential Circuits in 1978 as one of the first affordable polyphonic synths. Viewed as a major development, it would establish the classic eighties synth sound and boasted an all-important balls-out bass sound for Rev. While Marty was still exploring the Roland CR-78 drum machine, Ric also brought in the latest Sega 78, where buttons were pushed to get a beat.

Now might have been the time for Suicide to either amp up their song aspect or further explore the experimental paths of the first album with this new technology. Instead, they made a sleek, disco-inflected New York classic, which Marty likes to describe as a "psychedelic orchestral version of Suicide", which he says was backed up by a musicologist friend describing it as "the *Sergeant Pepper's* of electronics". Ultimately for Rev, the album was another phase in the ongoing journey which, a few years earlier, had seen him hammering colossal noise emissions out of a cheap, hot-wired organ.

This time, the recording process saw the live takes of the debut album replaced by meticulous overdubs. While Alan concentrated on honing and singing his words, Marty set to work like a scientist. He doesn't even see the album as representative of Suicide at that moment; more a high-tech detour. In retrospect, it was a perfect move. If the first album had set new benchmarks for sonic extremes and tapping into the dark side, Suicide now started their new decade by presenting a way of working with electronics which uncannily presaged things to come, from synth-pop to acid house.

"The second album was all recorded separately," says Marty. "Ric said, 'Lay down tracks,' so I would record part after part. It was all very fresh to me. I had the Prophet-5 and drum machines which, at that time, were very new and worth exploring. It was a big studio. I remember Ric was very far away behind the glass in the control room! Then Alan would put his vocals on separately, then I would come back and add things to what he did and we'd go to the next one. It was like one track after another; 'Let me throw all these colours'. It wasn't Alan and I really cutting it together. There were so many tracks it was kind of multi-layered, and it kind of worked for me like that. We had never approached Suicide that way. I suppose, in many ways, it was recorded like a solo record, so the tracks probably reflected that. It was really more of a studio album, whereas the first album had really been us cutting it live in half an hour!"

Marty had been given another new path to explore, which became another step in his ongoing musical quest. "The technology was always very much part and parcel of what my searching was all about. Sometimes you realise after you do something it's not really what you want to hold on to. I guess a lot of the second album came out of the fact that we now had access to all these instruments. One of the basic ideas in my mind as the album was developing was, 'Hey, what would it sound like with an instrumental approach?' With Suicide, everything's multi-faceted; it's like a ship in a bottle. It has its own special, fragile kind of song form from two people. It kind of works that way, but at some point it's like, 'Okay, let's try this without vocals! Let's try this with five vocals!' It just begs a lot more possibilities. On a simpler level, I was thinking, 'We haven't done that yet, what would that sound like?' So that's a basic idea that gets you started. It was definitely out of what I was doing with Suicide but, in the working out of it, turned into something else."

Sonic exploration aside, recording at the Power Station was a memorable experience thanks to the neighbours working in the other studios, including Chic, who were producing Diana Ross' multi-platinum career-revitalising *Diana*. Also around was Carly Simon, and Bruce Springsteen, who since March had been working on his epic double album *The River*. "Bruce was next door just a few feet away," recalls Marty. "I think he already knew of us by then. When we felt the album was pretty much done, he came into the control room one night, and listened to the whole playback. He said something to Alan, while I was sitting off to the side listening. Then he came over to me and said, 'I really like what you guys do'. He was familiar with us already, which was saying something because we'd only had the first album out."

"Bruce came in and flipped!" recalls Alan. "He liked it right away. When Bruce was there, his roadies would stay with him, because they really love the guy. I used to hang with him a lot. His manager didn't want him to be drinking or anything, but I used to keep a bottle around all the time. It was like kids in school, going to the bathroom to smoke cigarettes. He's just a great guy." Alan also recalls, "Carly Simon heard Suicide and gave this disgusted look. No one wanted to be around her, man, although Diana Ross was friendly."

After Ric brainstormed the selection and running order, Suicide's second album was ready. It was called *Suicide: Alan Vega and Martin Rev.* The cover, which Marty reckons has "a disco feel", features a blood-splattered bathroom.

Rob Partridge sent me an advanced test pressing (in a black sleeve marked 'Suicide album' in white pencil), so I made it the lead review in that April's 100th issue of *Zigzag*. 35 years ago I wrote the following first impressions, which I still stand by.

'Now Suicide have emerged again. They're being told "their time has come" but they're still ahead... by miles. This album is so startlingly new, yet perfectly danceable, that it can comfortably sit with early Velvets, Roxy's first, Bowie's best, Metal Box and any other future-pointing landmark you care to mention.

Side one and 'Diamonds, Fur Coat, Champagne'. Suicide's words often consist of the title repeated over and over, plus lung-racking, distended screams and crazed murmurings from Vega. This track rides a mesh of drum machines, counter-riffs and ridiculously propulsive bass. 'Mr Ray (For Howard T)' is a churning, steaming whack in the guts. Vega's voice gets more guttural and rasping until he disappears under one impossibly long scream. 'Sweetheart' is Suicide's love song. Only lyrics are the title and "I love you", which Vega croons in an Elvis vibrato. The backing swings softly and coos. 'Fast Money Music'; hectic and whooping, the drum machine on chattering overdrive. 'Touch Me' is another scorching, metronomic feast, like letting off a fire extinguisher in your trousers. There's so much going on beyond the jigsaw construction of the beats and melodies. The odd, stepping momentum set up here is totally danceable. Can't believe it's produced by one of the Cars!

'Harlem' opens side two with a nightmare ride and a menacing throb. Screams in the night echo for miles, the sirens are going but the eerie fascination keeps you rooted to the danger. Suicide in their element. 'Be Bop Kid'; pure rock'n'roll bass-line, roller-coaster beat, piping keyboard punctuation, insanely catchy. 'Las Vegas Man' is the other mid-side slowie, almost a night-club croon, vocal-wise. 'Shadazz'; relentlessly 'up' deranged calypso. 'Dance'; down to the black bones of an electrocuted thrash, and a spine-freezing riff, under which voices moan and speed up into a sort of demon chipmunk.

This'll be acclaimed, everybody will suddenly have liked 'em all along, and that's great. They deserve it. Suicide – shuts all other competition in the kami-khazi.'

It's funny reading those words now; written by biro to be sent to a type-setter at a time before drum machines had really strayed beyond Moroder/ Kraftwerk and synth-pop had yet to storm the charts. Electro was still a gleam in Afrika Bambaataa's belly, rappers were still using Chic records as backdrops, acid house and techno were still five years away. There was nothing else to hold Suicide's album up to.

There was also no inkling that, instead of propelling Suicide to their deserved global stardom, the record would actually herald a barren stretch and the world wouldn't see another album from the duo for eight years.

NINETEEN

Maybe symbolically, Suicide's first gig of the eighties was their last at the club which had opened all the doors for them in the previous decade. By now, Max's was in the downward spiral which would see it finally close its doors the following year. "At that point, Max's was beginning to go to hell," says Peter. "Tommy got lost in the blizzard. I was doing the best I could within a club that was physically falling apart. Max's never came back after Tommy lost his restaurant manager in early 1980. The quality of the food went down, and the place wasn't kept up. It looked seedy and falling apart. There was a slow two-year decline, during which I put on lots of great bands and had some wonderful shows, but to no avail. We were also facing competition from the Mudd Club, Danceteria, Peppermint Lounge and a slew of lesser places, which thinned out the audience, so it was becoming more and more difficult to stay afloat."

Peter was left adrift and skint when Max's closed. "I had to go get a job," he says, ruefully. "I had worked at Max's for subsistence wages. When Tommy asked me how much I wanted, I told him what I needed, rather than what I should have done. That was the stupidest thing I *ever* did. I should have said, 'Give me a dollar a head on the door'. I'm not a very good businessman. Same as with being Wayne's manager. I made the same kind of mistakes. I was an artist really. I made Tommy Dean a millionaire and he was able to buy the building, but I didn't make anything for me. I looked for jobs, and found one in a place that books studio musicians. I made sure it was the evening shift."

It seems unjust that the guy who built Max's back to glory in the last half of the seventies, and gave Suicide their first breaks, now had to look

241

for a position away from the downtown action he helped create. Recent years have seen him try and round up original survivors for his annual Max's reunion.

Suicide's last show at Max's on January 18 was actually a blinder, as shown on *Attempted: Live At Max's Kansas City 1980* (released by Marty Thau on Sympathy For The Industry in 2004). Their set starts with 'Harlem' and Rev's drum machine scooting along at top-speed turbo-rattle under Alan's bitter street growl, before 'Radiation' mutates the riff from Barrett Strong's 'Money'. 'Dream Baby Dream' is similar to the original single, with Alan soaring over its pumping drum machine tattoo as Marty weaves sepulchral new organ melodies. 'Ghost Rider' is a vicious rework over the rhythm from 'Fast Money Music' and 'Dance' is already unrecognisable from the new album, stoked by an organ riff shaped from the Crystals' 'Then He Kissed Me'. '96 Tears' mounts a Latin shuffle. 'Rocket USA' also gets a savage makeover with its chain-dragging speed-shuffle. Alan starts inviting punters onstage, including a hammered Cheetah Chrome barooing through 'Be Bop A Lula'. The 'Touch Me' rhythm pops up behind 'Night Time', while 'Jesus' revisits early set stalwart 'Junkie Jesus' with Rev in Spanish doom-chord mode under the Latin beat. All told, it was fresh evidence that, as Rev says, the second album was a luxurious diversion and a work unto itself. Meanwhile, Marty carried on using his newly acquired machines to further evolve Suicide's sound in a live setting, along with marking the release of his own album with a solo show at the Kitchen, along with Peter Gordon's Love Of Life Orchestra.

While they waited for their album to be released in March, Suicide returned to Hurrah on March 11 for a ZE Revue Night. Lizzy Mercier Descloux opened, Kid Creole & the Coconuts played their first major showcase and ZE's disco princess Cristina made a brief showing before Suicide topped the bill.

Suicide: Alan Vega And Martin Rev still sounds like a blueprint for all synthesizer-based music that's come since. It perfectly fit ZE's exotic New York dance mission, delivered Suicide-style with its icicle disco textures, exotic piston rhythms and Alan's tour de force masterclasses in animated expression. The opening 'Diamonds, Fur Coat, Champagne' saw Rev painting the era-defining picture of glitzily decadent nightclubbing at that time, while Alan says his lyrics were also inspired by Marvin Gaye's 'Inner City Blues (Make Me Wanna Holler)' from 1971's seminal *What's Goin' On*.

"'Inner City Blues' was the story of guys like us," he says. "I thought about it when I wrote 'Diamonds, Fur Coat, Champagne'. You might not see the similarities, but just in terms of the pathos. Here's the poorest guy on the planet, who doesn't have a pot to piss in, talking about giving a girl diamonds, fur coat and champagne. But that would be impossible, completely off the charts. It'll never happen. That's what Marvin's song was about; You can't get your cheque, you can't get anything. It was us!"

Suicide could only glimpse that world they so perfectly evoked in the song. When their album was released in May, they would have settled on seeing the record in the shops and promoted in the media. Instead, they fell victim to the paranoia starting to grip the US music industry when ZE got the thumbs down at a board meeting at Arista Records, its US distributors. "The option came up on ZE and Arista passed, just as our record was coming out," says Marty. As a result, the album stalled and ZE shifted its game plan, pushing Kid Creole, who would sign to Sire, along with new acts such as Detroit's Was (Not Was) and Bill Laswell's Material.

Robert Fripp talked about the "sense of terror" gripping the music biz when we met again around this time and inadvertently explained Suicide's fate. "It's difficult to convey how hot New York is for rock'n'roll at the moment. There are clubs springing up, new groups, great ideas and enthusiasm. The only thing that's wrong is the music industry. New York is bursting with groups but the industry has no idea what to do with them." Fripp blamed the US music business being more interested in its ludicrously extravagant expenses budgets than taking a chance on releasing records that were going to sell less than 100,000 copies. He predicted that, unless the high-end greed was tempered, artists with a more specialist fanbase, like himself (and therefore Suicide), might never see the light of day in the future.

Suicide had ended the seventies being air-lifted into a situation which should have seen them reaping long-overdue rewards and acclaim. Given the state-of-the-art means to make the album of their dreams in a top New York studio for a happening label, Suicide had risen to the occasion by creating an album which upgraded their sound and foretold musical developments in the oncoming decade. But their bright new record would now sink in the face of ignorant indifference and problems at the business end. Instead of scorching through the new decade in triumph, Suicide found themselves playing the clubs again.

Ironically, at the same time, those dressing room kids from the 1978 UK tour were busting out all over in various permutations of electronic pop. Suicide had been at the front of this charge before it got beyond the starting blocks but now had to watch as their trailblazing crusades were buffed up for global success by those with big bucks backing and the requisite grasp of glib commercialism.

Although Suicide's original radar blips were assuming depth-charge impact, it would be wrong to say that every band which picked up the drum machines and keyboards which earned Suicide such abuse in the seventies had consciously ripped them off. Many of these acts didn't even know they existed. Take boffin-friendly *Keyboard* magazine's 2011 compendium professing to tell *The Evolution Of Electronic Dance Music* through the magazine's back pages. The book starts with chapters on Kraftwerk and a reprinted June 1982 piece on 'New Synthesiser Rock', which focuses on Depeche Mode, Soft Cell and Japan. The "now-defunct" Suicide are mentioned in a list of names that used "digital boxes". It's their *only* mention as various pale reflections go on to name their influences; usually starting with Kraftwerk.

When Suicide were first active, they were obviously heard only by a tiny minority. Those who took their template often failed to credit them, such as in BBC4's documentary on the birth of electronic pop and rock in 2010, which ignored them completely. Soft Cell were an exception. After storming the charts with 'Tainted Love', the Leeds duo were a cut above the shiny-trousered synthy-warblers on *Top Of The Pops*, hinting at forbidden pleasures and sleazy underbellies while establishing their own personalised agenda. Soft Cell took pains to trumpet their love of Suicide, and covered 'Ghost Rider' in encores. After Marc Almond saw Suicide in New York in the early eighties, he ranted evangelically to me in the Some Bizarre offices one afternoon about how great they had been. "It was performance art! It was the sound of the New York streets." When we put Alan in *Zigzag* in December 1983, he said Soft Cell had made some good records, but had first described them as "Suicide the easy way" (which had hurt Marc).

Ultimately, Suicide felt they were on their own, going nowhere again as they gigged sporadically around New York for the rest of 1980, returning to Hurrah, playing a new place called the 80s Club on 86th Street and making their first appearance at the new Danceteria on 37th which, in a few years, would be the hottest club in the city. The latter set was filmed by the club's video lounge masterminds Pat Ivers and Emily Amstrong for their weekly *Nightclubbing* show on Manhattan Cable TV.

If Danceteria pointed at clubbing's future, CBGB was battling on as a last bastion of New York's punky past. It was usually empty but filled up for events such as Alan's solo return on August 21. Suicide saw out their last active year as a duo for a while with further club dates and two more hellish encounters with enraged stadium ignorance when they supported the Cars at arenas in Hartford, Connecticut, and Providence, Rhode Island, in November. It was the usual rain of coins, bog roll and booing, which was so loud Alan compares it to a hurricane. This time, roadies found a knife sticking in the drum riser.

"There was another limbo between scenes," says Marty. "A couple of years of no wave and that was it. There wasn't a lot happening for Suicide, and in New York in general, so we concentrated on solo things, Alan on a more high profile level." While Marty worked on the "vision" he had of "building an orchestra of pure electronic, more abstract sounds," which would eventually appear as *Clouds Of Glory*, Alan embarked on the solo career which would consume his next few years. It would also lead to him meeting his soulmate and muse.

Alan had already started playing solo gigs, at Max's and at the new Squat Theatre in March. Inevitably, his next move was to record his first solo album. Announcing "I had always wanted to do a rockabilly record," Alan decided to go against the then current grain of synths and big productions and reach back to his rock'n'roll roots.

The idea had got under way when he met Texan guitarist Phil Hawk banging on a piano at a party in SoHo. The blond-quiffed guitarist had just moved up from Texas with his Fender Telecaster. "Shit, he's like a blond Elvis Presley," thought Alan. The urge to strip down to rock'n'roll's unadorned guitar-drum roots grew, manifesting on the minimal 'Jukebox Babe', which was released as a single by ZE to test the water for a whole album. The song's combination of Alan's Elvis intonations, clanging guitar riff and skipping rockabilly groove was an instant hit in Europe, going Top 5 in France. Its success clinched the recording of the album, which was released that November. "I think I cleansed my soul with that one," says Alan. He knew that, with Suicide on the way out with ZE, the move was a last ditch lifesaver.

Reaching back to rockabilly was a logical, even masterful move on this third album to emerge from the Suicide camp in the space of a year. While Marty's set had presented his vivid electronic visions, Alan had taken the other road in Suicide's sound – stripping back to its rock'n'roll roots and concentrating on his singing as a focal point. *Alan Vega* was recorded at Skyline Studios on 37th Street, which was popular with names such as the B-52's, David Byrne and Steely Dan. The sound is intimate and microscopic as uptempo numbers such as 'Jukebox Babe', 'Fireball', 'Kung Fu Cowboy' and 'Speedway' deal out ankle-tugging brush-strokes on the rockabilly groove. The slowies, notably the pleading 'Love Cry' and desolate 'Lonely', plant Alan in previously unfamiliar soul crooning territory, which he makes his own with exaggerated pathos. The dubbed-up scrub of 'Bye Bye Baby', with its screams, yelps and grunts, is the closest thing to Suicide, while 'Ice Drummer' is the title which remained on the shelf after the first album sessions. Delicate and haunting, it presented a skeletal new form of American roots music; Manhattan fried, Vega-style.

Alan even got a decent review in the *Village Voice,* where Debra Rae Cohen wrote of the album's "stylised postures of Sun country and spaghetti westerns", concluding "The result is a kind of hypnotic neo-rockabilly that's more expansive than Suicide's oppressive New York throb, but just as wisely soulful, woven from scraps of Americana."

The year 1981 saw two last Suicide shows before Alan's solo career took over. On September 17, they played Chase Park on Broadway and Houston, topping a bill which included Lydia Lunch's new 13:13 and post-no wave outfit Ike Yard. Since Teenage Jesus, Lydia had moved through a string of resounding projects, including her orchestral noir masterwork, *Queen Of Siam*, on ZE. Her new band's first album moved her confrontational bloodletting up to another, richer level and Lydia further along her road to becoming one of the longest-lasting and loudest harbingers of the original no wave spirit.

Meanwhile, Ike Yard were making their debut as one of the New York bands which showed a tangible Suicide influence in the form of the jittering synth action, topped with deadpan vocals, on that year's *Night After Night* EP. Mainstay Stuart Argabright, now a respected no wave archivist who still makes music, recalls Chase Park as "a venue right out of *Diamond Dogs*" on Lower Broadway. "That was a cool night," he recalls.

"Everyone played tight and there was a good crowd, but I remember we had to wait to get paid by the promoter! Certainly, some of what we did in Ike Yard was influenced by Suicide. We worked it out so we could play those multiple parts from three or four synth keyboards live, playing together and improvising along the grooves for that bustling urban synth funk. After that show, Alan was very gracious and complimented the group. After that, I kind of thought of them as relatives, fathers to Ike Yard, in some sense."

Two days later, Suicide were on the alien turf of Minneapolis, playing its Walker Arts Center for what was billed as their "Tenth Anniversary Show". As documented on the *Ghost Riders* CD, they played one of the most remarkable, unusual sets of their career. Alan was on supercharged form, unleashing some of his most full-throated screams and constantly cajoling the polite-sounding crowd. Rev hit a startling new sound on his Prophet-5 and had never sounded like this before, gouging out seething, almost harmonium-like tones and frequencies. 'Harlem' stretches into an extended Death Valley maelstrom and there's a new epic afoot in the anti-smack 'Sweet White Lady'. Sometimes it sounds like they're clinging on for dear life.

As David Fricke's liner notes say in the original 1986 ROIR release, this set is about survival and celebrating a decade together: "...all battling barroom goons, starving and scantily recorded while Suicide-come-latelys like OMD and the Human League were up to their pencil necks in platinum. All that energy, frustration and indestructible pride comes blasting through in this recording... *Ghost Riders* is the sound of hard-won victory."

Ironically, considering Suicide was about to go on pause, they were further eulogised that September when ROIR released the *Half Alive* cassette put together by Rev, which boasted a fascinating bunch of live recordings (including their 'Sister Ray' at the Marquee in 1978) and demos, complete with cover designed by Jim Sclavunos. I managed to snarf one when I visited ROIR boss Neil Cooper at his Manhattan office in 1983, where he'd been operating for two years. He had big plans for his cottage industry and soon it seemed like every downtown luminary had a ROIR release.

Lester Bangs' liner notes placed Suicide as the real originators of terms being bandied about such as "new music", "minimalism" and "industrial", maintaining "What they have been all along is primal prototype street punks (with the best of hippie) thrown in on the side… All you have to do is take a gander at all these worthless synthesizer-art bands around now to realise how far ahead of his time Martin Rev's approach to keyboards was, and how much more soul he's always had. It's just a real shame they got so little credit for what others turned into piddle." Lester concludes, "I don't know where you live, but like the Velvet Underground's, the Dolls' and damn few others, Suicide's music is truly the sound of New York City for me."

Suicide's final recorded shout for a while was 'Hey Lord' on that December's *A Christmas Album*, ZE's festive project which initially came on snow-coloured wax and also featured Material, August Darnell, the Waitresses and Cristina. At the time, it was looked on as the first decent seasonal collection since Phil Spector's. Suicide's track is a supremely moody, sonorous drifter; the ghost of Christmas future. Zilkha had asked for another Suicide track, but Marty had left to visit Mari in California so Alan dubbed up the rolling electronic groove and rapped over it.

By now, ZE had changed somewhat from the idealistic enterprise started by Zilkha and Esteban, who had recently split. "I lived in New York most of the time between 1976 and 1981, and they were great creative years," says Michel. "In 1981 I did not think New York was the centre of the world any more, and wanted to travel, so I came back to Paris and went to Africa and Brazil."

The second Suicide album had provided Rev with impetus and instruments on which to make his next two solo albums, *Clouds Of Glory* and the next decade's *Cheyenne*. *Clouds* was mainly what kept Marty busy creatively when Alan stepped up his solo mission ("otherwise it was just continuing your own journey, as usual").

Started at Blank Tapes in February 1981, *Clouds* is the record Marty Thau had wanted to cut with Rev after the first Suicide album. "I had this very clear visual idea for my next two albums," explains Marty. "*Clouds* was a natural progression from the second Suicide album. I used that Prophet-5 live for a while on shows, which allowed me to get deeper into what could be done with it."

Marty's main inspiration came from travelling across America between coasts, "because, at that time, Mari and I were based between California and New York. I took one of those three-day Greyhound bus excursions, which was my chance to see America for the first time. It was incredible going through all the deserts in Texas, Mexico and Arizona. I got this feeling of this American landscape that I had in my mind as a child but never really saw. This expanse of terrain, landscape and all those new sensations greatly influenced my visual concept. They all had that same kind of colour, which was in my mind for a long time. A lot of the time the music was just visual ideas relating to those journeys across America, using the sounds I was getting in the new instruments. When I went into the studio I already had such a clear idea at least where to start. It was a very auspicious moment because it was all floating around my mind fairly clearly."

While the album was started in a flurry of inspiration, it wouldn't see release until Marty Thau clinched a deal with France's New Rose label in March 1985. Rev remembers he had sent the label a tape of the album, which New Rose believed "was just a demo for actual songs. When Marty Thau sent them the final tape, they thought we had pulled something over on them because there were no vocals. But that was the record they signed."

The album is a richly panoramic feast, the only familiar reference points coming with the Suicide-like bass lines which snake through pieces such as 'Rodeo', 'Rocking Horse' and the title track. 'Whisper' sounds like a hallucinogenic dub of 'Sweetheart' and the widescreen doo-wop procession of 'Metatron' is an atmospheric peak. 'Parade' is indeed a vivid representation of wild America's most spectacular expanses, endless and glowing.

In his memoir, Thau describes the album as "wondrously ahead of its time, featuring music that Rev and I believe will someday be recognised for its integrity, originality and wildly unrestrained hypnotic rhythms. A fascinating electronic work, replete with space, ambient, trance and other techno elements, it marked the return of our studio collaboration and resulted in some of Rev's most startling and accessible work."

As 1981 came to a close, Alan recorded his second solo album at Skyline Studios. The sessions marked the first time he had worked with a band. Not just any band, as the rhythm section was drummer Sesu Coleman and bassist Lary Chaplan from the Magic Tramps, who were Mercer veterans and massive Suicide fans. "It was a thrill," says Sesu. "Alan wanted to put a band together that reflected his rockabilly influence. He loved Elvis, Buddy Holly and Gene Vincent and wanted to reach in that vein. He had guitarist Mark Kuch in mind. Alan and I were both raised on this style of music, and he explained he wanted to keep it basic and real. He wanted the influence to combine with an organic tribal jungle sound, allowing him to dig deep into his soul and make it personal. Originally there was to be no bass player, but I suggested Lary. It worked well as Lary and I were tight and could feel each other's musical vibe live. With Alan knowing us from the Magic Tramps, it worked perfectly."

Alan explains the album as continuing his mission to celebrate "that core essence of rock'n'roll." Much of it consists of spirited rockabilly tear-ups such as 'Outlaw', Buddy Holly-inspired 'Raver', 'Rebel' and 'Magdalena', which enjoyed an August Darnell remix on 12-inch single. The band also steam through covers of 'Ghost Rider' and Gene Vincent's 'Be Bop A Lula', while 'I Believe' is a spine-tingling gospel ballad, reaching a screaming soul peak.

"Recording *Collision Drive* in New York City was a spiritual and magical project for me," says Sesu. "Mark Kuch was an instant fit. I stripped my drums down to a basic set. Alan knew what he wanted. He told me he hadn't worked in a band with a drummer and said 'I'll be listening to you – keep it simple, solid and strong. Keep us on track.' So it's basic and to the point. Re-making 'Ghost Rider' was bold yet it has its own personality and strength."

Everything which came before couldn't help being overshadowed by the 13-minute 'Viet Vet'; a sonorously heaving epic with the band writhing like a snake-swamp colossus. Along with 'Ghost Rider', the song was the other towering masterpiece which was directly inspired by the Vietnam War to come out of the Suicide camp. "You owe me a debt!" hollers Alan in livid, frustrated rage at the claustrophobic climax. It was as disturbing as 'Frankie Teardrop' and more graphic than 'Harlem'.

Sesu recalls the dimly lit studio having "a Vietnam-Cambodian jungle feel" when the track was recorded live. "We were all in one musical moment and living the song, which was about a soldier returning from the horrors of war hell with a bloody stump for an arm, trying to adjust to civilian life, never to be the same. The story, along with Alan's howls, groans and screams of pain was so real. All of us playing it together was an out of body experience. Recording this album helped put music in perspective as to what it was supposed to do - provoke, yet celebrate. It was the most emotional recording I've ever done. It's simple, yet connects with the inner soul. I'm honoured to be on that album. It changed my life."

Billy Idol told Sesu that *Collision Drive* "was his favourite all-time album" and he played it non-stop on his tour bus. *Collision Drive* also incurred the best reviews of Alan's career. *NME*'s Barney Hoskyns cited Alan as "one of the great rock'n'roll singers" and praised each track, particularly 'Viet Vet', which he described as "Vega's most extraordinary nightmare vision yet… Forget *Apocalypse Now*, put yourself through 'Viet Vet' and learn the truth." *Sounds*' Jeremy Gluck (writing under his Ralph Traitor *nom de plume*) simply declared "Alan Vega is a true original. We need him."

Ironically, when Alan took his band on the road he was bemused to find himself being heckled for appearing with a rock group and not doing Suicide songs! "Where were they when I was dodging bottles?" he mused. Around that time, I caught his major London show at the Venue in Victoria; a nice old theatre with no seats, like a cavernous Marquee. 'Jukebox Babe' was the extended centre-piece, before the encore featured his version of 'Jailhouse Rock'. It was strange seeing Alan in a normal band setting without Marty, who himself had recently opened solo for Iggy Pop at New York's Peppermint Lounge.

In June 1982, Alan opened his first one-man show since OK Harris at the Barbara Gladstone Gallery in New York. He sold all but one of his 13 pieces based around "crucifix type things". He still moved in those circles, having long known Hungarian art critic Edit DeAk, who let homeless artists stay at her loft, including himself in the past. Through Edit, Alan met the doomed Jean-Michel Basquiat, who he sadly remembers being "drugged out a lot".

In July 1982, *Zigzag* carried an interview with Michael Zilkha, who said Alan had assured him he was going to make "the most commercial record ever this summer" by going to Detroit to work with Was (Not Was). But by the following year, ZE would be winding down. In a parting shot, Zilkha got Alan a deal with Elektra Records. Instead of going to Detroit, he recorded his next album, *Saturn Strip*, at the Cars' Syncro Sound studio in Boston. He used his band, with Ocasek producing and Ministry's Al Jourgensen playing keyboards.

Alan's schedule at that time was so hectic he was writing lyrics on the drive up to Boston. Released that September, the album's manifesto is best illustrated by the pulsing, keyboard-driven 'Video Babe'. The version of Hot Chocolate's 'Every 1's A Winner' was an unexpected choice. Fronted by the gleaming pate of Errol Brown, Brixton pop-soul outfit Hot Chocolate were *Top Of The Pops* regulars in the seventies, riding the glitzy disco-pop boom with smashes such as 'You Sexy Thing', 'So You Win Again' and 'Every 1's A Winner', which reached number six in 1979.

Alan returned to the UK in late 1983 and played the Venue again. He had swapped the band for two synth-players, with only guitarist Mark Kuch remaining from the band. He talked about his wild times on the road with his rock'n'roll band in *Zigzag*, explaining, "I got that band together to have some fun and as a kinda holiday but I was having such a good time I couldn't bring myself to put an end to it... I couldn't see it but a lot of people who I respected told me it was time to start work again."

While Rev further retreated into his ongoing personal journey, Alan went to another extreme of record company boardrooms, limos and promotional campaigns, and was about to face the most demoralising artistic experience of his whole career. It turned out to be the best thing that could happen to him.

TWENTY

"Time's definitely running out. The kind of stuff that happens in New York is like a modern Rome, the epitome of decadence and moral decay. But that's what happens before destruction. I'm really affected by what happens on the streets because I'm there. It's my life. There's a lot of energy there. New York offers me the electricity, gives the music a buzz." – **Joseph Bowie of Defunkt,** *Zigzag* **1982**

It was only when I was fortunate enough to visit New York in 1983 that I could really understand why Suicide had sounded like they did. From the moment I got out of the cab outside Danceteria, there seemed to be an intangible electric energy that coursed under the sidewalks and sparked larger-than-life craziness all around. Titles of immortal songs came to life in the street signs, and around-the-clock black music radio stations such as WBLS, KISS FM and KTU were a revelation.

Since the cab ride in I already believed those who said they were never the same again after first seeing the New York skyline, but the defining moment came the morning I was standing on the subway platform at Union Square. A rumble in the tunnel swelled in volume until it had become a deafening eruption of flashing sparks and howling metal. There it was; the uptown 6, covered from top to bottom in an eye-blasting barrage of cartoon figures and wild style lettering; like a mobile art gallery screeching up from the bowels of the city. From now on, New York's essential artery became a perennial source of awe and fascination, its coruscating steel wheels sounding like early Velvet Underground feedback or Suicide. *Particularly* Suicide.

My New York adventure started at Danceteria, then under the guidance of its serene booking agent Ruth Polsky. The club was now in its most famous location on 21st Street and seemed like a living embodiment of the city's artistic substrata thriving off each other's energy. On the same night that Frankie Goes To Hollywood were having their US launch party, Run D.M.C. were performing their debut single, 'It's Like That', in another room. In the ground-level live room it was possible to see anyone from Bo Diddley to world class local bands such as Certain General and the Band Of Outsiders. Two more floors catered for dancers, with DJs booming out disco and electro. The top floor's Congo Bill bar was a ground-breaking TV lounge, reflecting the appearance of MTV and coming visual age. Artists such as Keith Haring and Basquiat were regulars. So was Alan, who I would sometimes stumble into there. Although still as down-to-earth and friendly as ever, he looked like a rock star now.

The clubs were still under the hold of two records made in New York City the previous year which had helped reshape music: Grandmaster Melle Mel's 'The Message' and Afrika Bambaataa and the Soul Sonic Force's 'Planet Rock'. 'The Message' was almost like a rap version of Suicide, like Frankie goes to the South Bronx with its seething refrain and bleak images of broken glass, rats, poverty, junkies, whores, dead kids and brutal cops. Bolstered by its ground-breaking electronic backdrop, the track proved to be a brutal reality breakthrough for rap and marked the maturing of New York hip-hop. When I got to New York, Mel was rapping about 'White Lines' on another kind of anthem for the times.

Meanwhile, 'Planet Rock', which Rev describes as "one of the originals", had kick-started the electro movement. Coming up in the Bronx River Projects, Afrika Bambaataa had tried to steer his fellow Black Spades gang members away from thug life with his parties. Now he wanted to record a global anthem. "I was always into 'Trans Europe Express', and after Kraftwerk put 'Numbers' out, I wondered if I could combine them to make something funky," he told me in 1984.

Bam's dream was realised at Intergalactic studio, the New York studio now being operated by the same Jay Burnett who engineered 'Dream Baby Dream'. For Bam's session, Jay engineered with a team including up-and-coming producer Arthur Baker, keyboards maestro John Robie and Bambaataa directing. "That record was interesting because no one knew what they were fucking doing, but it turned out really great!" says Jay. Inevitably, Kraftwerk were not amused and the ensuing lawsuit got them the composing credit.

Ironically, Suicide were nowhere to be seen as these two milestones helped legitimise the drum machine as an essential tool, and established electronic-based music as a vital modern development. They did make a one-off return appearance the following August at Irving Plaza, churning through 'Radiation', 'Ghost Rider', 'Dream Baby Dream', Alan's 'Bye Bye Baby', '96 Tears' and 'Harlem'. David Fricke reminded the world of their existence in a glowing *Melody Maker* review, bursting with lines such as "Dominating centre stage, like an evil Hispanic bat with his black leather cape and hair combed in a tall black statuesque arc, Vega whooped it up like a real Elvis from hell, barking and shrieking through a '96 Tears' charged with tenement blues fury." *NME*'s David Keeps remarked that time and solo success had not dulled Suicide's "abrasive aesthetic... as brilliantly relentless as ever, a confrontational blow to the nervous system, yet still defiantly rock'n'roll."

Alan also found time to sing on the debut album by San Francisco-based accordionist Angel Corpus Christi's debut album, *I (Heart) NY*, which was released on Criminal Records in 1985 and sees her covering songs by Reed, Hell and Suicide in her quirky style. Produced by Howard Thompson, who was now head of A&R at Elektra, Alan adds a male counterpart to 'Dream Baby Dream' and 'Cheree'.

Paradoxically, Alan's next solo outing, *Just A Million Dreams*, released in late 1985, marked the nadir of his major label experience, complete with pouting cover photo ("I looked like fuckin' Rudolph Valentino, man!"). He had started on the album with Ric Ocasek but the latter's work with the Cars (who had been rocketed to global stardom with their Live Aid-bolstering smash 'Drive') prevented him continuing, leaving Elektra to find another producer. With next choice Arthur Baker too busy, they spent over a year looking for the right candidate, eventually settling on old school muso Chris Lord-Alge. Making the album was two years of aggravation that felt like 10, rumbled Alan in a special 'stop gap' Vega edition of Lindsay Hutton's faithful *Next Big Thing* fanzine, in which he describes being thrown out of the studio, Elektra hating what he was doing, and being absolutely perplexed and even mortified at what was being done to his music as titles such as 'Hot Fox' and 'Cry Fire' were

255

resprayed with twiddly guitars and big eighties drums. While he admitted that it got him radio play, he expressed feeling as though he'd had to sell his soul to get there.

If *Just A Million Dreams* was the low point of Alan's major label solo sojourn, its launch party at the Palladium on 14th Street would change his life after he met future partner and collaborator Liz Lamere there. Though she came from the high-powered world of Wall Street law, something clicked that night and the couple have been together ever since.

Liz was born and grew up with two older brothers in the predominantly Irish suburban town of Milton, Massachusetts, just south of Boston. "My dad's father was Italian and when he married my Irish grandmother the Irish were more socially advanced in Boston. I think her family had some reservations about her marrying an Italian man, so they changed the spelling of the name to make it look more French! My name looks like it's French but the original spelling had an 'i' at the end, so that's why it's pronounced Lameri."

Milton was an easy subway or car ride into Boston, where Liz's father worked as an attorney in a law firm. She was sent to Catholic school and taught by nuns "in a very strict, structured environment. I was always a bit of a rebel and acted out a bit. I pierced my own nose when I was 15. This was back when the only people I had seen with pierced noses were Indian women on the subway. On the weekends my girlfriends and I would get on the subway, go into Boston and explore the big city. I would see these Indian women standing on the subway in their long dresses, with the jewels in their noses and go 'oh, isn't that beautiful?' I thought that was so cool. At high school, we'd sneak into the men's room – because the only one who'd use the men's room would be the janitor – to smoke cigarettes. I'd pierce people's ears, cut their hair and we'd write on each other's uniforms but, at the same time to please my parents, I was always a straight-A student because I thought that would piss the nuns off. Supposedly, I could be a trouble-maker but academically they couldn't fault me."

Liz was "a bit of a tomboy, always very physically active", playing Varsity soccer for four years and skiing, but also a regular at the Rat Club in Boston. While her older brother played his stone age Uriah Heep records, Liz was attracted to more lively current outfits such as the Dead Boys and formed her first band at 15 with a guitarist boyfriend called Brian Pike. She decided drums were the perfect instrument, reasoning "How hard can it be, banging on things and trying to keep a beat?" She was allowed to rehearse in the basement at home. "As long as my grades were okay I got away with a lot."

After attending Tufts University in Somerville, Liz studied law at Columbia university. She would take the train to CBGB, becoming a regular at the club when she started working for a law firm in the cut-throat world of Wall Street. Dressing "over to the extreme of conservative" by day in three-piece power suits, "by night I had the thing in my nose and dressed punky". She continued playing drums in bands for fun, including one called Moral Turpitude and another with two undergraduates from Columbia and Barnard called SSNUB (Sergeant Slaughter's No Underwear Band). "I've always been into music. I am very passionate about creating and performing, but we didn't have any great aspirations of making a career out of it."

At this point, Liz had never heard of Alan Vega or Suicide. All that was set to change after her close friend Dori Kachinsky, whose brother was Alan's guitarist Mark Kuch, invited Liz to accompany her to the launch party for *Just A Million Dreams*. Ironically, the low point of Alan's career was about to provide a high point in his life.

Liz and Dori's plan was to go with Mark to pick up Alan from the Gramercy Park Hotel, the lovely vestige of old school New York, complete with piano bar, where he had been living. Liz recalls the moment they knocked on Alan's door. "Alan appears and sweeps us in. He's all hyper-energy with his hair all up and he's got the bandana on. The room was relatively dark, but he's got these light sculptures on the wall. I thought, 'This is really intense, what's going on here?' But the focused way he looked at me was like 'Wow, who is this guy?' I had an immediate visceral reaction. There was some serious energy radiating off this person. I remember looking at the lights on the wall and thinking, 'What is this?' Alan and I met on October 23, 1985. I remember because it was exactly one week after my twenty-seventh birthday. You remember these things because that was it – boom! – the day I met Alan. The interesting thing was I read my horoscope that day and it said, 'You're going to meet a lamb in wolf's clothing.' At one point before we were leaving for the Palladium, I suddenly noticed Alan's belt and it had silver studs with the word 'wolves' written all over it. I got chills when I saw that."

The party hopped over to the Palladium, which was overflowing with liggers, fawners and freeloaders all looking over each other's shoulders to see who'd just walked in. "All these people were hovering all over Alan, but he kept breaking away and coming over to where Dori and I were standing, saying to me, 'So what's your story? So you're a lawyer?' Dori kept saying to him, 'Go away, she doesn't wanna talk to you'. I think that was part of the attraction too! All these other people were trying to pull Alan to them, but he kept trying to get away and find out what my story was. I had the same kind of reaction, like 'Who is this guy? There's something amazing about this person.' Then he went off on a tour, so I didn't see him for six weeks, but I kept thinking about him the whole time. Dori was going 'Forget about him, I'm sure he's trouble.' She was probably trying to protect me."

While on tour Alan found his time with Elektra was coming to an end as they were preoccupied with panto-rockers Mötley Crüe and silky soul MORsters Simply Red. "*Just A Million Dreams* was the beginning of the end," says Liz. "He went on that tour and discovered they weren't going to push the album as they'd made an executive decision at Elektra that they were going to push Simply Red and Mötley Crüe. So they pulled the plug on that. He knew the writing was on the wall. When he came back I called him at the Gramercy and he immediately said, 'Wow, Liz, where are you? Can you come over now?' It was a Thursday night and I left work and went to him. We sat in the lounge by the bar and stayed up all night talking. It was like we were catching up with each other's whole lives in that one night to the point where I felt like I had known him for many years by the time we parted. I can remember going to my office that day with virtually no sleep and going back to see him that night. We were pretty much together from then on."

Liz now divided her time between staying with Alan at the Gramercy on weekends and the feverish intensity of her "crazy Wall Street job, which included a lot of all-nighters; this crazy career doing securities offerings for people like Drexel Burnham, the investment bankers who later got in a lot of trouble. I'd sometimes go two or three nights, just take a shower at the office or at the printer, because back in those days we'd go to print. The clients would disappear into the bathroom, where I suspect they were snorting coke to keep up with the ridiculous number of deals they were juggling. For 'entertainment' breaks they would make late night phone porn calls and put the ladies on the speaker in the conference room. I was a bit outnumbered as there were not many women practicing high stakes corporate law in those days. It felt like I was back at a college fraternity house! Meanwhile, I'm thinking 'What the hell am I doing here? These corporate finance deals are deadly boring, and I hope this deal dies so I can go play drums with my band!'"

Back at the Gramercy, Alan was revisiting his electronic roots by experimenting with electronic junk and effects; exorcising his pop star period by going back to the experiments he had conducted at the Project. Liz was enthralled by her intense new boyfriend, who was about to resurrect the band she now knew about and couldn't wait to experience.

By summer 1986, I had made the big move and relocated to New York. My neighbourhood was always the East Village which, at that time, could still be dangerous, but was still where artists, musicians, anarchists, junkies and hustlers managed to co-exist amidst the bedlam. At that time, hip-hop had become the sound on the streets and radio stations. The big label was Rick Rubin's Def Jam, whose first eight singles had established a new sound built on bare, granite-slab beats. While the form would manifest during the following decade in Alan's solo outings after he got into gangsta rap, this brutal new street sound piqued Rev's curiosity in a musical form he had long been aware of as the latest phase in R&B. "For me, rap and hip-hop was part of that same root. There was that authentic thread of continuity. There was a guy who used to be on the corner news-stand here on St Mark's Place and Third Avenue. He would rap as he was giving you your newspaper. He was doing that really early. Rap was more and more permeating but, to me, the age it really broke through was on those early LL Cool J records. That was my beginning with rap."

Jay Burnett had helped Rubin forge this cavernous new template for the first key Def Jam releases, including LL Cool J's 'I Need A Beat' and former punk band the Beastie Boys' 'Rock Hard', which had sampled the guitar riff from AC/DC's 'Back In Black'. Jay and the Beasties' MCA further influenced coming electronic percussive manoeuvres with 'Drum Machine', a remake of a track which Jay had released in 1982. Rubin gave Jay the name Burzootie and five grand cash to produce the track for Def Jam. Burzootie achieved his influential sledgehammer beatbox sound using the Oberheim DMX and EMS sampler, recalling "That drum sound evolved over a couple of records. Every time I got a really good sound using the DMX, I'd sample another sound on top of it and put on a bit of reverb, sample that, then add something else for the next record. The pinnacle of that was the MCA and Burzootie record and a couple of things for LL Cool J that wanted the big drum sound."

While this aggressive form of beatboxing would underpin several Suicide tracks, Marty saw hip-hop more as a kind of parallel street music created by striving to convey a message by any means necessary. "I recognise the similarities with the original approach, but it also confirmed to me the role of necessity being the mother of invention; making art out of necessity and what you had, not what was coming down from up top. Rap wasn't coming from up top or the big studios. It was coming from the people on the street who just wanted to make music. That's why it was so new. They had maybe a turntable and some vinyl and just had to find some old rhythm machine. They had a DJ and an MC, then you had groups all over the place. All of a sudden, Suicide was not the only one. I can appreciate the similarities. I knew that was the next genuine phase of rhythm and blues too, combining rock and the whole new technological thing of collaging sound, which had never been used before."

But, like disco, hip-hop was another influence on Marty which would be subliminal rather than pronounced. "I was already in a place where I didn't feel I've got to do that, or I've got to be like that. Like most of the things I've heard all the way through the years, it kind of gets assimilated and absorbed. I was already using electronics and whatnot. As much as I appreciated and respected rap, I didn't feel to the need to emulate it. I never wanted or needed to emulate anybody!"

By September, I was living at 437 East 12th Street by kind courtesy of Joe Drake, bassist with the Band of Outsiders. This was the famous 'Poets Building', whose residents had included many famous artists, writers and musicians. When I moved in, Allen Ginsberg lived in the apartment below, Richard Hell was my next door neighbour, and I would exchange smiles on the stairs with mysterious avant-disco producer Arthur Russell, although I only found out who he was after I'd moved out (and that Luc Sante had written *Low Life* here too).

On the night of September 7, I was supposed to meet Ruth Polsky outside the Limelight, the converted church on Sixth Avenue which was now a hot local night-spot. She was managing my close friend Parker Dulany's Certain General, one of downtown's most evocative but overlooked bands, who were playing that night. I was late getting to the venue, but shocked when I arrived to find a yellow taxi lodged in the church's old doorway. All night everyone wondered where Ruth was, then were stunned to discover it was her that had been under that taxi. Parker and I had to go and identify the body.

After his band's Limelight set, Parker went to a bar on 12th and Second called W.G.A.F. (Who Gives A Fuck), where Alan could often be found at that time. "It was before confirmation of Ruth's death and I poured my heart out to him," recalls Parker. "He had already heard the rumours of it possibly being her under the cab. Ruth loved Alan but I had never spoken with him, partially out of competition because of Ruth's affinity for both of us. But that night he was very calming and sweet. He knew who I was and he knew how much I loved her, and he really was a gentleman to me. We both knew it was a dire situation. I was already spiralling downward and he was trying to keep me afloat."

Three weeks later on a cool, clear evening, Suicide returned to CBGB on the night of September 27. The first time I had seen Suicide on their home turf remains the best gig I saw in my years in New York City. Returning to the club they'd first played 12 years earlier, this time they got a heroes' welcome. The energy was incredible as Marty, sporting red hat, shades and studded black shirt, disdainfully spat out pulses and intricate micro-rhythms from his setup, with a tweak here and a flick there. The first track was built on a pile-driving groove and resonating rock'n'roll motif, prodding Alan, in leather jacket, black bandana and fingerless gloves, to turn up the Elvis 'un-hunhs' and yelps. 'Devastation' invoked the ghost of 'Peter Gunn', before another intricate rhythm web underpinned a glorious 'Cheree'. Next, Alan dedicated 'Rock'N'Roll (Is Killing My Life)' to Ruth; a relentless locomotive of clanging riffs. Words haven't been invented to describe how I was feeling by now. Here were Suicide, 10 years after I'd first heard them on the Max's album, back again to smash the club which once hated them. Alan changed the words of 'Rocket USA' to include 'Jailhouse Rock' while Marty sent out sonorous helicopter throbs and surgically mangled monster-grooves. They played for just over half an hour and it was magnificent. As we spilled out of CBs on to the Bowery afterwards, my girlfriend of the time bit a chunk out of my face, providing a lifelong souvenir of that magical gig. Above anything, that appearance showed that Suicide were back. Surely the next step would be to record that long-awaited third album?

Over in the UK, Suicide had been enjoying new recognition following their name being dropped by former Generation X bassist Tony James, whose stack-haired Sigue Sigue Sputnik had emerged as their most blatant heist and affectionate tribute. Tony's former Generation X comrade Billy Idol was now a US megastar, who had praised Suicide in interviews, but Tony seemed to be basing his entire new future-mission on 'Ghost Rider' and Alan's first two solo albums. Billing his band as "Hi-tech sex, designer violence, and the fifth generation of rock'n'roll", Tony came on like a 21st century update on McLaren, wielding his "Fleece the world" slogan as he, reportedly, signed a multi-million pound record deal with EMI and insisted on Giorgio Moroder producing the group's first album, *Flaunt It!*

"It was after punk, in about '82 or '83, that I really studied and obsessed about Suicide," says Tony. "I had to buy every album, bootleg and tape I could find. I immersed myself in their sound, while I dreamed my dreams of how to create my rock'n'roll band from the future. In the early days of Sputnik we listened over and over to 'Ghost Rider', 'Rocket USA' and 'Frankie Teardrop'. In our first rehearsals we would play endless versions of their songs with our two drummers hammering out the beat and me playing a two-note bassline. Often, in time honoured tradition, you would mutate a song to finally make it your own, changing the lyric and tune. We applied that to Cochran, Elvis and Suicide. Suicide showed us you could just play one riff over and over. But we'd have hit pop tunes as well. That was what had held them back, as far as I could tell, because they deserved to be massive. Also it was the confrontational nature of their sound. We took that too – pummel the audience to death by riff."

Tony adds that Alan's first solo album was just as great an influence on the band. "Here was a way of playing minimalist rock'n'roll with a whole band. The early Sputnik went and saw Vega play at the Venue. I wonder if he saw this band of pink-haired freaks staring up and studying him with their imaginations on fire. We saw the future. It was another piece of our jigsaw puzzle. Then we just had to add T Rex, violent movie trailers, Donna Summer and put it all in dub. The Sputnik sound was born."

Even if Sigue Sigue Sputnik wouldn't last for long, the press attention hadn't done Suicide any harm at all. Now the high-profile stage of Alan's solo career had ended, the return of Suicide was further cemented when Marty Thau told Alan and Marty about the renewed buzz around them. London booking agent Paul Boswell came on board and booked a four-date European tour in late 1986, consisting of dates in London, Amsterdam, Berlin and Paris. These European mini-tours would be the norm for the rest of the decade, including UK dates supporting long-time fans Siouxsie & the Banshees in 1988.

"Everything had pretty much dried up with Suicide so we did the solo things," says Rev. "Then sometime in the mid-eighties, there was this turnaround when Sigue Sigue Sputnik and a lot of these groups started mentioning Suicide in the press. When we toured in '78 we left under an impression of 'What was that?' as they still hadn't totally understood what we meant. We weren't asked to come back. Now we had all these groups saying we were an influence. Marty Thau picked up on that and approached us about doing a tour. He said, 'You're gonna have an audience now', and put us in touch with Paul Boswell, who was very interested in doing it. That's when we came back and we would do maybe two two-week tours a year for the next four years. Sometimes you have to wait. It's been like that ever since."

In October 1987, Ric Ocasek invited Suicide to Electric Lady studios on Eighth Street to record the album that would become *A Way of Life*. "Ric was doing more production and wanted to produce us," says Rev. "He said, 'It's time to do a new album, let's do it.' He just wanted to do a record, then would let us try and get a label to release it; 'It's your record, do what you want'. He just gave us the records. He was generous that way. He just wanted to do it out of sheer enjoyment. At that time, Ric pretty much had Electric Lady as his own studio. He said, 'Get to the studio, we'll do a session about noon.' He figured we'd have to set up and soundcheck, or whatever. So Alan and I came down and set up. Ric came down at around two then left the engineer to get the sound. He said we might as well record, so we started writing a few things right there and did them live. Ric strolled in about 3.30 or 4 and said to the engineer from behind the glass, 'What have you done so far?' The engineer said, 'I think they already recorded the whole album'. That was day one. Ric was pleased about that, but then we spent time listening to it and going over each track."

Rev sees similarities with the way the debut album was recorded live, then subjected to the mixing process, although there would be a lengthy break while Ocasek attended to Cars activities. "I always think of it as being closer to the first album in ideas," says Marty. "I was going back, personally; not to recreate it but I got ideas. Again, we recorded it right there, then the rest was Ric's mixing. He had to take a break on that record for about a year, then he called us into another studio, where we did 'Dominic Christ'."

The album, *A Way of Life*, rode in on the booming grind and twisted electro beats of 'Wild In Blue', which had been written on the spot in their first hour at the studio. 'Surrender' is a surreal doo-wop love call with swooning backing chorale, soaring mellotron and Alan quivering with Elvis ballad passion. 'Sufferin' In Vain' and 'Devastation' are sharp examples of the stripped-down rockabilly sensibility underpinning Rev's sublimely propulsive grooves, boosted by an Emulator for subtly employed guitar samples. 'Jukebox Babe' even gets a Suicide-style makeover, heightening the feeling of Alan's earlier solo outings dovetailing into Rev's mission to recast classic rock'n'roll motifs with new machinery. 'Love So Lovely' resonates like an exercise in pressure-cooker tension, while the claustrophobic thump of 'Heat Beat' echoes the subterranean electronic innovations taking place in Detroit techno.

Suicide's anger was now being stoked by New York becoming overrun by yuppification in the decade dominated by doddering cowboy Ronald Reagan, who inspired an incensed Alan to write the incendiary 'Rain Of Ruin'. "Marty and I are both political and we were not too happy with the way things were going down, especially in those Reagan years," says Alan, citing 'Rain Of Ruin' as the track which summed up how he was feeling at the time and also as one of his favourite Suicide tracks. The plight of the homeless is graphically portrayed on the searing 'Dominic Christ'.

"It was pretty bad, anywhere you were sitting," adds Marty. "The politics got very conservative. The album might be the most reflective of that, and the way it felt that anyone under or slightly above the poverty line had started to really feel under duress. That had been there before but it had increased and expanded. There was this feeling that the government was more and more brazenly working for the upper classes. Under the Reagan administration, social programmes that had been in place since the sixties or even before were being dismantled. There were these years of feeling there was less and less of a future for people like us, and people left out of the system so long. It was becoming a more right-wing kind of time."

Closer to home, Suicide's return had coincided with Alan's blossoming relationship with Liz, who happily applied her legal expertise and organisational skills to their affairs, including finding a record deal for the new album. "I started representing Suicide," she recalls. "They didn't really have proper representation or somebody who had their best interests at

efiant: Suicide at Club Europa, Brooklyn, May 2008.

Rev celebrates Suicide's first music award at the 2007 MOJO Honours.

The author and Alan at the MOJO Awards.

's my favourite photo of Alan and I." Alan & Liz Lamere at the Ramones Beat On Cancer benefit, NYC 2007

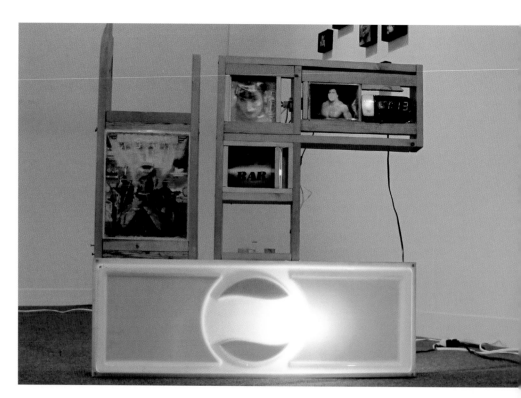

Three of Alan's 'In Prison' pieces at Gallerie Laurent Godin booth at The Armory Show, NY, March 2015.

Liz & Dante Lamere 2013.
MARIE LOSSIER

Dad & Dante 2013.
MARIE LOSSIER

Rev performing *Stigmata* at Barbican, London, July 2015.

vine Enfant.

Suicide play to rapturous welcome at New York's Webster Hall in March 2015.

heart. I never said, 'I'm gonna manage you guys.' I kind of fell into it de facto. It was kind of like, 'Oh Liz can you look at these papers and discuss it with Thau?' Both Alan and Marty are very street smart. Rev has a brilliant mind; he could have been a lawyer or an accountant, because he thinks that way. He's very logical and detail-oriented, while Alan is more abstract. Marty has always been very keyed into the business decisions and is co-pilot on the managing stuff. He just understands the mechanics of the business side of things in a way that Alan really doesn't. Alan understands it globally, but he's not really interested in drilling down the details. You just tell Alan the big picture and he'll go yay or nay. The challenging thing about Alan is that it was always, 'No, no, no' and 'You've got to get me out of this thing'. As a manager, you think you're gonna hear 'You have got to get me this'!"

"Liz had a very positive influence on Alan and Suicide," says Marty. "In the eighties, when we started going to England, she acted as our manager, co-ordinating it all. *A Way Of Life* was done and we felt fine about it, but it wasn't going anywhere because we couldn't get a deal for it. Suicide has always been an uphill entity. Liz and I used to do a lot of strategising, so we put our heads together and said, 'Let's call Paul Boswell and ask him'. So early next morning we had a conference call with Paul, even though he wasn't in the record business. He had the idea to send it over to Chapter 22 Records and they came right back and wanted to do it."

Chapter 22 released *A Way Of Life* in Europe in 1988, before US industrial label Wax Trax put it out the following year. At that time, I was assistant editor of *Dance Music Report*, Tommy Boy Records' monthly NYC tip-sheet, and delighted in placing Suicide at the forefront of the electronic revolution gripping the clubs, radio and overseas markets.

Suicide were back for the age they had always predicted, although the living would still be far from easy.

TWENTY-ONE

At the same time as its poorer areas were being hit hard by AIDS, crack cocaine and the homeless problem, New York City started undergoing the gentrification which has led to today's situation where only the rich can afford to live in Manhattan (unless they have a rent-controlled apartment or own their place). It was time for me to return home to the UK, prompted by a vicious mugging on the 6 train, which capped a stretch spent traversing the extremes of the city's darker sides.

For Marty and Alan, the nineties saw an increased swell in the sea-change of recognition which had started later in the previous decade when Suicide were cited as a major influence by industrial groups such as Nine Inch Nails, Front 242, Ministry and Nitzer Ebb. R.E.M. covered 'Ghost Rider' for the B-side of their Vietnam-addressing 'Orange Crush' single, and Bono said U2 were listening to 'Cheree' when they wrote 'With Or Without You'.

While continuing to represent Suicide, Liz had been through a hectic stint working in legal head-hunting. "It's kind of like being a talent scout and I thought it could be interesting," she says. "At the very high end of the market there might be a dozen people in the world that do what my clients are looking for. I figure out who those key people are, approach them and then help negotiate the deal." But she had become tired of Wall Street's wolf-packs, including a spell working on mergers and acquisitions with the notorious Carl Icahn. "He was doing hostile takeovers of major companies and the work demands were coming at a grueling pace since so much money was on the line. So after doing that for less than a year I started representing fashion designers. I always loved contracts and negotiation, rather than rule-driven law like securities, which is so fricking boring! I didn't like being in a law firm setting because it controlled your time and your life. Representing fashion designers put me in an industry that I enjoyed a lot more and was closer to home because I was in essence representing talent."

Liz also kept working on music with Alan, who was reacting against the stultifying regimentation of his major label period by going back to the primitive DIY ethos he explored before Suicide. "Alan had these various guitar pedals, just kind of jerry-rigged together," recalls Liz. "He was just making sound. He was trying to strip things down to almost like a minimal tonal order. You could never be off key because there were no keys or notes. Alan's previous girlfriend, Anne Deon, had toured with the Vega band and apparently it eventually became difficult for them to work creatively with each other. It had got really intense, so Alan would say to me, 'We're never going to work together because that never ends well.' I was like 'No, that's fine, I got my band. I'm not interested. I just really love listening to this.' But when it came time to bring it into the recording studio, he said, 'Why don't you come in and we'll see what happens?' I suggested working at 6/8 Recording Studios because my band, SSNUB, used to rehearse there."

Liz introduced Alan to the studio's owner and engineer Perkin Barnes and they immediately clicked. Alan has worked with Perkin at the studio located in the Cable Building on Houston and Broadway ever since. He had played with downtown disco-punkers Konk and has engineered Vega's solo work ever since. "Alan first had me play like a live drum kind of thing, then we'd run it through these effects," recalls Liz. "Perkin had just bought this big rack of effects and we would change the settings on the effects machine to the beat. Everything was live. That is how *Deuce Avenue* evolved over the next several years. We didn't have a plan that we had to release a record. It was really Alan rediscovering sound and getting back to the purity, with no thinking along the lines of 'Oh, we're going to make an album and then release it'. Part of that was a response to the other extreme of being with Elektra. He was not interested in anything else but getting back to the most stripped down, pure experimentation. We pretty much never stopped going into the recording studio. For me, that became like going to the gym, just as a regular thing. It wasn't like, 'We're working on an album,' it was more like 'We're in the studio creating sound'. Sometimes he'd just keep revisiting the same thing. I used to say it was like painting over, because back then it wasn't computerised like it is today. He literally would record over tracks on the tape. I'd be like, 'No, don't do that, record it on another track instead of covering that track!'"

The plan was to finance the album, keep the rights and license it to a label, which they did after being approached by a French imprint called Musidisc. "Alan could obviously still afford to live at the Gramercy Park Hotel. There was always an interesting contrast between Alan and Marty's living situation, because Marty was paying for a lovely rent-stabilised apartment. He had a great deal, while Alan was paying a pretty fair chunk of change every month to stay at the Gramercy Park."

The album was finally released in February 1990 as *Deuce Avenue*. Underpinned by Liz's metronomic treated drums, it explores a taut urban funk which takes the post-punk sound to another level on the opening salvo of 'Body Bop Jive', 'Sneaker Gun Fire', 'Jab Gee' and 'Bad Scene', while 'La La Bola' recalls the New York boogie sounds coming out of black radio stations. Alan's vocals and the angular basslines are the most upfront constant elements, although experimentation is prevalent throughout, such as the sampled metal guitar stabs on the title track, abrasive scratching on 'Future Sex' and 'No Tomorrow' with its new take on the ethereal ballad. The 'On Broadway' chords on 'Sugee' are a subtle nod to the eternal city whose electricity jags through the grooves. It was good to have him back.

Alan and Liz were on a roll and *Power On To Zero Hour* came the following year out of the same ongoing creative pattern. 'This album is dedicated to FRANKIE' says the cover, fronted with a bleached-out photo of Alan sporting poodle-rock wig. Vega is credited with vocals, guitar and keyboards, and Liz with vocals, drums, machines and keyboards. The sound continues along the surrealistic wired city funk path of its predecessor, joined by sampled guitar stabs and electro-flavoured drum patterns on tracks such as 'Fear', 'Doomo Dance' and 'Jungle Justice' (which boasts piercing treated screams). 'Cry A Sea Of Tears' plants a yearning Vega love ballad over sampled proto big-beat.

"*Power* came quickly because we hadn't stopped working," says Liz. "We did a bit of sampling, and looping. Alan's sources for samples would be interesting. It would be stuff off the TV or sounds in the street; open the window at Perkin's and throw out a mike, then turn that through effects and loop it. Perkin would buy a new machine and have no idea how to use it but would let Alan on it. The beauty of Perkin was he would always let Alan go hands on with his machines; just touching and turning and flipping things. Alan was like the director of sound. He would go 'I like that', and throw it onto a track. Perkin would just get it down. Alan was discovering sound randomly and Perkin is just such a cool guy. He's perfect for Alan, because he is super chilled and Alan's energy is so 'ggggzzzzz'. Alan and I would be killing each other, going 'Fuck you!', 'No 'fuck you!' and he'd go, 'Wow, I just love your relationship'."

The album earned Alan and Liz a support spot with crusty techno-jigglers Pop Will Eat Itself at London's Town and Country Club for two nights. The couple found themselves heckled and pelted by luddite piss-heads, having to fend off beer-filled plastic cups, coins and even a large chunk of mirror from the bathroom. Alan treated the imbecilic element with disdain honed from countless Suicide gigs, taunting and rushing the front rows to spark cowardly mass retreats. Eventually, security stopped the set. The next night was packed with press hoping for carnage to report but the promoters begged Alan not to play. Liz finally negotiated a higher fee for NOT playing. The following day's *Libération* in France depicted Alan, squatting on the bog, pants round his feet, counting his cash. The headline shouted 'Paid More Not To Play, Vega Doesn't Give A Shit'.

While this was going on, Ric Ocasek invited Suicide to record their fourth album. "*Why Be Blue* was another great opportunity," says Marty Rev. "Ric said 'You guys haven't done a record for a while, let's do one.' By that time, he had a studio in his basement. So we started recording in the summer of 1990 and then we had to stop because Ric had a schedule. I don't think we continued working on it until the following summer. We had a great time doing it, we'd go over every track with Ric. It was a very relaxed situation being together in his place, with no pressures for time. Ric would mix and produce it on his own time, when we weren't there. When he sent us the final album that was gonna go out, I had to call and tell him not to put it out. It just wasn't finished. It's a fine record but it was the least Suicide in the sense of being brought to that place which was us. Ric was producing it in his time when he wanted to, even when he would wake up in the middle of the night. He played it for us and the sound and production were great but it didn't have that final footprint which would have made it Suicide."

Rev still wouldn't be happy with the album when, after Cars manager Elliot Roberts couldn't sell it to any majors, ROIR's Neil Cooper had found a deal with Munich-based Enemy Records and *Why Be Blue* was released in 1992. It was always an occasion to receive new Suicide material but the album did seem to miss their essential street edge and challenging electronic innovation (although maybe that could also be seen as Suicide's reflection of New York at the time). 'Chewy, Chewy' and 'Hot Ticket' even hark back to Alan's textbook radio-rock outings, although the rumblingly plaintive 'Universe' is a towering heartfelt exception. Alan has called it one of the best Suicide songs of all time. Rev finally had his say when Mute reissued the album in 2004. He put it through a blender of effects and strove to take the album to where it might have ended up if Suicide had been involved in the original mix. "I can live with the reissue," he says, "but I couldn't have lived with it before. The running order was wrong. It just needed to be crazier, further out, more electronic; like us. I think it is now."

Tracks such as the sleek 'Mujo' sport a new dance-floor sensibility. Suicide had already been cited as an influence when acid house and techno appeared in the late eighties, from drum machine foundations to innovative electronic textures. Like disco before it, Marty had heard house and techno on the street which, again, became a subliminal rather than obvious influence on his creative muse. "It was in the environment. I guess it was different in New York because it was different house music. It wasn't really industrial, it was right out of disco. All the cars passing by had it blasting out. It was very club-oriented, just with a different twist. To me, it was definitely there to be exposed to. Some things take you really deeply and you hear right away. I heard it right away and felt I could play around with aspects of it in what I was doing. That came through in some of those mid-tempo things. I always tend to go for what I feel I don't know and what is challenging me that day; 'What's going on here? How do I accomplish it as a technique?' I would hear techno and go 'Okay', so I guess I didn't really study it as closely as many people did."

The year 1991 saw Rev finally release his retitled instrumentals from the second album sessions, which were joined by later widescreen sound paintings to make *Cheyenne*. Complete with Mari-designed cover depicting a black bucking bronco rider, the album was released on France's Marilyn label and by Alive in the US, but was hard to find until its 2007 reissue on Mind Expansion (which featured three bonus cuts led by the lustrous doo-wop swoon of 'Coyote', which came from 1990's Czarist Productions sessions; 'Pony', recorded with Charles Ball in 1992; and 'Durango' from the *Why Be Blue* sessions).

The idea for revamping the backing tracks he had cooked up at the Power Station had been gestating in Marty's head for years. "Towards the end of the second album sessions, Ric had mixed what he called 'TV tracks', in case we were going to do something on TV. We were sitting in the control room and he had two large quarter-inch reels in boxes and just gave them to me and said, 'You take these, these are yours'. I thought this reflected another approach. It's another sound when you treat it instrumentally. When you work with someone else it's like two people working on one painting. When you take the track on its own, it gives you a visual sense of something different. There were so many layers on that recording it worked for me that way. So I had that in my mind for a long time and just kind of had 'em on the shelf. Then the opportunity came up with the French label through Neil Cooper, so I went into the studio and worked those tracks in a way that satisfied me as instrumentals. The pure backing tracks were very close but their form needed to be arranged a little more. I put them together as an album with some newer tracks."

It's fascinating, sometimes even spine-tingling, to hear tracks so embedded in the consciousness refashioned as instrumentals in their own right. 'Touch Me' becomes the title track, 'Harlem' provides 'Red Sierra', 'Prairie Star' is 'Diamonds, Fur Coat, Champagne' while 'Sweetheart''s gorgeous metamorphosis into the swooning 'River Of Tears' could have enhanced any David Lynch love scene. Even second album out-take, 'Super Subway Comedian', transforms into 'Dakota'. Rev saw the tracks as visual illustrations of his travels across the country, as in "the whole American Western culture" – one reason he retitled them drawing inspiration from Native American Indians.

The year 1993 saw Alan back with his eighth solo album, *New Raceion*, again recorded at 6/8 with Perkin. This time he said he was trying to bring different kinds of music together as a new race, reflecting America's modern multi-ethnic society. "That album was a little different," says Liz, "because now people wanted to come in and play, so we had guitars. Alan was thinking, 'Let's see what we can do'. It was amazing." Axe-men who cameth included Mark Kuch, Cie Vega, Ric Ocasek and Roger Greenawalt, who joined Liz on keyboards and drums. There's a noticeable hard rock edge, with 'Viva The Legs' even careering into speed-metal and

'Gamma Pop' adding industrial weight. Liz's co-write with Alan, 'How Many Lifetimes?', is a subtly evocative highlight.

Meanwhile, Suicide continued to be recognised by the electronic dance community, cited as seminal by new electronic gods such as Moby and Aphex Twin. I had been making techno records since returning to the UK, which were released on a label called Sabres of Paradise. It was run by Andrew Weatherall, who was then the UK's most uncompromising but visionary DJ and producer. He made no secret of his admiration for Suicide, even appropriating the first album's blood-splattered image for a T-shirt. In 1993, the sixth release on Sabres was by a genially manic French Suicide nut called Bruno Catali, whose 'Vegagod' (under the name Jack of Swords) was his techno tribute, complete with 'Cool As Ice' and 'Harlem' mixes.

Suicide's long-awaited payday came the following year when Henry Rollins covered 'Ghost Rider' on the soundtrack of *The Crow*, the goth blockbuster based on James O'Barr's comic, which told the story of a rock musician revived from the dead. The soundtrack, which also featured the Cure, Nine Inch Nails, JAMC, Violent Femmes and Rage Against The Machine, went on to sell six million copies, resulting in the most money Suicide had ever seen (and making their fifth album a possibility).

Rollins had recently become another ally after being blown away by the first album, which he rated next to the first Stooges and Velvets albums. 'Ghost Rider' was the first song he had worked up in his hardcore punk group Black Flag. In 1994, Rollins' 2.13.61 publishing company released *Cripple Nation*, a book of Alan's drawings, poems and lyrics.

"Henry came over to our house one afternoon," recalls Liz. "Alan's room is very interesting. It's full of piles and piles of the notebooks that he writes in, like for his sanity or mental health. He would go to the pub, then come home and write, or do his crazy portrait drawings. That's always been Alan's process. When it came time to do the album, the very last thing would be the lyrics and titles. Everything will be like 'Song A', 'Song G', 'Song Q', then it will become what it becomes. Henry knew Alan must be a writer. He shows up and he's like a kid in a candy store. First of all, he's flipping out that he's meeting Alan Vega. There's like an immediate kind of kinship where they can feel a like spirit. Alan completely connected with Henry. He was into all kinds of music, including the jazz stuff that Alan's been into. They were just off and running, talking about everything. I think Henry stayed like eight hours that first day because the two of them were having too much fun just talking. Then he decided it was a disgrace that Alan's music was really only being heard in Europe. Henry is like the archaeologist of culture because he's got this intrinsic need to understand how this evolved. That's very similar to Alan's philosophy and way of looking at things. "So Henry created a record label under the 2.13.61 umbrella, to be distributed by Warner Bros, mainly as a vehicle to reissue the first two Vega solo albums, *Deuce Avenue, Power On To Zero Hour* and *New Raceion*. He also put together a beautifully packaged promo compilation including both Suicide and Vega solo tracks. Henry was living in New York then and his office was in the Cable Building, so he was right on the front line."

December 1994 saw a unique one-off happen when Alan, Alex Chilton and Ben Vaughn got together in Dessau recording studios, on the second floor of an old building near City Hall, and recorded *Cubist Blues*. Alan was already working there with Liz on his next solo album when he got the call from his old friend Ben, asking if he fancied recording some "late night blues music". Alan agreed, on the condition he could go in with no preparation and just see what happened. When Ben mentioned the upcoming date to Alex Chilton, he revealed he was a big Vega fan and asked if he could play guitar. He was in adventurous mood, having recently recorded the *Cliches* album of solo jazz standards, and even offered to pay for his air-fare up from New Orleans. Alan lights up at the mention of Chilton, who died in 2010, robbing music of one of its all-time great idiosyncratic talents. "I really love Alex. I met him when he used to hang out at CBs all the time. He was always in the bar across the street. Years later he was saying he liked Suicide."

When Chilton arrived, he hooked up with Ben and the pair went around borrowing equipment, including guitar, bass, drum machine and synth, which went with the studio's knackered old upright piano. Studio engineer Drew Vogelman was a drummer, and had a kit. On the first night, Alex and Ben started cooking up sounds, while Alan scribbled lyrics on a copy of the *New York Post*. Seven minutes later they had the bluesy shuffle of 'Fat City'. Alan suggested adding some downtown street noise, so dangled a mike out of the window.

With lift-off obtained, the session went on for the next few hours. They improvised a skeletal noir-blues called 'Sister', with Alan reporting what he saw going on outside the window. The songs kept coming, with minimal overdubs being added before moving on to the next one. "By

273

the last song, my brain was burning up," recalls Alan. "The music just kept coming… We were meditating on sound, and time was suspended." More tracks followed including 'Candy Man', 'Promised Land', 'Come On Lord', even 'Dream Baby Revisited'.

Six more songs sat in the can by the time they wound up at three in the morning. The trio repeated the exercise the following night, followed by a third for mixing. Job done. When Henry Rollins heard what the trio had done he knew a special moment had been captured and released *Cubist Blues* on his 2.13.61 label, while in Europe it came out on Last Call.

The trio were asked to appear at the Transmusicales Festival in Rennes, France, in December 1996, and warmed up with a show at the Mercury Lounge on Houston Street. Alan wasn't at the soundcheck but, resolutely keeping to the spirit of the album, turned up at show-time and sang a whole different set of lyrics as he hadn't heard the music since he improvised over it in the studio. "It was just stream of consciousness for me," he recalls. Next day they went to Rennes and played another stormer to a packed house with Suicide's 'I Remember' as an encore. After the show, Alan did battle with the French press at a conference, suggesting they take it outside when a journalist called them dinosaurs.

By 1995, Alan and Liz had unleashed *Dujang Prang*, the album they had been recording at Dessau with Drew Vogelman, and guitarist Mark Kuch still on board. It was wrapped in a fold-out comic strip by Mark Bright which illustrated a bleak Vega poem. The music had moved on to explore a disturbing kind of claustrophobic urban future vision; like a graphic novel come to life in the dense, surreal swirls of the title track, 'Flowers, Candles, Crucifixes', 'The Kiss' and 'Hammered'. Gritty funk is still in evidence, notably the remake of 'Saturn Drive', although the beats also encompass techno on 'Big Daddy Stat's Livin' On Tron'. After the years of sonic laboratory experiments, Alan and Liz seemed to have moved on into a fresh new strain of big city funk (at a time when the city itself was undergoing its systematic soul-sucking car-wash at the hands of Mayor Rudy Giuliani, who had come into power in 1994 and seemed to be blitzing everything funky and great about the city every time I returned).

Meanwhile, Rev reached right back to his doo-wop roots for 1996's *See Me Ridin'*. Released on ROIR with striking cover painting by Mari, it's his first full vocal album, full of love songs to his eternal sweetheart, who co-wrote 'Small Talk'; their own doo-wop teen anthem. Marty's wistfully innocent vocals over his skeletal, dreamy backdrops beautifully evoke the spirit of his beloved doo-wop tempered with Buddy Holly-style innocence. Rev explains the doo-wop undertow in his music as "inevitable. When you're born into something it's just so much a part of you." Nearly 20 years on *See Me Ridin'* sounds even more audacious and timeless. The production is ground-breaking in its intricate manipulation of microscopic electronic ingredients, such as 'Ten Two''s deceptively complex jigsaw collage, which weaves together a gamut of riff snippets, melodic flare-ups and sound effects, or 'Mari Go Round', with its misty melodic clouds and clockwork momentum. 'Secret Teardrops' works its magic using just a synth-pulse, sporadic stick cracks and pizzicato string flourishes, while 'I Made You Cry' is built on just a single resonant shimmer; half-whispered, breathy and haunting. The closing minutes of 'Post Card' boast some of the richest alien synth tones Marty had yet explored. Maybe this often overlooked or misjudged album could actually be the ultimate statement of Suicide's impassioned New York doo-wop skyline transplanted into the future.

So far, the nineties had been a time of low-key regeneration. The latter half of the decade would finally see Suicide's time arrive, before the 21st century brought their last album after an appalling tragedy in their beloved city.

TWENTY-TWO

"American Supreme will be looked at again in years to come. There's something about this album, which I think is on the level of the first one, definitely. There's something about it because it's kind of strong and radical. It's amazing the way the first and second albums got caught up with." – **Martin Rev**

"All our albums seem made for history. No one gets it the first time." – **Alan Vega**

Since 1980, Suicide had only seemed to enjoy sporadic periods of activity. With no firm foundation to build on, building anything resembling a career had been out of the question. As Marty says "We never had a major label. We never even had two consecutive records out on the same label!" But as the nineties entered their second half, the duo found themselves riding an arc of triumph, recognition and solid business support which has actually continued.

It started in 1998 after Paul Smith, the Sheffield Clash tour veteran, signed Suicide to his Blast First label, which was distributed by Daniel Miller's Mute Records. Suicide would now see their past albums reissued, and their new work coming out all under the same roof. Paul has also been closely involved with their European activities ever since.

Paul's entry into the music business came through hooking up with Sheffield electronic pioneers Cabaret Voltaire and starting Doublevision, originally to tap into the new medium of music videos, before becoming a record label. He went on to start Blast First, releasing early Sonic Youth albums and other experimentally leaning missives, before contacting Suicide in 1996 to open a projected new arts venture on London's South Bank. "David Sefton, the head of contemporary music at the South Bank Centre, was always looking for interesting things. We'd have dinners and exercise our fandoms, as he too was a child of punk. There was talk about turning the south side of Charing Cross railway arches into a South Bank-controlled club space. He asked me which band I would choose to open the space as some kind of mission statement. I said Suicide. He said, 'Go get 'em.' So I tracked down Alan and Marty through my New York contacts, both said yes and two days later we had a deal in place. Eventually it became clear the space was never going to happen, but it turned out the rights to their first album had just become available. Blast First was able to pick that up and re-release it, which was an unexpected bonus."

The wheels started cranking into motion in January 1998, with 'Reinventing America', an art installation celebrating US culture at London's Barbican Centre. This was deliciously ironic for a band so ostracised in their own country, especially since the event was sponsored by American Airlines. While nearby stood the Harleys ridden by Marlon Brando and Peter Fonda in their famous films, Suicide appeared on a foot-high stage in the corner, ripping through 'Mr Ray' and 'Girl'. The crowd included acolytes from Primal Scream (who had recently covered '96 Tears' Suicide-style), Depeche Mode, Soft Cell, JAMC and Pulp.

"Feeling kind of embarrassed" when the South Bank project collapsed, Paul Smith booked Suicide four nights at North London's the Garage in early March (prefaced by a session for Radio One's Mary Ann Hobbs). "The first night, when all the press and VIPs came, they were pretty poor," recalls Smith. "Vega was the wrong side of a bottle of vodka so there were a lot of slow songs. I remember standing at the side of the monitor desk thinking, 'Oh shit, I've killed a legend'. We'd planned an after-show party upstairs and when Alan and Marty were leaving they stood waiting on the stairs for a cab to take them back to the hotel. I heard Vega say, 'Marty, we're fucked, these kids are actually listening to us!' Happily, the second night, they walked in through the back door, straight on stage and absolutely slew that audience. They sounded as ahead of the game as they did back in '78. From there we were off and running."

A recording of one of the nights accompanied a later reissue. It displays an on-form Suicide blasting through 'White Man' (splashed with avant garde keyboards), a vindictive 'Harlem', supremely spooked 'Surrender', electro-disco 'Show Me Tha' Money', stretched-out 'Girl', supercharged 'Rocket USA' and encore of 'Jukebox Babe', which is amped up "in deference to Gene Vincent" before Alan manages to homage Lou Reed, Iggy and Hot Chocolate before leaving the stage shouting, "Every one's a winner!" Neil Thomson's academic declaration in *NME* that Suicide had managed to keep their edge across the decades, which qualifies them for the title vastly influential, typifies the sort of late praise which would come their way from now on.

Suicide were invited by Jason Pierce to join Spiritualized in a rendition of 'Rocket USA' at *NME*'s annual Brat awards held at London's Astoria. Pierce cited them as a major influence on his previous band, Spacemen 3, who had recorded a tribute track called 'Suicide'. This late revival activity was compounded by the reissue of the first album, complete with a bonus disc featuring *23 Minutes Over Brussels* and a 1977 CBGB set. It brought a fresh barrage of plaudits, the more astute including *The Wire*'s Biba Kopf's comment that "No record summarises better the big hurt of a continent still angry in the aftermath of defeat in Vietnam" (plus his punchline "This kind of music is what electricity is for"). I couldn't help thinking back to the reception the album got in 1978, when jazz buff Richard Williams beautifully 'got it' but *Sounds*, then pushing its 'New Musik' manifesto, was scared off.

The Wire appreciated Suicide as more than the 'synth-pop pioneers' they were now being painted as but never aimed to be, as evidenced by the prime selection of rockabilly, jazz and Lou Reed's *Metal Machine Music* which Edwin Pouncey played Marty and Alan for the magazine's 'Invisible Jukebox' feature. Elvis's gospel track 'Inherit The Wind' prompted Alan to recall being stricken with pneumonia the week after Presley died. Sinking into fitful sleep, he dreamed he was at "Elvis Presley School", being whipped by the King to wake up when the phone rang. Alan answered to hear the caller asking for "Mr Presley". It turned out his apartment's previous resident was called Mr Presley. Meanwhile, Rev described Miles Davis as the closest musician he ever had to an idol.

Long-time supporter John Peel invited Suicide to join the Jesus And Mary Chain on a bill for his Meltdown festival on July 4. Starting with 'White Man', the set was broadcast live on the great man's radio show.

Meanwhile, Alan's creative snowball careered on. Through Paul Smith, he was introduced to Finland's Pan Sonic, whose Mika Vainio and Ilpo Vaisanen were major Suicide fans after discovering the first album in the late seventies in a local hardware shop. The result was *Endless* by the newly christened VVV, a stark workout which saw Alan railing over coruscating electronic pulses generated from Mika's home-built machines. Considering the bucolic wilderness where Pan Sonic hailed from, the duo's ability to evoke the atmosphere of dirty old New York with scorched circuit minimalism is uncanny. It brought out the best in Alan as he drew from his wad of scribblings to deliver titles such as 'Desperate For Tha Miracle', 'Sick Sick USA' and 'Disgrace' in single takes. "Thank God there was another group out there I could finally get off on," he says.

Alan had also been working with Glaswegian producer Stephen Lironi as Revolutionary Corps of Teenage Jesus. The pair went into New York's Cutting Room studio to see what happened. I had met Stephen when he was guitarist with late seventies post-punk popsters Altered Images. Now he was showing Alan some respect from the city which had thrown an axe at him in 1978 by planting him in modern techno/breakbeat soundscapes. The first fruits were three 12-inch singles released on Stephen's Creeping Bent label – an oddly effective dance version of 'Frankie Teardrop', 'Protection Rat' and 'Pay Tha Wreck, Mr Music King'. The *Righteous Lite* CD from 1999 corralled them all together.

In 1998 Alan was approached by French director Philippe Grandrieux to supply music for his bleak psychodrama *Sombre*, about a serial killer who went after prostitutes. The director told Alan that he played Suicide's music every time he took a break in filming, and that lead actor Marc Barbe was a major Vega fan. "It was exciting and fun to be creating music for this film," said Alan in the soundtrack liner notes. "This film itself is great with all kinds of images that played with my mind... which, ultimately got me to do things musically, beyond my own expectations of what could be done with sound." Alan also contributed eight tracks to the noise-loop poems on Ric Ocasek's experimental *Getchertikitz* album, along with Gillian McCain. His titles included 'Smell War', 'Living Crazed', 'Gangland Scag', 'Metal Eyes' and 'Shoot The Fucker'. 'Alan also found time to visit a Brooklyn studio to sing with his old friends the Fleshtones, who were still battling on. "Alan came out to Flatbush and sang a lead vocal for 'Gentleman's Twist', a very basic rock'n'roll song," recalls Peter Zaremba. "I always thought that Alan had the right attitude to sing it, although a lot of people would be surprised by that. It came out on some obscure B-side, and a Fleshtones 'obscurity' is really obscure!"

Alan's experiments with Perkin at 6/8 seemed increasingly bent on steering extreme machine noise into vaguely song-like apparitions. This fertile period also saw him guest on an album called *Re-Up* by French-based brothers Eric and Marc Hurtado, aka Étant Donnés, along with Lydia Lunch and Genesis P-Orridge. A mangled new version of 'Ghost Rider' rears among the pile-ups. Then came 1999's *2007*, Alan's darkest solo work yet, which seemed like a grim warning of some kind. The black clouds of aural ectoplasm and mutant electro beats on tracks such as 'Meth 13 Psychodreem' and 'This Is City' crystallise a fathomless essence beyond anything else going on around that time; techno, industrial or otherwise. Although 'King' manages to take its dismembered heavenly chorale on an opium trip, by the closing 'End' Alan has just let the pulsing machines take over.

Liz only appears on 'Hunger Wonders' and 'Sewer Deep' due to her and Alan recently adopting Dante Miguel Angel, to whom the album is dedicated. While changing the dynamic at home, Dante made Alan aware of the dangers in the world in which they were bringing him up. "That was when I stopped going into the studio for every session with Alan," says Liz. "Up until that point we were attached at the hip in the studio. We always went together and I always worked on stuff with him. It was very much a collaborative process. Alan was the director of sound, but he always gave me a writing credit when I came up with something and it was clearly from me. On *2007*, Alan started noodling on the keyboard. The tone of the album was really dark. He was thinking, 'We have this child, we didn't bring him into the world but what kind of world is my son coming into?' He was very reflective during that period. He also had premonitions. It's really scary because I think there was some foreshadowing of the attacks on 9/11. He was sensing that something really significant was gonna happen soon in Dante's lifetime. That comes through in that album. Even Henry Rollins didn't get it. He thought it was *too* dark. Alan thought that was a really good sign, because people who were normally were like 'wow, everything Alan does is amazing' would hear it and were silent."

Although Alan had gained a son, he lost his brother Robbie in 1999. "He was only 50-something," says Alan. "He was a scientist who lived in Washington all his life. We used to share a room together. He was a really smart guy. When I went to the funeral I had to go down to Maryland and saw an old freight train. I wrote a song about him."

Suicide-wise, June 1999 saw the duo play a magical set at that year's Sonar festival in Barcelona. Marty remembers performing in a "half awake" state of trance after travelling most of the previous night, and concentrating on creating electronic textures. As the major global showcase event in the electronic music calendar, the date further consolidated Suicide's acceptance as key figures in the electronic arena, which was backed up with the reissue of the second album. The package, fronted by a cover shot of Alan and Marty at the Mercer in 1972, also boasted the 'Dream Baby Dream'/'Radiation' 12-inch and 'Super Subway Comedian', Alan's vivid narrative about characters to be found on New York's subway system, which had been too long for the original album.

Most excitingly, the second disc gathers 14 tracks from the 1975 demo sessions at the Project. Along with 'A-Man' being commissioned for a Tia Maria advert, Suicide were again favourably reviewed in most of the UK's major music publications, who again focused on the duo predating synth-pop. More insightful was Ken Hollings' *The Wire* review of the also-reissued *Ghost Riders*, ROIR's recording of 1981's tenth anniversary show, which declared "No one understood the maniacal, grinding energies at the heart of modern American music the way Suicide did." Apart from setting aside conventional rock instruments, Suicide had embodied American life at the time through the microcosm of New York City; thrusting together all its violent contradictions and atrocities as futuristic harbingers of the blues.

The new century started voluptuously with *Strangeworld*, Rev's startling new solo work, which was released on Finnish label Sahko. The album continued the late fifties pop vocal experiments conducted on *See Me Ridin'*, now fleshed out, rocked up and sprinkled with hallucinogenic glitter-dust and buckets of reverb. Doo-wop tracks such as 'Solitude' and 'Cartoons' shimmer like dream sequences, while the instrumental 'Splinters' lives up to its name. A meaty synth riff would seem to take 'Chalky' into Suicide territory but ultimately these solo works were all concentrated facets of a unique ongoing mothership ethos. "*Strangeworld* was definitely coming out of *See Me Ridin'*," says Rev. "It gave me the motivation to go on from there in a similar context, but take it further out."

Suicide started the new millennium by playing the New York Festival of Electronic Composers and Improvisers at the Knitting Factory on Houston Street, which had opened in 1987 as downtown's prime experimental hotspot. It was Suicide's first New York show in eight years and the two nights in January broke the attendance record as they headlined bills including Detroit's Carl Craig, Morton Subotnick, Pan Sonic and a returning Silver Apples. In October, they played the Los Angeles Knitting Factory. This was followed by return visits to London's Garage and New York's Knitting Factory. With these new, enthusiastic crowds, it seemed the right time to record a new album. But this time would be different, on Suicide's own terms. With the money from *The Crow* soundtrack, Suicide could pay for time at 6/8 Studios. Working with Perkin meant they could take control and produce themselves.

This time, Marty wanted to try a different approach, explaining "I didn't feel we were going to approach making the record by going in and doing it live because we'd done that already. So first I gave Alan all the central tracks without going into the studio." Marty then took off for Montreal where, at that time, he spent several months of each year with Mari in a rented condo. "I said, 'Why don't you fool around with these, write some words and, when you're ready, I'll come back'."

"We always wanted to do an album on our own, without a producer, and we had the technology now," says Alan. "We finally had enough money to be able to go in together and do it from start to finish. I told Marty, "We've really got to try something new and experimental, that's what Suicide's about'. So we did it differently this time. He gave me the music to about 23 songs to work with, but I couldn't do it. After all the years we've been together, Marty and I don't have to rehearse. We just walk in off the street and do a show. But this was something different. 'Holy shit, I can't do it!' It was terrible. Marty gave me a curve ball. I had to choose about 12 for the album."

At first, Alan found it difficult as tracks were built on grooves constructed in a similar manner to hip-hop producers. He cites the track which became 'Televised Executions', with its funky rhythm laced with squelching wah wah guitar and popping Bootsy Collins-style bass. But, after a while, as Alan realised Marty had introduced everything from hip-hop to Thelonious Monk and free jazz into Suicide's sound, he started to get into it. "I realised that I had to do something new here, something a little different than as a singer trying to sing to these songs. I like that. I try and do that with my solo stuff. I try to make the kind of music that I can't sing to, then I know I have something. That's what happened to Marty with this thing. It was tough at first. It took a while until I got the right lyrics. It was a bit of a different lyrical approach."

Then came the unimaginable horror which arrived suddenly that morning of September 11. Nothing was ever the same again and the effect on Alan was seismic. Dante was a day away from starting pre-school, five minutes' walk from the twin towers. Alan can't bear to think what could have happened if the strike had happened then. He remembers the white ash falling from the clear blue sky, everything going grey as the sky filled with "Just tons and tons of white stuff coming down. It was like an instant change from day to night, summer to winter." If the towers had toppled instead of coming straight down they would have crushed his building.

Now marooned in a death zone, Alan couldn't get a bus, cab or train, had to walk an hour through military checkpoints to get food and carry a passport and letter certifying residence to get back into his neighbourhood. "The remains of the buildings were like the most horrific things I've seen in my life. It was like a sculpture that no human being in the world could make. After 9/11 suddenly my whole world was turned upside down. Cos I live right there. I was in the middle of all that shit. I couldn't believe the lyrics I'd written before any more. My life was drastically different now. I'm like that. I like to reflect what's happening in my life. That's why sometimes I find it so hard to do the old songs. Some of the lyrics seem so stupid now. I had to redo pretty much all of the songs because I couldn't believe the lyrics I'd written before that came down. Now I felt angry. I did before 9/11 already, because we had a shit old president who was fucking up anyway. I knew he'd pull something like this off."

Thirty years earlier, it had been Vietnam, now it was on the doorstep. Suicide had always reflected New York City and this was its darkest hour. They would now plug into the city's agonised psyche in a bleakly compelling statement which has been called a *There's A Riot Goin' On* for the 21st century.

Marty was in Montreal when the towers came down. "When it happened, we were staying at this condo we would rent by the month. There were a lot of different places. We would go from one to the other. We had this nice little modern place for maybe two months in the summer. It had a TV bracketed up high on the wall and we were sleeping on a low mattress on the floor. Mari would often sleep with a little transistor radio on. She might start with a show that was interesting to her, like music or a talk show, then during the night it would morph into news, which is not the greatest thing, but she could really thrive on that stuff. She would usually never wake me up that early but, with the intensity of what was coming through, she nudged me and said, 'You gotta hear this'. Then she took the remote and put on the TV so we could actually watch. Then it happened the second time. I mean, it was incredible."

Marty stayed in Montreal while Suicide cancelled shows booked in Belfast and Dublin. "Alan said they wouldn't even let cabs come in the neighbourhood where he was. We had to cancel those shows and then I just stayed up in Montreal. I wasn't anxious to go back. Everything was very ominous down there. So I stayed there until October when Liz contacted me and said, 'He's ready, he's got the words'. I was now ready to take it to the next step, so I came in and then we produced the album. 9/11 was now so much a part of the environment that it seeped into everything you felt and did at that point. When I came back in October there was still a very anarchic sense down here. It was just frazzled emotionally and you could still smell it too. The mood of that time in New York had a definite effect on what we were doing and definitely influenced us. It influenced Alan's writing because he witnessed the whole thing. He was there. The vocals were a literal reflection of that period. I came into the studio and redid everything too."

"Marty and I really worked very well together on that thing," says Alan. "I basically let him do the board. Marty was so hot and so in tune. We had 11 songs and he would sit down with each one, then add a new line or two then play the fucking thing. He's always like that but this was different. Sometimes he used to drive me nuts but with this one he walked in and went 'Bam!' Perfect. Next. There was no stopping him. He was like a machine going from one song to another. It took him as long as each song was. He was unbelievable. Playing live he's pretty amazing anyway, but what he chose to play that night was *really* fucking amazing. It was a real eye-opener, man. I was sitting there going 'This is unbelievable'."

American Supreme was one of the few albums to directly tackle the aftermath of 9/11, subtly evoking its grisly impact on New York and the American psyche, while asking sensitive questions. Paradoxically, behind the cover's bleached-out flag writhed Suicide's most danceable album yet. 'Televised Executions' invokes an old school block party with its James Brown guitar and the Champs' quintessential hip-hop organ stab. This is the song Alan initially had troubling adapting to but he now uses it as a vehicle to attack the American media's long-endured bloodlust for broadcasting the most harrowing events. 'Misery Train' is Alan's desolate reflection on his brother Robbie's death ("Dearest brother, fly, fly"), now working in 9/11 imagery about the "sulphur sky" over Marty's mournful riff. 'Swearin' To The Flag' rides a hectic disco groove, splattered with acid squelches and synth-drum pellets, as Alan reflects how the landscape's different now. Even the roaches are leaving town. Although the track's built on disco rhythms, the dancers are distant spectres and the mirrorball flames a fiery red at the wake for this ultimate tragedy, before everything collapses in a roar of dust and dismembered machines. 'Beggin' For Miracles' apocalyptic on-the-one gothic funk groove paints a graphic picture of lawless New York the day "the nightmare came". It's almost like a 'The Message' for the 21st century with its images of rape, overdoses and corpses dragged down dark alley ways. 'American Mean' rides the kind of skipping, organ-propelled house groove which soundtracked the city's dance clubs in the early nineties, albeit put through the Rev machine.

In many ways, *American Supreme* can be held up with late eighties Bomb Squad productions or RZA's sinister evocations for the Wu Tang Clan as barrier-blasting sonic jigsaws constructed from the entire history of music. 'Wrong Decisions' samples brass derived from Syl Johnson's 'Different Strokes', which had become part of hip-hop currency on Wu Tang's 1993 classic 'Shame On A Nigga'. "Mom's not breathing" vents Alan in his chilling refrain. 'Power Au Go Go' hoists another minimal hip-hop beat. By 2001, rap had become the biggest selling form of music in the world, although often glossed up and riddled with the pantomime cliché syndrome which afflicted punk in the seventies. Suicide were revisiting hip-hop's original ethos of bare beats and rhymes as Rev pieced together funk-fuelled tapestries for Alan to use as launch-pads for his observations on America today. Meanwhile 'Death Machine' sees Rev recalling the jacking acid house sound of early nineties Chicago, using a stomping kick gouged with squelching 303 motifs as Alan unleashes his "Body count" hook. 'Dachau, Disney, Disco' is a war chant harking back to free-form origins with its beat-less mass of synthesised explosions and computer game abuse laced with Sun Ra-like organ noodling.

After 'Child, It's A New World' has reached back to early seventies conscious soul to rise out of the wreckage as a beam of optimism for Dante, like a dad's advice to his son, the album goes out on the merciless terror of 'I Don't Know'. This is the track which had drawn Alan into starting the album. Framed by Rev's chattering, deranged techno skeleton, he begins in total confusion, crawling out of the twisted ruins with a scrambled mess of questions, mainly where's the girl he loves. Set against a kaleidoscopic melange of psychotic breakdown sounds, 'I Don't Know' ranks as the most intensely hard-hitting Suicide track since 'Frankie'. It's excruciatingly easy to picture the song's bewildered subject scrabbling through the dust and rubble looking for his girlfriend, wondering if she's alive, or if he should get a gun and kill someone. It was like all Alan's memories of living with his loved ones in the heart of the towers' destruction had coalesced into a frantic rush and could be the most graphically honest and disturbingly poignant depiction of the devastation his city had just suffered. Sheer confused desperation has never been captured so vividly and heartbreakingly.

American Supreme was released in October 2002 with a striking cover image by Scott King of Crash depicting a bleached-out stars and stripes. It seemed like a dust-covered headstone for the country. When I complimented the duo, who were sitting in front of me, Alan said "Thank you but Marty had a problem when I suggested *American Supreme*." Rev then explained, "I just hate using flags, man. I just thought 'Oh no, why? Not the flag!' If you're calling it *American Supreme*, why use the flag?" I took his point but, on this occasion, it seemed chillingly appropriate.

The most reviews Suicide had ever had were also the best, summed up by *The Wire*'s Martin Carlin writing about 'I Don't Know': "You can almost breathe the dust. It is the only possible conclusion to this brave, bleak yet compassionate record."

While they were still recording the album, Suicide's next UK gigs had been two shows in October 2001 promoted by London club-runner Sean McCluskey under his current banner of the Sonic Mook Experiment. I'd been DJing at its nights and was thrilled when Sean asked if I'd like to warm up for Suicide at London's ICA on the 28th. At the time, there was another new musical fad doing the rounds which cited Suicide as prime inspiration, but 'electro-clash' was really just a brash eighties electro hijack which would go on to blueprint the appallingly soulless racket which cleans up today under the term EDM. I made a mental note to steer clear of that at the ICA and instead played some choice Stooges-heavy punk and electronic New York post-punk oddities. It was fantastic seeing Suicide again and they played a blinder, starting with now traditional opener 'White Man'. We hadn't heard the new album yet, but it was great to see them again, still firing on all cylinders.

Alan had never stopped creating his sculptures out of street junk, light-bulbs and pop trash, despite all the intense musical activity of the previous two decades. "Our apartment walls were covered with light sculptures and hanging pieces," says Liz. In 1999 a photographic book was released of his light sculptures called *100,000 Watts Of Fat City*, put together by Anna Polerica and introduced by Julian Schnabel. In February 2002, he held his first exhibition in the city for years with *Collision Drive* at Jeffrey Deitch's Deitch Projects gallery on Grand and Wooster. Hundreds attended the opening night, including Moby and Bjork, and Suicide played at the end. Deitch had first met Alan in 1974, after seeing one of his exhibitions at OK Harris, which he always remembered as one of the few shows he considered to be genuinely seminal.

"Alan does art for the same reason he breathes, so he had never stopped," says Liz, "though sometimes his focus shifted to different forms. He was always adding sculptures to the walls. It always comes from a pure place, without any conscious intention to exhibit it. It was decades between the shows at Barbara Gladstone in the eighties until Jeffrey Deitch came back in 2002 and, sure enough, Alan had continued to do the sculptures. A couple of Jeffrey Deitch's assistants came to Suicide's Knitting Factory show on New Year's Eve 2001, went back to the gallery and said Suicide were amazing. Apparently Jeffrey said, 'What, is Alan Vega still doing music? I wonder if he's still doing art.' He sent one of the girls to track us down. Then Jeffrey showed up and couldn't believe it. He was the one responsible for bringing Alan back into the art world."

When Suicide played two nights at the Cartier Foundation in Paris, Alan was invited to make a sculpture to be permanently installed in the front of the building. Back in New York, when the Museum of Modern Art asked Jeffrey Deitch to suggest a band to play at the opening of MoMA/PSI in Queens it balked at his suggestion of an outfit calling itself Suicide.

Musically, Alan had also been collaborating with the European dance music fraternity. He sang two tracks on German techno producer DJ Hell's album *NY Muscle*, and laid into media coverage of violence when he supplied vocals to big beat producer John 'Mekon' Gosling's 'Blood On The Moon', which also boasted a rap from Bobby Gillespie.

The year 2002 also saw Suicide's 'Girl' show up in a scene at the Bada Bing! strip club on HBO's *The Sopranos*, albeit performed by Californian shoe-gazing band Vue. The track made *The Sopranos: Peppers And Eggs* soundtrack album, guaranteeing a handy wodge of publishing dollars.

Marty had been continuing his long-standing creative relationship with filmmaker Stefan Roloff, which had started in 1988 with videos for 'Dominic Christ' and 'Surrender'. They had met when Roloff was experimenting with blending painting with digital media at the New York Institute of Technology and pioneering 'moving painting' (which led to him collaborating with Peter Gabriel on the prototype for his ground-breaking 'Sledgehammer' video). By 1997, Roloff was working on a documentary for German TV called *Die Rote Kapelle (The Red Orchestra)*, which concerned his late father, who had been part of the Resistance group during WW2. Roloff asked Rev to write the electronic score, and the film was incorporated into the United States Holocaust Memorial Museum's permanent exhibition.

The year 2002 also saw Marty's first solo album reissued on CD by ROIR, with bonus tracks. It had already seen a Belgium reissue in 1997 on the Daft label, which had added two tracks recorded in 1991 in the shape of 'Coal Train''s quirkily resonant lounge-music and the aptly named 12-minute 'Marvel', which stretched to the cosmos on an atmospheric beat-less glide twinkling with ephemeral brass and twinkling electronics. The new reissue included three further Rev-style ventures into the unknown via '5 To 5', 'Wes' and the inter-planetary doo-wop of 'Daydreams'.

Marty remembers the later recordings being something of a reunion with co-conspirator Charles Ball. "I hadn't seen him for many years and he said he'd love to do something. He was living up towards Westchester and there was a studio there he had access to. I took the train quite a few times up there and cut 'Marvel' and everything else on those bonus cuts. When ROIR wanted to put it out, we had still never released any of that material so I went back and listened to the DATs."

Rev had already started recording his sixth solo album before *American Supreme* but *To Live* didn't see the light of day until it was picked up by Chicago's File-13 label in 2003. After the doo-wop innocence of the previous albums, Marty had moved into a harder form of electronic rock, opening with the title track's cavernous beats, growling whispers and abrasive riffs. It was closer to Suicide, but denser and heavier. "It's pretty rough sound-wise," says Marty. "We were already playing some of these things live in Suicide which we hadn't recorded, so I was already using a track or two; with different words, of course."

It's fun hearing Rev booming like a rock sex god with no regard for overloading on the relentless grind of 'In Your Arms', then realising it's another take on Suicide's 'White Man'. 'Black Ice' and 'Shimmer' are monstrous walls of wildly treated sound, while 'Gutter Rock' comes on like a cinematic mid-period Marvin Gaye. 'Places I Go' reaches back to a perfect pop twang, albeit put through his current effects mill. There's also an ongoing electro tint to the beats on 'Lost In The Orbits' and 'Jaded', which plants jazz xylophone over Rev's whispers. The noise collage of 'Stormy' sounds as if Rev is tuning in the sounds from a distant radio. At a time of Coldplay blandness, this positively raging album came like a raw shot in the rump.

Suicide activities had been continuing through these years with short European tours and appearances at high-profile festivals such as Roskilde and old downtown mucker Vincent Gallo's All Tomorrow's Parties in Camber Sands. In 2005 came expanded reissues of *A Way Of Life* and Marty's readjusted *Why Be Blue*, along with a DVD of Suicide's performance at La Locomotive in Paris that January.

The footage is an intimate document of the 21st century Suicide who have nothing to prove and everything to celebrate. In black leather and huge shades, Rev seems to delight in kicking up the next song's mechanical groove, striking keyboard superhero poses with a malevolent grin, while Alan strides and points, now the consummate MC interacting with the crowd. As ever, rather than promote their latest product or supply greatest hits to demand, the set is weighted with unreleased material, such as the opening 'White Man' and disco guitar-loop of 'First Come First Serve' and 'Stay Alive', although Alan's 'Wipeout Beat' is reworked as 'Uptown Line' and the last Suicide album is represented by a crunching 'Wrong Decisions' and 'Death Machine'. 'Cheree' is now a haunted doo-wop sparkle and 'Ghost Rider' taken down the same lonely highway if it was overbuilt with overspilling nuclear reactors. There's also entertaining interviews with the pair at home in New York. While Alan bemoans the invasion of his city by machine-like young professionals, to the point that he welcomes bumping into a rare bum, Rev is asked about his shades collection and stands talking about punk outside their old haunt CBGB, whose days were now numbered due to the astronomical rent. As I found out myself when I visited New York the following year, everything was changing irrevocably. Even the perilous Avenue D was now safe to walk.

Meanwhile, Marty and Alan's lives were both about to be drastically challenged.

TWENTY-THREE

"I'm always looking for something unexplored, that's fresh for myself that I can process. You always search to find that road that hasn't been travelled and then it's like 'Wow!' The desire is to marvel at the things you're finding." – **Martin Rev**

"Who knew I'd spend 45 years doing this? Suicide was meant to be death, but we're still alive. Now I listen to all this shit and everybody's influenced by Suicide. That's what's so damn scary." – **Alan Vega**

It's June 2007 and Suicide are in London to receive the first award ever to have been bestowed on them by the music industry, and to play a high-profile opening spot for long-time fan Nick Cave's Grinderman. But first, I'm in a room at the Holiday Inn on Old Street to take Alan and Marty through their career for a projected film about them. It was now nearly 30 years since I had first met them on the 1978 Clash tour. Then Suicide were treated as outsiders, even outcasts. Now they were being hailed like old gods; trailblazers who'd almost died for everyone's sins.

Rev is uncannily timeless in his space-age shades, genially radiating quietly subversive cool as he declares, "Suicide has always been a commentary on America, on the direction we felt it was taking, and how we felt about it as a place to live." He also seems to relish reliving the revolutions his music has sparked over the previous four decades, especially as the extreme reactions it caused now sound like the receptions given to some of his jazz heroes. Alan is a chain-smoking ball of Brooklyn energy, unfailingly good-humoured as he fires out one-liners but still crackling with intense passion for his art, whether music or sculptures. As his recently released *Station* album shows, he is still mad as hell at society's injustices, although getting him going today are England's new smoking ban ("It's the fourth reich, man!") and New York's ongoing clean-up ("The funk has gone!").

The memories fly, along with the laughter, as Suicide traverse their story, then reflect on their place in the present. "Suicide gets credited with influencing every new thing that comes out," ponders Alan.

"We're the act that comes on as the curtains are closing," adds Marty. "No, it's not quite like that," interjects Alan. "When we finally get on they decide to close the curtains because we're going the wrong way. We're always deemed the least successful band but we're still here. I'm not going to retire anyway. What would I do? How can I stop making music? It would be like stopping breathing."

The following night Suicide are due to be presented with their Innovation In Sound award at *Mojo* magazine's annual awards ceremony, held at a converted brewery near the Barbican. I was writing for the magazine then and was asked to chaperone Suicide for the evening. Alan was still pinching himself when he arrived at the venue with Liz, Rev, Paul Smith and Howard Thompson, who'd flown over from his home in Connecticut for the occasion. "I said to Liz, 'This is probably going to be the first and last time I walk down a red carpet. I should cut out a piece of it'," he said.

After hailing Suicide as "utterly revolutionary", *Mojo* editor Phil Alexander brought on Nick Cave to introduce them. Alan and Marty took the stage to a standing ovation. "I was nervous, man," recalled Alan. "I thought I'd get up there and not be able to say anything. I was just so lucky to get any words out of my mouth!"

After the ceremony came the traditional team photo in an on-site studio created by photographer Ross Halfin. Suicide managed to incur the wrath of Sharon Osbourne, who claimed Alan was obscuring her venerable husband. Alan was too busy digging this alien experience to notice. "The great thing was that so many things were happening. The people that were around were all my favourites. I ran into Mick Jones and he was really nice. At the photo shoot, I'm sitting on the floor and right behind me is Alice Cooper, Iggy and Ozzy. Alice was really great, and Iggy was really friendly. Sharon was being an obnoxious bitch. 'You in the red hat get down, you're blocking Ozzy!' Ozzy just said, 'Shut the fuck up already'."

"Alan was convinced it was all a joke, or that I paid *Mojo*'s publishers scads of cash to buy the award," says Paul Smith. "We were originally supposed to get Classic Album but a major label dropped a wad of advertising support (the reissue of Bob Marley's *Exodus*) and suddenly we were offered a different category. It was so very much the music biz! Our publicist Sarah Lowe snuck us into the big stars' photo because we weren't actually invited."

"I was extremely happy when *Mojo* decided to give them that honour," says Howard Thompson. "Recognition from anyone other than a few fellow artists has been hard to come by for Suicide, but I think they'll get it in the end. Those 'in the know' know who Suicide are and what their contributions have been. I'm sure history will sort it all out in their favour."

The following night, Suicide played a low-key warm-up gig at London's Buffalo Bar. Lindsay Hutton recalls hearing 'Ghost Rider', 'Che' and 'Girl' at the soundcheck, and an awesome show. "It was like being in church. I managed to burrow almost to the front for 'Frankie Teardrop'. The crisp, clear shards that were evident earlier were being absorbed by the wave of bodies that formed a solid mass in the tiny venue. It wasn't comfortable and it likely wasn't meant to be."

The Grinderman show at the Forum came the next night. After Suicide, hobo sensation Seasick Steve, and Grinderman's infernal blues explosion, the whole cast assembled for a cacophonous romp through 'Mr Ray' and 'Harlem'. Preparing for this encore had sent Alan back to listen to his old songs. "I had to write the lyrics down and thought, 'Wait a minute, this is what's happening now.' It brought back all the memories of writing lyrics to these things and what I was thinking. It was like going through an old diary. I actually listened to the first two Suicide albums. It was so long since I'd listened to them. I went, 'Holy shit, this is fucking amazing'. I didn't believe what I was hearing, man. People would ask me 'What kind of music is this?' I said, 'This stuff is country'n'eastern music. East Coast instead of western."

Jim Sclavunos, who now played drums with Grinderman, hadn't shared a stage with Alan since a dimly remembered jam at Max's with James Chance. "I was on the floor playing percussion," he remembered. "Smashing cocktail glasses with a microphone. I don't recall it being a very coherent performance. It must have sounded pretty obnoxious. That was to be the only time I shared a stage with Alan until the Forum. At the soundcheck we had all rehearsed together but when we got up for the actual encore, Marty started playing something totally different. It was utterly chaotic sounding and afterwards Alan seemed a bit flustered, but I found it very amusing. It seemed entirely in keeping with what I perceive as Marty's proclivity for bamboozling musical anarchy."

On the recording front, Alan had participated in a return session with VVV, resulting in 2005's *Resurrection River*. It's a finer tuned but angrier selection, ramming grime-scoured hip-hop and electro beats under Vainio and Vaisanen's weightless textures and scabrous drones. The trio seemed to have arrived at their own ominous city soundscape on simmering missives such as 'Desperate Nation' and "Chrome Z-Fighters'.

2007's *Station* came as the ultimate peak of Alan's creative torrent, which had started 20 years earlier with Liz. He said it took the elements of his previous work "all the way". Alan had actually started the album 10 years earlier, when he submitted an early version to Blast First called *Mutator*, followed by further incarnations. Some leaked on to *2007* but he seemed to have been striving for an even more extreme manifestation of the raw, ugly noise he saw befitting his current world-view. The album is dedicated to his late brother Robbie.

"Alan had continued working with Perkin, putting tracks and tracks of sound into the vault," says Liz. "When Dante got a bit older, I started joining Alan and bringing Dante in with us. Eventually, we started focussing on the next album, *Station*, which coincidentally was released in 2007. Dante can be heard calling out 'Momma' when I stepped into another room to take a call. Dante had been singing in the Trinity Wall Street Youth Choir since the age of seven, and still does. He has been playing trombone since age nine. When we did a tour of Europe in the summer of 2007, he joined us on stage."

Reviewing the album on the *Trakmarx* website I said, "*Station* is possibly the most brutal, unsettling, ANGRY torrent of vein-busting rage to emit not only from Vega's gullet but really from anyone I can think of. Here, Vega is trying to paint the bleak realities of life in the 21st century by screaming his simple messages as loud as he can over the ugliest backings he can muster. Rusty-nail radio static shadows of riffs and nerve-crunching, jackhammer drum machine beats. Monolithic back alley behemoths with nothing resembling the ballads, rockabilly or techno with which he's dabbled previously. This is inner city psychosis pushing the limits of mental derailment. Sometimes it's like Lou Reed's *Metal Machine Music* with nuclear beats. On 'Psychopatha' an icy melody creeps in, Vega sobs and cajoles while voices chant 'psychopath'. Occasionally Dante cries 'mummy'. Halfway, Vega gurgles, cackles and shrieks with chilling malevolence."

'Traceman' is offset with Liz's unsettling vocal hook, while '13 Crosses 16 Blazin' Skulls' is the track cited by Alan as the album's most extreme breakthrough. 'Devastated' winds up this bludgeoning soundtrack for a country drenching itself in escalating psychosis and unnecessary deaths, thanks to its gun laws and urban neglect. About to celebrate his seventieth birthday, Alan was still out on the front line.

Alan didn't want this roll to stop, telling me just after *Station*'s release "I've been working on another new Alan Vega record. I just reached a good thing on *Station*. The songs really took me into a new place. I just wanted to continue from that place and not stop working."

Even suggestions of Suicide celebrating the 30 year anniversary of the first album seemed to get in the way. "I'm not sure what's going on any more. It's a big mess. The thought of coming back and doing the Suicide 30 year revival... We're supposed to do a show with Suicide playing exactly the same. Marty hasn't quite been co-operating. He'd have to remove all his equipment and just use the old Farfisa and drum machine. I'm not too keen on it either. We do what we do now."

Meanwhile, Liz continued to manage Suicide's affairs. At the same time, she started developing an interest in boxing, and boxing management. After getting her licence in 2013, she now devotes much of her energy to her management stable, which includes hot title hopeful Angel Luna. "With Suicide I've really been more like the gatekeeper," she says. "It's been amazing how all these years I'm basically just fielding things that came to us. I'm not going out there trying to find opportunities because that really hasn't been my mission, especially with respect to Alan. His emotions are on his sleeve. The beautiful thing about Alan is that you always know where you stand. He's 100 per cent honest. He will never tell you what he thinks you wanna hear. He will always tell you exactly what he's feeling or thinking. You always know that you're getting complete honesty from Alan, which is great. I love that."

Marty was on his own creative trajectory, one which would result in his masterpiece. After *To Live* he had recorded the sparkling *Les Nymphes* (which would eventually see release on File-13 in September 2008). It sounded like his surreal take on house music as he laced cathartic melodies with hallucinogenic reverb and spoken interjections. "*Les Nymphes* started with certain definite elements, kind of a loop idea, then, in that process, I discovered new things," explains Marty. "There was a lot of arranging. It was kind of expressing myself through that, just making it a different way of using vocals and space."

While 'Sophie Eagle', 'Daphne' and 'Cupid' hoist the kind of ecstatic keyboard riffs which had been gripping dance floors since the previous decade, 'Nyx' propagates a luxurious strain of fusion dub, complete with rare vocal contribution from Mari, and astral jazz flourishes pepper outings such as 'Triton'. Continuing the Suicide interaction, 'Venise' replants the haunting motif which underpinned 'Misery Train' in an exotic house garden.

Marty's next album would be unlike anything that he had ever done and would take on a far greater significance and poignancy than he could ever have imagined when he first arrived at the next phase in his ongoing creative journey. "Most times you start an album with a nice idea in your mind but it's not gonna work," explains Marty. "When I start a new one I've got all these ideas from the last one but, with every record, there's a big difference between expectation and reality. It's like an adventure that starts from scratch every time. This one was the same. I just had these tracks and didn't know at first how I was going to treat them. Certain things that might have worked for you a year ago; certain values, now all of a sudden it's doesn't work for you any more. You've changed, which you only realise in the process of working."

Mari's "incredible music and art essence" had a major impact on Marty's working process as he started hatching what would become his modern electronic classical epic *Stigmata*. "Mari knew and had experienced so much about classical music that when she listened she heard it in comparison to maybe 10 other versions. It was incredible what she knew about art and music. I remember being at a classical concert somewhere. There was an encore and somebody played something which I didn't recognise. Mari just turned to me and said 'Scarlatti'. At that time, I couldn't recognise Scarlatti. Now sure, but she just knew it right then."

Marty had an idea to inject his new classical compositions with his own wordless vocals. "I realised I could do this vocal idea that I'd had: I didn't know it was gonna come through this particular time or album. The religious aspect is there, but it's also a link with a tradition which has such a strong basis in the history of music by itself. In Montreal, Mari was listening to Alessandro Scarlatti, the afore-mentioned Domenico's father, and Vivaldi. One time after I had been away, she had taped this Vivaldi version of *Stabat Mater* that I had never heard before. Sometimes you hear something that hits you and you go, 'That's exactly where I am now and I should really take off on that'. It could be one year old or 600 years old, but, 'Yeah, that's the way to use vocals.' It was just right at that time. Then I started listening to other things that related to that kind of search. I wasn't necessarily thinking of atmospheric vocals but they came off very well like that. I'd been exposed to religious music from the baroque period for some time. It was in my mind, but soon after that I heard just *how* much. We were also listening to Pergolesi. He had a big influence on me."

Giovanni Pergolesi, who died at the age of 26 in 1736, was an Italian composer who also wrote sacred music, including his *Stabat Mater* for soprano, alto and string orchestra, written for an annual Good Friday meditation in honour of the Virgin Mary. "Pergolesi had a big influence on my thinking then. It hit me that this was the perfect scenario in which to approach my vocal parts. I've been into falsettos ever since doo-wop. The baroque falsetto musical culture is incredible. The falsettos were like the rock stars of their time. That was all in my mind when I started doing the vocals. I thought, 'Wow, it's working'. I now had a definite idea of what I wanted to do. A lot of my music has been found music for a long time too; finding tracks that were already made and then working with those. I'll find maybe two bars and make a piece out of them. It's very contemporary. *Stigmata* is probably still an enigma to many classical people too. Is it classical music? It doesn't matter."

Marty was working on the album when he came to the UK in June 2007. "When I left, I said to Mari, 'Listen to this and let me know what you think.' She always listened to everything I did but I especially wanted her to do that. When I came back she had made a whole list of notes for each track. I remember we had some great talks about it at the time."

By February 2008, Marty was starting to consider the album almost finished. Then Mari, his beloved lifelong muse, suddenly passed away, igniting "the most tumultuous time of my life". When *Stigmata* was released in 2009 its cover carried the dedication 'Angel Mari, spread your wings in joy and fly to the loving arms of the Divine'. Her impact on Marty's life and music was highlighted for the first time when I talked to him for a 2010 magazine feature about his solo work.

"It's very simple. Mari, my wife, left the world, very suddenly. It happened pretty much simultaneous with the live Suicide box set. The cover had been something that she had done years before for a poster for Max's. Ironically, Paul happened to choose that without knowing that it was hers. Time has thankfully provided some clarity. I was with her my entire life, from before I was 20 years old. She *was* my entire adult life. Sometimes we lived in separate states, going back and forth, but she was the essence of my life all the way through. She was with me most of the time I recorded *Stigmata*. She heard it pretty much close to its final master stage."

Since then, I have had further conversations with Marty about his remarkable soulmate. A smile seems to creep into his voice when he says her name. Mari died on February 16, which also happened to be her birthday. "It's kind of significant," says Marty in 2015. "In many mystical religions, especially Judaism, the highest kind of righteous person goes on their birthday. As a young girl, and always later, Mari would tell me 'Mart, I've been dreaming since I was a young girl that I'm gonna die on my birthday' and she saw the age come to her. She actually died on her birthday at that very age, but with the numbers reversed. But she was really convinced that was gonna happen until that year passed. Then we never really spoke about it again, although I realised it later."

Thankfully, Mari was in New York at Marty's apartment when it happened. "Luckily we were together. It was Valentine's Day. I said, 'Happy Valentine's Day, it's your day. Whatever you wanna do, let's do it.' Usually I was always looking for time to do my own work, but I said, 'I've just got to take the whole day off and do whatever she wants to do.' At first she wanted to see *Persepolis*, Marjane Satrapi's movie, but we got to the theatre and she said, 'Do you think we could see this another time? Let's not see it today, let's go to Chinatown.' She loved Chinatown. She had Chinese ancestry. She always felt so good in Chinatown, like it was so sane. So we went to Chinatown and walked around. She loved those markets and bought vegetables and things. We had a great day. She said, 'This is such a beautiful day.' The next day I got up a little early because

Sabine, my agent, wanted to hear the demo of *Stigmata*. So I got up first to put it in an envelope and get it to the post office. About an hour later, Mari said she had things she needed to send, so she sat on the floor putting them in envelopes, and that's when she was struck by something. Mari had to go to the hospital and the next day she passed."

Thankfully Mari heard the album she had put so much care into at its final stages. *Stigmata* is a brilliantly executed excursion into modern electronic classical music, wrapped in religious imagery with most titles in Latin. Only 1969's *Moondog* by blind street composer Moondog, or maybe Walter Carlos' *A Clockwork Orange* soundtrack, have flown in any remotely close orbit. Cinematic, soaring and other-worldly, its translucent grand passion is perfectly enhanced by Marty's haunting wordless vocals. Tracks such as the delicately celestial 'Te Deum' now assume a heart-breaking poignancy and tangible spiritual dimension. The city now had a towering new rhapsody and Mari couldn't have wished for a more beautiful requiem.

"I met Mari a few times at Suicide shows," says Liz. "She always radiated very intense energy, much like Alan. And she always gave it to you straight, no apologies. She was obviously a very bright and creative woman. I can see why she had a very significant, very muse-like effect on Marty. Someone once said she made Alan seem relatively calm."

The year 2008 also saw Marty unwittingly contribute to a song which would later become embedded in the consciousness of the British public after he supplied lyrics to Irish producer David Holmes' 'I Heard Wonders'. The song was featured heavily in the BBC's 2012 Olympic Games coverage after Danny Boyle picked it for his opening ceremony soundtrack. I first met David when he was a young, aspiring techno DJ from Belfast. After carving a reputation for vibrant eclecticism with a cinematic soul, he went to Hollywood and scored blockbusters such as the *Oceans* series before returning to his beloved Belfast and directing films. 'I Heard Wonders' was the opening track of David's *Holy Pictures* album, which movingly pays tribute to his parents.

Like many in the early nineties, David heard about Suicide through Andrew Weatherall, while director Glenn Leyburn (of *Good Vibrations* fame) turned Holmes onto Rev's solo albums. "I was blown away by Marty's style, especially on *Strangeworld* and *See Me Ridin'*," recalled David. "His songs are so visual and I really love his voice. Those songs blew me away. Before I decided to take the huge leap into writing songs and singing myself, I approached Marty to collaborate with me as a singer rather than a keyboard player. I was working on 'I Heard Wonders' and tracked Marty down. He dug the track and wrote a beautiful song around the title. By then, I was writing so much myself and, although I loved what he did, I decided the only person who could do this was me as I realised I was writing about the death and memory of my parents after the passing of my dad. I had written the vocal melody, the first two verses and half a chorus when I hit a wall. I quickly revisited Marty's lyrics and thought they sat perfectly with what I was writing and added them to finish the song. It was a beautiful moment and a great meeting of minds even though he was in New York and I was in Belfast. When I spoke with him, he was so humble and gracious and I was just so happy to have collaborated with not just a true pioneer of electronic-based music, which I had loved for 20 years, but a total gent and all round great and generous guy. 'I Heard Wonders' went on to be one of the most well known and loved tracks I ever produced and to collaborate with such greats as Marty and Leo Abrahams on guitar is something I'll never forget. During the London Olympics, Danny Boyle chose the track to appear over a montage of the torch being carried through Britain. The track was reborn and became an instant hit overnight."

In 2008, Alan celebrated his seventieth year on the planet. Paul Smith released a series of 10-inch singles to mark the occasion, housed in covers illustrated by artists Alan had influenced. "Suicide are not really recognised for their influence on music culture," he says. "Lots of artists owe them big time. So I used Alan's seventieth birthday to try to address that, even though Alan was not at all a willing participant in this. He didn't want the world to know he was 70 at all!"

Released in October, the first single was a recording of the version of 'Dream Baby Dream' that Bruce Springsteen had played through 2005 on his *Devils & Dust* tour. In keeping with his album of the same name, the tour was just Bruce, accompanying himself on guitar. For the final encore he would sit down at a pump-organ and plug into the core optimism of Alan's words like a religious mantra, sometimes for up to 10 minutes. "Bruce is a gentleman and a true fan of Alan's work," says Smith. "His office made it very easy to do. Oddly enough that was pretty much why Blast First Petite came into being as Mute didn't want me to do the series."

Alan went to see Bruce's tour in Bridgeport, Connecticut, that July. "Bruce finished the soundcheck and came over and gave me a fucking bear hug and signed a photo for my son. I hadn't seen him in over 20 years but it was like the old days all over again. We were talking for an hour or so. He's just such a great guy." Bruce dedicated 'Dream Baby Dream' to Alan that night and blew him away with his rendition. "I'm freaking out!" Alan recalled. "I thought, 'I'm never gonna do this song the same any more.' Then the show ends, the lights come up and my song 'Dujang Prang' came on. It's one of Bruce's favourite songs. It's weird shit, but he loves it."

The second release featured the Horrors covering 'Shadazz', Howard Thompson's recording of Suicide performing 'Radiation' at Irving Plaza in 1984 and Nik Colk Void's sultry electro take of 'Rocket USA'. November saw Primal Scream's Glitter Band-style version of 'Diamonds, Fur Coat, Champagne' with German electro chanteuse Miss Kittin on vocals. The flip featured Conrad Standish's version, joined by Suicide's 1976 demo of 'Ghost Rider'. The next single saw Lydia Lunch rise to turning 'Frankie Teardrop' into her personal nightmare cauldron, still a highlight of her live set today. The B-side featured Suicide's stark 1976 demo when the song was still called 'Frankie Teardrop, The Detective Meets the Space Alien'. Rev's two-note riff and bubbling drum machine are the only similarities with the known version as Viet vet Frankie goes to the race-track and shoots the space man after confessing he's already killed 100 people.

'June 2009 saw Sunn O))) and Pan Sonic getting together to take 'Che' to the pits of doom while the following August witnessed the Klaxons tackling 'Sweetheart'. A huge knob sculpture adorned Peaches' playful 'Johnny' in May 2010 ("Before she became a performer she'd never heard of Suicide," says Alan). Finally, Gavin Friday and Dave Ball got together to play 'Ghost Rider'.

Recent years have seen Alan encouraging and working with young bands he has inspired. "A.R.E. Weapons are two guys who admitted they wanted to be just like Suicide," he says. The New York electronic noise-rock trio were formed in 1999 by Mathew McAuley, Brain McPeck and Ryan Noel. Their 2001 singles 'Street Gang' and 'New York Muscle' betray requisite confrontational elements and abrasive delivery. By 2004, they had released their eponymous debut album, gained synth-player Paul Sevigny (brother of actress Chloë) and Noel had died of a heroin overdose. In 2008, Alan joined the band for a two-track 12-inch single consisting of 'See Tha Light' (startlingly built on the ringing guitar riff from the Gun Club's 'Yellow Eyes') and their electrolysed take on Edwin Starr's 'War'.

Then there's Vermont's psych-drone duo the Vacant Lots, who released their debut single, 'Confusion', in 2011, followed by 'High And Low' and '6AM', which Alan remixed. The group also covered Suicide's 'No More Christmas Blues' for a 2013 compilation called *Psych-Out Christmas*.

In 2009, Alan enjoyed a major retrospective art exhibition at the Museum of Contemporary Art in Lyon, curated by Mathieu Copeland, which included over 40 light sculptures, 96 portrait drawings and 30 small box paintings of boxers. The following year, he teamed up again with Marc Hurtado to create *Sniper*, another stark excursion with track titles such as 'Fear', 'Sacrifice' and 'War'. 'Saturn Drive Duplex' glimmers with swelling melodies while Lydia Lunch makes a demonic cameo in 'Prison Sacrifice'.

That year also saw Suicide buckle and play their first album at selected shows, including opening for Iggy & the Stooges at Hammersmith Apollo in May. Like Marty taking the stage at the Village Gate years before, it was another way of reconnecting with past heroes. "It was really more for Alan, but when we played with Iggy, that was like a lapsed time warp too," says Marty. "Iggy had already made his first record on Elektra when I was eating crackers and peanuts and we couldn't get a show. He wasn't a household name then, but now here we are playing side by side, both doing our albums. I just kind of observe and smile a bit. It's just another of those divine comedy concepts that can happen."

The following May saw Suicide play the first album at festivals, including alongside Grinderman at Barcelona's Primavera festival, where Nick Cave introduced them as "the reason we're all doing this". But Suicide's show at Moogfest 2011, held over Halloween weekend in Asheville, North Carolina, would be their last for nearly three years.

On March 16, 2012, Alan suffered a massive stroke and heart attack. Liz recalls the night that everything changed and she nearly lost him. "We have a loft, so upstairs are two sleeping areas; one is Dante's and one is mine. Alan's got a workspace and sleep space downstairs. Alan woke up at about three in the morning. There's a window in Dante's which overlooks Alan's. He was calling out and thank God Dante heard him. I kept trying to pull him up but he kept lurching to the side. I called an ambulance. He said, 'I can't feel'. I thought, 'Shit, he's had a stroke', plus he'd also had a heart attack. His arteries were 95 per cent blocked. There was one good artery that had enough of an opening to get a stent into, but they said he could die on the table. 'If we nick it, that's it, game over, but if we don't do it he'll probably be dead within three months.' I rolled the dice and thank God, and Dr Wong at Weill Cornell Medical Center, he's still kicking! He's a total survivor. He should have been dead. The doctors were blown away. His heart was pumping at about 10 per cent of the level rate of a normal human being for years before he had that stroke. They couldn't believe that he hadn't had a massive event before that. And they couldn't believe he was sitting there in the hospital going 'Whadda ya talkin' about? I'm fine'. His life force is so strong. His cardiologist is truly shocked at his level of performance activity, and attributes it to very strong force of will."

Alan was allowed home after three weeks in hospital. He now mainly spends his days doing sculptures, writing and watching TV. "He's on about 10 different medications," says Liz. "He's basically kept alive through the medication he takes. It was very challenging because he still has difficulty speaking and finding words. When it first happened it affected his whole right side. He was writing with his left hand and, after a week in hospital, was drawing these crazy portraits upside down because he was getting bored. Right after the stroke he was really lucid, but I guess the blood in the brain and everything started destroying some stuff after a while. A lot of it has come back but there was a period where it was really difficult for him to find words. He'd get very confused. He still gets confused at times. His knees are almost totally riddled with arthritis, making it very difficult for him to walk but that's a blessing, because he's not like running a marathon. He's very conservative with his physical energy. It's like his singing. It's amazing that he can sustain the notes that he can."

The first time Alan ventured back into the studio was to cover Screamin' Jay Hawkins 'I Hear Voices' for a small Italian label doing a benefit album for the owner's disease-stricken child. "We didn't even know if Alan would be able to sing," continues Liz, "because he couldn't even talk much, but he put the headphones on and went in the vocal booth. Perkin and I both started to cry when we heard him start to sing because it was the most plaintive wailing. The tone of his voice was like nothing we had heard before from Alan. It was so poignant. Then Alan suddenly switched from that high end wailing voice into crystal clear classic Vega. Perkin and I looked at each other and our jaws dropped. It was as if he was saying 'Ha ha, I'm still in here!' It was one of the most intense moments in the studio ever."

In 2014, the Vacant Lots hooked up with Alan for a split 10-inch single on Fuzz Club Records, for which Liz supplied 'Nike Soldier' from the extensive Vega vaults. "We've got so much in the vault it's not even funny," says Liz. "There are hundreds of hours of soundtracks that Perkin and I have on computer files from all the years that Alan worked at 6/8 Studios; just going in to create sound, which evolved into song. It was similar to how Suicide worked in the early days. We just opened the library and there was the title 'Nike Soldier'. We basically put that track together, then I played it to Alan and he said, 'Sure, go ahead'."

Suicide's old manager Marty Thau was trying to nurture some of the city's other new artists when he relaunched Red Star before he sadly passed away in February 2014. His final project was a compilation called *Variations: Modern Sounds & Modern Beats*, including Rev and Jeremy Gluck among new discoveries such as Lola Dutronic.

Although Alan has a new album entitled *IT*, which he was working on before his stroke, ready for release on Blast First, according to Marty, the subject of a new Suicide album "doesn't come up any more. It used to. Once in a while I think about it. It would have to be in a different way, maybe just a live album in the studio." Recently, Craig Leon, who has carved a highly impressive career in recording classical music since the eighties and has recently been revisiting his seminal early eighties electronic work *Nommos*, has said he would love to record Suicide again. He even pitched a concept involving avant garde artists, Rev solo works and a live section with Alan. "We could have a Suicide album on Sony classical!" he says. "Let's do something that's really a challenge, a whole new blueprint. We did that album in 1977. Now let's do something that would be as unexpected to those that are expecting to get 'Frankie Part 2'."

Marty is close to finishing his next solo album. "I'm working daily. It's now approaching demo stage. I started it with *Stigmata* in mind but you have all these possibilities bubbling in your mind then it's like 'No man you did that already!' Again, it's like a search from nothing. That's what makes it great, because it's like a process from nowhere. I can never really count on what I did before. It is what it is. An album is a composite of many pieces; it's a big chunk of your life. For me, it's a very psychological, obsessive thing to find something so crazily fresh. You learn things at gigs that you never could learn anywhere else. There's something in the focus of the performance. Art is like a bird that takes off into something new. Gigs are always different. It's a different room, a different sound. Your life is different. Records can only be that way too. For me anyway."

Alan was back in action just months after his stroke when Laurent Godin mounted an exhibition of his work at his Godin Gallery in Paris and in his booth at FIAC. "Both exhibitions did quite well, with pieces being sold to major collectors," says Liz. "Miraculously, Alan was able to travel to Paris for the exhibitions and Alan, Dante and I did a combined concert in Paris in celebration, performing tracks from *IT* and *Sniper*. If you had told me the prior June that we would be doing that in the fall I would have found it hard to believe!"

Suicide's first shows after Alan's stroke were at the MIMI festival in Marseilles and Paris' La Gaîeté Lyrique in July 2014. The latter was accompanied by an exhibition of Rev's drawings at a nearby gallery. In March 2015, Suicide played a rare New York show at the Webster Hall, which coincided with Alan being the sole artist in the Godin Gallery's booth at the Armory Show and an exhibition of his portrait drawings at the Invisible Exports Gallery on Eldridge Street.

"Alan and Marty had no idea what the other person was gonna do," says Liz. "It was great, it was pure performance. Alan had not physically seen Marty since they did the show in Marseilles. Marty had a dressing room on the second floor and Alan couldn't get up there 'cause of the stairs. Marty arrived just before the set, so they came on to the stage from separate entrances. They literally had not seen each other before walking on the stage. There was no set list, it was supposed to be totally freestyle and it was absolutely brilliant. It was a shoulder to shoulder packed house and people were mesmerised. Nobody left the room during their set. It was unbelievable. It really was amazing and there was so much love in the house. There was this encore with Alan and Dante singing together and it sounded so beautifully ethereal. It was transcendent."

"It's come like full circle," says Alan. "I know it was a great gig but I don't remember a fucking thing about it. That's the way things used to be. It doesn't matter at this point because Suicide is such a thing already. We can do anything. I love Marty. We never do any soundchecks or rehearsals. Are you kidding? If I can't do it now we'll never get it right! They went crazy and nobody left. We could have played another hour. I can't dance much now but we were getting so into it I don't know what happened. I don't remember leaving the place. What, was I drunk? I had a white wine. I only drink white wine. I was so exhausted from the thing. I can't remember anything. I like that; I don't *want* to know. Apparently, it was great."

"No, we didn't see each other," says Marty. "I showed up and he showed up. Apparently it went over quite well. I know when it's good and it was fine at my end but the audience were great. That's the way we tend to work these days. We just do what we do. I'd rather Alan doesn't try to remember words. That's what we've been doing since we expanded out of the first album."

Their old friend Howard Thompson was there to witness what was possibly the best reception Suicide had ever received in their 45 years. "It was an odd one. Each song ended with huge applause, shouting and screaming! Marty has fucked with his sounds to the extent that it's sometimes difficult to make out what the fuck they were playing. But it didn't seem to matter – the crowd ate it up. Marty sounded gigantic and Alan was Alan, albeit a bit slower and far less threatening. It was good to see them enjoy some adulation. I was conflicted by the gig. I've watched them be much better and get practically bottled off stage. This was almost a love fest but the songs are so different now. I think it's just me. I've seen too much! On the other hand, they're not resting on their laurels, so points to them for moving it forward. I will say that, whenever I saw Suicide, I always felt I was in the presence of greatness, however frightening, confrontational, ill-attended, brutal or just plain shambolic the gig might have been. There's something underneath that radiates a beauty, a truth, a reality that I only occasionally got from other performers. Suicide never seemed like entertainers to me, just artists. *Pure* artists. And great ones, to boot."

At the end of that month, Rev played a solo set at a warehouse in Hackney Wick as part of the Bad Vibes festival headlined by krautrock legends Faust. It turned out to be the ultimate DIY shambles but, "It was fun," laughs Marty. "It was the chaotically organised festival that I expected, from setting up to things breaking down. It was a very street-level affair. Right before the show they discovered they didn't have any power on one of my sound sources. They were very worried and upset. Half the entire rig went, but it's one of the best sets I've ever done. The sound was great. The speakers were old and dusty but really powerful, and that makes all the difference at the time, especially for me. I was glad I did it just to explore some additional territories."

For the last few years, French filmmaker Divine Enfant has been making sumptuous, sparkling videos for Marty's solo tracks, which now number over 40 and can be found on YouTube. After Hackney, Rev took part in her rock art show in Dijon, playing to some of the films. "For me, they are very fresh," says Marty. "We did it together. Divine Enfant is a brilliant visual artist I met in Europe. I really dug her work so she did the *Stigmata* cover from a photo she took of me in a doorway near Times Square. We've been combining on photo and video shoots. She would pick the track and combine those. Now, because our world is so visual and virtual, every time you put some works on YouTube it's like a reflection of you. I wasn't crazy on it at first but take away the money aspect and you're totally free. You can do anything you want to and it's totally accessible all over the world. That's an incredible phenomenon. I feel good about this as another new direction to be explored."

Marty still walks the lower Manhattan streets he has been traversing since the sixties, brushing against the ghosts of Ornette Coleman, Rocky Boyd and other former jazz comrades. Thankfully, the gestation and rise of Suicide coincided with that time when New York was being electrified by great artists. "I have to always admit that New York must have been essential to something in the sound," he says, "the environment, the architecture, the tension, the intensity, the *particularity* of it."

Alan remains in the financial district and is still dismayed by the inexorable change in his city's dynamic. "I walk around New York like a stranger in a strange land now," he says. "The real New York types are going. Now the new types are coming in and I do not want to be part of it. Where is the funk? The funk has been lost. Everything is shiny now and lawyers are moving in across the street. When the business people came and moved in it killed the art community. I used to come home with all this shit from the streets. I loved it. It was unreal. Now you can't get anything on the streets. It's too clean! There's nothing. It's the worst."

As New York turns into another city, Suicide's job seems done. They have come full circle and will finally wind down as the live performing entity they started as 45 years ago, although Marty and Alan's individual journeys through their artistic obsessions will inevitably go wherever their lives take them. But they can be safe in the knowledge that, sometimes against all odds, Suicide ended up leaving some of the biggest footprints in New York's musical history behind them. These are now as immortal as the beleaguered skyline.

As Marty says, "You can't be the same person you were then, but if you feel the same sense of edge or intensity about what you're doing then you are still there."

Forever.

EPILOGUE

July 14, 2015: Helen and I are sitting with Marty Rev in the restaurant of the rather self-consciously hipster Ace Hotel in Shoreditch. After the months of intense memory-wrenching and word-honing which have gone into this book, there's a refreshing calm, and even a sense of achievement in the air today as we tweak the finishing touches.

Marty then reflects on Suicide's landmark 'Punk Mass' evening held during the 'Moog Concordance' nights as part of the Barbican's Station To Station event. His long and personal journey has taken him through over 50 years of amazing shows, jamming partners and extreme gig scenarios. This unusually lavish presentation and public display of the lifelong camaraderie between Marty and Alan could well be seen as closing the circle and very probably the last time the pair take the stage as Suicide, although offers continue to flood in.

The show had started coming together in March, so whenever I spoke to Marty for the book he inevitably started thinking aloud about what Suicide might be doing. As the night was being billed as a 'Punk Mass', his first thoughts had been to take that literally, which could have meant something of a religious nature, maybe echoing Howard Thompson's idea a few years ago to stage *Stigmata* at a New York cathedral. But back in March, Rev was mischievously considering taking the 'Punk Mass' at face value and reaching back to "this wall of sound kind of thing," he said then. "That's really my orientation on what I'm looking to do. It's not going to sound *exactly* like that, note for note, but the intensity that I feel is really the same. I love doing different ideas for live shows, but to simulate something? That's really not us, not Alan, and not Suicide.

You have to remember the original Punk Mass was a very raw affair! It wasn't attempting to imitate, intimate or duplicate an actual mass, it was *our* mass, just what our gigs were at that time."

By May, Marty was talking about how Moog had come on board and that Suicide would be ensconced in their hotel for a week with a roomful of Moogs in the basement, which was a novelty as he could never afford one. "It'll look like kind of spacey onstage, which will be cool, although that might be the extent of the Moog part, I don't know!"

Eventually, Suicide's night, which I was mortified to miss through the combination of a tube strike and charity bike race putting the city in lockdown, which precluded any chance of making it past the M25 in time, took the form of three sections: after the Feral Choir's stab at challenging vocals and a 'Liturgy of the Word' about Suicide from Henry Rollins, Marty came on with a burst of the Del-Vikings' doo-wop classic 'Whispering Bells', then played tracks from *Stigmata* with embellishment from Finlay Shakespeare and his Moogs and gospel trio Sense of Sound. A brave but beautiful thing to hurl at a Suicide crowd. "It was a gas," says Marty, "although it could have been louder."

A few weeks earlier, Liz Lamere had told me that Alan would be performing four tracks from his new *IT* album, joined by her and Dante. On the night, the trio blasted out 'Prayer', 'Vision', 'Screaming Jesus' and 'Stars' as a coruscating tech-noise assault. Maybe if the reviewers commenting on Alan's restricted movement and big throne-like chair knew the full extent of his struggle since the stroke they might have been more sensitive with some of their comments. He pulled it off but still had to face a Suicide set as part three of the evening's programme.

"It doesn't make sense to try and recreate a liturgical-oriented production because that's not us," says Marty. The duo piled through 'Cheree', 'Ghost Rider' with Henry Rollins, 'Rocket USA' (with different words), 'Frankie Teardrop' and 'Dream Baby Dream' as an encore, with vocal support from Bobby Gillespie and the Savages' Jehnny Beth. The most touching moment was 'I Surrender', the two old friends still together on a stage after 45 years, one now dealing with a much bigger struggle than an oafish crowd. Now they were being applauded and showered with love.

"I was pulling him in, saying 'you wrote these words,'" Marty says. "As I said to Alan, if this is our last gig it's perfect, because it has broken through into a new place for us, which is so new and fresh and if it's going to end here why not have it end just this way?"

ACKNOWLEDGEMENTS

Firstly, I have to thank Marty, Alan and Liz for agreeing to be such a major part of this book, and for their endless encouragement along the way. I wanted to give Suicide their long-deserved literary due, in the context of the music and events which influenced them and the city which spawned them, showing why they are one of the most important bands in history. It soon turned into the biggest, most ambitious project I have ever embarked on, but also the most rewarding.

A particularly massive thank you goes to Martin Rev, who allowed himself to be prodded and probed for hours in a series of epic conversations where he revealed everything from his previously untold story, from immersing himself in Manhattan's sixties jazz scene to falling in love with Mari, his lifelong muse and inspiration. Marty's priceless memories and tireless guidance helped shape the whole book, along with his diligent editing and correcting as it went on.

I have to thank Alan Vega for fabulous conversations over the years and more recently, and his partner Liz Lamere, who was a ball of enthusiasm and a mine of information on the solo projects. Alan might have become a little hampered after his stroke in 2012, but his intense spirit burns as bright as ever.

I would also like to thank all my interviewees, both recent and past (listed separately in the source notes). Key figures in Suicide's story rose to the occasion, notably long-time champion Howard Thompson, who supplied DVDs, CDs, memories and many priceless photos, and gave the book its first mention during his spectacular two-hour Suicide special on his North Fork Sound radio show in March 2015. Also Peter Crowley, who gave Suicide their first breaks both gig and record-wise, Craig Leon for his detailed account of producing the first album, and a posthumous salute to the great Chairman, Marty Thau, for his inimitable accounts of his time as Suicide's manager and record label boss. I'm glad I got to know him.

I also want to thank Lydia Lunch for taking the time out from her hectic touring schedule to write the soul-searing foreword. Suicide were her first New York friends and she doesn't forget. Also cheers to Cypress Grove for making the introduction. Thanks to Adrian Boot for the magnificent cover shot, and to all the other photographers who have contributed.

Others who deserve a big shout for their input, however indirect, or just words of support include Chris Stein, Daniel Lee Needs, Dante Lamere, David Holmes, Divine Enfant, Jay Burnett, Jeremy Gluck, Jim Sclavunos, Lindsay Hutton, Madeline Bocchiaro, Marc Mikulich, Mike Garson, Miriam Linna, Parker Dulany, Paul Smith, Peter Zaremba, Sarah Lowe, Sesu Coleman, Slim Smith, Stuart Argabright and Tony James. Thanks also to Ric Ocasek, even if schedules didn't allow an interview. I would also like to thank David Barraclough for commissioning the book, Chris Charlesworth for taking on the task of editing it and everyone else at Omnibus Press. Also, I have to hail Pete Frame for getting me started in the first place and giving me his doo-wop collection.

Just as I was revving up the engine, my beloved soulmate Helen Donlon was finishing her own book, *Partyinsel Ibiza*, a beautifully evocative account of the White Island's history of pirates, freaks and parties. Helen's forensic attention to detail and eloquent prose became a template to aspire to. I can only thank her for lending her expertise to reading and making suggestions about my own words, especially after they started turning into a skyscraper. Helen was also a major pillar of support at those times when the task seemed too huge (along with Jack the 'Doig' and Binky and Cookie, our zen-like bunnies). Thank you baby x.

SOURCE NOTES

List of interviewees

Argabright, Stuart: Producer, singer; chapter 19: Interview by e-mail April 2015

Bambaataa, Afrika: Hip-hop overlord; chapter 20: Interview in London, November 1984. Quote first appeared in Needs, Kris, *Some You Win Some Zulus*, *Zigzag*, December 1984

Bocchiaro, Madeline: Writer; chapter 15: interview by e-mail, April 2015

Bowie, Joseph: Singer, trombonist; chapter 20: Interview in London, May 1982. Quote first appeared in Needs, Kris, *Too Fierce For Radioland*, *Zigzag*, June 1982

Burnett, Jay: Producer, engineer; chapters 17, 20: Interview by phone in May 2015

Chance, James: Sax maniac, songwriter; chapters 15, 16, 18: Phone interview in June 2010. Some quotes first appeared with CD review in *Record Collector*, August 2010

Coleman, Sesu: Drummer; chapters 9, 10, 19: Interview by e-mail April 2015

County, Wayne/Jayne: Singer, DJ, trans-punk trailblazer; chapters 5, 10: Some quotes from interviews at her Earls Court abode in March 1977 and July 2013 by e-mail. Some quotes appeared in *NY Punk*, *Zigzag*, April 1977, others in *Vive Le Rock's* CBGB special, September 2013

Coxe III, Simeon: Silver Apples mainstay, The Thing manipulator; chapter 5: interview by phone October 2012. Some quotes first appeared in *Record Collector*, February 2013

Crowley, Peter: Max's Kansas City booker, downtown dynamo; chapters 4, 5, 11, 12, 13, 14, 19: phone interview, April 2015

Darnell, August, aka Kid Creole: Singer, songwriter, producer; chapters 2, 17: Interviews at Island Records, London in June 1982 and by phone March 2008. Some quotes also first appeared in Needs, Kris, *Kid Creole*, *Zigzag*, July 1982; and my liner notes for Strut Records' *ZE Records Story 1979–2009*

Dulany, Parker: Singer, songwriter; chapter 20: e-mail exchange in March 2015

Eno, Brian: Musician, producer; chapter 17: Interview in London, 1977; Some quotes originally appeared in Needs, Kris, *An Interview With Eno*, *Zigzag*, January 1978

Esteban, Michel: ZE Records founder; chapters 18, 19: Interviews by phone and e-mail in May 2009; Some quotes first appeared in liner notes for Strut Records' *ZE Records Story 1979–2009*

Frantz, Chris: Drummer, songwriter; chapter 10: Quote from e-mail interview in 2013 for *Vive Le Rock's* CBGB Special.

Fripp, Robert: Guitarist, producer; chapters 18, 19: Interviews at Polydor Records, London, April 1979 and 1980; First appeared in Needs, Kris, *Robert Fripp*, *Zigzag*, May 1979, May 1980

Garson, Mike: Pianist; chapter 3: interview by e-mail, May 2015

Gentile, Elda: Singer; chapters 5, 9, 10, 11, 12: Interview by e-mail March 2015

Gillespie, Bobby: Singer, songwriter; chapters 12, 16: quotes from e-mail exchange for liner notes of *Kris Needs Presents Dirty Water: The Birth Of Punk Attitude*, Year Zero, 2011

Harry, Deborah: Singer, songwriter; chapters 10, 17: Interviews in Bournemouth, June 1977 and Park Towers Hotel, London, January 1980. Some quotes first appeared in Needs, Kris, *All Aboard For Funtime! Zigzag*, August 1977; Needs, Kris, *The Art Of Class*, *Zigzag*, February 1980

Holmes, David: Producer; chapter 23: Interview by e-mail, May 2015

Hutton, Lindsay: *Next Big Thing* editor, chapter 23; e-mail in April 2015

Innes, Andrew: Guitarist; chapter 16: 2011 e-mail

James, Tony: Bassist, Sigue Sigue Sputnik mastermind; chapters 16, 20: Interview by e-mail March 2015

Jones, Grace: Singer, songwriter; chapter 18; Interview at Island Records, London, June 1980. Some quotes first appeared as Needs, Kris, *Grace*, *Zigzag*, July 1980

Jones, Mick: Singer, guitarist; chapter 16: from phone chat in 2007

Lamere, Liz: Vega collaborator, manager, lawyer, drummer; chapters 20, 21, 22, 23; Interviews by Skype in March and June 2015

Leon, Craig: Producer; chapters 11, 13, 14, 23: Main interview by phone April 2015; also by phone in 2011 from which quotes appeared in Needs, Kris; Porter, Dick, *Blondie: Parallel Lives*, Omnibus Press, 2012

Linna, Miriam: Drummer, Red Star press officer, Norton-KICKS supremo; chapters 12, 13, 15, 16, 18: Interview by e-mail May 2015

Lure, Walter: Singer, guitarist, the Heartbreakers; chapters 10, 11: Interviews by phone June 2013 and e-mail July 2013; Some quotes first appeared in *Vive Le Rock's* CBGB Special, September 2013

Mizrahi, Sylvain: Guitarist; chapters 9, 11: Interviews by phone in 2005; in London and NYC, March 2006; Some quotes first appeared in Needs, Kris; Porter, Dick, *Trash! The Complete New York Dolls*, Plexus, 2006

Nolan, Jerry: Drummer; chapter 9: Interview at Track Studios, London, March 1977; quote first appeared in Needs, Kris, *NY Punk*, *Zigzag*, April 1977

Peacock, Annette: Singer, songwriter; chapters 4, 8: Interview by e-mail, June 2011, published in *Shindig!* August 2011

Philips, Binky: Singer, guitarist; chapter 10: Interview by e-mail July 2013. First appeared in *Vive Le Rock's* CBGB Special, September 2013

Ramone, Johnny: Guitarist, songwriter; chapter 10: Interview outside Dingwalls, London, July 1976; Quote first appeared in Needs, Kris, *Ramones*, *Zigzag*, October 1976

Rev, Martin: Suicide instrumentalist, solo artist, songwriter; quotes throughout come from interview at Holiday Inn, Old Street, in June 2007, phone conversations in 2009, 2010, 2011 and between March and June 2015, plus numerous e-mails; Some quotes first appeared in Needs, Kris, *Suicide*, *MOJO* November 2007; Needs, Kris, *Martin Rev*, *Clash*, 2009; liner notes for *Watch The Closing Doors: A History of New York's Melting Pot*, Year Zero, 2011

Sclavunos, Jim: Drummer, producer; chapters 14, 15, 16, 23: Interview by e-mail May 2015

Smith, Paul, Blast First honcho; chapters 16, 18, 22, 23: Interview by e-mail June 2015

Stein, Chris: Guitarist, songwriter; chapters 10, 14: Quotes from phone interviews and e-mails in 2010, 2011, 2013. Some quotes appeared in *Vive Le Rock's* CBGB Special, September 2013

Thau, Marty: Chairman of Red Star Records, former Suicide manager; chapters 10, 12, 13, 14, 15, 16, 18, 19: Interviews in London, 1980, and by phone in 2011. His story first appeared in Needs, Kris, *Marty Thau*, *Zigzag*, August 1980. Some quotes also appeared in Needs, Kris; Porter, Dick, *Blondie: Parallel Lives*, Omnibus Press, 2012.

Thompson, Howard: A&R champion, DJ, producer; chapters 15, 16, 18, 23: Interviews by e-mail March 2015

Thunders, Johnny: Guitarist, singer; chapter 9: Interview at Track Studios, London, March 1977; Quote first appeared in Needs, Kris, *NY Punk*, *Zigzag*, April 1977

Vega, Alan: Suicide, singer, artist; quotes throughout the book come from interviews at the Holiday Inn, Old Street, June 2007, then phone conversations through 2007, 2008, 2009 and early 2015; some quotes appeared in Needs, Kris, *Suicide*, *MOJO* November 2007

Zaremba, Peter: Singer; chapters 6, 12, 13, 15: Interview by e-mail June 2015

Citations & Further Reading

One
Frame, Pete, *The Restless Generation*, Rogan House, 2007
Sutphen, Van Tassel, *The Doomsman*, FQ Books, 2010

Two
Goode, Mort, liner notes, *The Paragons Meet The Jesters*, Jubilee, 1959

Three
Baram, Marcus, *Gil Scott-Heron: Pieces Of A Man*, St Martin's Press, 2014
Cleaver, Eldridge, *Soul On Ice*, Dell, 1968
Gioia, Ted, *The History Of Jazz*, Oxford University Press, 1997
Jones, LeRoi, *Blues People*, William Morrow, 1963
Spellman, A.B., *Four Lives In The Bebop Business*, Pantheon, 1966
Albert Ayler quote from interview with Kiyoshi Koyama for *Swing Journal*, recorded July 25, 1970, in Saint-Paul-de-Vence, France; on Disc 9 of *Holy Ghost* box set, Revenant, 2004

Four

Velvet Underground review by Grace Glueck, *New York Times*, January 14, 1966

Five

Davis, Miles, *The Autobiography*, Simon & Schuster, 1989

Six

Miller, Henry, *Remember To Remember*, New Directions, 1961

Warhol, Andy, *Popism: The Warhol Sixties*, Harcourt Brace Jovanovich, 1980

Seven

Bangs, Lester, *Of Pop And Pies And Fun; A Program For Mass Liberation in the Form of a Stooges Review Or, Who's the Fool? Creem*, November 1970

Jahn, Mike, *The Stooges*, *New York Times*, September 8, 1969

Nine

Hollingworth, *Roy, You Wanna Play House With The Dolls? Melody Maker*, July 22, 1972

Hollingworth, Roy, Suicide review, *Melody Maker*, October 21, 1972

McCormack, Ed, *New York City's Ultra-Living Dolls*, *Rolling Stone*, October, 1972

Riffs column, *Village Voice*, November 9, 1972

Ten

Thau, Marty, *Wishing Upon A Red Star*, unpublished memoir

Miles, Barry, *In The Seventies: Adventures In The Counter-Culture*, Serpents Tail, 2011

Zone, Miki, *Playground: Growing Up In The New York Underground*, Glitterati, 2014

Eleven

Sewall-Ruskin, Yvonne, *High On Rebellion: Inside The Underground At Max's Kansas City*, Thunder's Mouth Press, 1998

Twelve

Moore, Thurston, Suicide, *The Gulcher*, issue 5, 1976

Thirteen
Persky, Lisa Jane, Suicide, *New York Rocker*, May 1976

Fourteen
Thau, Marty, *Wishing Upon A Red Star*, unpublished memoir

Fifteen
Bangs, Lester, liner notes to *Half Alive*, ROIR cassette, 1981
Bangs, Lester, *The Joy Of Suicide*, *SoHo Weekly News*, May 28, 1978
Carson, Tom, *Suicide Is Meaningless*, *Village Voice*, January 30, 1978
Thau, Marty, *Wishing Upon A Red Star*, unpublished memoir
Williams, Richard, *Suicide Is A Solution*, *Melody Maker*, January 21, 1978

Sixteen
Dadomo, Giovanni, *Suicide: The Third International Science Fiction Festival, Metz, France, Sounds*, June 17, 1978
Joe Strummer quote from Don Letts' film *Westway To The World*, 2001
Thau, Marty, *Wishing Upon A Red Star*, unpublished memoir
Tyson, Ian: www.glasgowapollo.com

Seventeen
Chatham, Rhys, *New York Now!*, *Zigzag*, March 1980
Masters, Marc, *No Wave*, Black Dog, 2007

Eighteen
Committing Suicide, St Petersburg Times, Los Angeles, September 29, 1979
Trakin, Roy, *Martin Rev*, *New York Rocker*, 1980
Needs, Kris, *Suicide*, *Zigzag*, April 1980
Thau, Marty, *Wishing Upon A Red Star*, unpublished memoir

Nineteen
Bangs, Lester, *Half Alive* liner notes, ROIR, 1981
Cohen, Debra Rae, Alan Vega, *Village Voice*, November 9, 1980
Doerschuk, Robert, *The New Synthesiser Rock*, from *Keyboard Presents The Evolution Of Electronic Dance Music*, Backbeat, 2011
Fricke, David, *Ghost Riders* liner notes, ROIR, 1986
Hoskyns, Barney, *Collision Drive*, *NME*, January 23, 1982

O'Reilly, Paul, *The Truth Is Known*, *Zigzag*, December 1983
Traitor, Ralph, *Collision Drive*, *Sounds*, January 23, 1982

Twenty
Fricke, David, *Suicide*, *Melody Maker*, August 24, 1984

Twenty-Two
Carlin, Martin, *American Supreme*, *The Wire*, November 2002
Hollings, Ken, *Ghost Riders*, *The Wire*, August 1998
Kopf, Biba, *Suicide*, *The Wire*, March 1998
Pouncey, Edwin, *The Invisible Jukebox, The Wire*, March 1998
Sombre: Musique Originale Alan Vega, liner note, Zelie, 1999

Twenty-Three
Needs, Kris, *Station*, *Trakmarx*, April 2007

Further Reading

Aletti, Vince, *The Disco Files 1973-78*, DJHistory.com, 2008
Beeber, Steven Lee, *The Heebie-Jeebies At CBGB's: A Secret History Of Jewish Punk*, Chicago Review Press, 2006
Berman, Marshall; Berger, Brian, *New York Calling: From Blackout To Bloomberg*, Reaktion, 2007
Bonomo, Joe, *Sweat: The Story Of The Fleshtones, America's Garage Band*, Continuum, 2007
Carr, Ian, *Miles Davis: The Definitive Biography*, Quartet, 1982
Chessman, Caryl, *Cell 2455, Death Row: A Condemned Man's Own Story*, Prentice-Hall, 1954
Darling, Andrew, *Ghost Rider: The Visual Guide*, Dorling Kindersley, 2007
Fletcher, Tony, *All Hopped Up And Ready To Go*, Omnibus Press, 2009
Gendron, Bernard, *Between Montmartre And The Mudd Club: Popular Music And the Avant-Garde*, University Of Chicago Press, 2002
Gribin, Dr Anthony J., Schiff; Dr Matthew M., *Doo-Wop: The Forgotten Third Of Rock 'N' Roll*, Krause, 1992
Grimshaw, Jeremy, *Draw A Straight Line And Follow It: The Music And Mysticism Of Lamonte Young*, Oxford University Press, 2011

Groia, Philip, *They All Sang On The Corner*, Phillie-Dee, 1983

Hermes, Will, *Love Goes To Buildings On Fire: Five Years In New York That Changed Music Forever*, Faber & Faber, 2011

Jost, Ekkehard, *Free Jazz*, Da Capo, 1972

Kahn, Ashley, *The House That Trane Built: The Story Of Impulse Records*, W.W. Norton, 2006

Kiedrowski, Thomas, *Andy Warhol's New York City*, The Little Bookroom, 2011

Lauterbach, Preston *The Chitlin' Circuit And The Road To Rock 'N' Roll*, W.W. Norton, 2011

Lawrence, Tim, *Hold On To Your Dreams: Arthur Russell And The Downtown Music Scene, 1973-1992*, Duke University Press, 2009

Musto, Michael, *Downtown*, Vintage, 1986

Nevius, James & Michelle, *Inside The Apple: A Streetwise History Of New York City*, First Free Press, 2009

Nobakht, David, *Suicide: No Compromise*, SAF, 2005

Perchuk, Andrew; Singh, Rani, *Harry Smith: The Avant Garde In The American Vernacular*, Getty, 2010

Pye, Michael, *Maximum City: The Biography Of New York*, Picador, 1993

Reynolds, Simon, *Rip It Up And Start Again: Postpunk 1978-1984*, Faber & Faber, 2005

Ross, Alex, *The Rest Is Noise: Listening To The Twentieth Century*, Harper Perennial, 2009

Russell, Ross, *Bird Lives!* Quartet, 1973

Sante, Luc, *Low Life*, Farrar, Straus & Giroux, 1991

Strausbaugh, John, *The Village: A History Of Greenwich Village*, Harper Collins, 2013

Stubbs, David, *Future Days: Krautrock And The Building Of Modern Germany*, Faber & Faber, 2014

Sullivan, Denise, *Keep On Pushing: Black Power Music From Blues To Hip-hop*, Lawrence Hill, 2011

Vega, Alan, *At Random*, Kyoto Shoin, 1990

Weiss, Jason, *Always In Trouble: An Oral History Of ESP-Disk: The Most Outrageous Record Label In America*, Wesleyan University Press, 2012

Wilmer, Valerie, *As Serious As Your Life: The Story Of The New Jazz*, Allison & Busby, 1977

Werner, Craig, *A Change Is Gonna Come: Music, Race And The Soul Of America*, Plume, 1998

Wolcott, James, *Lucking Out: My Life Getting Down And Semi-Dirty In Seventies New York*, Doubleday, 2011

Websites

Ghost Riders: Suicide Discography
Gothamist
New York Dolls chronology; From The Archives.Org
New York Songlines: Virtual Walking Tours of Manhattan Streets
Rock's Back Pages.com
Suicide Chronology: From The Archives.Org

INDEX